NOT YOUR LUCKY DAY

A MURPHY'S LAW FARM MYSTERY

L. R. TROVILLION

HIPPOLYTA BOOKS

Not Your Lucky Day

Copyright © 2023 by L. R. Trovillion

www.lrtrovillion.com

All rights reserved.

No portion of this book may be reproduced in any form without written permission from the publisher or author, except as permitted by U.S. copyright law.

This book is a work of fiction. References to real events, establishments, organizations, or locales are intended only to provide a sense of authenticity, and are used fictitiously. The characters portrayed are fictitious. Any similarity to real persons, living or dead, is coincidental and not intended by the author.

First Edition

HIPPOLYTA BOOKS

Printed in the United States of America

ISBN: 979-8-9880714-0-2 (ebook)

ISBN: 978-0-9908995-9-4 (print)

Cover: Get Covers

Editor: Kimberly Hunt, Revision Division

A Medical Laboratory in Western Maryland

Prologue

THE LABORATORY WAS HOUSED in a squat, brick building nestled in the cleavage of western Maryland's mountainous landscape. This small town's residents passed by it without thinking twice about what went on there. They assumed it was one of many other similar looking industrial buildings with few windows and featureless brick walls—perhaps an office building, a physician's suite, or a tech company's satellite office. If anyone noticed at all, it wasn't considered odd that cars rolled up its long driveway in the middle of the night. The building was rendered nearly invisible by virtue of its bland commonality. And that is why it was selected.

Guided by the light from the full moon on a clear night, the driver backed the trailer to the oversized bay doors behind the building. Two men dropped down to the pavement from the cab of the truck. The short, muscular one took charge of the shipment. He opened the top doors of the trailer and checked on the live load. The horse craned her neck, struggling against the ties attached to her halter, to look behind her and see what was happening. The other man—tall, lean, with an air of authority, disappeared into the building.

Before the shipper could unload the horse, a woman dressed in dark scrubs appeared at the back entrance with the tall man at her side. Her gray hair was cropped short like a helmet. "Wait," she ordered and strode with purpose to where the short man was unhooking the ramp in preparation for lowering it.

The woman strained on tiptoes to peer over the top. A smile crept over her face when she caught sight of horse's haunches rising above the edge of the ramp. "That's her alright." She stepped aside. "Get her inside. Quickly."

The man lowered the ramp and went around to the horse's head to walk her off the trailer. Even in the weak glow from the security lights, the horse's strange coloring was visible.

"Weird-looking horse," the tall man commented. He stood far away from the dancing animal. The mare's nostrils flared, sucking in the strange scents on the night air. Her hooves ground up the gravel underfoot, spinning on the end of the short lead. The man jerked the lead with a chain over her nose with two quick snaps. Instead of yielding, the mare strained her neck, holding her head high and swiveled her dark eye, watching. The moonlight reflected the white edges of her eye, giving the horse an otherworldly look.

The woman took the lead rope and spoke to the mare in a voice one might use with a visiting dignity—respectful, deferential. "Welcome to the lab, my dear. I've got some exciting plans for you."

She brought the horse through the rear of the building into a room lined with small animal cages where the scent of cedar shavings and sharp chemicals competed in the flow of forced air.

A thousand small, black eyes followed her progress as she led the mare into a stall. The tall man followed a few feet behind her.

The mare spun in her stall, sniffed the hay, and called out in a high-pitched whinny. The man flinched.

"Is she going to do that all the time?" he asked.

"She'll settle down."

His lips pressed into a thin line. "What's with the tiger stripes?" He flicked his hand at the mare's haunches in a dismissive gesture. "And her eye...it looks weird."

The woman's smile returned. It was not a warm smile, but one of self-satisfaction, one that said she knew more than most people around her and she might be gracious enough to bestow her knowledge on them, if she cared to. This evening, she would, because she was pleased with her new acquisition.

"You refer to the color striation of her coat over the hip—the mix of colors. It is one outward sign of how incredibly special this particular horse is on the inside. She's a chimera, and that will make all the difference to my work here."

The mare lifted her head, startled by the clang of the trailer ramp and truck engine roaring to life in the still air. The churn of the tires on gravel signaled the horse transport had left.

The woman turned her attention to a computer, preparing to enter new data and waiting, with a bit of a smirk, for the inevitable question.

"Chimera? What's that mean?" he asked.

She prepared a syringe. First step, she thought, will be to draw blood. She didn't look up to answer his question. "It means she's a single organism made up of genetically distinct types of cells, from two or more individuals—in fact, this mare has two sets of DNA." She entered the stall without looking at the man or caring whether her answer was sufficient. She had more important things to do. Inside the stall, she swabbed the horse's neck with practiced precision and thrust in the needle. The syringe swirled full of dark blood. She capped the syringe and exited the stall. "Tomorrow, I'll insert a port so I don't have to keep sticking her."

The lab animals stirred in their cages. Otherwise, the room was quiet. The intense light of the work area didn't reach into the back corners of the lab where the larger pieces of equipment were stored. Waiting their turn. Expensive diagnostic equipment that later would be used to test her theory. The research she'd been working on for decades. Research that others had tried to stop.

The man appeared to read her thoughts, calculating the cost of his investment. He rubbed the back of his neck. "How close are you to perfecting the drug do you think?"

She labeled the blood vial. "Close."

He stood with hands on his hips, staring at the strange horse. "I hope so. It better be worth it."

The woman's rubber soled shoes made no noise as she walked over to where he was standing. She was forced to tilt her head up to look up at him, but she didn't flinch from his questioning gaze. "It will be worth it, thanks to her." She watched the mare pull at a few strands of hay. "Finding Regalo de Suerte again was my lucky break."

Chapter 1

Pia Murphy, Pimlico Race Course

Six Years Ago

All her life, Olympia Murphy had a complicated relationship with luck. Luck and horses.

Olympia—known as Pia by friends and family—rested her elbows on the cool metal of the racetrack's guardrail and craned her neck to catch sight of the horses near the start. For the past several weeks she'd hauled herself out of bed early for a precious few hours at the track before heading to the office. The racetrack's siren call still lured her into the city in the wee hours so she could catch the early morning workouts. She entertained the notion for a few sweet moments that she was still in the game, that she had a future here, that her family's racing stable wasn't dead.

She was the sole inheritor of a failing racehorse training farm. Her dad, fully embracing the family's capricious fate with luck, had named their place Murphy's Law Farm. Pia never changed the name. That would be bad luck.

Like it could get any worse. The farm was a hundred acres of dilapidated barns and fences held together with baling twine and a prayer. Pia swept a stray strand of dark hair out of her eyes and stuffed it back into the ponytail that brushed across her back. She straightened and rolled the stiffness out of her shoulders. She hadn't slept well. Still, she got up and out once again, floating on a wisp of hope that this horse would be different. The one to turn things around. Regalo de Suerte was her last racehorse and her last hope.

The weak dawn sunlight hit the moisture evaporating off the track, creating the illusion that the horses were mystical creatures standing in a shimmering oasis. Ever since her dad first threw her up on the back of a horse, she'd always seen them as magical beings.

The illusion shattered when the pack breezed by at a gallop, spraying up clods of earth that clanged against the guardrail. Pia leaped back. With a second look, she caught the swish of a tail, churn of hind legs, and the rhythmic thrusting motion of the exercise jock.

A man standing next to her checked the time. "With any luck, he'll run like that again when it matters," he said, walking away with a smile. He was counting on luck. With horses, it was always about the luck.

Pia needed a heavy dose of it. And soon. Her office job was holding things together. For now. But her salary wasn't going to feed a string of broken-down ex-racers retired to a farm that was collapsing around her.

Her dad, Patrick Murphy, had been the king of second chances. Even as a respected trainer with a sound knowledge of bloodlines, he'd ended up with a collection of permanent ex-runners on the farm. Ones that didn't turn around on the racetrack and no one wanted in the sales ring. And her softhearted dad could never quite bring himself to part with them as they grew older. She loved that about her dad. But now...

Pia turned away from the rail and considered getting into the office early to rack up some overtime when she heard a familiar voice.

"The racetrack's no place for a lady."

Uncle Cosmo, with a big grin plastered across his face, walked toward her. His signature fedora was tilted over his right eye and he had an unlit cigar clamped between his teeth. She wondered whether he realized what a cliché he was.

Cosmo Vassiliki was her mom's big brother, but more importantly, Pia's racehorse backer. When he proposed a partnership, Pia scoffed. "If by backer, you mean someone who pays the majority of the bills, then you're on," she'd told him. He took on day-to-day expenses of Regalo de Suerte in exchange for a share in her winnings. Which hadn't been much lately.

Pia stood next to her uncle, her lean frame towering over him by a good six inches. She'd inherited her mother's Mediterranean warm skin, almond-shaped eyes with sweeping brows, and thick, dark hair, but it was her dad's Celtic warrior ancestors that gave her an almost six foot stature. She'd outgrown any hope of being a jockey by the time she was eleven.

She usually met her uncle to get an update on Regalo's progress and to exchange track gossip. They'd watch the morning workouts as a familiar, companionable silence settled between them. But this morning she sensed something was different. Something was up.

Cosmo took a hard look at the unlit end of his cigar. "I sure miss actually smoking these things."

The enticing scent of brewed coffee and bacon grease floated on the air from the café causing Pia's stomach rumble in response. Before leaving that morning, she'd scarfed down an old granola bar she found in the car chased with a cup of stale coffee. There was nothing in the house since she hadn't been grocery shopping for a couple weeks. Not very responsible behavior for a grown woman on the backside of twenty-five, she thought, and vowed to do better. She'd have to. She was getting married soon and Ron wasn't used to her erratic lifestyle. Lifestyle! Ha, she didn't have a lifestyle. Her life was more like a constant emergency reaction force. She wanted to do better. For him. To start their new life together like a scene from Leave It to Beaver, not Game of Thrones.

Pia lifted her face and sniffed like a bloodhound on the scent. Uncle Cosmo caught her longing glance. "Let's grab a cup of coffee. Sit down for a while, like normal people. Besides, I've got something I want to talk to you about."

And there it was. A flicker of apprehension ignited in the very bottom of Pia's empty stomach. She could sniff out bad news and had come to expect rotten luck. Like an emergency room physician, she had learned to hold her emotions in check while she probed the latest casualty. Her voice modulated, even, she asked, "It's Regalo?"

He squeezed her elbow and that little flame of worry flared. Uncle Cosmo, who usually treated Pia like one of the guys was acting as if she were made of glass. He nodded toward the entrance. "Let's sit down."

Inside, the blast of air-conditioned coolness raised goose bumps on the back of her arms. She grabbed a table near the big windows overlooking the track, while Cosmo went to the counter to order.

"Make mine a large," I called to his back. "And an egg sandwich if they've got 'em."

He waved a hand at his niece. "I've got it, I know."

While he was gone, Pia pulled a handful of napkins out of the dispenser and wiped the table as her mind slipped into its well-worn worry groove. *The filly. She's hurt.*

He returned with a tray holding steaming to-go cups of coffee and one sandwich wrapped in greasy paper. Pia stirred her coffee in jerky movements, her hand holding the little stirrer stick a bit too hard. "So, what did you want to talk to me about?"

His gaze skittered away to the group passing by their table and the side of his mouth hitched up.

She wanted to rip the bandage off this bad-news wound, whatever it was. "Is something wrong with Regalo? If there is, just tell me—"

He returned his attention to Pia. "There's nothing wrong with her, except that she's not a racehorse."

Her mouth fell open as a long queue of arguments lined up in her head. Cosmo held up a hand.

"Wait, I know what you're going to say, but hear me out first. You know she's not running well. We could put her in cheaper races, see if we could earn back some of the money, but is that the right thing to do to her?" His black eyebrow arched.

Pia looked down and shook her head.

Cosmo's voice softened. "She's a class horse, well bred, but she doesn't have the heart. Doesn't care about winning. Do we want to keep running her, putting her in cheap claimers, risking her breaking down?"

"Of course not." Pia lifted her head and held her uncle in her gaze. "There's no way I'd agree to putting her into a claiming race where she could end up with God knows who. I'd never risk her getting hurt or ending up in a bad place."

He made a sucking noise through his teeth. "So here's the thing. We have to let her go. For her own good, you see."

"See what?" Pia leaned forward. "You want to sell her? But—"

He crushed the napkin balled up in his fist. "Pia, I'm tapped out. The last divorce took what I had left and Regalo's not earning her keep. You can't afford her either and it's not fair to a young, healthy horse to just stand around. She needs a new job. One she can be good at. For a long time, not like racing."

The muscles in Pia's neck clenched as she whispered "no" even as her mind shifted through what he was saying and knew it made sense. "But she's all that's left..."

Pia's words choked off like a car sputtering to a halt. She didn't say *all that's left of Dad, who gave me this special horse because he believed in me.* She shook her head, shaking the thoughts away. *I'm an adult. I'm responsible for maintaining the farm, keeping my job...I can't cry over one horse like an infatuated teenager.* But the ring around her throat tightened as she envisioned Regalo getting on a trailer and driving away. Forever.

When Regalo goes, so would her hope of keeping the Murphy's Law racing stables alive, her dad's legacy. Her whole life up until this point was collapsing.

The warmth of Cosmo's hand covering hers pulled Pia back to the present.

"I know, kiddo. I know. When your dad gave her to you, we were all excited about her future. It's not every day you come across a horse with her breeding—a Luck horse. But let's face it, your dad was a poor businessman. He didn't know how to cut his losses."

Cosmos Vassiliki was the opposite of Paddy Murphy. He was a very good businessman and as such, there was little to no room for sentimentality. The Greek side of Pia's family was all business while the Murphys leaned heavily on Hail Mary saves, magic, and prayer. Pia saw a clear-eyed vision of what must be done in Cosmo's eyes and heard it in his clipped statements. He was like his sister, her mother. Hard work and the bottom line were what mattered. Pia recalled her mother looking out the kitchen window at the herd of "useless" horses and clicking her tongue with disgust. "Each one of those could be a vacation or a down payment on a new car or repairs to this place," she'd say, waving her hand at the water-stained ceiling or the peeling linoleum kitchen floor. Dad, sitting at the table with his racing form, would laugh and tell her a warm horse greeting in the morning beats a shiny new car any day.

"Dad believed Regalo would change everything. Change our luck," Pia said. She recounted to her uncle's impassive face how her dad had poured over Thoroughbred registries, studying the bloodlines, searching for one special horse. Paddy Murphy, a true Irish horseman, believed success depended on superior bloodlines, a good trainer, and luck. And by luck, he meant the Luck bloodline. For years he'd searched for a horse descended from the Argentine mare, Luck, who not only had an impressive racing record, but also kept running well into her mature years. She was imported into the United States and bred, but apparently producing offspring was not her strong suit. Luck progeny, although very fast, were rare.

"He wasn't wrong, not really," Uncle Cosmo said. "The filly is a unique find and should have been a great runner."

"So we breed her. Like you said, she's got the bloodlines."

Cosmo grimaced like he was having gas pains. "Expensive. Poor return on investment." He took a sip of coffee. "And risky. Admit it, we're both tapped out." He set the cup down and pushed it aside.

"So what's *your* solution?" Pia didn't mean for the words to have a biting edge, but she knew he wouldn't have brought this up if he didn't already have an answer in his back pocket.

"There's someone who wants to buy her." He rubbed his chin as if he were still considering the option, but Pia wasn't fooled. He was sold on the idea. "Not to race. We're keeping her papers to make sure of that. The woman's a show jumper. Seems like a nice lady. She says she's been looking for Luck Thoroughbred lines and she found Regalo and contacted me. She had a horse with almost the same breeding and is anxious to find another. And as you know, there aren't many out there." He leaned in, raising a brow. "And she's willing to pay."

"How much?"

"A lot. More than we'd normally get selling a racehorse that doesn't run."

Pia looked down at the congealed grease from the half-eaten sandwich. "It's not about the money." Her words sounded noble but made her cringe. Of course it was entirely about the money right now. She didn't have any. "Regalo would have to go to a good home, to someone who cared about her. Maybe we could even write in a buyback clause if she didn't work out." Pia's words rushed out. If she said them out loud, if she made some sort of provision for the mare's future, it wouldn't be so bad. Maybe she'd feel better. It wasn't working.

What other choice did she have? She couldn't support the horse by herself and Cosmo was losing his shirt carrying the larger percentage of the partnership. She had to think about her future, her new life with Ron. Sure, he had a great job and came from a family of some means, but what was she contributing to the marriage? A broken-down farm, a horse that didn't run, crippling tax bills, and the salary from an entry level job in an insurance fraud investigation firm. Not a good start to a marriage. The sale of Regalo would help.

Her uncle picked up his cigar and rolled it between his fingers. "Racing's a business. You have to watch out for the bottom line, do things that are hard sometimes." He held Pia's gaze and seemed to look into her private thoughts. "And you're getting married..."

One side of her mouth twisted up. "Finally. You forgot to say finally."

He pointed a finger in her face. "You didn't give me a chance. And it's about time you did marry. He's not Greek, but I hear he comes from a good family. With the money from the sale, you can fix up that old place, better yet, sell it. You have to think about your future now."

Pia cocked her head, waiting for a brilliant vision of her future to emerge. A vision of her wedding or of Ron surprising her with a special gift... Her thoughts remained stubbornly blank. Instead, the image of Regalo looking back at her with an accusing stare flashed before her eyes.

"What if she's not taken care of? If the new owner doesn't love her and—"

Uncle Cosmo barked out a cynical laugh. "Regalo will be taken care of. Who pays that kind of money for a horse and doesn't take care of it, right?"

Pia spat on her hand and made the sign of the cross.

He smirked. "Warding off the evil eye?"

"Not taking any chances. You know it follows me." A breeze swept over the table, lifting the napkins and sending them skittering across the surface. She slapped her hand down to keep them from flying off.

He waved in a dismissive gesture. "I'll write up a sales agreement. Every horse deserves to be some rich lady's pampered pony. Regalo will love it. Don't worry..."

"Buyback clause. Put that in the agreement. We get first refusal if she wants to sell her."

"Right, right." Uncle Cosmo stood.

This was happening. Regalo was going to a new owner. She had to think of what was ahead—a new life with Ron, new plans, new dreams. Pia gathered up the trash and dumped it in a nearby bin, but froze. It felt wrong. Like betrayal.

Uncle Cosmos stood beside her. His heavy hand thumped on her back. "Don't worry. It's a perfect situation for Regalo." His hand lifted but the cold shadow of its absence remained between her shoulders. "After all, what could go wrong?"

Chapter 2

Captain Jonah Watkins, Forward Operating Base (FOB), Afghanistan

Six Years Ago

THE PRE-BRIEF WAS HELD in an interior room of the most secure building in the complex. That said, the Razor Talons FOB was not much more than a conglomeration of shipping containers turned into housing units, makeshift storage sheds, and poured-concrete bunkers, surrounded by concertina wire atop a HESCO barrier. Thank God for that wall. Just outside lay landmines, Taliban snipers, enemy sympathizers, and a bunch of locals who switched loyalties more often than most guys here changed their socks. And the mission in this God-forsaken sandbox—or, as some of the men called it, litterbox—was to convince those locals that we were the good guys.

Captain Watkins nodded to the soldier posted at the door. Since the FOB was designated a no-salute zone for safety, Watkins's seniority was acknowledged with a slight nod. He entered to find the entire team already assembled. A quick glance at the time told him he was not a minute late—1500 local. Hanging on the wall next to the digital clock were old-fashioned analog clockfaces showing GMT—Greenwich Mean Time—as well as the time in Washington DC, London, and Bagdad. A final clockface on the end perpetually indicated it was five o'clock since its batteries had died months ago. Some joker had labeled it Margaritaville. Not strictly regulation, but the captain let it go. *If we lose our sense of humor out here, we're done for.*

Chairs scraped as the occupants rose to their feet. "Be seated, gentleman. We'll make this quick." Watkins tapped the stack of briefing folders against the table to straighten them and took his seat at the head of the table. He'd just pinned on his captain's bars a while ago and was anxious to succeed in this new assignment. It would ensure his promotion to major. So far, he had climbed the ranks "below the zone," meaning well ahead of schedule. And planned to continue at the same pace.

He opened the top folder. The mission briefing, captured in colorless military lingo, boiled down his assignment in this remote province into a simple catch phrase—a slogan if you could call it that. Winning the hearts and minds kind of stuff—blah blah blah. The brass in Washington liked slogans, but the mission here was much more complicated than a catchy phrase. Watkins had spent the last nine months piecing together a relationship of trust with local leaders in order to sway their support for the presence of US and multinational forces in the area as a counterweight against further Taliban incursion. This little scrap of dirt was a strategic location and would be disastrous if it fell completely under hostile control.

Watkins had worked tirelessly, orchestrating an intricate dance between patrol leaders on goodwill missions, who meet with local merchants and minor officials. The effort eventually gained the cooperation of local police forces and tribal elders. All that work had then paved the way for the mission Watkins faced today—meeting with Amardad Mukhtar and Elders of the Jurga to obtain their backing and support against the Taliban. In exchange, Mukhtar's community would receive US protection, medical assistance, and not a small amount of good old-fashioned infrastructure investment. Mukhtar was more than a tribal elder. He had climbed to prominence as a leader and maintained power over a vast number of Pashtun tribal groups. He had the ear of many far-reaching leaders in the region as well. It was up to Watkins to convince him to take the deal.

"Okay, let's go over the final arrangements and make sure we're all clear on our roles this afternoon," he said looking around the room. "First off, who's the assigned translator?"

Relief washed over him when he saw Reza raise his hand. He was the best. Watkins turned to Lieutenant Brody, Alpha Platoon Leader. He had worked closely with PsyOps in Kabul and had a reputation for winning the trust of the Pashtun leaders. "Give us any special protocol we should follow for this meeting."

Brody tapped the folder in front of him. "You're probably not going to like this, Captain, but you need to go in there unarmed. Also, no body armor."

A throat cleared to Watkins's left. He swiveled to lock eyes with the head of security—a civilian contractor sent in especially for this high-level meeting with Mukhtar.

"Captain, I want to assure you that security has cleared the venue and is in place, ready for any contingency," the security expert said.

"Thank you, Mr. Morrow. I should hope so." Morrow had given Watkins a bad feeling from the get-go. It was unusual he was here. Added to the fact that the captain didn't like being responsible for civilian contractors in a FOB no matter what his qualifications. But Watkins followed orders. Ones that came from some high-level intelligence official back in DC who vouched for Morrow's expertise.

Watkins's attention moved back to Brody. "Anything else? Removal of helmet, I understand. Maintaining distance from Mukhtar to ensure security..."

"Ah, Captain." Morrow again. He got up and moved to Watkins's side, pulled out a folder from underneath the stack, and opened it. "The venue has been moved. It's in a neighboring village, Girdi Dara. Mukhtar's reps approved when we pointed out it would be more secure."

"More secure?" The captain turned to Morrow, hovering over his shoulder. "Meaning, you've managed to set up security to our advantage?"

He reclaimed his seat at the table. "Without body armor, we considered it an unacceptable risk. At Girdi, we can have people around the perimeter, on top of buildings in line of sight."

This was the exact thing Watkins had promised Mukhtar would not happen. He'd given his word that they would meet on equal footing. "Why wasn't I consulted? And why am I only hearing about this now?" A glance at the clock told him this would require moving the departure up considerably. In fact, they'd have to leave almost immediately to make it in time. "Dammit, what a cluster. Assemble the intel group, the support van. Is it possible to get word to Mukhtar? I want to assure him about this change in plan."

Brody shook his head. "No, not if he's on the road. Security ordered a comms blackout before the meeting."

Watkins seared Morrow with a look that told him he had better make himself scarce when he got back.

"Brody, Reza, you come with me. The rest assemble at the security checkpoint outside the rendezvous site. We do have the coordinates, is that right, Morrow?"

His dark complexion colored a bit. "Sir, these are Afghans. They may show up two hours late or two days late. No need to hurry."

Watkins strode across the room and leaned into his face so close Morrow winced. Watkins's voice remained controlled, but barely. "Your inability to follow communications procedures through chain of command could have obliterated six months of work. Since it is my job to see we succeed, I'm going to do everything in my power to ensure this meeting is the first step. And I intend to run down exactly how this change was overlooked when I get back. Do I make myself clear, Mr. Morrow?"

He shifted his eyes away. "Yes, sir."

A staff sergeant stood in the doorway. "Your vehicle is ready, Captain."

Totally against convention, Watkins decided to drive to keep his mind from circling back over what had just happened and instead focus on how he would approach this first meeting with Mukhtar. Lieutenant Brody jumped in the passenger seat and shot Watkins a questioning look, but decided against taking note of this break in procedure. Nothing about this mission was "regular." The hum of the all-terrain tires on the rough roadbed made conversation nearly impossible. Brody checked the Blue Force Tracker mapping system, then scowled at the paper map flattened out across his knee. His head lifted to scan the horizon. It looked the same no matter where you turned—dirt road, rubble, mountains shrouded in dust.

"Captain, this rendezvous site is outside of our AO on the edge of a Taliban stronghold. I don't know what they were thinking moving it."

"Morrow claimed the first location was compromised. Taliban was informed of the meeting somehow. Security Ops wanted it moved at the last minute."

Reza, sitting the back seat, scooted forward to look out the windshield. "Girdi is the next town over from where Taliban set fire to houses last winter."

He didn't need to describe what happened there. They all knew.

Watkins turned to Brody. "I'm going to call in our position and ETA to SecOps and let them know we're on the way. That is, if you can get a channel out here." He picked up the unit and punched in the code. "Alpha Base, this is Whale Boy, reporting in. On our way to Op Peaceful Warrior, just past mile marker twelve in Delta quadrant headed north-northeast."

Brody looked askance. "Whale boy?" The corner of his mouth curled up.

Watkins shrugged. "Some SecOp smartass gave me the handle when I came in country. Because of my name."

Brody's blank look told me he wasn't following.

"Jonah. And the whale. You ever go to Sunday school?"

Brody's eyes brightened. "Oh, yeah. Five years of Parochial school with the nuns in Chicago. Got the ruler marks on my knuckles to prove it."

Brody was a great guy. He was headed back stateside in a few months and Watkins hoped their paths would cross again in the future.

A voice overlaid with static crackled in Watkins's ear. *Whale Boy, you're not in the right quadrant for Op Peaceful Warrior. You're headed into...* the comms broke off.

"Dammit." The handset dropped to the floor of the vehicle and he kicked it aside. "Try to reach them again."

Brody retrieved it and looked up through the windshield. His eyebrows marched together, forming a furrow in the middle. "Where's Morrow's security? No one has stopped us at the perimeter and we're approaching Girdi now." He punched in a number, but the comms were dead.

Watkins slowed the vehicle and checked behind him. Nothing. The Quick Reaction Force vehicle had stopped a quarter mile out, as directed, awaiting further instructions. A group of buildings clustered around the road shimmered in the afternoon heat. Everything was dust-colored—the road, the structures, the scrubby vegetation. Were there spotters on the rooftops? He didn't see anything. A group of men squatted under the sparse shade of a juniper tree. A boy ran down the road, turned, and disappeared into a courtyard.

"Check the time," Watkins asked Brody.

He reported they were on time.

"That means we're early," Reza chuckled.

The men under the tree turned their faces toward the vehicle as it approached. From one of the buildings, midpoint along the road, a tall figure stepped into the street. He was bearded, as most men, wearing a flat dark cap and drape over his shoulders. Four men stepped into positions surrounding him. Mukhtar.

"I don't like this," Watkins said. "Where are Morrow's guys?"

Reza leaned forward in order to look up at the buildings. "If they're here, they're damn good at lying low."

Watkins opened the door.

Brody grabbed his arm. "Wait. Something's not right." He let go of Watkins's elbow. "Captain, I suggest we wait for confirmation." His eyes implored Watkins to hear him out.

A quick glance at Mukhtar. He stood under an awning, watching the vehicle. *I'm making him wait*, Watkins thought. *I'm tipping the balance of honor, respect.*

Watkins pushed the car door open. "You wait here. Keep the others back. I'll go in first." He removed his helmet and dropped it in Brody's lap. "It'll be okay, I promise."

Outside the vehicle, the sun glinted off the tops of the buildings. A fly circled his sweating head and distracted his attention for a split second as he waved it off. A louder buzzing, a roar broke over the silence. A motorcyclist appeared at the far end of the street. Watkins made a quick assessment of the figure—dressed in dark clothing, face covered, a backpack strapped on his shoulders. He leaned over, gunning the bike.

"Mukhtar!" Watkins shouted, waved. "Take cover!"

A stunned face amid his guards. The smell of churned up dirt, dust. The cyclist raced down the road as Watkins sprinted toward the group, waving. Out of the corner of his eye, he noted the men under the tree had disappeared.

Watkins's hand groped his side, but the weapon wasn't there. Not armed. No body armor.

The cycle's engine whined and then a wall of black. A noise like a siren screamed in his head, rattling inside his skull. Blood and dirt filled his mouth.

Then nothing.

Chapter 3

Murphy's Law Farm

Present Day

Pia shut the mailbox and trudged back up the driveway toward the farmhouse. Shuffling through the stack, she saw they were mostly junk mail flyers, advertisements, and—ugh! The vet bill. This one would be a biggie and there wasn't any room left in what she jokingly called a budget this month. She folded it and shoved it in her coat pocket out of habit—so she wouldn't have to listen to Ron complain about money spent keeping the old horses alive. Now that Ron was gone, she didn't have to worry about what he'd say. Now she had to worry about how she'd pay.

The back door screeched and scraped across the floor when she pushed on it. The hinges were loose and it needed rehanging. It was on the to-do list since last summer. Ron had promised to do it, but somehow he never had time. Pia dropped the mail in a bowl on the kitchen table and yanked opened the refrigerator. She could eat leftovers again. For the past five years, leftovers had been banned. Ron informed her she was never to serve them, along with several other mandates. Never wake him up early on

Saturday mornings—his only sleep-in-late day (Sundays he was up early for golf), never launder his dress shirts—they had to be professionally cleaned and starched, and never, ever ask him to get on a horse again. Pia slammed the refrigerator door shut. Before they were married, he'd been a different person.

Pia sat at the long kitchen table and spun the bowl containing the pile of bills. Seemed they were always short of both time and money. At first, the sale of Regalo helped pay off some taxes and fund the wedding, but wasn't near enough to get the broken fences, sagging barn roof, leaking pipes, and rotted floorboards fixed. The house was a charming money pit sitting on a hundred acres of neglected, but prime, real estate. Ron had a dream of developing it and making a financial killing. Pia had a dream of restoring the house and barns. Growing a business. A horse business.

"Horses aren't a business," Ron would say. He got testy whenever he was paying the bills. "They're a hobby. A hobby for rich people who can afford something that just keeps racking up expenses and never returns on the investment." Ron always handled the bills and Pia had been more than happy to leave all the household finances to him. She took after her dad—not great with money. Ron was a businessman and a financial adviser, after all. And she knew how hopeless she was with money. Another thing she had in common with her dad. Ron didn't have much tolerance for horses. A horse that didn't make an ROI—return on investment—in his mind was a walking, eating, pooping, financial liability and waste of time. That's when he started in on his land development campaign. "Look at this," he'd say, swinging the laptop around for her to examine a spreadsheet she didn't understand. "If we divided this place in quarter-acre lots, allowing for common areas, with the price of land in this county we'd clear at least 6.5 million." His eyebrows would shoot up, waiting for Pia to calculate what she could do with that kind of money, waiting for her to come to her senses...

Ron was difficult, she knew that, but had such expressive, dark eyes. They were deep and round and deliciously inviting; Pia would fall into them, forgetting everything else. She recalled how they looked up close when he was kissing her. Staring into hers. Holding her captive. She'd always wanted to say or do anything to make him happy. To keep his eyes smiling on her.

It started with their arguments over the farm. It was a fissure that grew and spread over time. The farm had been Pia's home. She couldn't watch as developers ripped apart the fields where she'd galloped ex-racers, or tore down the house containing the bedroom where her mother lay sick for months before she died. She could not watch a two-hundred-year-old barn be crushed into rubble for the sake of a cookie-cutter mansion.

Fights over selling the farm were like water sloshing over the bathtub rim into other fights. Not just money. The time she spent with the horses. His lack of interest in fixing up the farm. Why she didn't want to attend his company dinners. But the one that hurt the most—her supposed lack of interest in her appearance. That one stung.

It all came to a head the day she sat down at the kitchen table and opened his laptop. Looking back, she wasn't sure why she did it. Probably to figure out where all the money was going. The question irked her. Ron handled their finances and he always told her he had it under control.

A mug with coffee dregs and a plate covered in crumbs attested to the fact that Ron had been down for breakfast. *Why he couldn't put the dishes in the sink, I don't know.* The plate rested on the lid of his laptop. He must have been checking email before work. She listened. Overhead, the pipes clanked. He was in the shower, getting ready for work.

Pia pulled his laptop closer and opened the lid. She was too lazy to go upstairs right now to get her iPad, so if his was still logged on, she'd look up the accounts, check the balances, get a better idea of where—

The account page displayed balances in all the accounts: savings, Mastercard, loans...

This can't be right.

The retirement account balance was less than what would carry them through two months of expenses. She recalled he had her sign something months ago. He said he was moving the fund into a more aggressive investment portfolio. She should have asked, but at the time, she was dealing with contractors fixing the barn roof and a dozen other problems.

She clicked on savings. It looked about the same, but then again, it never was anything to shout about. A line with a code she didn't recognize. Auto bill payment, so it came out every month. She logged out of the bank's accounts and rested her hand on the edge of the lid, ready to close the laptop when a message flashed in the bottom corner of the screen. The sender's name was Valerie MacQuoid. No one Pia knew. The pop-up message faded, but not before she read the first few lines.

If you want to start your day off with a hot deal, meet me...

The rest was gone.

"What are you doing?" Ron stood in the doorway, his hair still wet from the shower. His face bloomed red.

Pia slammed the lid. "I needed to look something up and mine's upstairs."

That was the beginning of the end. A week later Pia had the evidence. She was, after all, good at finding out things.

The truth came out over dinner. Pia pressed for the name of the new fund holding their life savings.

Ron put his fork down alongside the plate with deliberate attention. She held her breath.

"Pia, it's time we talked about something." His words were even, like a professor addressing a class of nervous freshmen. "You've asked about money that simply doesn't exist anymore."

"What are you talking about? That's our retirement. What do you mean *doesn't exist*?"

He rubbed his chin. "How to I explain this?"

"You stole it, that's how you explain it." She picked up her plate and tossed it into the sink with the silverware, making a clatter that set her spine tingling.

"That's quite an accusation. I'd watch it."

He was so damned calm. "Then what would you call it? Money doesn't just disappear. Not that much money." She leaned against the peeling countertop.

He spun in his seat to look at her. "I borrowed against it. It wasn't stolen because you signed the papers. Remember?"

"No, I don't remember." Her voice was shrill, piercing heavy air. "I don't remember giving you permission to spend all our money." Her gaze traveled to the window, to the black Tesla sitting outside. "That's how you paid for that car."

Ron stood and brushed past her, leaving his dirty plate on the table. "You have the farm, dear. You got what you wanted, what you wouldn't share. So I took what's mine—what the farm's worth in liquid assets against the investment portfolio—which is now defunct." He loomed over her, his face twisted in an expression she'd never seen before. Hate leached out of his eyes. Hate for her. Their life together.

He waved an arm through the air like a game show host. "So now you have all of this! The broken-down house, the crippling real estate taxes, and the beloved Murphy's Law Farm, the money pit of horse racing. What a name. What an effing perfect name your dad gave this dumpster fire of a place."

He shoved her aside and stomped upstairs. She heard drawers slamming shut, the jingle of coat hangers. In no time, he was downstairs with a bag packed.

His hand reached for the doorknob.

"Off to Valerie's place?" Pia lobbed the taunt at him. She expected a stiffening of his back. Shock that she knew. Instead, he turned and smiled. A smile of satisfaction, like after a great meal or a particularly good glass of bourbon.

"As a matter of fact, it would be more correct to call it your place. You bought it for her."

He slipped through the door and was gone. Pia stood in the center of the kitchen, almost exactly where she was standing now, not moving. Not willing to absorb what the man she thought she knew had told her. Betrayal's not like how the storybooks describe it. It isn't hot anger, violent eruptions, or slicing pain. It's more like being submerged in a soundproof chamber of ice water, or like being cast out on a frozen lake where you can't get your feet under you no matter how hard you try to make sense of things. There's no ground anymore. It's bottomless.

Chapter 4

National Security Agency

Present Day

Watkins sat in his car in the parking lot outside of the National Security Agency's main headquarters and stared up at the clouds reflected in the glass-faced cubical buildings. He never imagined he'd end up working at a desk most of the time, but all in all it wasn't a bad compromise after he separated from the army. He was still working hot topics—the pointy end of the sword as they liked to call it—working intel projects in support to Homeland Security's Special Reaction Team.

He stowed his phone in the console and dug out his badge. It was about a fifteen-minute walk to the door, but he always parked outside the perimeter fence line and as far away from the building as possible. Not just for the exercise, but because he knew it was the safest exit strategy in case of an attack. Some habits die hard.

Inside the front door, Watkins waved his badge over the turnstile and punched in his PIN. His fingers moved by habit over the numbers without a conscious thought. He nodded to the guard and walked down the hallway past a gallery of cryptologic achievements in history and a black granite memorial—*They Served in Silence* etched across the top. Another monument to dead heroes. This morning, like every morning since he began working here almost five years ago, he stood a moment and scanned the list for any freshly-engraved names. And took another moment to remember the ones he would never forget: Brody, Reza, Holofield... The sticky bomb the motorcyclist slapped to the side of the vehicle had killed them instantly.

Even though it was only six thirty in the morning when Watkins stepped on, the elevator was crowded and reeked. Chicken liver Thursday, he thought. Thankfully, this pungent breakfast treat was only served once a week.

He waved his badge over another reader outside his office door and waited for the click. It was dim inside with the blinds drawn and only every other light turned on. The analysts—especially the ones working geo-plotting on the curved, high-def monitors wanted it that way. It was quiet aside from the click of keyboards and the drone of the air handlers.

Watkins tossed his keys on the desk, sunk into his chair, and logged in. While he waited for the triple-monitor computer to boot up, he unlocked his drawers and pulled out a report file he'd been working on.

A young analyst dressed in torn jeans and a Dr. Evil T-shirt walked by his desk and raised a hand in greeting. "Hey, Jonah," Darren said loud enough for several heads to pop up like prairie dogs above their cubicle walls. He held a finger over his lips and shushed himself. "So-orry."

Watkins shook his head and smiled. Good kid, smart as hell, but no sense about what's expected in a professional setting. He'd known a lot of fellows like Darren in the military. They would have been booted out if not for the unique skills they brought to the table. This kid was the same. A pro at gaining access to all sorts of computer systems. Thank God he was on our side.

Like Watkins, Darren had been recruited recently for the special Homeland Security cell inside of NSA. The two agencies collaborated on terrorist and criminal activity from different angles, but their roles complemented each other when a threat moved from the international arena to the US and its territories.

A heavy woman in a sweeping skirt and cowboy boots stomped across the floor and collapsed in the desk chair adjacent to Watkins. She flung her oversized purse into the bottom drawer and kicked it shut.

"Good morning, Marion." Watkins greeted her as he scrolled through his emails, deleting most of them.

"What's good about it?" she answered.

It was the same sarcastic exchange they had every morning.

Watkins spun in his chair and smiled at her. "What's good about it? You woke up this morning with another chance to save the free world."

Marion made a noise like a pig rooting around the trough. "Ha. I'm here for the money, same as you, sweetie." She slurped from her coffee travel mug. "Just eight more years and I'm outta here, not that I'm counting."

Watkins liked Marion. He liked her dependable banter, something he could count on. Regular. Unchanging. He found he didn't like surprises much these days.

"So you got any big plans for the weekend, handsome?" Marion teased.

He wasn't so sure about her calling him *handsome*. Sure, she was an old-school Baltimore native and called most of the guys "hon" or "handsome" or the sarcastic "sweetie," but in his case… Watkins ran a finger over the raised scar that ran down the side of his face from the edge of one eye and disappeared behind his ear.

The ear that lost 50 percent of its hearing.

He turned the damaged part of his face away and mumbled, "Nothing special, Marion. How 'bout you?" But didn't hear half of what she was saying about a family get-together in Fells Point. The background clatter of the office faded as his mind spiraled back to the rehab hospital. Six years ago and he could still distinctly remember the exact, peculiar noise of the machine that was keeping him alive.

※※》 《※※

The sucking noise it made was at once annoying and at the same time comforting. At the end of each long, drawn suck it sort of popped and started all over again. The probe—what did the nurse call it?—cannula up his nose and the tubes trailing to the inside of each elbow made him into less than a human. When he awoke after the bombing, he wasn't sure of the extent of the damage. Relief flooded him when he saw two limbs extending from his body under the thin blanket and could wiggle toes.

The ICU nurse showed him a button. It connected to a metered bag hanging on a stand nearby. "It's for pain. You can push the button every two hours for a dose when you need it. Don't wait too long, however." She wagged a finger. "It takes a while to have an effect." She pushed the tray table nearer. It held a plastic glass with a bendy straw sticking out of the top. Apparently, he was not expected to be able to drink from a glass either.

After she tucked the blanket in and set the button device within reach, she headed to the door. Before leaving, she paused in the doorway. The look of pity in her eyes steeled his resolve. Watkins vowed he was not going to push that button and dissolve into a fog of painkillers. He was going to get out of there. But first, he was going to get some straight answers about what happened.

"Captain Watkins." A doc in camo stepped into the room. "I'm Major Hastings. I wanted to check on how you were feeling now that you're awake." Hastings didn't wait for him to answer, but pulled a chart out of the sleeve on the end on the bed and frowned.

"Don't believe everything you read," Watkins told him.

He set the chart aside and clicked on one of those annoying little pen lights to shine in Watkins's eye. His breath smelled of mint, when he leaned over to encircle his wrist, checking his pulse. check more vitals. "You're lucky, you know."

"Sorry, but I'm not feeling too lucky right now."

Hastings caught his bottom lip with his teeth. "Of course. Foolish thing for me to say. I apologize."

The room became quiet aside from the wheeze from the machinery. Watkins shifted in the bed. "I can move my feet," he said. "I'm still alive. I guess I am lucky."

The doctor's face relaxed. "The blast threw you back several feet and buried you under a pile of rubble. The search dogs found you." He lifted his eyebrows, as if to signal *Do you remember?*

His memory was a big, blank hole. The last piece Watkins could retrieve was getting out of the vehicle. Brody pulling him back, yelling something. But he had to wave off Mukhtar. Warn him. The motorcyclist with the backpack sped toward them. Then just sound. Sound so shattering that it felt like blackness. And pebbles raining down.

The doc was talking to him again. "So your vision is not affected in the right eye."

"What?" Watkins probed the bandage over the left side of his face, covering from the forehead down over the left eye, cheek, ear… "My eye's gone?" The shiver in his voice betrayed the fear and revulsion.

"Not gone, but damaged. We can't say yet, but most likely you'll regain full vision." He rubbed a hand over his mouth as his gaze skittered away.

"But there's more." Watkins's voice was flat.

His attention shot back to Watkins. "Yes. The skin was severely damaged on that side. The ear was reattached but will require further plastic surgery for reconstruction and you've likely suffered significant hearing loss."

There are no mirrors in these military medical units. Good decision.

Watkins nodded, acknowledging the facts. He resolved to evaluate them later, when he was alone. Facial disfigurement, vision and hearing loss…he wouldn't be fit for in-theater combat areas ever again. Everything he'd worked and trained for… Not now.

"Could be worse," Watkins said. He tried to smile.

"Just take it easy. The staff here will keep me posted on your progress." Dr. Hastings tucked the medical file under his arm. "One more thing."

Now Watkins thought real hard about pushing that pain button. *What else?*

The doc shot a glance at the door. "There's a Colonel Abramson to see you. If you're up for it?"

"Sure, I'm okay." *Who says "no" to a colonel.*

"He said he wanted to go over some of the facts of…your accident." The doc shot the file back in the sleeve at the end of my bed and beat a hasty retreat to the door.

Big Army would want to debrief him on the incident. There were a lot of lose threads that didn't add up. But they wouldn't send a colonel to conduct an investigation. There was something else going on here. Yeah, that pain button was looking mighty tempting now.

Not thirty seconds later a man with a number one buzz cut, metallic gray on the temples, and wearing a uniform with such sharply defined creases down the front of his pants he certainly never sat down, stood in the doorway. Despite his condition, a twinge urging Watkins to stand and salute shot through his body.

"Colonel Abramson," he greeted the officer. "Come in."

"Captain Watkins." He pulled up a chair and sat. "Are you up to giving me a few minutes?"

When Abramson pulled the chair over to his good side, Watkins studied the insignia on the uniform. He's an Intel guy. *What did he want?*

Abramson leaned closer. "I want to offer you a job."

Chapter 5

Burke and Hingham Insurance Investigations, Inc.

When Pia finally got in to work—a half hour past her usual arrival time—the office reeked like someone had microwaved a fish taco. A few days ago. She was late for the morning stand-up meeting—not that it mattered. Mr. Burke mouthed the same platitudes about client privacy, increased productivity, and attention to detail every Monday morning. It got so her friend, Deliah, started keeping a Burke Company buzzwords bingo sheet she'd sneak into the meetings.

Pia edged into the conference room and took the only empty seat. Heads swiveled in her direction when Mr. Burke voiced a sarcastic greeting. "Nice of you to join us, Mrs. Harcourt." Pia flinched, hearing herself called Mrs. Harcourt—her married name. She was working on changing that.

A sharp heel landed on her foot under the table. Pia's head snapped up to catch Deliah twiddling her pen and smirking at her. She passed her a bingo card under the table.

Mr. Burke was a small man with hair thinning in the back where he couldn't see it. He walked fast, gestured in staccato motions, and talked like someone was going to interrupt him any moment. He opened the meeting with a review of the outstanding insurance fraud investigation cases. That was how the company made money—as a third party insurance investigator. At first Pia had been hired for her data input and management skills, but she soon proved her abilities in fraud investigations. In the case of a suspected arson investigation, she had uncovered a silent partner among the building's financial backers who was underwater financially. She directed the company's contracted private investigator to look into his connections, which led to the arrest of an arson-for-hire. The PI, a squat guy who looked like a human pug dog named Bart Wiggins, had also convinced her one day to act as bait in an entrapment scheme. He was investigating a workers' comp claim on a guy who supposedly hurt his back, but when he saw Pia struggling to load bags of mulch outside the Home Depot, he leaped to her aid. Wiggins was there with a camera, filming the whole thing. Pia didn't like acting as Wiggins's bait, but it made sense to stay on his good side. Her job was to feed him information and leads she dug up, so when he got the evidence to prove fraud, it made her look good. And she needed to keep her job.

"Mrs. Harcourt, did you hear me?" Mr. Burke pinned her in his gaze.

"Yes, of course." Pia straightened in her seat. Her faced blazed when heads turned once again in her direction.

"I asked for your input." Mr. Burke stood at the head of the table.

Someone tapped a pen against the polished surface. Deliah's eyebrows shot half way up her head as she mouthed a word Pia couldn't make out.

Mr. Burke sighed. "Your input on strategies for increasing recovery from fraudulent insurance claims. The stats show a drop off this month and I'd like your take on what's causing this."

"Close the loopholes, increase penalties for convicted fraud, demand more transparency when conducting investigations..." She parroted back Mr. Burke's favorite war cry, ticking off a few tried and true bingo catch phrases, but he wasn't buying it today.

"No, I'm looking for innovative solutions from your unique perspective having worked this problem for several years now." He placed a palm on the table and leaned toward Pia.

Innovative? Unique? Since when did Burke want to hear anything that smelled like it might be risky.

She clamped her bottom lip between her teeth and shifted focus away from his needy, pale eyes. Her home account's bank balance figures floated there, superimposed on the oatmeal-colored conference room walls. She couldn't keep the farm afloat on what she was bringing in now. But a promotion might tip the balance. A raw emptiness hallowed out her insides. Her words grew louder to cover the sound of blood pulsing in her ears, fueled by anger. Anger and frustration over Ron's underhanded pillage of their savings ignited all the financial frustration and fear festering in her.

"What we need to do is catch these bastards who think they're above the law. Every one of them thinks they're smarter, exempt, more deserving or whatever it is they tell themselves to justify their slimy acts. They need to be caught. They need to know I'm not fooled by their lies and I'm coming after them."

Mr. Burke groped behind him to pull up his chair and sank into it. "Well, yes, I agree. And while I admire your ardor, we do have to work within the law." He shot Deliah, the company's legal counsel, a significant look. Pia wondered if the message was *Keep an extra close eye on this one.* He flipped open the folder in front of him. "Moving on, let's hear from Joe on the new AI project..."

Wiggins leaned over and murmured, "You go, girl." His breath smelled of a mix of Everything bagel and peanut butter. "Get your PI license and team up with me."

He winked. Pia shuddered.

She knew her self-control was slipping. If Wiggins wanted her help, she'd been way out of line. The meeting continued another forty minutes but she walked out without taking a single note. As soon as she was outside the conference room, Pia bolted for the ladies' room. Inside, she splashed cold water on her face. When she looked up, Deliah was standing directly behind her. She sauntered to the bank of sinks and perched on the edge.

"So, you want to explain what that was all about?"

Pia dabbed her face with a paper towel. "What?"

"Don't give me *what?*" Her eyes went wide as she mimicked a stupid look. "You went all Rambo in there. Burke the jerk shouldn't have pressed you for an answer to embarrass you, but wow, Pia. Before that, you were catatonic." She shook her head, causing her long braids to swing across her shoulders, and folded her arms across her chest.

Pia sighed, dumped the paper towel and pulled open the door. She held it as Deliah followed her out and stopped in the hallway. Her friend wasn't going to let it go.

She sighed. "Ron. He's the problem."

"Up to something else? Something besides cheating on you and stealing half your money?"

Pia winced and glanced around to see who might have overheard. She lowered her voice. "Yeah, more than that. He wants the farm."

Deliah's dark eyes shone with a cold heat. "What's going on?"

"Calls from listing agents, a mysterious bill that turned up from a surveyor, a political candidate's election chair who keeps calling asking for Ron to discuss zoning issues... Zoning?" Pia's voice had risen from hushed tones to outraged rant. "He's always wanted to break up the farm and sell it. I'm afraid he's cooked up some kind of land grab scheme but I can't figure out what it is."

When Pia glanced over Deliah's shoulder, she crumbled. Wiggins had walked up right behind her. He'd heard everything.

"Your ex is a cheating, conniving creep," Deliah said, unaware the PI was behind her.

"Cheating husbands are my specialty," he said, inserting himself into the conversation. "You want to catch him in the act, get the goods on him?"

Deliah tugged her away. "This is a private conversation, Bart."

He called after them. "Put a tracker on his vehicle. Catch him dead to rights, that's what I advise. Hey, I'll leave one on your desk. Think about it." He turned and headed in the other direction.

Deliah called after him, "Wouldn't be legal!"

He shrugged, waved away her comment, and headed down the hall.

Deliah guided Pia in the opposite direction. "Forget him. C'mon, let's get a coffee and talk about this."

The coffee shop downstairs was a popular rendezvous spot because it had tall plushy booths that allowed you to hide from prying eyes and eavesdropping colleagues. Deliah ordered at the counter and nodded to a booth in the very back.

They had sat a minute before a waitress put a thick-walled mug of coffee in front of each and a plate of chocolate croissants in between.

"I couldn't resist," Deliah said and lifted one onto her plate. "I prefer chocolate to whiskey when you've got to get something off your chest." She took a huge bite.

"I don't have anything to get off my chest," Pia said.

She looked up at Pia under a fringe of dark lashes. "I think you do. Fill me in on your farm—what's your income stream?"

"No income, just outflow." Pia tore the napkin she was holding into tiny strips. "Thing is, I grew up on this farm. My dad bred and raised Thoroughbreds, mostly for the track. He raced some, sold some." She hitched a shoulder as to say, no big deal.

"You have racehorses?" Deliah's eyes grew wide.

Pia held up a hand. "Old ones. Before you start imagining some ritzy racing stable, let me assure you, it's not like that. Murphy's Law is a hundred-acre-fixer-upper."

Deliah sat back and folded her arms. "Girl, still, a hundred acres? It must be worth a fortune."

"That's what Ron says. It is. He checked it out."

Deliah squirmed in her seat. "I don't know, I might be with Raunchy Ron on this one. Sell that place and move into a deluxe condo somewhere."

"That's not me." Pia picked up a piece of croissant and set it down. "What kills me now is I sold the best horse I ever had—a gift from my dad—to get out of debt and finance the wedding. Can you believe that? I lost a great horse in exchange for a horse's ass." Pia took a sip of the scalding hot coffee and dumped more cream into the cup. "Ron made no secret of wanting to sell the place. When we got married, I made it clear that wasn't an option, but he went ahead and got an estimate on it. That really upped the ante. We fought more, he came home less. Then, the money in our 401(k) went missing. 'Not really missing,' he said. Claimed he'd moved it to a portfolio with better return, but he never mentioned where."

"Hold up." Deliah held her hand up in a stop sign. "You signed financial papers without reading them?"

A flush spread over Pia's cheeks. It was stupid. "Ron's an investment broker. We were married. I figured he—I don't know—he knew more about money than I did, so I left it to him to handle."

She sucked her teeth, making a tsk-tsk sound. "So, the property produces no income?"

"Just a tenant farmer who leases some fields for hay. And a woman, Hillary, who rents a trailer on the property. She helps with the horses for part of her rent."

Deliah kept shaking her head. "You're in a world of hurt, it sounds like. And that side action of your hubby's, what's her name again?"

"Valerie MacQuoid. Works for the county exec."

Deliah snorted. "What kind of service does she provide?" She thumbed to a search window. "Here she is." She held the screen so Pia could see it. Pia already knew what Valerie looked like. The opposite of her. Deliah swiped the screen and displayed another picture of Valerie, this time with her hair up in a French twist (with a few stray strands caressing her blushing cheekbones) and wearing a severe business suit with a triple-strand of pearls.

Pia frowned. "Triple-strand. Overcompensating for something."

"Yeah," Deliah placed her phone face down on the table. "For being a—" She bit off the word when she looked up into Pia's face. "You still have feelings for this guy?"

Pia's head made a jerking motion back and forth. "No. Not really." She swept up the napkins shreds from the table and dropped them on her plate with the uneaten pastry.

The jumble of bangles on her friend's hand chimed when she slid it across the tabletop, grasping Pia's. "Damn."

It was real. All the excuses Pia had told herself since discovering the missing funds, all Ron's "sensible" explanations vanished and were replaced with the glaring, naked, hard truth. The truth that she'd been cheated, would likely lose her home, and worst of all had financed her disastrous marriage with the sale of the biggest gift her dad had ever bestowed on her sat like a cement block dragging down her insides, making her bones turn to putty. Her whole body collapsed on itself. Her future, her identity, her dreams were a lie—a lie Ron had fed her as long as it served his purposes, all the while planning God knows what.

"You better protect yourself. Get a top-drawer lawyer," Deliah said. She rummaged in the huge purse at her side. "Here. Take this." She held out a business card. "It's a guy I met at the last legal conference." Her lips on one side curled up. "You tell him you're a friend of mine. It'll put you to the top of the list, trust me."

Deliah had a string of guys all lining up to do her favors.

"Thanks." Pia took the card. She dreaded what would come next. The marriage was well and truly over so now she had to focus on keeping her home. "This is unbelievable," she whispered.

Deliah shook a manicured finger. "Believe it."

Chapter 6

Military Hospital Rehab Unit

Six Years Ago

Watkins entered Dr. Merkowski's office and was surprised the psychiatrist sent to conduct the checkout eval was a lot younger than he expected. And a woman. He didn't know why he'd envisioned the head of the psych department to be a grizzled, war-hardened Colonel or a Freud look-alike, but it taught him he had a lot of preconceived notions he'd need to get rid of.

That kind of thinking wouldn't fly in the intelligence game.

Ever since Colonel Abramson tapped Watkins for the new assignment, he'd continued to warn him it wouldn't be easy. The battlefront wasn't clearly defined, something you could plot on a map, but was rather a strategy game of the mind. If Watkins walked into an intelligence debrief with personal prejudices or expectations, he could at best cloud the information, at worse, totally misinterpret what was said and possibly get someone killed.

He'd already done that. He wasn't making that mistake again.

Dr. Merkowski, a civilian, was dressed in a navy blue suit with a pale-colored blouse, blending well with the backdrop of a military hospital. Her blond hair was pulled back at the nape of her neck. She got to her feet as he entered and gestured to a group of chairs clustered around a coffee table. After she'd seated herself, Watkins sunk into another chair and turned down her offer of something to drink.

"Well, let's get to it, then," she said and rested a folder on her lap. He assumed it was his jacket—a personnel record containing everything about him, including his recovery. Or lack thereof.

"I'd appreciate that," he said. Decisive. His respect for the doctor went up a notch.

"Captain Watkins, I'm gratified to see you've made a remarkable physical recovery. Occupational therapy reports your hearing is improved, you've regained 90 percent vision in the damaged eye, and you—"

"My name is Jonah. You can call me that." He had to get used to being a civilian.

Her shoulders dropped. Maybe she sat back a little more comfortably in her chair.

"Thank you, Jonah. You can call me Lena if you wish."

They sat in a tense silence as the air conditioning hummed. Watkins was anxious to receive his checkout evaluation.

"Dr.—ah, Lena," he said. "Your show. What's on your mind?" He'd guessed she had a mandate to clear him mentally for the next assignment. Therefore, his objective was to say or do or whatever she wanted.

"I want to know what priority you would give to these three things: honor, pride, and forgiveness." She crossed her arms.

"What?" He had heard. He just wasn't sure he understood.

She didn't repeat the question. Just the three words: honor, pride, forgiveness.

"Well," Watkins steepled his fingers in front of his lips. "They're all priceless."

Dr. Merkowski—or rather his new buddy Lena—leaned in. A smile curved her polished lips. "Cut the bullshit. That's a fortune cookie answer."

Watkins met her stare. "An answer to an open ended, New Age bullshit question. You want to know something, Doc, just ask me straight."

She frowned and gave a small nod. Watkins inched back in his seat and wondered on some level, *Did she just win? Was this a tactic?*

"You've refused to answer certain questions at debriefs about the Peaceful Warrior incident, you've started fights in PT, and have gone silent with every other therapist so far. So, okay, I'll get right to the point. I'm your last hope, Captain."

We're back to Captain.

Watkins rubbed a hand over his chin and looked away. She was right. If he didn't pass the psych eval, he didn't have a career. Or a future.

There were chunks of memory that were still missing. But some were coming back and he didn't like what it showed him. He'd made serious mistakes in judgment during the mission. Mistakes that cost lives.

The doc was waiting. Relaxed, hands resting on the arms of the chair like she had all day to wait for him to cough up something she could put under her shrink microscope and examine.

"I don't remember much after the explosion."

She nodded.

"I broke with procedure and endangered others in my unit." This had all been established in the debrief and he accepted responsibility.

Her face showed nothing.

"Responsibility for a failed mission as well as loss of lives." If she asked him how he felt about losing Brody and Reza, he was going to jump out of his chair and leave. Damn the career.

"You were betrayed, Jonah. The responsibility is not yours to accept. It lies elsewhere."

The words had the effect of making the ground shift under him. A jumble of thoughts fired in his head. *Not mine to accept? Of course it is.*

Her voice, modulated like she was talking to a spooky horse, related the same story he'd heard from the post-ambush investigation team. Morrow had been the Judas, sent to destroy the peace mission, to incite an escalation of violence, so he could continue to feed weapons to his customers on both sides. Morrow had insinuated himself as a security adviser. A perfect ploy to set up the ambush.

Dr. Merkowski's words penetrated his thoughts, but not his heart. "No matter what you did that day, it was going to end in death—for Mukhtar and his entourage as well as your men. Morrow set it up that way."

"And this is supposed to make me feel better, how?" The sarcasm wasn't lost on the doctor.

"It's not my job to make you feel any particular way. I'm here to point out to you the truth. The truth that you are not responsible for what happened. You can't take that upon yourself any longer. Instead, we have to move on to deal with something much deeper."

He couldn't give in, let go. He chewed over what she'd said. "So, what's deeper than guilt over getting men killed because of my ambitions that kept me from double-checking the situation? What would that be, doc?"

Her mouth twisted. Good. She was much too cool for his liking.

"I'll tell you when you finally decide to put down that cross you've been carrying up the hill, waiting for someone to crucify you. Wanting someone to punish you for what isn't your fault. Get over yourself so you can get on with yourself."

His hands clenched the chair arms. Anger? *Was I angry at her?* His face flared hot. Shame. It was shame her words elicited in him... Shame over being pitiful. But he had to get through this.

He swallowed the lump creeping up his throat. "Okay. You don't mess around with it, do you." It wasn't a question.

"No, I don't mess around with it. So I'll tell you what you need to deal with now. Grief. Then forgiveness."

"Who am I supposed to forgive? Morrow, the traitor? The suicide bomber, or hey, maybe the Taliban who cleaned up afterward by shooting my backup team in their heads at point blank range?"

At least she winced.

His heart felt like a fly trapped in a jar, banging against the glass walls. "Forgiveness is for Sunday school lessons." But a germ of what she'd said kept echoing in his head. Grief. He hadn't let himself feel any grief. Not for the death of his men, the failure of his mission, the wreckage of his face... Let alone forgiveness.

She leaned forward. "The forgiveness is for you. But you have to accept it."

The clock in her office had a loud tick as the second hand swept through, marking a minute's passage.

"For living, when no one else did," he said.

"That's a start. You lived, so make something of it." She tapped the folder still resting on her lap. "You have family or anyone in Maryland?" The casual question lightened the air. A reprieve. Watkins was due to report for training at a base in central Maryland, if he was cleared. Her question raised his hopes.

"I've got a brother living just over the border in Pennsylvania. My folks are gone."

"What about your fiancée?"

A look of surprise on his face alerted her.

She tapped the folder on her lap with one perfectly manicured finger. "In your file."

"Well, it needs to be updated."

She arched an eyebrow. "Care to explain?"

Now it was his turn to point. At the side of his face. At the silvery red skin that stretched from the middle of the eyebrow along the cheekbone to wrap behind his ear. The ear that is missing the bottom half. "The plastic surgeon told me it would fade to a more normal color, but the scar would always be visible. My eyesight's not great in that eye and I can't hear worth a damn if you're sitting to my left."

"You think she broke it off because you were injured?" she asked.

"I know she did. She told me as much."

Dr. Lena Merkowski, professional psychiatrist, murmured something that did Watkins more good than any previous advice.

"Shallow, useless bitch."

Her lips hitched up to one side when she realized he'd heard her. With his bad ear. She turned crimson, but Watkins laughed. She joined in.

"I beg your pardon. That was totally unprofessional." She wiped her eyes.

"No, no. We're dealing with the truth here, right, Doc?"

She shook her head and smiled. "When you get to Maryland, I want you to make an appointment with Dr. Amy Wong at Bethesda Naval Hospital for a follow-up and therapy referral."

"More therapy? I don't think I need therapy. I just need a job."

Lena handed him a prescription slip with the name and address written on it. "I think you'll like it." She nodded to the paper in his hand. "Based on your background, I'm recommending you work with an old friend of mine, Selma Bennett."

Her handwriting was clear and blocky. Not feminine at all. It said, *Pegasus Equestrian Center.*

"Horses?" He looked up to see if she was joking.

She wasn't.

Chapter 7

Pia

THE SUN SET EARLIER in the evening these days. Pia dreaded the fall, only because it meant winter wasn't far behind. Standing at the back of the barn looking out over the fields, she wasn't seeing the beauty of a farm, but instead the broken fence boards and pastures in need of mowing. All that would have to be done before winter set in, that and more. She stooped to yank out the persistent weeds that sprouted by the doorway. She could still do something about the weeds.

"Pia, I think you'd better take a look at this," a voice called from inside the barn. Pia turned toward the sound of Hillary's voice on the far end of the barn. She was bent over the water hydrant.

She strode down the aisle. The hollow drip of water hitting the bottom of an empty bucket plucked at her nerves. "What's up?" she asked.

"There's something wrong with the hydrant. I shut it off, but a trickle of water leaks out sometimes." Hillary nudged the bucket with her toe.

"That's just great," Pia words bit off any further conversation. Hillary's mouth slammed shut. Pia was blaming her for the bad news, but that wasn't fair. "I'm sorry, I didn't mean to bite your head off."

"That's okay. I know you've got a lot going on," Hillary said and forced a tight-lipped grin. Her silvery hair, backlit by the setting sun, looked like a shimmering halo. She was a saint, in a kind of old-fashioned hippy with ideas about spirit animals, energy forces, and karma sort of way. But at the same time, she could hold a couple Jack Daniels and would stand between you and a pack of trouble without being asked. Pia wouldn't have wanted anyone else living in the old trailer behind the barn.

"Do you want to tell me what's going on?" Hillary sat on an old tack truck and patted the spot next to her.

Pia's sighed. "Same old stuff." She sat hunched over like a deflated mylar balloon. "Money—or I should say the lack of it—men, and horses. All put on earth to break our hearts."

"I don't know about money and men. They can't make you happy, but horses always can." Good ole Hillary maintained the horse-crazy love of a teenaged girl. She took Pia's hand and traced an index finger along the palm. "Your love line stops and branches, see, right here?"

"I don't believe in palm reading." Pia drew her hand away and tucked it under her thigh.

"Neither do I." Hillary barked a laugh, then grew serious. "Ron, now that guy was all wrong for you. Wrong for this place. Bad energy. I know it's hard to hear now, but you might be better off without him." Her lips pressed together and she paused as if debating her next words. She sat up and blurted them out. "He's been here, when you're at work. I've seen him pull in with that fancy car of his and drive around the place. And he wasn't alone."

This was news, but it didn't surprise Pia. More evidence. Ron was putting together a plan and she'd be left on the curb.

Pia kicked her heels against the tack box. "After Dad died, I thought I could manage with Ron's help. Keep this place going. He promised he was on board with it. He promised..." The words trickled to a halt. "Just my luck, hooking up with a guy who can't keep a promise. Or marriage vow."

"Your dad hoped he would step up. But he never had much faith in Ron."

Pia's head spun back to check Hillary's expression. "You knew my dad felt that way and no one ever said anything? I'm finding out all kinds of things about Dad, now that I can't do anything about it."

Hillary's gaze slid away. "Sorry. Shouldn't have brought it up. Bad karma to review the past unless you're willing to do something about it."

You can change your karma? Your bad luck? Pia smirked. "Boy, if we could, I'd do some things different." She looked around the quiet barn and listened to the horses munching hay. The sound wrapped her in warmth and comfort.

Hillary stood, put a hand to her lower back, and stretched. "Like what, besides the Ron thing?"

What would she do if she had a do-over? Pia's brain buzzed like a swarm of insects, swatting at ideas, knocking them away only to have them zooming back. She would have told her mom she hated the water before she forced Pia into swim team tryouts. For college, she would have tried for a few of those reach schools just to find out. And that high school boyfriend—she would have dumped him first. But most of all, the image of Regalo popped in her head. The Luck-bred horse. Things went downhill the day she sold her. She let out a burst of a laugh that was more an explosion of air than an expression of mirth. "For one thing, I'd have kept Regalo and not let Uncle Cosmo talk me into selling her. She was my heart horse." She looked at an empty stall, door open, swept clean of bedding and imagined Regalo in there, munching hay and settling down for the evening. "God knows where she is now."

Hillary hooked her hands in her pockets and looked down. "So find her."

It sounded so simple.

"She was bought years ago. I don't know where to start..."

"At the beginning. Who bought her? Call and find out. Hey, you can't change the past, but you can improve your karma. Find out where she is at least." She sauntered down the aisle, then stopped. "And something else. I told you your love line branched. I didn't say it ended."

⁂

The sky had turned dark by the time Pia returned to the house, ate some leftover pizza, and trudged upstairs to the bedroom. It was time she stood up for herself. Stopped letting people make decisions for her—bad decisions. She had to face the fact that Ron was not going to have a change of heart, nor give up on his grab for the property. She emptied the contents of her purse on the bedspread and rooted through the clutter for the lawyer's business card Deliah had given her. She plucked it up and leaned back against the headboard, steeling her resolve. The lawyer, Desmond Cornell, was a distinguished looking man in a severe business suit. A touch of gray frosted the temples of his close-cropped hair. According to Deliah, he was an expert in family law. A specialist in property settlements. Pia never thought she'd need such a thing. She let her hand fall to the bedspread. Her fingers unfurled, releasing the card. She had to face talking to a stranger about her failed marriage and how foolish she'd been.

If the farm was in jeopardy, she also had to confess to the rest of the family. Her dad had been the only one of seven siblings who wanted to stay on the land and who actually thrived out in the county. His brothers all took off to pursue careers in air-conditioned office buildings and sought lives in houses that didn't require a diesel tractor to mow the yard. But when he passed, they'd all pitched in, helping Pia out with the taxes and some of the upgrades. She'd promised to pay them all back. She really thought she could.

She rolled off the bed, bent over, and swept her hand across the surface of the bedspread to corral everything back into her purse. A tube of lipstick—one she hardly used but expensive—tumbled onto the carpet and disappeared under the bed. Scrunched down in what looked like a yoga child's pose, she lifted the edge of the spread to search for it. She swept an arm along the dusty carpet feeling for the metal tube. Instead, her fingers crashed into something hard. She probed the edges. Wooden, a box. She flattened to the floor and wedged her body underneath the frame in order to get some purchase on it. She didn't remember ever putting anything under the bed. It was wedged under a broken support. Probably something Ron stuck there.

With some wiggling back and forth, she managed to pull it out. As soon as she saw the lid, a ring tightened around her throat.

It was something her dad started years ago. It was packed full of pictures of sweat-soaked horses in the winner's circle, racing programs with the winning horses' names highlighted, newspaper articles, Jockey Club papers for horses long since gone... Her vision blurred. The box smelled of old paper and cedar. She pictured her dad poring over his clippings, writing notes with that leaky fountain pen, and circling their horses' names in the programs. She pulled out a wad of old photos held together with a rubber band and flipped through them, each horse coming back to her in exquisite detail down to individual quirks and habits. Shuffling through the photos like a deck of cards, her hand froze. The last racehorse—Regalo. In the picture, the mare looked back at her through big, intelligent eyes. Such a young face, cocky, kicking up her heels about something while the groom turns, his eyes registering alarm. Regalo was always a handful.

Although she'd never seen this photo before, she knew it was the day Dad bought her, because he told the tale of how the filly nearly leaped into his trailer to come home with him. Pia always knew it was a fanciful story, but loved it nonetheless. It was taken just before he spent the last of his "big win money" on her. Before she changed their lives with her magic. Everything was wonderful in those years, even when she wasn't winning. They floated on an intoxicating cloud of hope.

She turned the photo over. A pain sparked in her chest when she recognized her dad's handwriting.

The blue smudged ink, now faded, echoed his words, his voice, so clear she could hear his deep voice in the silent bedroom.

Dear Olympia,

Aside from the day I married your mom and the day you were born, this is the happiest day of my life. Today I finally found my Luck horse and made her mine, now yours. Keep her forever, my dear girl. She'll bring you joy and protection when I'm no longer around. Love, Da.

She sat back against the bed and barked her spine against the metal frame. Arching away from it, she rolled onto her knees and brushed the other pictures back in the box. Pia held the message in front of her eyes until the handwriting burned into her retinas and she could see a ghostly image of it on the bare wall when she looked away. When did he write this? There was no date. More than six years ago, before she was sold. He'd never wanted her to sell Regalo, and yet Uncle Cosmo said nothing about it. He must have known, yet said nothing to her. *Joy and protection. Dad must have known he was sick when he wrote it. Before he told anyone.*

Her hand, clutching the photo, fell to her side. Staring at the pattern in the carpet, the ring of her cell phone was like the snap of a hypnotist's fingers, dragging her back to attention. She picked up the phone from where she'd left it on the dresser and saw it was Uncle John, her dad's brother. Once a week, he called to check on her. She debated letting the call go to voice mail, but decided it was a chance to ask some difficult questions, ones she wasn't entirely sure she wanted to know the answers to.

"How's my favorite niece?" he joked. Pia was his only niece.

"Okay." Great or even fine were too close to outright lies.

There was a pause on the other end.

"You sure?" he asked. Pia heard her Aunt Cecelia's voice in the background. *Just ask her*, she urged. Uncle John went on. "It's just that—well, we wanted to check. In case you needed anything." He wouldn't outright ask if she needed money. "It's your Aunt CeeCee made me call. Thought there might be something wrong. You know, she's got the sixth sense. A regular Irish witch." There was a pause. "Ouch!"

Aunt Cecelia must have punched him for the crack about being a witch. But it was true. She knew things. No one in the family could figure out how. They'd all stopped wondering and decided to find it amusing. And now she was right again. She must have snatched the phone away from her husband because her voice boomed in Pia's ear.

"Pia, Sweetheart, I had the worst feeling about you and made John call to check up. What's up? And none of that 'I'm fine' malarkey."

The picture, clutched in her hand, was now stained with a thumbprint in the right corner. She stared at the four walls of the bedroom she shared with Ron and felt her thoughts float away. He used to hold her in bed, spinning elaborate tales of how they'd fix up the farm and rebuild up the horse business. Soft kisses and dreams of kids learning to ride bratty ponies and big family holidays with everyone gathered around the dining room table swirled through her head. In six years, there was never one occasion when Pia had to put in an extra leaf to make more room at the table. "You're right, Aunt Cecelia. Everything's not okay." She had to get out of this room.

Pia got up and wandered into the tiny spare bedroom used as an office and flopped into the desk chair. "I don't know where to start." She placed the photo on the desk. Was it her imagination, or was Regalo's eye turned to her with an accusing look?

"Well, that's easy. Start at the beginning."

"Oh my God, Aunt Cecelia. That's the thing. I don't even know when it started. I was completely fooled all this time." Her voice escalated in pitch. She swallowed, to get it under control. To get anything at all in her life back under some control.

"Who fooled you?" A knife-edge crept into her tone.

"Ron." His name spun out from the bottom of her stomach riding on wail. A flame of heat flashed through her body. Shame. Admitting she was betrayed. She was stupid and trusting. "You know he's left me, but it's more than that." She spun out all the details she hadn't admitted to her aunt and uncle.

Aunt Cecelia hissed, *I told you it was him!* to Uncle John, who must have been standing nearby. "Good-riddance to garbage I have to say."

When Aunt Cecelia got worked up, her Boston accent flared up. It was now on full-on Southie Cecelia.

"You get yourself the best lawyer. Your uncle and me will pay for it."

Pia didn't have the energy to protest and was relieved, because she was pretty sure Mr. Cornell didn't accept a payment plan. She focused on her diploma hanging on wall. Her degree in business mocked her. "Of all people, I should have known better. I earn a living catching insurance fraudsters and financial shysters. I never dreamed I was living with one." She spun around to the desk, getting ready to make an excuse to hang up because a big tumbler of Woodford Reserve was calling her name, but the photo of Regalo caught her eye. "Hey, by the way Uncle John, did Dad ever say anything to you about Regalo?"

A deep sigh echoed down the line. "I knew he loved that damn horse. Why?"

"Because I found a picture Dad must have kept in his box of mementos. It was a photo of Regalo but he wrote something on the back, addressed to me. But I've never seen it before."

Her aunt's voice softened. "What did it say?"

"He told me to keep her forever. I didn't know he felt that way. Uncle Cosmo never told me—"

Aunt Celia made a harrumph noise. "Figures. He was all about the business. No sentiment in that man."

Pia thought about what that meant. What Celia was saying—that Uncle Cosmo likely knew how her dad felt about Regalo, but kept it from her in order to make the sale. Now Uncle Cosmo was gone, too, and there was no one to ask. In the end, she was to blame, too. She hadn't tried very hard to save the mare.

She heard the pop of a bottle top being opened. Uncle John allowed himself one beer at night. His voice boomed back on the line. "Your father sure loved that horse. Thought she was something magical."

"That's the other thing," Pia glanced down at the handwriting again. "He wrote something about Regalo protecting me after he was gone."

A few more swallows and noises that called to mind Uncle John swiping a meaty fist across his mouth before he spoke. "Your Dad knew horses alright. You know her strange patch of dark hair on one hip and that spooky eye she had. Looked like it was two colors, dark with the lighter ring around it?"

She remembered thinking her eye looked as if it had been damaged, but the vet assured them she was fine. "Sure, hair that looked like tiger stripes."

"Paddy did a lot more research on her when he had the time. When he was getting sick and none of us knew yet what was going on. He learned she was a chimera." Uncle John cleared his throat. "Your Da wasn't doing too well then, remember. He took to believing in a lot of things the rest of us thought was a bit off. At the time, he was worried about leaving you. He knew he was sick. He might not have been thinking clear. I wouldn't put too much stock in it."

"But he didn't want me to sell her."

"Paddy." Uncle John spoke her dad's name like that was the only explanation needed. She imagined him slowly shaking his head as he said it.

A tear slipped over the edge of her lid and tracked down one cheek. She didn't bother to wipe it away. "I loved her, too."

"Then get her back." Aunt Cecelia voice piped up. Like that would make everything all better. Like she'd even have the money to buy her if she could find her.

"I can't. I don't know where she is."

"Then find her."

This was crazy. The second person in a few hours to tell her to find Regalo. The idea lit a tiny flame in her chest. Hope. She tried to extinguish the flame with sense and reason. Even if she found her, she didn't have the money to buy the horse. Besides, it would take an enormous amount of hunting and even more, it would depend on a lot of lucky breaks. Yeah, and that's something Pia had in short supply.

She looked at the picture and the little spark flamed brighter.

Chapter 8

The Pegasus Equestrian Center

One Month Ago

Gravel from the rutted drive spit pebbles up under Watkins's SUV as he rolled down the dirt road. The farm's sign at the head of the long driveway showed a horse with angelic wings wrapped around a heart. The first time he saw it about six years ago, he almost turned around and went home. *Schmaltzy.* He wasn't going to waste time at some kiddie riding academy that threw a bone to veterans as a sideline. He changed his mind when the barn came into view. The yard in front was raked gravel. Two rockers sat under a portico at the entrance. The shutters flanking a dozen windows along the side of the barn were open and freshly painted. The place was neat and squared away. The way he liked things. Six years ago, when he'd pulled up to the barn, his heart lifted with an unfamiliar feeling—hope.

Now the woman standing at the entrance with gray hair swirling about her face was a familiar and welcome sight. Selma Bennett was more than a therapist. To Watkins, she'd also become a friend. She propped her broom against the wall and lifted a hand in greeting.

Selma tracked his progress in her direction without saying a word. She didn't talk just for the sake of filling the void, and he appreciated that. The first day he'd arrived, he'd expected a cheery greeting, a too-friendly overture to make him feel welcome—the chipper uptick in voice modulation he found gratingly false in people. Worse, were those who pretended they didn't see his injury.

But this Selma woman, she didn't say a word.

When he'd stopped at the entrance, her eyes, so pale blue the light shone through them like a Husky's, swung up to take in his face. His ruined face. Out of habit, his hand rose to the scar, to feel its rough edges. She looked, but her face remained unreadable. Curious? Repulsed? He couldn't tell.

The silence stretched between them. Until he broke it.

"I'm Jonah Watkins. Dr. Merkowski sent me."

"Do you intend on riding?" she'd asked.

He held a neutral expression. What did she mean by that? "It depends."

The woman scrunched her mouth to one side. "Depends on what?"

She was an odd old bird. But direct. He had to respect that. "Depends on whether this is going to be a pony ride pity party or if I'm going to learn anything worthwhile." He could be direct as well.

"It depends." A triumphant smirk spread across her face. She turned her back and walked into the barn.

Watkins was left standing. What the hell? He followed her to the far end where she stood outside a stall. She watched him walk toward her as if he were a horse she was assessing for soundness and conformation.

"Depends on what?" His voice had a hard edge that surprised him. Was this eccentric old woman getting under his skin?

"Depends on you. I won't put anyone on one of my horses if they're carrying around an attitude. Negativity. Anger. Or hiding fears. Horses know it and they don't deserve it. So, like I said, it depends on you."

Her eyes held his and didn't turn away. He felt the heat flush over his face, no doubt making the damage stand out—remaining pale in comparison. She shifted her weight to her other foot. Waiting him out.

"Fair enough," he said.

Her body seemed to let go, all the muscles relaxed as if she had crossed swords with the adversary and won. A smile, a warm one, spread across her face.

"Lena—Dr. Merkowski that is—tells me you've done some riding in the past." She took in his full seat breeches and well-fitting boots. "But we do require every rider to wear a helmet here, no matter how accomplished you are."

Now it was his turn to smile. "Good policy. I'll get it." He turned to head back to his vehicle but she grabbed his sleeve.

"Wait. I want you to meet someone special first. A horse I think will be perfect for you." She slid the stall door open and beckoned him inside. "This is Regalo de Suerte."

He ran his hand down the mare's neck and she leaned into him.

Selma stood in the doorway watching. "She's an exceptional girl. But it will take an extra special person to reach her." An eyebrow shot up. "Maybe that's you?"

The mare had the refined beauty of a classic Thoroughbred but was heavier boned and muscled like a warmblood. With a very unusual swirl of dark and chestnut coloring over her flanks. Watkins couldn't say what it was about her, but she caused a longing ache behind his breastbone that he hadn't felt in years.

The mare rubbed her head hard against his hand releasing the earthy scent of sweat and sweet clover leaching from her skin. He wanted to take her into a field and let her show him what she had for muscle and speed and heart. He wanted her to be his dance partner.

He noted the brass nameplate on her stall. "Regalo de Suerte. Interesting name. Gift of Luck." Her liquid eye watched him. "But not so lucky lately, I'm guessing."

Selma's mouth pressed into a flat line. "Like a lot of ex-racers. But luckier than most. Typical Black Beauty series of owners—one worse than the previous one. Went from pampered show horse to being dumped here."

"Sound? No injuries?" he asked.

"Nothing serious. Physically at least." She tapped the side of her head.

Watkins understood. He'd seen horses pushed past their limits too quickly, ones that had been intimidated into submission, or overfaced and now fearful. Once their trust was betrayed...their performance and even their health showed the damage.

"Did she race?" he asked.

"Not long. I heard tell her racing owners cared about her and sent her to a big-name show jumper. Didn't work out for some reason. From there, God knows what happened. Passed around a good bit and now she's here. But she's no therapy horse. Most of my clients I wouldn't even have them sit on her on a leadline. Don't get me wrong, she's not mean, just, well..."

"Exacting. Discerning." He felt the smile crinkle up his bad eye.

The mare stared at him, unblinking. He didn't look away. He didn't turn his head to hide the damaged side of his face. She took it all in, it seemed. And what of her? What damage did she sustain that didn't show? He wanted to know her. Earn her trust.

He leaned in and pressed his damaged face against her warm neck and inhaled her scent.

Today, after almost five years together, Regalo still greeted him in her usual way—a head butt to his chest. He ran his hand up her long face and clenched a bunch of her forelock to give it a shake. "My naughty girl." He held a pinwheel mint under her nose and listened for the shattering crunch of it being ground between her teeth.

He liked to spend an extra amount of time and attention on her grooming, losing himself in the rhythm of each stroke, lifting the dust and sweeping it away. Her tail hairs were gently separated until it hung in a thick, chestnut-colored waterfall that swayed with the slightest motion. He also liked to come visit when Selma was busy with her other clients—the ones he deemed more worthy and needing her attention. But he wasn't always successful at dodging her and her probing questions and her piercing eyes.

At first, he only came to the barn when most of the regular clients were gone. He didn't want to run into the other soldiers who had lost so much more than him. He also didn't want to chat with the stable girls who always looked at him a bit sideways, their eyes sliding away from his scars. He had no interest in their friendly overtures and only wanted to be left alone to ride.

In his sessions with Selma, he had shared much of what happened to him but limited it to the facts of the attack. She wanted to know what he felt, but he didn't have the words to describe it. He'd become more peaceful, less anxious, more forgiving and less rigid—but that wasn't enough for Selma. She was still digging at him.

Tonight for some reason Selma dogged his heels like a terrier pup.

"You know, this isn't a boarding barn. You're here for a reason."

Jonah swept the soft brush over Regalo's back. "I know. I'm here to save this horse from the horrible riders she's had so far." He tried out his most charming smile.

Selma wasn't having it. "And who is saving you?" Her hooded eyes bored into his.

He walked away to pick up the saddle pad. "I don't need saving."

"Then why do you avoid the others? Why do you shun people like yourself? People you could encourage, maybe even help?"

Jonah flinched. The best defense was a strong offense. "Maybe because I think they need to help themselves." His eyebrows rose in a challenge to this volley.

"Bullcrap."

"If you're going to psychoanalyze me, hurry up. I want to get on this horse."

"What's the difference between your relationship with Regalo and other riders she's known?"

Watkins stopped brushing. Selma threw him a curve with this new line of attack. He knew it was psychological entrapment, he just couldn't see far enough down her train of logic to figure it out yet. But he was intrigued.

"I don't know. Maybe the fact that I'll listen to what she's telling me."

Selma picked up a brush and worked to untangle the horse's tail.

Jonah could wait her out. He'd played this game with all sorts of adversaries, from Afghan elders to army psychiatrists.

"How would she know that? I mean, before she got to know you?" Selma didn't look up from her task. Her arm swept the length of the tail, causing the hair to halo out with static.

"How would she know what?" Watkins asked.

"How would she know she could trust you? That you'd be different from others who looked like you, were as strong as you? How would she know that it wouldn't be just more of the same?"

Watkins adjusted her bridle by straightening the noseband. "She wouldn't."

She tossed the brush in the grooming box and stood beside him. "She wouldn't know you were any different. So why would an animal who could kill you in a minute, and probably had plenty of built-up resentment and fear of people, trust you instead of her own instincts?"

Watkins rubbed a hand over his face. "Whatever you're getting at, why don't you just come out with it?" He sounded cross, peevish even. He turned away. "I'm sorry, that was uncalled for."

The warmth of her hand bled through the back of his shirt. "Jonah."

She had never called him by his first name. It was always Captain Watkins. He turned and her hand dropped. "You're right. She didn't know. But she kept a small door of hope open, just in case this guy was different. She didn't shut down completely. Instead, she let you prove it to her that you could be trusted."

Watkins ran his hand down the mare's muscled shoulder. "And I'm to take a lesson from the mare? Keep an open mind, hoping people won't disappoint or betray me again?" He held Selma's eye as one eyebrow rose. "Is that it?"

She stepped back. Perhaps he'd been too callous.

Instead of retreating, she squared her shoulders. "Horses are our mirrors. She's trusted you so far, but there will come a day she won't if *you* don't change."

"I've changed," he fired back.

Watkins led the mare into the indoor arena, mounted, and performed their usual warm up. When he moved into the trot, he sensed something was off. Regalo laid against his leg and stiffened her jaw. She refused to yield, but instead jackknifed, went crooked, or tried to run through his hands. The suppling leg yields he'd taught her would not come. Tonight, the mare said no but it didn't make sense. She wasn't sore, she wasn't confused, she simply would not yield. His arms tensed as he came down the long side and tried again, but she lifted her neck and tossed her head.

He took a deep breath, swallowing down the frustration. Making the turn down the centerline again, he used his whip on her haunches with two smart snaps. Regalo shot forward.

He stopped her in the middle of the darkening arena and slumped in the saddle.

"What's wrong, girl?" he asked as Selma's words echoed in his ears. *A horse is a mirror for our emotions.*

The overhead lights blazed on. Selma stood by the light switch.

"You been there long?" he asked.

"Long enough."

"Got any ideas what's wrong?"

Over the years he'd learned this woman who was built more like a rugby player than a rider had a lot of knowledge about horses. Or more precisely, horses and riders. "The horse isn't the problem. It's the rider we need to fix," she told him. "What's bothering you tonight?"

Watkins slumped in the saddle.

Selma touched his leg lightly. "Tell you what, do something she's good at and enjoys. End on an upbeat note, then let's talk." She tilted her head toward the viewing lounge. "I've got some brews on ice and something to tell you for a change."

Watkins noted the flat tone to her voice. It sent up a red flag. Within a half hour, he had the mare tucked in her stall, cleaned the tack, and was sitting with Selma in the lounge, her hand wrapped around the neck of a beer bottle. Watkins wasn't sure if he'd ever seen her drinking before.

She fingered the bottle top. In the slanting light, she looked older, more frail than he'd ever seen her. Selma had always been a force. A small mountain of energy and hope and kick-ass no-excuses commitment. Now her face sagged.

He had spent more than a few hours across from Selma at this table. She had always been the one in control, the one to open the discussion, drawing painful revelations out of him. Now he had to take on that role.

"Selma, you've always been direct with me and I've appreciated it. Now, it's your turn. You want to tell me what's going on?" he said.

She lifted her gaze. Her eyes were always so clear, so direct. "I wanted you to know first, Captain...Jonah. Pegasus is in financial trouble. It has been for as long as I've run the place, but now a lot of the financial backing has dried up. I have to make some hard decisions in order to stay open."

She looked at him, waiting for something. Recognition of what she was saying? He made some sort of noise acknowledging her words but waited, not knowing for sure where this was going.

"Regalo isn't a therapy horse." Her hand snaked across the surface of the table and grabbed his. It was rough and cool to the touch. "She'll be the first to go. I have to get rid of others, but she's the hardest to place."

He lifted his chin and glanced away at the corner of the ceiling. He knew what she was saying. Regalo wasn't an asset to the therapy business...she was kept on, fed, vetted, and cared for because of him. What she had done for him.

"I understand." His head spun, calculating the cost and logistics of keeping a horse. The board, vet, farrier, care when he was away... "When do you have to place her?" His words were calculated. Precise. He was dealing with facts, not emotions. He could figure out a solution.

Selma's hand drifted off his, leaving it feeling exposed and cold in the air. "As soon as possible. The lease here is up and we're looking at downsizing."

The comforting noise of the horses moving in their stalls, knocking into buckets, munching hay drifted in under the door with the cool of the evening air. It was the quiet, the order, the peaceful rhythm that Watkins craved, needed to heal. It would be taken away. Regalo would be taken away. His savoir.

He squared his shoulders. It was clear what he had to do. The decision freed him. It lifted him beyond all the worries about money and logistics and how... "Don't sell her until I get back," he said. "I have a trip upcoming...er, business...but I'll be back. I'll take her. I'll work it out, I promise."

Selma lifted her eyes and searched his face with hope. Her eyes narrowed. "There's not much time..."

Watkins phone pinged. He was conditioned to respond. Sometimes it was a work emergency. "Excuse me," he said and looked at the screen. It was his brother, Caleb.

I'm in jail in Lancaster. Bond posted, I'll pay you back. I promise.

Chapter 9

Pia

Rain hit the farmhouse's windows like fingernails tapping on glass and ran down the rickety gutters almost as loud as a metro train rattling through a tunnel. When lightening flashed, Pia moved away from the window. Regalo's official Jockey Club papers were folded in three and stuffed into an envelope tucked inside the memento box. She hadn't looked at them in a long all time—not since the day she'd gotten a call from the famous jumper rider who had bought Regalo. The woman had decided to sell her less than a year later. Per their agreement, she offered Pia the right of first refusal but the asking price at the time was so high—and she and Ron had no money—that Pia had to let Regalo go a second time. In desperation, Pia had scribbled the name of the second person who bought her on a Post-it note and stuck it to the mare's papers. All she knew about the new owner was that he was an event rider based in Middleburg, Virginia, but from there the trail went cold.

No number. No farm, just a name.

Pia pulled her laptop out and Googled him. A photo came up of a man probably in his midforties, but with such a weathered face he may have been much younger. She read about his success with eventers whose names she recognized. She clicked around the website, hoping to catch a photo of him on Regalo. No such luck. After all, she reasoned, it had been quite a few years and event horses don't compete forever. She noted the phone number on the contact page.

It only rang once when a voice boomed in her ear.

"Yeah, what you got?"

"Mr. Reinhart? Denny Reinhart? My name's Pia and I'm calling about a horse."

His voice turned to velvet. "Oh, I apologize. I thought you were the vet calling back. I'm waiting on a pre-purchase exam. What can I help you with? Which horse are you're interested in?"

Pia scrolled through the website's horses for sale. Impressive eventers with warmblood breeding and price tags that would require her to take out a second mortgage.

"I'm calling about Regalo. You bought her, well, it's been several years ago now—"

"Sorry, don't have one with that name." He muffled the phone but she could hear him yell to someone in the background. "What level you riding and what are you looking for? I can have my assistant help you."

"No, Mr. Reinhart. I'm looking for that horse. You purchased her in," Pia shuffled the papers in front of her and did a quick calculation in her head. "Must have been in 2017 or so? She was pretty distinctive. Had a mark on her hip like tiger stripes with coppery hair running through it on the off side. You got her from—"

"Wait." Pia heard a clunk like the phone was slammed down on the counter. In a minute a woman's voice picked it up. "Sally Reinhart here. Denny says you're asking about Regalo. We don't have her anymore. In fact, it's been several years. She was quite a horse, but couldn't manage when we moved her up to prelim. Sold her to a nice young lady who was training level. Sorry." Her voice was rushed, like she was ready to hang up.

"Wait! Do you have her name? Where I can contact her?"

"I dunno." The woman's voice faded as if she were physically distancing herself from the conversation.

"Please. I have to know if she's okay. You see, she was a present from my dad and he's dead now—"

"Julie Harlow," she said. "She rides at Fox Haven Farm now in Poolesville. Moved from this area after she bought Regalo. That's all I know."

Pia wrote down everything the woman said before she forgot it. "Thanks, thanks so much for your help."

The phone clicked in her ear.

Pia continued all afternoon researching and calling the next name on her list, begging for people to help her, to listen, to give her any tidbit of information as to the mare's whereabouts. It seemed Regalo changed owners perhaps four times in just the first year after she was sold. It wasn't the life Pia had imagined for her. All day she tracked Regalo's course and learned her fate from first living at top farms as a show horse with professional riders, to a junior riders, then a short stint as a school horse at Garrison Forrest, a private school near Baltimore. From there, who knows what happened, but a middle aged lady bought her who wanted to trail ride. Regalo turned out to be too much horse for her, she told Pia. But she loved the horse and wanted her to go to somewhere safe.

"I donated her to a riding center," she told Pia. "They do therapy there and it seemed like a nice place."

Pia silently groaned. Nice or not, it wouldn't be a good fit for Regalo. Now she worried if next she would be told the mare had been shipped off to an auction, bought by the kill buyers, or had died alone and neglected in someone's backyard.

Her stomach rumbled when she looked up at the clock. The sky had cleared outside the window, but the day was almost gone. She swallowed hard and picked up the phone again to punch in the numbers for the last call. As she waited for someone to answer, her mind filled with images of a place run on a shoestring budget, stocked with hallow-eyed half-dead horses who had lost their will from being led around in endless circles. That was no life for Regalo.

The phone rang four, five, six times. Pia waited for the answering machine to pick up but it kept ringing. She moved it to the other ear and thought about hanging up.

"Hello, Pegasus Equestrian. Selma here." The voice sounded like a nice aunty, unlike the stressed, harried horse people she'd been dealing with all day, cajoling them into giving up two minutes of their day to speak with her.

"Oh, hello. Sorry, I was going to hang up," Pia said.

"I'm glad you didn't. What can I do for you?"

Pia's shoulders dropped a few inches from where they were hovering up around her ears all afternoon. "My name is Pia. I'm trying to find a horse I used to own—a really special horse. She has unusual markings. Stripes on her hip—"

"Oh, you're talking about Regalo."

A tingle shot through her hands as she reached for her notepad. She found her. It sounded like she found her at last.

The voice chirped on. "But we always called her Reggie…"

Called? "Do you still have her?" Pia clamped the phone between her shoulder and cheek to free her hand for writing.

"No, sorry to say I don't." The woman's voice was warm. Despite the disappointing words, it felt like honey in hot tea.

"You don't?" She couldn't stifle the whimper of disappointment that climbed up her throat and escaped. "It's just that I've been searching for her. It's important. She was a present from my dad. He never wanted me to sell her but I had to..." She didn't know why she was spilling her sob story to this woman, Selma.

"I understand. I do," she said. "I hated to let her go, but you see she wasn't suitable for most of my clients. On top of that, we've lost the lease on this place and I'm downsizing. Since we live and breathe by donations and grants, I just couldn't afford to keep her, as much as I wanted to."

Her words rolled through the phone line, in Pia's ears, and bounced around in her head. Another dead end. Another step down the food chain. Who takes a horse from a therapeutic program? It's usually the end of the line for crippled or aged horses. Pia squeezed her eyes shut and asked.

"So, she's dead?"

A laugh like a bell shot through her ear. "Of course not, no. A client had a mom with a small farm, willing to keep her. Until I could find a home."

A whoosh of air escaped Pia's chest. So close.

"Funny you called, however." The woman's voice prattled on. "The fellow who always rode her, a Captain Watkins, expressed interest in taking her, but he's been out of town I suppose for these past few weeks and I haven't heard from him. I had to find a place to put her because we're moving—"

"No!" Pia's fingers gripped the phone. "I mean, she was my horse and I really want her back. Tell him, whoever he is, that I'm—"

"He phoned and told me he was headed over there today to get her."

"What's the address? Do you have their phone number? Do you have his number, so I can talk to him before he takes her?"

Pia scribbled down the address where Regalo was being kept and a phone number for this guy. She looked at the time. The town was at least a forty-five minute drive if she left right away. Or, she could call and tell whoever this Watkins guy was that Regalo was rightfully her horse. She hurried to thank Selma and pushed disconnect. As soon as the dial tone restored, she punched in the number for a Jonah Watkins. The call went to voice mail, where she left a desperate message—one that she was sure made her sound like a crazy woman.

"Just don't take her, I'm on my way." She ended the call and grabbed her barn coat on the way out to hook up the trailer.

Chapter 10

Caleb

One Month Ago

Watkins drove the two hours to Lancaster, Pennsylvania, in the driving rain. On the way, he battled the idea that he should let Caleb stew in jail and face whatever consequences were coming his way. That's how he'd handle a raw recruit when he got in trouble. That way they learned. Took responsibility for themselves. But he couldn't do that. Watkins had made a promise to take care of Caleb. He never broke promises, and it was his brother after all.

Watkins paid and signed at the front desk, vouching for Caleb. Promising he would appear for the misdemeanor charge. Drugs again. Watkins signed his name with a swift scribble that caused the pen to rip a small hole in the paper. Instead of taking a seat in any of the plastic chairs bolted to the floor, he paced. How was he supposed to keep his promise to watch over Caleb when he lived two hours away? Now he was faced with ensuring he showed up for court. Frustration boiled inside, forcing his feet to move faster, wearing a path on the polished floor. He was leaving on TDY in a few days. If he did bring Caleb home with him, he wouldn't be around to check on him. But then again, he would be away from the dealers he knew who he thought were safe, away from his "friends."

A door at the end of the hall opened and Caleb was escorted from the holding area into the waiting room. His shirt was filthy around the collar and stained with brown splatters. His hair was greasy and matted. As he brushed past without a word to retrieve his possessions at the desk, Watkins detected the sour smell of vomit. He'd have to drive with the window cracked and get his car cleaned afterward.

"You ready to go?" Watkins asked, not knowing what else to say. His question elicited only a grunt as Caleb's eyes shifted away.

His baby brother was no longer a kid, but for some reason Watkins never understood, continued to act like a sullen teenager. He'd quit college at Franklin and Marshall, but continued to hang around Lancaster, working at a local restaurant enough hours to pay rent at a townhouse apartment he shared with four undergrads, buy beer, make car payments, and party with kids that were increasingly younger than him every year.

Watkins headed past the college campus, down Harrisburg Avenue, and turned toward the highway access.

"Hey, where we going?" Caleb spoke for the first time since Watkins rescued him. "My place is back there." He spun in his seat and hooked a thumb back toward town.

"You're coming home with me." Watkins stared straight ahead.

"The hell I am." Caleb pulled his phone out. "Let me out. I'll call someone to get a ride back."

Watkins jerked the wheel and pulled the SUV over onto the shoulder with a squeal of tires. He threw the gearshift into park and turned to Caleb. "Look. I've just dropped ten K to get you out of there." He flinches, recalling the bank balance earmarked for Regalo and her boarding expenses. He pushed the thought away as a lava of anger roiled in his gut, threatening to erupt. "Second offense. And what *were* you thinking? Swinging at an officer?" A throb had started up a rhythmic thump in Watkins temple, causing his right eye to water. The windshield wipers slapped at the pouring rain, sluicing it away in sheets.

Caleb said, "I should've known you'd make a bigger deal of this."

Watkins rubbed his forehead, breathing. Taking his voice down a notch. "Be realistic, Caleb. Who the hell would you call? Your friends are all frat boy kids or druggies. Who would put up the money to get you out? Did you think of that?" He gave his brother a hard stare.

"That's what Bail Bondsmen are for. They don't take you from one jail so they can lock you up in another. Like you."

Watkins made a guttural noise signaling his dismissal of Caleb's comments. "When are you going to grow up?" He didn't expect an answer, but put the car into gear and eased back onto the road.

They traveled the two hours back to Watkins's townhouse in silence. The rain had let up some, but the descending darkness wrapped them in its cold and damp embrace. Caleb shivered in his thin shirt. On the doorstep, Watkins turned at the sound of a faint chirp. Yellow glowing eyes peered from under a bush. The small black cat shrunk back out of sight.

"Hey there, MacArthur. You out of food?" Watkins stooped down and brushed aside the bough of a juniper bush to check the bowl he'd filled that morning.

Caleb snorted. "Still rescuing strays. Still gotta be the hero, the big guy."

Watkins stood. "The cat doesn't deserve what happened to her. She didn't crap all over her own life." He shot Caleb a look that said *like you*, before turning to unlock the door. Inside, Caleb dropped onto the couch and flicked on the television. Watkins pulled some clean clothes from his dresser, gathered some toiletries, and pointed Caleb to the shower.

When he heard the water running for a few minutes, he fished through Caleb's wallet, his pants pockets, and the small backpack he always carried. His face flushed with shame and his skin prickled, waiting to be caught in the act of violating his brother's privacy. It wasn't the first time he had done this. He started searching Caleb's stuff when he first started using, when they were much younger. Watkins would find it, destroy it, before their father could find out. Not much had changed.

It was a decade later and they were still stuck in the same endless dance. Watkins riding in to save him. Caleb, not wanting to be saved. But he knew he had to. He knew Caleb's addictive behavior. His bent toward self-destruction. He wasn't sure what he was searching for—any drugs the police surely would have confiscated—but more likely a contact number for a dealer. A suspicious name on the back of a matchbook. A hint of what Caleb might be up to. Or worse. A dark glimpse into his life. A life headed down a frightening path.

Caleb always accused him of wanting to save the world. Watkins pocketed a slip of paper with a phone number. *No, Caleb, I've tried to save the world and failed. Now I'm just trying to save my little corner of it.*

Chapter 11

Pia

THE ROAD NARROWED TO the width of the horse trailer. The directions on her phone indicated the farm was a few minutes over the rutted, single lane. She hoped she wouldn't run into someone coming in the opposite direction since there was no place to pull over. What if this Jonah Watkins person was pulling out with Regalo just as she arrived? She could block the road. Get out. Talk him into transferring the mare to her rig. Pia patted her purse with the farm's business checkbook inside. There wasn't much left in the account, but she'd write a check for Regalo if she had to and figure out how to make good on it later.

The covering of mature trees cast the farm in shadows as she pulled in. A light shone over the back door of the house. She parked at the entrance to the bank barn. It stood on a stone foundation with low ceilings and a single row of light bulbs illuminating the center aisle. Pia checked her phone one last time. She'd called earlier to say she was coming but there was no response, no messages. Her truck door creaked when she opened it, but no one stepped out to see who had arrived. She approached the entrance to the barn.

"Hello?" she called. Horses stirred in their stalls. A tabby cat jumped down out of nowhere and curled around her leg. She looked back at the house and noted a Ford Ranger parked between the house and the barn. Maryland plates, with a US flag decal on the bumper. Probably him, the army guy. Total poser. If he were a real horseman, he'd have a full-sized truck. The only other vehicle parked near the house was a full-sized truck all right, but it looked like something Jed Clampett would drive.

She should go to the house and ring the bell, but if Regalo was here she wanted to see her first. Her heels echoed against the cement floor as she walked deeper into the barn, peering into each stall. So far, only a pinto pony and an ancient shire horse lifted their heads.

"Who are you?" A voice demanded from a dark corner.

Pia spun around and froze. A waterfall of adrenaline dumped into her bloodstream. "I'm sorry. I called, but no one answered."

A figure stepped into the light. She was dressed in heavy rubber boots probably a size too large and held a pitchfork in one gloved hand. It was hard to tell how old she might be, but Pia had the sense she was a teenager. She walked closer under the light, opened a stall door, and tossed a flake of hay to the pony.

"What do you want?" she asked.

Pia was right. Catching sight of her face under the bill of a baseball cap, she estimated her grumpy host was about sixteen.

"I *did* call," Pia stammered. "About a horse you have, Regalo."

"You with that guy?" The girl tipped her head to indicate somewhere beyond the walls of the barn. "My grandma's talking to him around here somewhere."

Pia looked behind her. "So he is here."

Before Pia could ask another question, a man and an older woman entered the barn. The woman was dressed in an outfit almost matching the teen—rubber boots, grubby barn coat, and a ball cap shading her face. But Pia's eyes locked on the man at her side. He wasn't wearing a coat despite the cold. The army green jersey clung to his muscled shoulders and arms. A guy who worked out and liked to show it off. His hair was dark and cropped close to his head. He turned to her. The light hit his eyes, making them turn golden and a bit menacing under dark brows. Pia stepped back, feeling like a field mouse spotted by a hawk. He nodded at her revealing a scar that ran up the side of his face near one eye. She decided then and there this man was certainly not going to get Regalo.

"Grandma, this lady's here about the horse, too," the girl said by way of introduction. She gripped the handles of a wheelbarrow and disappeared down the aisle.

Pia removed her glove and extended a hand. "Hello, Mrs. ..." Damn, she forgot her name. "I'm Olympia Harcourt. I called you earlier about Regalo."

Her outstretched hand was ignored. She dropped it to her side and wiped her pants. Like that's what she meant to do all along.

"As I was explaining to the captain, I don't have her anymore," the woman said. "Told Selma when she needed a place for the mare that I'd take her for a week or two. Selma's a great friend, but she's got no sense of time. I had the horse nearly a month and couldn't afford to feed her. That's when I met a fella at the feed store who offered to take her up to the auction for me."

Auction. A searing burn shot across Pia's empty stomach, causing her to press her hand into it. Auctions attracted a lot of the wrong kind of people for a long list of very bad reasons. The worst of which were the meat men. Bought horses for cents per pound and handed them off to slaughter across the borders.

"Which auction?" Pia blurted.

"When Mrs. Krankowski and I spoke earlier, I explained my interest in the horse. It's too bad I didn't make it in time to find her here," the guy answered. His voice was deep, commanding.

Damn, he *was* the guy Selma said wanted the horse. Some army dude. And double damn, he remembered Mrs. Krankowski's name at least. Pia took the hint. She straightened and resolved to backpedal her enthusiasm for the sake of being polite and winning over the old woman. But what she really wanted to do is shake her and demand to know what she was thinking sending a horse off with God knows who to an auction.

"I'm sorry to just drop in on you. I called ahead to explain..." she repeated, but let the words run out. Obviously no one answered the phone around here or listened to messages. "I used to own Regalo. I've been trying to find her again." She widened her eyes as if to say, *do you understand how hard this has been?*

The man turned to where her trailer was parked. "Did you plan on bringing her home with you?"

Pia stiffened. "If she was here, yes." *But it's none of your business, actually.* Mrs. Krankowski pulled her coat around her as a stiff breeze swept across the yard. Pia's feet were freezing. She didn't want to stand in the wind much longer, but she couldn't afford to be shut out, to miss some key piece of information that would put her back on track. Her lips curved into a forced smile. "Yes, actually I was hoping to find her here. I was prepared to make a fair offer."

"She was your horse, you say?" The old woman tilted her head and looked askance at her. "Why'd you sell her?"

Pia looked down and toed the gravel with her boot. "It wasn't really my idea."

That smarmy Watkins guy touched Mrs. Krankowski's arm. "Ma'am, you probably should go inside. It's cold out here." He caught Pia in his hawk-on-the-hunt gaze. "Ms. Harcourt and I can talk about this out here."

A stab of fear flared behind her breastbone. *Stay out here, in the dark, with this strange guy? Nope.*

The dim light in the barn illuminated the planes of his face. He was handsome—except for that scar—in a rugged, deer-hunting, sports-watching, flannel-wearing, sort of way. Definitely not her type.

The woman shook her head. A strand of gray hair came loose and blew in her face. "No, all of us, come inside. I'll make some coffee." She turned and headed to the back door.

Captain Watkins gestured for Pia to go ahead. "After you, ma'am."

"Mrs. Harcourt," she corrected him. She had no idea why.

He walked behind her to the house and held the door. The kitchen looked like a time capsule from the sixties. An aluminum-framed kitchen table was circled by four chairs with cracks in their vinyl seats. An avocado green refrigerator hummed in the corner. Mrs. Krankowski kicked off her boots and padded around the kitchen in stocking feet.

"Sit down," she said indicating the small table. When it was ready, she poured three mugs of coffee.

Pia sat opposite the captain. Under the harsh kitchen lighting, the damage to his face was more distinct. A purplish scar ran from a few inches under his eye to his ear. A bit off the bottom was missing. The skin on that side of his face was not quite right. It looked waxen and too shiny. She noted the shadow of his unshaven cheek on one side did not match the damaged one. Was he in an accident? she wondered. Maybe a fire. A jolt of realization hit her—maybe during the war.

Mrs. Krankowski placed mugs on the table and sat with a groan. She pushed a covered dish of sugar in Pia's direction along with a quart of milk. "Don't know how you take it," she said.

Pia was careful to pour a small amount of milk into her mug, not that she intended to drink much of it at this hour. She'd be up all night. Or maybe she should, if she was going to hunt down the guy who took Regalo. Watkins stirred two spoonfuls of sugar into his. She noticed he didn't wear a wedding ring.

"Captain Watkins came here looking for the same horse. What's the chances of that, huh? Some luck, two people show up for her a few days after I send her to the sales." The older woman shook her head.

Some luck is right. Bad luck, as usual.

"You mentioned you'd look for the man's name," Watkins said. His voice was like whiskey and honey. Masculine, with a bit of grit, but had a deep and almost soothing quality under it. She could easily imagine him giving orders.

Apparently, Mrs. Krankowski thought it was an order. She jumped to her feet with unusual agility for her age and disappeared into the back of the house. Pia could hear drawers opening and shutting and the soft rustle of papers.

"How do you know my horse?" Pia asked.

He stared over the brim of his cup at her before answering. "Your horse? You mean your former horse. You never told us what happened. Why you sold her."

Pia launched into the story of Regalo's failed racing career and the financial decision that forced the sale before she realized he had sidestepped her question with one of his own. She forced herself not to stare at his damaged face, but the strange scar pulled her eyes back to it. She'd act like she wasn't seeing it, like everything was normal.

"She can't be raced, you know. We kept the Jockey Club papers when we sold her," she said. This Watkins guy probably wanted to race her. Just make a buck off her.

"She'd be too old to race now, wouldn't she?" he said. He rested his hands around the coffee mug, his tone condescending. "Besides, I'm not interested in racing. I'm against it."

A small shudder rippled through Pia as if she'd been slapped. *Who was this arrogant jerk?*

"She's not a trail horse, either. She's from racing bloodlines and is not exactly an amateur's kind of ride."

He smiled. It was an exasperating, condescending sort of smile. She noticed the scarred skin near his eye didn't wrinkle up like the other one.

"I'm sure. Tell me, Mrs. Harcourt, when was the last time *you* rode her?"

Pia had never ridden Regalo. She opened her mouth to tell him she'd ridden plenty of other ex-racers, when Mrs. Krankowski returned.

She slapped a paper down on the table and resumed her seat. "Here's what I was looking for. I wrote it all down. This man, Mr. Cavanaugh, said he'd take her to the auction and make sure she got a good home. He promised she sure wouldn't go for cheap."

"Friend of yours?" Pia asked.

"No, no. He gets a cut from the sale price, so it's worth his while to take the horses through the sale. And that way I know he'd make sure she got a good price. Not meat prices."

Pia gripped her coffee, which was bitter and undrinkable. It sounded more like a guy who found horses to feed up and dump into the slaughter caravans. "Do you remember him telling you which auction he takes them to?"

Mrs. Krankowski squinted at the paper and tilted it toward the light. "He signed his name here but I can't make it out. He takes them to a couple auctions. Ones over in Pennsylvania, some around here, he said."

Notorious places. Pia wanted to grab the paper out of her hands.

Watkins leaned over her shoulder to look at the paper. He pulled out his phone and swiped the screen.

"How long ago did he take her?" Pia asked. She glanced at Watkins, fooling around on his phone.

"Oh, must have been last Wednesday I suppose. I had to get to the feed store before closing and I remember he was late coming by to get her."

Watkins frowned at the screen. "We might find her in the auction manifest if we find the right one. I can look for where a Mr. Cavanaugh consigned horses last week."

"That's a great idea." Pia leaned closer across the table. "If you can match his name with Regalo's, we can find which auction she went through. Then find the buyer."

He stretched his neck to double-check what was written on Mrs. Krankowski's paper. His thumbs danced over the screen. In a few minutes, he stood, picked his car keys off the table, and pocketed the phone without a word.

"Did you find anything?" Pia asked. She spun in her chair as he headed to the door.

"Thank you, Mrs. Krankowski, for all your help," he said.

"Did you find the auction?" Pia got to her feet. *What is wrong with him? Why isn't he answering?*

"I did." He walked out.

Pia followed on his heels back to his car. A cold wind had kicked up. "Are you going to tell me or what?"

He opened the door and paused. "No. I'm not."

"Why not?" Panic and frustration squeezed the words from her throat.

"Because Regalo will be better off with me." He slid into the driver's seat and shut the door. Pia stood rooted to the spot watching the red taillights disappear down the gravel driveway.

"What an a-hole," she whispered, her words frosting into a cloud in the cold night air.

Chapter 12

Pia

When Pia finally arrived home from that useless wild goose chase, she was starved, had to pee, and was mad enough at that arrogant GI Joe to put her fist through a wall. What did he mean Regalo would be better off with him? It was dark and all the horses still had to be brought in and fed, along with the barn cats. She worried about her dog, Ryder, who had been locked up in the house most of the day. What to tackle first? When she stepped out of the truck, the yard lit up with a flash of lightning. Fast on its heels came the thunderclap and the sky darkened.

"What else you got?" she looked up and shouted at the sky.

By the time she'd gotten all the horses in, the dog out, and all the mouths fed, rainwater was dripping from her hair and down her back. She tracked puddles through the house, stripping off wet clothes as she went. It was almost ten before she sat down in front of her laptop in dry clothes with a Tupperware container of reheated spaghetti. She placed the scrap of paper with the guy's name on it—the turd, Cavanaugh, who shipped Regalo to the auction for his cut in the sale.

Where to start? She wouldn't have to go through this if army guy, Watkins, had only given her what he'd found. How did he find the name of the auction so fast? And did he also have the address of the buyer? What's his magic formula? She pounded the keys, wondering if he was on his way now to lay claim to Regalo.

Her best hope was to find a manifest online for when Regalo went through the sales, sometime during the last week or so. Besides not having an exact date, she didn't even know where to focus her search. There were half a dozen big and small livestock auctions in the Delaware, Maryland, and Virginia area where Cavanaugh could have taken her. If he took her to auction at all. She tried a Google search of his last name linked with Regalo de Suerte, hoping it would hit on something. No luck. She tried using various parts of the mare's name, her Jockey Club registration number, different spellings of his name. A bust.

She got up to put the dirty Tupperware in the dishwasher and nudged the door shut with her hip. How did Watkins find it so fast? What was she doing wrong? She padded back to the laptop and stared at her results. A guy named Cavanaugh hit on an auction list for a place up in Pennsylvania—New Holland. She shivered. Lots of meat buyers go there to get horses. For this sale, Cavanaugh had brought in a pair of horses, but they were ponies and it was over six months ago. There was no contact information for him, not even a first name. She sat down and tried searching New Holland and Regalo's name without his. Nothing.

She pushed the laptop away and leaned back in her chair. *Think!* When they were sitting around Mrs. Krankowski's table, what did she say? Did Watkins have more information than just Cavanaugh's name? She struggled to remember the exact words spoken. She recalled the older woman came in with the paper with Cavanaugh's name and said he'd approached her about taking the mare off her hands. Mrs. Krankowski said she wasn't sure if she could trust him, but she had no other options for finding a home for Lucky.

Pia heard the woman's voice in her head, thin and frail as tissue.

Lucky. She called Regalo by a nickname.

Her fingers flew over the keyboard. Lucky plus New Holland plus Cavanaugh.

Bingo.

A long manifest listed a mare, the same age, Thoroughbred, color marking matched. It had to be her. The timeframe fit. Pia scanned the manifest to find the name of the buyer. Blank.

A click of toenails on the linoleum and Ryder dropped his big head in her lap. Ignored, he collapsed at her feet and sighed. It was way past the usual bedtime and he wouldn't settle down until she did. Pia leaned over and scratched the old dog's head.

"A few minutes longer, then I'll give up," she promised.

She pulled a sweater off the back of her chair and wrapped it around her shoulders. The old house was cold. She couldn't turn up the heat. Too expensive.

"Work smart, not hard," she told herself. Who can help me? Pia had never been to one of these auctions and wasn't even sure how they worked. Who did know? Horse rescue groups often turned up to save the ones they could, people looking for cheap horses for riding schools sometimes picked up horses at auctions, rent-a-horse trail riding outfits, and...she sat up straighter. Regulators. Representatives from the track sometimes go to check out whether Thoroughbreds were being dumped at auctions for slaughter. And she knew just the person to call.

A sleepy voice picked up after the third ring.

"Good, you're awake," she said. "This is Pia and I need to ask you something really important."

"I'm awake *now*," a voice gravelly with sleep replied. "You'd better be stranded in a ditch to call me at this hour."

Pia checked the time. Ugh, it was after eleven thirty. "Sorry, Gary, I lost track of the time. And it is an emergency, sort of. I'm looking for a horse that went through an auction last week up in PA and I know you cover a lot of the bigger places, keeping an eye out for ex-racers being dumped there."

Gary Paulson was an enforcer. He worked for the Maryland Racing Commission, keeping an eye out for any owner or trainer who might dump a slow racer illegally. It was against the law, not to mention a ticket to being banned from the track, and he made sure everyone played by the rules. He haunted the auction floors, checked up on shady trainers, and generally made life difficult for anyone who didn't treat his beloved Thoroughbreds with respect.

He stifled a yawn. "Last week? And this couldn't wait, why?"

Pia heard his wife in the background ask who's calling. Pia cringed with embarrassment. "I got a lead on a dealer who brought the horse to New Holland, but I can't find the name of the purchaser. I know you have an in with a lot of the auctions and I thought maybe you could look up in their records database and give me the name."

"You know I can't do that," he said. "I can't violate the trust these places have shown me by providing access to records only to give out information willy-nilly to anyone who wants it. There has to be a reason—a stolen horse, an illegal acquisition of a horse, or a horse in immediate peril—loading on a slaughter transport."

"She's in trouble," Pia said. She shifted the phone to her other ear. "She may be hurt or in bad shape. She's been tossed around a lot and now this guy dumped her at an auction and who knows where she is now. I've got to get her back and I just need a name."

"Wait. This isn't a horse directly off the track?" he asked.

"Well, not really." Pia fingered the edge of the sweater. "It's Regalo. I don't know if you remember her—"

Pia heard rustling and a female voice asking where he was going. The distinctive chime of a computer booting up rang out.

"Why didn't you say so?" Gary asked and made a few old man noises clearing his throat. "Your dad's Luck horse, right?"

Gary knew his racing bloodlines. He always liked Regalo and was disappointed when she left racing.

"Yeah, my dad never wanted me to sell her, but I never knew that. I want her back. At the very least, I have to make sure she's okay, ya know?"

His voice was whispery, like someone who'd smoked too many cigarettes. "I know. Give me a second. New Holland, right?"

"Yeah. You'll look it up for me?"

"No one has to know where you got this information, understood?" He was gruff.

"No, of course not. I'm going to contact the buyer and, I don't know, make an offer."

Pia had been so intent on finding the buyer, she hadn't figured out how she would pay for buying the horse back. She had credit cards in both their names, if Ron hadn't shut those down by now as well. She could maybe get a line of credit on the farm... She'd just have to worry about that later. Now, she had to find Regalo.

Gary's voice boomed in her ear. "Got a name."

"Great! Thanks, Gary. What is it?" She held a pen over a notepad.

"Before I give it to you, you have to promise me something."

"Sure."

"No, you listen to me before you agree. I don't want you running out to some place all by yourself. You don't know what kind of person you're dealing with and I don't want to be responsible for something happening. You keep me posted, okay?"

"Okay." Her voice glowed with a smile.

"The buyer is a woman named Dorothea Strauss and King's Grant in Lancaster. No other info. Sorry."

"Thanks so much for your help. I owe you one. And tell your wife, sorry I woke her." She clicked off before he could levy any more conditions on her.

Ryder huffed at her feet. "Just a second more."

Pia looked up King's Grant in Lancaster. According to their website, it was a riding school. Looked like it catered to beginners—up downers—and little girls with big dreams. She had trouble imagining how Regalo would fit in there, but then again, she hadn't seen her in years. Watkins's parting shot echoed in her ears, *She'd be better off with me.*

She rubbed her eyes and shivered. In a few hours, she had to get up for work. And try to sneak in a call to this King's Grant place.

"Let's call it a night, Ryder." His soulful eyes turned to her, but he didn't rise to his feet. "You've given up on me?" She trudged into the guestroom, unable to face the California King-size bed she'd shared with Ron. Ryder circled once and collapsed on the floor with a huff. Pia pulled a comforter over her and dangled her hand down over the edge of the bed to stroke the old dog's head. What a day. What was she hoping to gain by getting Regalo back? She flipped over and kicked at the covers to free her legs. The sheets held her in a knot. Maybe this was wrong. She remembered the leaking hydrant, the broken gate… Maybe she should sell the farm and forget horses. Forget the worry, the money drain, the backbreaking work. She could get a condo closer to work, not have to mow grass ever again, and spend the extra money from not having to feed and vet horses on fancy restaurants and exotic trips. Like normal people.

Ryder snored as she rubbed his ears. Pia tried to picture it. A new life. A fresh start without Ron—it hurt but she could see it.

Maybe someday there'd be a place in her life for a new guy. Maybe. But a life without horses and the farm? Nope. Even if it would be more practical, it made her heart hurt. She couldn't see herself as that responsible, rational other woman who invests her money in sensible markets and comes home to an empty apartment. A tear slipped out and ran down into her mouth. Salt. She rubbed her face on the pillow. How had she gotten to this place? When had it all started to go wrong?

She tucked her hands up under the pillow into the cool, smoothness there. Her mind drifted, riding a dark wave back to the past. Before Ron walked out. Beyond the tough years, the financial troubles of their marriage, back past losing her dad, the problems plaguing the farm... Back to when she could handle what got tossed onto her path. When she was strong and optimistic and trouble was just a speed bump on her hopeful journey to where she was headed. Back when she had Regalo.

The mare's strange coat of swirled multicolor hairs glistened in the sunlight when she walked up the ramp of the trailer that took her away.

Another tear slipped out of the corner of her eye and wet the pillow.

That's when it started, the bad luck. Her life going off the rails. Pia was sure. It was the day she let Regalo go.

Chapter 13

Pia

Why did the break room at work always smell like burned popcorn, except when someone opened the refrigerator? Then it smelled like garbage. Pia tossed her heated up mystery lunch on the table—she couldn't remember what was in the container when she pulled it out of the fridge that morning. Sitting down opposite Deliah, she opened the lid and stirred the sludge inside.

Deliah looked up from a magazine. "You cooked a goat or something? It stinks."

Pia pressed the lid back on and tossed the whole container in the trash. "I know. Not hungry anyway." Her shoulders rounded. A flower wilting.

"What's up?" Deliah tossed her trendy red readers on top of the magazine.

"Nothing."

"Ron up to more bullshit? I'm telling you, you need to get Des on your case and fast."

Pia lifted her eyes. "Des, huh? You've gotten awfully friendly all of a sudden."

Her friend flashed a toothy smile. She lifted one shoulder and waved Pia's comment away. "You know. He gave me a call the other night and well, one thing led to another."

"Uh-huh." Pia stole a french fry from Deliah's plate.

"Finish them." She pushed the plate across the table. "God knows, I don't need 'em. And while you're stuffing your skinny bod full of salt and carbs, fill me in on what's up."

Pia's hand stopped on the way to her mouth. She dropped the fry. "Everything's a mess. I've met with your Mr. Cornell—er, Des—and he's going to try to get my half of our money back and go forward with divorce proceedings. In the meantime, I'm a little behind on the mortgage and everything is falling apart." Pia covered her face with her hands. "How did I let this happen? I trusted him. And I'm supposed to be a fraud expert."

When Deliah didn't answer and merely shrugged, Pia stood and dumped the plate of fries in the trash. Clinging to the back of her chair, her fingers dug into the padding back. "And now I've also found out some things about my dad I didn't know."

Deliah looked alarmed. "What kind of stuff?"

"Nothing big, like he was cheating or anything. Just, well, I found an old box with some of his things. Including a note he never sent me. He said some things that got me thinking. Years ago he bought me a special gift, because he believed in me. A horse. He said she was for good luck and I was never to sell her..." Pia huffed. "Maybe that's why my life sucks now."

"A lucky horse?" Deliah leaned back and waved the words away as if they were sheer nonsense. "I guess all horses would be lucky wearing four horseshoes around all the time." She picked up her readers and twirled them by one arm.

"I'm going to get her back. I have to, Dee. I know you don't get it about being so attached to an animal, but she meant a lot to me. And now I feel guilty, too. She was everything to my dad. He worked so hard to find her. To put the money together to buy her. And I let her go. But I'll fix that. So long as I can beat this guy to getting her first."

"Will you sit down," she commanded. "Makes me nervous with you hovering."

Pia sat.

Deliah blew out a burst of air. "Girl, you got bigger problems than chasing after some old horse. Besides, how you going to pay for it?"

"I dunno."

"And who's this guy who wants your racehorse? What have you been up to?"

Pia related the story of running into Watkins. "He's an arrogant jerk who told me the horse would be better off with him. God knows what he wants Regalo for. Probably thinks he can breed her and make money or something. Not without her papers, he won't."

"Arrogant jerk or not, why don't you talk to him? Explain why you want the horse back." Deliah pointed her glasses at Pia, emphasizing each word. "Did you talk to him?"

"Nope. And I won't." Pia swiped crumbs off the surface of the table with one broad pass of her forearm.

Dee's eyebrow lifted. "So now who's being a jerk?"

Pia ignored her friend and spun around to check the clock. "So I have to get up to Lancaster to meet with this woman up there. I talked to her the other day and the only time she could meet me was this afternoon."

"When do you have to leave?" Deliah lifted her purse off the back of the chair.

"Now. To get up there in time. Hey, why don't you come with me?"

Deliah stepped back and held up a manicured hand. "Nope, no way. I don't do animals and I'm afraid of horses. Besides, I got work to do."

"You don't have to get near the horses. Take the afternoon off and come with me for the drive. And in case this lady gives me a hard time."

"What am I going to do? Lasso her while you steal her horse? C'mon."

"You have lawyer skills. Lay some legal talk on her. Scare her if we have to. Besides, if that captain is there again and beats me to her—"

"You think GI Joe might be there?" A sly half smile crept over her face. "I'd like to meet *him*."

The time flew by and it felt like no time before they passed the Maryland border into Pennsylvania and they were zooming past an Amish buggy trotting along the shoulder.

"Wonder what dating an Amish guy is like," Deliah smirked. "Those funky beards and all."

Pia shook her head. She wondered what it was like to have a thought process where every piece of information slid into a groove that led directly to men and sex. Deliah turned heads and she knew it.

The main highway running through Lancaster turned into a two-lane bordered by dried-out corn stalks and no shoulder. It meandered for a few miles, before Pia spotted a mailbox with the farm's name on it. The GPS announced in a cheery voice, *You have arrived at your destination.* But Pia didn't feel cheery about it at all.

The gravel driveway was full of ruts. The fence line enclosed a pasture eaten down to the dirt with a few tall weeds. The sagging gate was held to the post with baling twine. Horses with their heads hung low stood under the one shade tree.

"Yup, looks like Churchill Downs all right," Deliah said, staring out the passenger window.

Pia gripped the steering wheel. She was getting Regalo out of this dump no matter what it took. She pulled up to the front of the barn and threw the car in park.

Deliah grabbed her purse. "Don't worry. We'll talk to this woman and get your pony back." She opened her door and stepped outside. "Ugh, what is that smell?"

Pia slammed her door and laughed. "Outdoors, Dee. It's called the country." She took a sniff. "Farmers around here use cow manure to fertilize their fields."

A man pushing a wheelbarrow overflowing with dirty bedding rushed past.

"Excuse me," Pia called. "Can you tell me where I can find Dorothea Strauss?"

The man set the wheelbarrow down and scowled. "Who?"

"The owner, Dorothea?" Pia squinted down the dark barn aisle.

"Oh, Dot. Sure can." He grabbed the handles again and jerked his head. "She's right behind you."

Pia spun around. A woman in a ragged barn coat led a plain bay horse out of the field. The horse was sore on its front left. As the woman approached, Pia raised a hand in greeting.

"Mrs. Strauss? I'm the person who called—"

"The horse is gone." Dot turned her back to fasten the gate.

"Gone where?" Pia's voice lifted into a plaintive tone. "I drove all the way up here—"

Dot walked the limping horse past them. "Look, I'm sorry. I've got my hands full right now." She tilted her head to indicate the horse. "Probably have to get the vet out."

Pia fell into step alongside the woman. Deliah kept back and leaned against the car. Pia turned, gave her a wide-eyed look and jerked her head indicting she should follow them. Deliah pushed off the side of the car and kept her distance.

Inside the barn, each stall was decorated in childish writing with a typical school horse name—Scout, Champ, Buddy—embellished with hearts and sparkles. Pia noted the neatly folded blankets, the swept aisle, and the generous amount of hay waiting for the occupants. She had been a judgmental jerk. Would people think the same thing of her broken-down place when they pulled in? Would they think that she didn't take care of the horses because some of her fence boards were held up by bailing twine?

Dot tossed the lame horse a flake of hay and slid his door shut. She turned to Pia and her hand went to her forehead, as if it pained the woman to look at her.

She heaved an exhausted sigh. "I'm sorry you came all this way. I had to get her out of here as soon as I could. The mare was a danger to the kids."

Pia's mouth fell open. "Why didn't you call me? What do you mean, get her out of here? Regalo would never hurt anyone," she said, shaking her head. *Did she have the wrong horse?*

"Hurt? She nearly killed a girl." The woman's brows scrunched together under her knit cap.

Pia couldn't stop shaking her head no. The mare she knew had excellent ground manners. She never even pinned her ears, let alone... "What did she do?"

The woman's gaze shifted past Pia over her shoulder. Deliah stepped to her side, scraping muck off the bottom of her shoes.

"Mrs. Strauss, this is Cordelia Taylor, my—"

"Nice to meet you," Deliah said. Her hands, jammed into pockets, tugged her coat around her tighter. "So where's the horse now?"

The woman's mouth flattened into a thin line. "Someone picked her up a while ago. Like I said, the mare attacked one of my students in her stall. The girl's got a few broken ribs and her parents are on the warpath. I had to get rid of the horse. I can't risk getting sued."

Pia felt as if the ground rose up and slapped her. *Gotten rid of? What did that mean?* "Where is she?" Her voice climbed up an octave.

The bay horse pawed the floor in his stall. Mrs. Strauss flapped her hands at him. "The mare's fine," she said. "They arranged to have her sent to someone more experienced. That's what I'm told."

Deliah stamped her foot. "Is there somewhere we can talk? Preferably inside and warm."

Dot gave a curt nod and led them to an office. A blast of overheated stale air splashed over Pia's face and Deliah wrinkled her nose. The couch pushed up against the corner reeked of wet dog. The show ribbons and pictures lining the walls were coated with dust and fly droppings. Dot gestured to the couch, but both Pia and Deliah chose to remain standing. She dropped into a squeaking chair behind the desk.

Pia stood with her hands crossed and feet spread. Her Wonder Woman stance. "Mrs. Strauss, you knew I was coming for my horse and instead you shipped her off. So where is she exactly?"

"She's safe."

"And I'm supposed to just take your word for it?" Pia felt the heat burn her cheeks. "Did you actually see what happened to the girl? I still can't imagine Regalo doing anything dangerous."

Dot pulled off her gloves and dropped them on the desk. "Not the same horse as you remember, then. How long has it been since you saw her?"

The question stung. It had been too long. Maybe she had changed. Maybe something had happened to make her defensive.

Mrs. Strauss continued. "The horse that came here was hot, circling her stall. She must have been drugged at the auction. I never would have brought her here acting like that."

Pia chest constricted with a sharp pain. What had happened to her horse in the years between when she saw her last? "Just tell me where she is. I'll go get her." Pia's voice sounded dead, tired, with hope draining away.

The woman looked away. "You have to understand. I take excellent care of all my horses, but I couldn't risk my students..."

Silence hung in the dusty air. The baseboard heater sputtered and shut off.

Pia waited. Her fists balled in her pockets. Her mind raced from one tragic scenario to another—why was this woman stalling? Was she lying? Did she hand Regalo to another meat man like Cavanaugh to drug and resell? "Where?" the word leaked out like air escaping a balloon.

Deliah's hand gripped Pia's elbow.

Dot pushed some papers around on the surface of the desk. "I'm not sure." She lifted her eyes to meet Pia's for the first time since entering the room. "The girl's parents are very upset. As you can imagine. At first her father insisted the horse be destroyed—"

Pia's mouth dropped open. "For what?"

Dot raised her hand. "I know. Outrageous. But listen, he's a lawyer, the father. Big-time personal injury lawyer. He relented, but insisted the horse leave the barn or he'd make trouble. He called this morning to say arrangements were made for the horse to be picked up and taken to a new owner."

Dot's eyes pleaded with unspoken words. Begging for her understanding. It was Pia's turn to look away. "What's the new owner's name? I'll contact her."

Dot bowed her head. "I can't say." "Who's this lawyer guy? I'll call him and straighten it out."

Dot shook her head. "I don't want more trouble."

The blood thumping in Pia's neck was so strong it felt like her head would blow off.

Deliah stepped in front of her. "Mrs. Strauss, did anyone see what happened?"

A vigorous shake of her head. "No. Just what the girl told us."

"And who found her? Was she in the horse's stall?"

"One of the other girls heard her scream. She ran from the ring into the barn and found her in the mare's stall. Well, not in exactly. Just outside the stall on the floor. The door was ajar."

"And this other girl called for help?" Deliah opened her coat in the overheated office and with both hands stuck in the pockets, flapped the sides fanning herself.

Dot nodded. "She ran and got me. Told me there'd been an accident and Caroline was hurt. Well, I thought she'd fallen off that horse she was leasing from me. He's a bit of a hothead and they don't get along. I've told her he's not a beginner's ride, but she, well...her family pays for leasing and lessons and you see..."

"I do see." Deliah cut her off. "If the girl—what's her name? Caroline what?" Deliah's arched eyebrow raised another notch.

Dot rolled her lips together. "I'd rather not say. She's a minor and the family is already upset—"

"Yes, okay. Then let me ask you this: if Caroline had her own horse to ride, what was she doing in this mare's stall? Did she work here at the ranch or have a need to go in a strange horse's stall?"

Pia cringed at the term ranch, but Deliah had a good point. Why was this kid going in Regalo's stall if she had no business with the horse?

Dot opened her mouth and stopped as if the question caught her for the first time as odd. She rubbed her forehead. "I'm not sure. Caroline always wanted to ride Regalo but she was strictly off-limits to the students. She was too much horse for any of these kids."

Deliah paced, head down. This was her thinking pose. No doubt her brain was churning through all the facts so far.

She stopped and turned to face Dot, drumming her lacquered nails over her lips. "Was an ambulance called when you found the girl? Was she transported to a hospital? After the doctor examined her, what did he say?"

Dot flushed. "No ambulance or EMTs. She was just shaken up a bit, I thought. But there was a lot of blood. Her nose was bleeding. It was all down her shirt and smeared across her face." Dot struggled to shuck off her barn coat. "I got her cleaned up. There weren't any cuts... That's why I felt so guilty when her family told me later she had serious injuries."

"So you only know she had broken ribs and a head injury from what the family told you? Nothing you observed yourself?"

A nod.

"And the bloody nose. There was probably blood on her hands. Right?"

Another nod. "Blood all over them from wiping her face. Dripped onto her shirt."

"Then there was also blood on the stall door. Maybe in the stall where it happened. Did you find blood on the door where she must have pushed it open afterward? When she tried to exit the stall."

Dot's mouth hung open. She slowly shook her head back and forth. "No. I would have noticed that…"

"No blood inside the stall or on the door? You sure?" Now it was Deliah's turn to shake her head. She made that tsk-tsk noise. "Did you think that maybe she was lying? That she might have gotten hurt somehow, maybe on her own horse, and made up a story to tell Daddy?"

Dot leaped from her chair and yanked open the office door. She stuck her head out and hollered for someone named Alice.

A teen slumped into the office. She was dressed like a typical barn rat: ball cap with a long, stringy ponytail stuck through the back, breeches with one peeling knee patch, and a coat so dirty it could probably stand up on its own.

"Alice, sit down." Dot pointed to the ratty couch. "These people are here asking about Regalo. You were the first person to find Caroline when she got hurt. We need to ask you a few questions."

Chapter 14

Pia

THE TEEN PERCHED ON the arm of the sofa and stared at the floor. Dot stood and came around the front of the desk to introduce us. Alice made a grunt of acknowledgment and went back to staring at the floor.

"And this woman," Dot said, cocking a thumb at Pia. "She used to own Regalo. Says the horse was never dangerous or spooky before."

Alice's head shot up. She had large, dark eyes in a pale face sprinkled with freckles. Her lips parted, as if to add something but stopped.

Dot continued. "They have a few questions about what happened the other day." A pointed glance at Deliah said *I'm handing this over to you* and she perched on the edge of the desk.

Deliah loomed over the teen and looked down at the top of her head. "Alice, right?"

The girl lifted her face.

"Tell us what happened." She held up her hand to stop Alice as soon as she opened her mouth. "And by that, I mean what really happened, what you saw, not what Caroline told you. Start with when you heard the scream."

Alice's face flushed. "Yeah, I heard a scream, like you said."

"Where were you at the time?"

"Um. The indoor arena."

"And where was the scream coming from when you heard it? The best you could tell." Deliah tilted her head.

"The barn. The far row of stalls."

"The indoor arena is attached to the stabling area by a short passageway," Dot said. "You can hear almost anything going on in the barn from the arena."

Deliah nodded. "What were you doing in the arena when you heard the scream?"

"Huh?" Alice hugged herself tighter.

Pia stepped forward. "Simple question. Were you riding a horse? Moving jumps?"

"Yeah. I was riding. I was on Tabasco." Alice looked over to Dot. "I get to ride him a couple days a week in exchange for doing stalls."

Pia nodded. "And so you had to put the horse away before you went to see who screamed? Where is Tabasco's stall? Near Regalo?"

One side of Deliah's mouth curled up. "Must have taken a bit of time." She shot a look at Dot.

The older woman sighed. "Tabasco's stall is at the other end of the barn from Regalo."

"Then I ran down the aisle because I saw Caroline outside of Regalo's stall." Alice said. "She was covered in blood and—"

"And the door was ajar, as if she had just left the stall. Correct?" Deliah said.

Alice nodded.

"She told you that's what happened. Did you witness it?" Pia asked.

"She said the horse attacked her, pinned her against the wall. I said I didn't think she was—" Alice's eyes widened and her mouth clamped shut.

"You didn't think what? That Regalo would attack anyone? Or that Caroline was allowed in the stall with the mare?" Pia wanted to grab the kid and shake her. None of this made sense.

"Or, you didn't think she was telling the truth about the mare hurting her?" Deliah's voice was honey-coated and lilting. This meant she knew she had the upper hand. She'd caught the kid in a lie. "You saw something, but you're not telling. Why is that?"

The girl's head dropped.

"Look, kid, whatever that girl said about Regalo got my horse sent off to God knows where. Someplace she doesn't deserve." Pia grabbed the teen's coat sleeve and gave it a shake. She knelt and looked her square in the eye. "My horse would never hurt anyone and I think you know it. I still have a chance of finding her before she ends up on a slaughter truck headed for Mexico if you tell me the truth."

Pia's teeth ached from clenching them together. She stood up and crossed her arms.

A single tear slid down Alice's face and slipped under her chin. "I'm sorry." She ran a grimy coat sleeve under her nose. "Caroline said she'd give me a couple pairs of her breeches and her old show coat if I didn't tell. If I said Regalo did it." She snuck a glance at Pia. "I never thought anything would happen to the horse."

"Yeah, that's the problem, you didn't think." Pia retreated across the room and leaned against the wall, glaring.

Dot sat on the couch next to Alice and put a hand on her knee. "Now's the time to tell us the truth."

Alice sucked in a ragged breath. "It was her horse, River, that hurt her."

Deliah let out a snort. "Figures. So why did she lie?"

"She can't let her dad know River hurt her. He'd make her quit riding or worse, maybe hurt the horse. Her dad's psycho." The words tumbled out. She bit her bottom lip and took a deep breath. "Caroline always wanted to ride Regalo but wasn't allowed. It was her way of getting back, I guess."

Dot shook her head and inched away from Alice.

"So the whole thing was made up." Deliah put a hand to her hip.

Alice picked at the torn patch on her breeches. "Caroline was mad at River. He was putting his head up, not letting her put the bridle on. She lost her temper. She always was smacking him around when no one was looking."

"You saw what really happened?" Dot asked.

Alice nodded. "When River turned away and gave her a hard time, she raised her hand to smack him in the face. Instead, he swung his head into her. Then crushed her against the wall. She had a bloody nose and maybe some sore ribs, but that's all. I swear."

Dot stood and opened the door. She jerked her head at the exit and Alice shot out the door. Dot slammed it.

"Damn kids. I'm sorry," she said.

"I think you need to get ahold of Caroline's parents and tell them," Deliah said.

Dot drifted back to her desk and moved some papers around on the surface. "Yes, of course. I'll take care of it."

Deliah shot Pia a questioning look. "Mrs. Strauss, are you going to sweep this under the rug or are you going to confront this girl's parents? Which is it? Because my client here wants to get her horse back."

Dot's eyes shifted to Pia and skittered away. "Yes, of course. I'll do it this afternoon."

"How about now?" Pia picked her cell phone up off the desk. "And while you're at it, find out where he sent Regalo."

The older woman's hand hovered over the phone. "It's a little delicate, you see." Her eyes lifted, imploring Pia to understand. "The girl's father threatened to have my farm license revoked if I didn't hand over the horse. Now, it's one of my best horses involved, River. I don't want him—"

"Taking one of your horses? But it was okay if he took Regalo?" Pia leaned over the desk to get in Dot's face. "Who is this guy? What's his name?"

Dot shook her head. Her lips rolled together in a thin line.

Pia glanced at Deliah, raised her eyebrows, and lifted her open palms in a universal gesture of *what now?*

One curt nod and Deliah stepped forward. "Mrs. Strauss, I think you've got other matters to consider besides what threats Mr. Big-time Lawyer has made against you." One side of her mouth twitched up. "For one, you're dealing with stolen property." Deliah held up her palm in a command for silence, cutting off any squeak of objection from Dot. "You see, that horse was sent through the sale illegally."

Dot shook her head. "But I didn't know that. I wouldn't have bought her if I knew—"

"Her transfer to the sales agent was not official, so, in essence, she *was* a stolen horse. A stolen horse worth a lot of money, so I might be tempted to call it grand theft. Next, you were in possession of said stolen property and passed it on without benefit of papers. Also, illegally."

Dot kept shaking her head as Deliah spoke.

"Maybe charges of fencing stolen goods? Moving stolen property across state lines?"

"Stop." Dot dropped her head into her hands. "What do you want?"

"For starters, a name. I'll call Mr. Caroline's Dad myself and we'll have a little legal tête-à-tête about criminal actions." Deliah's face thrust forward. She held Dot's eye in a hawklike stare. "Understood?"

"But if he finds out..." She clamped her bottom lip between her teeth.

Deliah leaned in. "Now *he's* in possession of stolen property. I'd bet he'll keep quiet about any other little issues."

Dot sat frozen. After a few minutes, she scribbled on a piece of paper and slid it across the desk. "Here's his name. Contact information."

"And the name of the shipper. You must know who came to pick her up," Pia said.

"The truck said Lancaster Equine Hauling. That's all I know."

Pia nodded. "Local. Okay."

Deliah slipped the paper into her pocket. "I think we're done here." She turned and yanked open the door. Before she left, she turned back. "Don't be hard on Alice. I know kids get pressured by the bullies. If anything, I'd kick Caroline's ass next time you see her." She waved the slip of paper. "I'll be taking care of her dad."

Pia followed Deliah out and grabbed her elbow. "I knew I needed you here with me today."

"No problem." Her friend waved away Pia's words.

"No, really, thanks. You were brilliant. But, I'm not sure about..." Pia leaned in and whispered, "the bit about the horse being stolen, per se."

Deliah shrugged. "Maybe not—technically speaking. But Mrs. Strauss doesn't know that."

Pia felt a flutter of hope. With her friend's help, maybe now she'd get somewhere. She hurried to get in the car and get going.

The car seat was freezing. Pia turned up the heat and headed back down the long driveway. Deliah's red readers perched on the end of her nose as she squinted to read the scrap of paper in her hand.

"I'm calling this guy right now," she said, looking down at the cramped writing.

The car lurched along the rutted driveway then Pia slammed it to a stop. Deliah looked up. "What the hell?"

A car rolled up alongside them coming in the opposite direction.

"It's him! GI Joe Watkins," Pia said between clenched teeth.

The driver made a circular motion to roll down the window.

Pia sat, hesitating.

"Go on, see what he wants," Deliah said and leaned toward the driver's side window.

A waft of frigid air flowed into the car.

Pia turned to look at Captain Watkins. A knit cap was pulled down over his head hiding the scarred side of his face. His chiseled cheekbones and intensely dark eyes would attract any woman's attention...until they got to know him.

"We meet again." He smiled.

Pia didn't return the smile. "Yes, but this time I have the information. I'm leaving now, Captain." She rolled up the window and put her hand on the gearshift.

"Hey," Deliah stayed her hand. "Before you drive off, you wanna find out what he wants?"

Pia's eyebrows knit together. "Same thing I want. That's why we're leaving."

She put the car in drive and pressed on the gas, sending gravel spray in a rooster tail behind them.

Deliah spun in her seat. "Too bad. He's kinda cute."

Chapter 15

Pia

Pia's chin jutted out as she floored the SUV down the gravel driveway, leaving GI Joe in her dust. It felt good to turn the tables on him this time.

"You might have given him a chance," Deliah said. She faced forward and clicked the seatbelt buckle.

"A chance to do what? Insult me again? No way."

"Humph." Deliah's brown eyes stared at Pia over the top of her glasses. "Seems the lady doth protest too much."

"What the hell does that mean? The guy's a jerk."

"What it means is there's got to be something going on for him to get under your skin like that. Maybe you're just a little bit intrigued by the guy?"

Pia made a retching sound. "Nope, you're all wrong." She flapped a free hand at Deliah's phone. "Just call that psycho lawyer and see what you can find out. I'm going after my horse. That's all I'm thinking about right now, not some guy."

"If you say so," Deliah said in an annoyingly singsong tone. She punched in the numbers.

Pia put both hands firmly on the steering wheel. "I do."

In a matter of minutes, Deliah had contacted Mr. Anthony DiMarco, Esquire—or rather his secretary—and had an appointment to meet with him at his downtown offices. Seems the mention of Little Caroline greased the skids toward getting a face-to-face that afternoon. Deliah also located the address of the shipper.

"Great, we have time to talk to the shipper first, before your lawyer slam-down," Pia said.

Deliah shook her head so hard, braids swung and whipped her cheek. "Hold on. No. I've had enough close encounters with the animal wild kingdom today. Drop me off at a café downtown where I can wash my hands, grab an extra large café mocha, and scrape the shit off my shoes before I go see DiMarco. You go to the shipper."

Pia agreed and dropped Deliah at the Prince Street Café, a block from DiMarco's office. She hopped out of the car and before shutting the door, said, "Meet me here when you're done." She tapped the side of the car and sashayed into the café.

It was nearing five o'clock. Pia hoped someone would be in the shipper's office before it closed for the day. The GPS brought her back along the country roads to a dirt driveway cutting through an empty cornfield. Cavernous Morton buildings with rusted aluminum siding stood in the distance next to a trailer home and a few big shipping vans. She drove closer, scanning the buildings for an office sign. Her hope focused on finding some kindly grandma type behind the desk in the office who would listen to Pia's sob story and open the company's shipping books to tell her where Regalo was headed.

She spotted a door marked Office.

The raw cold of the evening had descended when she stepped out of the heated car. The sun, dipped low behind the buildings, cast the whole yard into shadows. Pia shivered, not just from the chill. Her footsteps crunched. The emptiness of the barren fields echoed them back to her. The last of the milky sun hovered on the horizon.

Pia pushed open the door and faced a desk and some battered gray filing cabinets.

"Hello?" She stepped inside and looked around. The stench from the overflowing ashtray, the monster truck and pinup girl calendar, and the desk paperweight that read *Does This Look Like the Help Desk?* extinguished her hopes of finding a sympathetic ear.

The door behind her opened.

"Yeah, whaddaya want? We're closing in twenty minutes."

Pia turned to find a man with slicked back hair too dark for his aged face standing directly behind her. He glanced at his watch and locked the door behind him. "Don't want anyone else wandering in here after hours." He strode to the desk where he picked up a paper and didn't give her a second look.

"Yes, I'm sorry." Why was she always sorry? Pia took a breath and started over. "I was hoping you could help me." Pia spun out the story as the man picked up one sheet of paper after another, read them, and grunted. Her words trailed off. "So, you see, I really want to get her back. If you could tell me where she is, I'd really appreciate it, Mr. – umm..." She clamped her mouth shut to stop her babbling.

He dropped the paper on the desk and finally looked up at her. "You sound desperate." An eyebrow arched with a flicker before he snatched a pack of cigarettes off the desk and shook one out. He held it between stained fingers for a minute before tucking it behind one ear.

"I am, I guess." Pia shifted her weight to the other foot. There was nowhere to sit even if she wanted to.

"So what do you want me to do?" He asked in such way to imply he had no intention of doing whatever it was she wanted.

She lifted her chin. "Look through your records. If I had the name of the buyer, a way to contact her, or the address, that would be great."

He hitched his mouth up on one side. He wore a Carhartt jacket over a T-shirt with a frayed collar. The end of neck tattoo peeked out over the edge. "Don't know if I can do that, darling."

Darling? Her gaze shifted to the locked door and her heart did a little hiccup. *Why did he lock the door? Who the hell was going to walk into this place?*

The guy slouched in a squeaky chair behind the desk. "What's this horse's name again?" He cocked his head. "Real anxious to get it back, huh?"

Pia clutched her purse. Was he hinting for a bribe? What could she give him? A mental scan of the contents of her wallet revealed she was in no position to offer much of a cash bribe. All she had was a pathetic twenty-dollar bill she kept tucked under her license for emergencies. She extracted the bill and held it out. "I am, actually. And I'd appreciate your help."

He stood and snatched the bill. It disappeared into a back pocket. "Well, that'll buy you about five minutes of my time."

Pia's cheeks blazed. *What a jerk.* But she couldn't afford to piss him off. Not now, not until she got what she wanted.

"Of course, I'm willing to write a check for your trouble—"

An explosive laugh burst out of his face and rocked Pia back a few steps. "A check? Hey, girlie, what century you living in? I don't take checks from anyone."

Girlie? Pia wished she could channel Deliah's attitude and put this guy right back in his place with a cutting remark or killer look. "Okay, for the next five minutes then, maybe you could look in your records for the mare's shipment." She walked up to the desk and picked up a handful of the papers scattered on top. Maybe they were shipping manifests. Maybe she'd spot a familiar name. "Or let me do it. Her name's Regalo. She was picked up two days ago. From a place here in Lancaster called King's—"

He slid the papers out of her hand. "Sorry, confidential records." Another smile.

"Are you going to help me or not?" She wanted to slap that quirky smile off his face.

"Maybe I could look for you," he said and covered the top sheet with his hand. "These records probably show where your horse is right now. I might even recall hearing about a horse with that name, Regalo. Thought it was going on a transfer truck. You know what that means?" He raised an eyebrow. "Means it's headed across the border…"

Pia knew what he was hinting at. Horses on feedlots waiting for transfer out of the country. Her heart slammed against her chest, pumping blood so hard her neck throbbed. He was trying to panic her. "So, will you look?" The words squeaked out when she wanted them to sound commanding. Should she use Deliah's ploy that the horse may be considered stolen property? Somehow, she didn't think this guy would care.

He retrieved the unlit cigarette from behind his ear and rolled it between two stained fingers. "Trying to cut down. Just like holding one sometimes. Know what I mean?" He looked up at her and his face became hard. "You got something else to give me if I look in the records for your pony?"

His hand brushed her hair.

She jumped away. His hand hung frozen in the space between them. He shook his head as he let it drop. "Too bad. Too bad for your horse."

Pia's gaze cut to the window. Nothing around for miles but empty, open fields. And it was getting dark.

"Look, if you're not willing to help me I'll come back tomorrow. With my lawyer." She hiked up her purse on her shoulder.

He came around the desk and walked to the door. "Suit yourself. But maybe tomorrow'll be too late if your horse is on its way to Mexico."

He said Mexico in a fake accent. It annoyed Pia even more. He tucked a thumb in his belt buckle and cocked his head. "Or maybe we could go out right now and have a drink together. Whaddaya say?"

Pia shot him a glare that caused most men to jump back a foot. She reached for the door handle and tugged. *Damn, forgot. He'd locked it.*

He moved beside her. Too close. Breath like a seedy bar—tobacco and whiskey—blew into her face.

"C'mon, I'm not so bad."

The hand came up again and caressed her cheek with the back of his fingers.

Pia spun and slapped his hand away. "I told you. What part of 'no' don't you understand?" Her back teeth felt like they would shatter.

The other hand came out of nowhere. A burning slap caused her head to pivot like a tetherball. When she looked back, his eyes narrowed.

His voice was gravel, dark. "Slap my hand like a child? I'll show you, you're not too good..."

Pia didn't hear the rest. She unbolted the door and ran outside. The crunch of steps behind her, faster. She groped in her purse for the keys. The damn keys, where were they? Cold air seared her lungs as she dragged it in with gasping breaths.

He slammed her into the car door. His lips were by her ear. The frigid air wasn't enough to drown out the smell of stale cigarettes. "I asked you nice. Now you're going to apologize."

He grabbed her wrist, crushing the bones. She turned her face away from his fetid breath. Her shoulder screamed in agony as he bent her arm back, pinning her body.

His breath came harder now.

"You tell me you're sorry. Now." He slammed against her, wrenching her arm.

Pia screamed.

He jerked her arm upward. "I like a feisty gal. No one's here," he said, words slurring. "Scream your head off."

Bile rose up her throat. Her shoulder blazed in pain as she groped the bottom of her purse with a free hand. Fingers brushed the keys. Her hand closed around them, two spiked up between her fingers.

She lifted her boot and slammed it down on his instep. Her wrist was free. She turned to face him, the keys splayed like daggers in her clenched hand.

"Back off," she said, reaching behind her for the door handle.

"Damn you." He hawked up a glob of spit.

Pia yanked open the door, dropped into the seat, and slammed the door just as an oyster-sized blob hit the window.

Lights blazed on from somewhere in the parking lot, blinding her. *Someone is out there.* Footsteps on gravel. The next moment, the skuzzy shipper's body slammed against the car, rocking it. He slid to the ground.

There *was* someone else out there.

She started the engine. Her fingers were shaking as she reached for the shift.

A tap on the window. She jumped in her seat and turned. Was the door locked? The ghostly image of a face looking in.

The scar.

A sob of relief erupted through her body.

"Captain Watkins."

Chapter 16

Pia

Pia entered the café and spotted Deliah in a booth in the back, facing the door. Her head was down, thumbing the screen on her phone. Pia slid onto the bench opposite.

Deliah looked up. "Well, hey, you finally made it." She tapped her rose gold Bvlari watch face. "How'd it go? I bet you didn't have as much fun as I did."

"Oh, I don't know about that." Pia pivoted in her seat and gestured to Captain Watkins, standing by the door.

Her friend's mouth dropped open. A small consolation. It wasn't often she could surprise Deliah. He approached the table.

"This is Captain Jonah Watkins," Pia said. She stood to let him take a seat on the inside next to her. She always hated to be trapped on the inside of a booth. He stood beside her and she sensed his body go rigid.

He gestured for her to slide into the booth first. "Please, have a seat. I prefer to be on the outside."

Pia reluctantly slid across the worn vinyl. *Choose your battles.* "And this is Cordelia Taylor. A friend who's been helping me."

"Deliah is fine." The intense ruby lipstick contrasted and set off her thousand-watt smile. "Glad to see you finally caught up to us, Captain."

"Jonah is fine." He thrust out his hand.

Deliah grasped his hand and held it a bit longer than necessary. "So what happened?" She shut off her phone—something she rarely did. Her eyes narrowed. "What's up. Something went on." She pointed at Pia. "And what's with your face? You run into a brick wall or something?"

Pia touched the side of her face where he'd struck her. The cheek was blazing hot. "Something like that."

A waitress appeared to take their orders. A roaring hunger overtook Pia's better judgment so she selected a double cheeseburger with a side of onion rings. "You don't serve alcohol here?" she asked as the waitress collected the menus. It earned her an incredulous sneer. "Damn," she muttered.

Deliah made a *let's have it* gesture with her fingers. "Okay, give. What happened out there? Then it's my turn, but I have a feeling your story's going to be better."

"Depends on what you call better. The creep attacked me."

Deliah's mouth dropped open. "What creep? What the hell?"

Pia relayed the conversation leading up to the attack. "He just flipped out when I slapped his hand away and told him to back off." She rolled her neck and shoulder as it stiffened up. "He wanted me to apologize. For what? For standing up for myself? What a psycho."

"My God, girl. You're lucky Jonah here showed up," Deliah said.

"I was handling it." Pia shot the captain a look. "Like I told him before we headed over here, he didn't *save* me."

Watkins rubbed the raw skin on the knuckles of his right hand. "I'd headed straight there from Mrs. Strauss's place. It was almost dark when I arrived, but saw an altercation of some sort going on in the parking lot. Then a woman's scream. When I approached, this guy took a swing at me. Well, to make a long story short, I convinced him that wasn't such a good idea."

Deliah gave the captain a thorough up and down look, halting her gaze at his biceps. "I'd guess so." She reverted her gaze to Pia. "I shouldn't have let you go by yourself."

Pia squirmed. "Oh, come on. I practically grew up on the racetrack. I've had much creepier guys come on to me. I know how to handle it." But her words rang hollow in her ears. She'd been scared.

"The guy had been drinking." Watkins shook his head. "Not that that's any excuse, he's probably still an asshole sober."

He slid away from Pia. *What now? Insisting he didn't save me piss him off or something?*

He stood and tilted his head, indicating the direction of the men's room. "Need to wash up. And make a phone call in to work."

Pia scooted across the seat. "I've got to wash that slimeball off my hands, too," she told Deliah. "I'll be right back." Alone in the ladies' room she used extra hot water and lathered her hands up to the elbow as if she we going into surgery. When she glanced up from the sink, she inspected the skin on her cheek where it had bloomed into a speckled red blotch. *You could have shown up a few minutes sooner, Captain.* When she returned to the booth, Jonah was still gone.

Deliah leaned in. With a conspiratorial whisper, she asked, "So…?" She dragged the word out to a ridiculous length. "What's the real story with Captain Hottie rushing in to save you?" She held up her hand. "And don't tell me you had it under control. What happened afterward? How come he's here?" She wiggled an eyebrow.

"Because he wants the horse same as I do, that's all. Afterward, you know, after he slugged the guy, he wanted to drive me home. I told him—"

Watkins appeared at the table.

Pia stood to let him in. *Round two.* "I was just filling Deliah in on what happened afterward."

Watkins gave Pia a questioning look but slid in across the bench seat. He sat with his hands folded on the table. "Afterward? We went back in the office and convinced the guy to tell us what we came for." He glanced down at his hands but a smile teased at the corners of his mouth.

Deliah peered at him with narrowed eyes for a moment, sizing him up. "Back up. So, after you slug this guy groping my friend here, you got him to cooperate? Damn. I need you on my negotiating team."

The waitress dropped two mugs of coffee on the table and said their orders would be right up.

Pia slid a sideways glance at Watkins. He poured two sugars into the coffee and stirred it like he was in a trance. A man of few words. "Well, Captain Wat—I mean Jonah—pulled the guy to his feet and basically told him if he gave us the record of where he took Regalo, we wouldn't call the police. The guy was terrified of him, so he pulled up the computer record on the shipment, and printed it." Pia held up a paper folded into a square.

"You didn't call the cops on this perv?" Deliah asked.

Watkins set his spoon down. "Of course we did. I didn't promise, I said *maybe* we wouldn't call."

Deliah snapped a salute. "I knew I'd like this guy. You a lawyer by any chance?"

"No, but I've got a bit of experience engaging in some tense negotiations."

"That's one reason we're so late," Pia jumped in. "He followed me to the police station where I filed a complaint. He was a witness." She slumped in her seat. *Assault. Did that really happen?* Heat radiated off Watkins's thigh, pressed against hers. She didn't move away. In fact, her body craved the warmth. She fought the urge to move closer. Riding a tide of adrenaline, she'd been energetic and alert. Now that it was draining out of her, she shivered and stifled a yawn. "My God, I can't believe all this happened." She propped her chin in her hands. "I'm almost too tired to eat."

As if on cue, the waitress placed a platter in front of her. The scent of grilled onions and charcoal wafted up to her nose, making her stomach growl in response. Watkins picked up his sandwich and took a huge bite.

"Let me have that paper." Deliah curled her fingers in a give-me gesture. "While you guys eat, I'll see what I can find out."

Pia mumbled thanks between mouthfuls and slid the paper across the table. "And tell us about your meeting with DiMarco. Did you straighten him out?"

"At first he didn't want to believe I was telling the truth until I hit him with the fact that a witness had come forward. That conniving little liar had her father wrapped around her pinkie." Deliah held up her manicured little finger as she filled Jonah in on the background story of Caroline ratting out Regalo for her injuries so her father would not take away her leased horse. "I'd paddle her backside good if she were my kid."

Pia felt Watkins flinch when Deliah spoke about beating the kid. She checked his expression as Deliah continued the story.

"Daddy went all Perry Mason on the poor stable owner, Mrs. Strauss, threatening her with lawsuits and legal actions if she didn't turn over the horse. Probably terrified her. When Caroline came home with blood down her shirt and a story about a horse attacking her, the DiMarcos rushed her to the Emergency Department at the hospital. While he was there, he called his sister, he said. He wanted her opinion about what he should do. Told her the whole story. He asked whether the horse might be dangerous and should he insist on her being destroyed. Then he made the arrangements to have Regalo picked up earlier today."

Watkins's brows knit together. "And Strauss never pushed back or even asked where he was taking her?"

"I asked about that. DiMarco implied he'd take business elsewhere and even threatened lawsuits. Mrs. Strauss needed the income, so she caved."

"He's a real piece of work." Pia dropped the burger onto her plate. "Did he tell you where he sent Regalo? And who's this sister of his? What would she know?" A knot twisted at the top of her stomach.

"Get this," Deliah said. "His sister's a vet. That's why he called her. DiMarco said she's the one who suggested he pressure the owner to relinquish the animal, for safety's sake. Then she magnanimously offered to take Regalo someplace where the horse could be examined. Like it might have something wrong with it. She convinced him that the horse could be a rogue—how he put it—and it could be only a matter of time before she killed someone and tells baby brother she'll take care of it. Make all the arrangements. DiMarco thought he was being the responsible good guy, doing the right thing in all this."

"That's absurd." Pia balled up her napkin and tossed it on the plate. "And after you explained to DiMarco that he had the wrong horse, did he offer to get her back? Contact his sister and call it off?"

"I asked him to call her. I think he actually felt bad about the trouble his daughter caused." Deliah sighed. "His sister told him the horse was placed,"—air quotes—"besides, Mrs. Strauss didn't want her back. Just wanted to sweep this whole thing under the rug and keep DiMarco happy so her horse stayed safely out of the narrative. He asked his sister where the horse went, but she wouldn't say."

"Great." Pia probed the side of her face where it was sore. She rummaged in her purse and found a couple Advil wrapped in a tissue. They were faded and a bit furry, but she swallowed them down anyway. "We got a nutjob self-righteous vet involved and another dead end."

Watkins twisted the heavy ring on his right hand. "It doesn't add up. Why would the sister volunteer to take a horse with a bad rep, sight unseen? What does she want her for? She wouldn't be any good as a companion horse even. You don't take a horse with a violent reputation to babysit yearlings."

Deliah shrugged. "I wouldn't know."

Pia pointed at the sheet in her hand. "The shipper must have the sister's name. Or did DiMarco tell you? We can call her, get Regalo back, and finally end this thing."

Deliah peered over her glasses. "I asked her name. He wouldn't tell me."

"Why not?" Watkins leaned forward, his elbows propped on the table.

A shrug. "He said he preferred to leave his sister out of this." Deliah imitated DiMarco's pompous voice. "I pulled the stolen property card on him but he wasn't buying it. He said Strauss was the legal owner as far as he was concerned and she relinquished all claim to the horse."

Pia sighed. "So all we have to go on is the address."

Deliah made a sucking noise with her teeth. "Sorry. That doesn't look good either. Seems the address is somewhere near Morgantown, West Virginia. The weird thing is, doesn't look like a horse farm. It has a building surrounded by a huge parking lot." She waved her phone. "Looked it up."

Pia took the paper. Watkins moved closer and peered over her shoulder. A subtle scent of spice and musk floated past and was gone. He moved away to pull out his phone. After scrolling, he punched in what she assumed was the address.

"Yup, looks like a parking rest area where tractor trailers pull in, fuel, rest up." He held up the geo image of the address. "There's a large building, like Deliah said. Flat-roofed industrial building. Maybe a gas station–grocery store."

Pia looked at the small image on his phone. Again, that outdoorsy scent of men's cologne wafted in the air and mixed with burned coffee and grilled onions. Pia head felt fuzzy with fatigue. She sat back. "None of this makes sense." She picked up her phone. "Maybe the sister's name is Dr. DiMarco. We could look for a vet with that name, maybe in the Morgantown area?"

Watkins's mouth turned down. "Only if she isn't married or using a different name."

Pia tapped the address printed on the shipping manifest. "So do you have any ideas? All we got from that scumbag is this useless address that leads nowhere. We're screwed."

Watkins picked up the paper. "Not necessarily."

Pia's heart lifted in her chest and at the same time she immediately hated that he was giving her a spark of hope. "What can *you* do? I doubt DiMarco would appreciate another visit from us and it sounds like he's washed his hands of the whole thing anyway." She paused for a deep breath. Her body ached.

His eyes held hers. "You're right about not going to see DiMarco again. Besides, I have a feeling we shouldn't tip our hand just yet."

"Tip our hand? About what? DiMarco already knows we intend to find Regalo and get her back," Pia said.

"DiMarco was pretty straightforward when he learned there was a mistake. Except for one thing—his sister's name. Why's that?"

Pia shrugged.

"There's something going on that's not quite right, probably involving his sister, and I don't want DiMarco knowing we intend to find out what that is." Watkins's mouth pressed into a hard line. "It'll make things harder if he warns his sister."

Pia's mouth fell open. "What are you saying? She's a criminal or something?" Panic squeezed her lungs.

Watkins put his hand over hers for a brief second and snatched it away. "No, sorry. I didn't mean to alarm you. I only meant we should be cautious about our plans."

"This whole day's been a complete fiasco," Deliah said and placed her phone face down on the table. "I can't find any vets named Dr. DiMarco near Morgantown, around here, or anywhere."

Watkins rubbed his chin. The dark growth made a sandpaper noise. "Listen, depending on how tight this DiMarco guy has his social media locked down, we can probably find out his sister's name. Take Facebook for example. Maybe he's posted a picture of his favorite sister at a family function or the daughter's birthday and tagged her. We can cross-reference potential names with the registry of licensed vets in the area. It shouldn't take much. A little research. She'll turn up in some professional journal or clinic website, and we'll have her business address. Don't worry." But his face looked plenty worried.

Who was this guy? Pia studied his profile while he spoke. The weird thing was, the longer she looked at him, the less she noticed the scar. He was helping. For whatever reason—to help him find Regalo or whatever, he was helping, *and* he made a lot of sense.

A deep line formed between his brows. "The thing is, this address has to be a transfer point, not a destination."

She snapped to attention. He'd stopped talking and was looking at her. *Had she been staring at him?*

"Why use a transfer point?" she asked. "Why not book a shipment straight through to where you want the horse delivered?"

He leaned back and smoothed out the shipping manifest. "It doesn't make sense and that's what worries me. Why would she book a destination to a highway rest stop? Unless she didn't want anyone to know the final destination. Transfers are used when you want to lose a tail. Shake off the scent of anyone following you. Problem is, if Regalo gets on the next shipment we'll have no way of finding her. She'll be gone."

"You make it sound like the sister is involved in human trafficking or drug running, not just moving a horse. Why would she go to all that trouble?" Deliah asked.

"Good question. People use transfers when they're moving something illegally, which she is not, as far as she knows. But the whole thing's suspicious. Secret destination, obscured by transfer points. No point of contact on the shipping manifest. There's something wrong here. Very wrong."

They sat with the words hanging in the air between them.

Hide the destination? The image of starved horses milling through the mud in feedlots popped into Pia's head. But that didn't make sense either. Why would she bother to take Regalo? She'd just tell her brother what to do...

The waitress came by and asked if they wanted anything else. Pia shook her head and leaned away from her plate.

"I'll take that." Watkins raised his hand and snatched the bill. He rolled on his hip, crowding Pia as he reached for his wallet in a back pocket.

"No," she said. "We can split it."

He shook his head and smiled at her. He had a nice smile. One that crinkled up the outside of his eyes.

Deliah flapped her hand at Pia. "Stop. The man's being a gentleman. Let him pay."

"That's right." He slid a pile of bills under the check. "And this way you owe me." One side of his mouth tilted up.

"Owe you what?" Pia asked. The flutter of something stirred in her chest, like the wing of a small bird. *Was she flirting? Really, with GI Joe? The stranger question—was he flirting?* "You're the enemy after all."

"The enemy of my enemy is my friend. An ancient piece of Middle Eastern wisdom."

This guy had an annoying way of spouting out weird stuff and not explaining. The pain in her head made her eyes squint. She was exhausted. Discouraged. She didn't want to have to think much. "What's that supposed to mean?"

He sized her up, it seemed, calculating her worth as an opponent and forming an opinion of her. "I want Regalo as much as you, so in a sense I'm your enemy. You're right. But we both care about the horse, so right now you and I have a much bigger problem. The person who has her probably is not interested in Regalo's health, safety, or wellbeing. That woman—whoever she is—she's the common enemy." His finger pointed to her chest and back to his. "So I say we join forces."

"You make it sound like a military operation," Pia said. A sliver of fear flicking pain under her breastbone. "Like we're ready to go out on some black ops mission."

He held her gaze. "Maybe. I'm ready to do what it takes to get her back. Are you with me?"

Chapter 17

Pia

Watkins's eyes held Pia's in as tight a grip as if he'd actually grabbed her.

"Of course I'll do what it takes to get Regalo back," she said. "I was attacked by a sleazeball tonight. If *that's* not proof enough for you..." Pia dragged her gaze away with the pretext of looking for something in her bag.

"You're right." He relaxed against the booth's seat as if the air had gone out of him. "I was out of line."

Pia's snuck a glance to check his expression. *He was sorry?* Ron never apologized for anything in all the years they were married. She sure never heard the words *I was out of line* come out of his mouth.

"That's okay. We're all upset over this. And tired." Pia didn't even try to stifle a yawn. "But while we're on the topic, you've never explained what's your deal with Regalo. That lady at Pegasus Equestrian told me you were looking for her, too."

His expression softened. "Selma, right. I told her before I had some—ugh, family troubles—that I wanted to take Regalo because she was being forced out of her place because of financial issues." He arched his back and circled his head, making an audible crunching noise. "Getting stiff."

"Old football injury?" Pia's words sounded snarky. She didn't mean them that way. It was just that most guys she knew tossed that off as an excuse for aches and pains.

"Never played football. Why—"

"Never mind." She waved her hands like she was erasing the words from the air. "You were saying you met Regalo at Selma's place. Did you learn to ride on her?"

"Something like that." He tapped two fingers on the table. "She taught me a lot. About being a horseman, not just a rider."

Pia thought Regalo wouldn't be a good candidate for a therapy program. She was much too sensitive. But right now she was more curious about Watkins. She struggled with how to phrase her next question. The Pegasus Equestrian Center specialized in rehab cases. The scar. Was Captain Watkins physically messed up, or something else? Something to do with a mental condition? PTSD?

She decided on the direct approach. "How long were you in rehab there?"

A flinch of his brow. "Quite a few years."

Pia waited. No elaboration. *Quite a few? How long was that?* "And you rode Regalo for therapy? I mean, well, the director must have really believed in you, starting you out riding an ex-racehorse and all."

A strange smile broke over Watkins's face.

"What?" she asked.

"You assumed I'd never ridden before. That I was a beginner." He turned in his seat to give her his full attention. "Why's that?"

Her mouth fell open. "You said you learned on her...I just thought..."

Deliah's snort caught her attention.

Pia scowled at her. "Well, it was an honest mistake."

"It was an assumption he was a beginner," Deliah said. "He told you the horse taught him a lot, not that he'd never ridden before. See, I listen." She tapped her ear.

Pia shrunk in her seat. "Sorry. I...well...no excuse." She made a time out motion with the side of her hand. "Now I'm out of line." She dared a smile in his direction. A little tickle fluttered in her chest when he returned it.

"Not a problem. No one expects an army brat to be a dressage rider."

"Dressage. That's that fancy horse prancing stuff, right?" Deliah made a motion on the table with her fingers, imitating a high-stepping trot.

Watkins laughed. "Yeah, my dad used to call it 'damn horse ballet.'"

"So wait," Pia said. She bit her bottom lip as she wrestled with how to temper the bluntness of her question. "You were there for years and you already knew how to ride, so..." She squirmed and let the words die out. *How to ask, what was wrong with him?*

"I was there for those years because the outside healed a lot sooner than what's in here." A sharp tap on his temple.

Pia plowed ahead. "I already put my foot in my mouth assuming things I shouldn't, so I'll go ahead and ask. Was it an accident?"

Watkins shook his head. "Not the conventional kind, no. It happened during an operation in Afghanistan that went bad."

The side of his jaw pulsed.

"We were set to meet with local leaders and work out a sort of peace accord, but walked into an ambush instead. I was medevaced out of country to a hospital in Germany for a while. Then rehab back stateside."

"Horrible." Deliah said.

Pia nodded. What could she say? So now she knew. And now she felt like a shit for asking.

Watkins plastered on a bright face. "Not all bad. I got back into riding. Started a new job, a new life..."

His words rang hollow to Pia. She knew a faker when she heard one. After all, it took one to recognize one. "And I made a promise to Regalo." One side of his mouth twitched up. "That I'd be back for her."

Deliah drummed her lacquered nails against the edge of her coffee mug. "It's a horse, Captain. Give yourself a break. She isn't going to know you broke your promise."

"But I will."

A silence descended over the table. Pia snuck a side-glance at Watkins. He was dead serious. He wanted the horse back because he promised her.

"Okay," she said breaking the spell. "What do we do now? The problem is we have no idea who bought Regalo and no clue where she's going after Morgantown."

"You're right." Watkins slid the shipping papers closer to him and scowled. "We don't have too many options at this point. In the morning, we could try to get more information out of the shipping company—"

"Or we could go after them right now," Pia said. Two sets of eyes stared back at her. "No, really. All we've got is a transport van heading to Morgantown. What if we headed out, see if we spot it on the road. If not, at least intercept it at the stop in Morgantown. It's the only chance we have before Regalo gets put on another transport to God knows where." As she spoke, the idea took form. It became more realistic. Electricity pumped through her tired muscles.

"That van left hours ago," Deliah said. She glanced at her watch. "What's the chance you'd get there in time?"

Watkins folded the shipping paper and inched across the bench toward Pia. "We might make it. We can assume the van took the major roads, but it will be traveling a lot slower with a live load." One eyebrow rose. "Worth a shot?"

"You're asking me?" Pia pointed to herself.

Watkins scooted across the bench closer to her. "No sense in both of us being up all night. If you let me out—"

"No way." She blocked his exit. "If you're going, I'm coming with you."

Deliah held up her hand. "Stop. Did either one of you remember, I have to get home. I'm not tagging along on another of your horse posse adventures."

Pia dug in her purse and slid her car keys across the table. "I'll go with the captain. You can take my car."

"And how will you get home, my dear?" Her voice went up a few notches.

Watkins pulled out a pen, scratched something on the manifest paper, and slid it over to Deliah. "It's not a great plan, but it's all we have right now. Here's my phone number. I can drop Pia at home after we find the van. She lives close enough."

"And how do you know that?" Deliah cocked her head.

"We spent some time filling out a police report. If you're so worried about me, rest assured, they already have my address." He shot her a smile.

"It's settled." Pia stood up to let Watkins out. She punched a number and held her phone against her ear. "I've just got to call Hillary and arrange for her to feed Ryder."

"I'll grab us some coffees for the road." He walked across the café to the carryout register.

"Are you crazy?" Deliah struggled to get out of the booth and grab her purse and phone. "You don't even know this guy."

Pia turned to watch Watkins pull out his wallet and pay for two large to-go cups. "Yeah, but I know enough. He keeps his promises." She turned her attention back to the phone in her hand. "Hi, Hillary. I have a huge favor to ask…"

In a few minutes, Watkins returned and handed her a coffee. "You sure you want to do this?"

"I'm sure. Got an old saying for you, too, Captain. Keep your friends close and your enemies closer. Let's go."

He tossed his keys in the air and caught them. "Fair enough. And for the record, I'm not your enemy."

Watkins headed out the door without checking to see if Pia was behind him.

Pia hiked up her purse on her shoulder and leaned toward Deliah to whisper, "Don't worry. I'll be okay."

Outside in the parking lot, Watkins held the door as Pia climbed up into his black SUV.

"Tinted windows? Really low profile vehicle, Captain. People might think you're Secret Service or something."

A strange expression flashed across his face. A second of shock, surprise?

Watkins turned the key in the ignition, but Pia put her hand over his for an instant when he reached to put it in drive. "Hold on a sec. I want to make sure Deliah gets off okay." She leaned forward with her nose almost pressed against the windshield. Deliah stood in front of Watkins's vehicle and made a point of photographing his license plate number. A smile curved Pia's lips. *Good ole Dee. Always got my back.*

Chapter 18

Pia

Watkins programmed the Morgantown destination into his phone and clipped it into a holder on the dashboard. She gave him a go-ahead nod before he twisted around to back out of the parking lot. Her eye caught an employee badge on a Go Army lanyard, tucked into the console. While he was looking away, she fingered the badge, tilting it for a closer look. Beneath his picture—a very stern portrait in a dark suit—was a government seal with an eagle, its wings spread. US Department of…she couldn't read the rest. Who was this guy?

He turned back. She snatched her hand away and faced forward.

Watkins slipped the vehicle into drive. He looked askance at Pia and snapped the console shut.

After a half hour on the highway, the hum of the oversized tires combined with the heavy meal and overheated car normally would have Pia nodding off. But she was too jazzed, too on edge for sleep. She wriggled to sit up and reached for the dial to turn down the heat.

"Sorry." Watkins slid the temperature gauge to cool.

Pia unzipped her coat and cracked a window.

"I got used to the heat." He turned the vents in her direction. "Should pay more attention, but I'm usually riding alone."

Pia thought about that. *Rides alone. So what does that mean? He doesn't have a wife or girlfriend? He never carpools to work?* She reminded herself she had to focus on the task ahead of them and not let her mind wander into things that were none of her business. She squinted through the windshield. "Where are we?"

He clicked the phone to display a map with a large dot. "About seventy miles east-northeast of Morgantown."

Pia gave the map a casual glance. It meant nothing to her and certainly didn't tell her what she was asking. Just like Ron. He gave meaningless directions like "turn east on Route 100" when what she wanted to know was whether she turned left or right after the Starbucks. Something that made sense. She leaned back against her seat. "No, I mean how long till we get there?"

He stifled a laugh. "You sound like my brother when he was a kid" He consulted his phone. "About an hour."

"You haven't spotted anything that looks like the van, have you?"

"Not a thing."

"Yeah, me neither." Her gaze wandered to the passenger window. "Now that it's dark, we'd have to be right next to it." She pushed the button to close the window. "If we did, what then? This is kind of foolish, isn't it?" She stared at his profile, but he didn't turn to look at her.

He repositioned his hands on the wheel. "The objective is to learn where the horse is being shipped next, not to intercept or try to stop the van. We know two things: that Regalo is in a dark green horse van with red and gold lettering for Lancaster Equine Hauling, and we know it is scheduled to arrive in Morgantown. We can only focus on spotting and following the van en route or intercepting it at the rendezvous location. Does that sound foolish to you?"

His eyes never left the road.

Yeah, it kinda did now. "You know what color the van is? How?"

"I questioned Mrs. Strauss when she told me the horse was picked up by a transportation service."

"So you had a plan in mind?"

Watkins shook his head. "No plan at the time. Just gathering data in order to formulate one."

She crossed her arms. "You always have a plan? You don't just, I don't know, wait and see what happens?"

His brows crept together as if he was processing a question that didn't make much sense. "No."

Pia tugged at her seatbelt, loosening it against her neck. "Why not?"

"I don't like to wait and see what happens because too often I don't like it. Especially if I realize there were steps I should have taken to prevent it."

Pia regarded Watkins. He was a big guy. He took up a lot of space even in such a large vehicle. Physically big, but also big personality. Commanding. She felt a bit crowded out. She pressed her back against the door. Male energy. It always sucked up the air in a room and made Pia feel small. Especially with Ron. His words were always spoken with authority. Without hesitation. *What was it like to feel like you were right all the time?*

Her gaze drifted to the dark window. Another couple of miles rolled by in silence.

"How's your head?" Watkins pointed to her forehead. "Better?"

Pia nodded. "I've had worse."

"Spoken like a true horsewoman," he said. Maybe with a bit of admiration. *He thinks I'm tough, so that's good.*

Red taillights flared and Watkins pressed the brakes. Traffic in front of them slowed.

"What you were asking about before—being unprepared. Waiting to see what happens. It's not something I've had much success at," he said.

Pia's eyebrows scrunched. "Oh." She didn't have a clue how to respond. "Some people are planners and some just figure what's going to happen happens and there's nothing you can do about it."

His stole a glance away from the road in her direction. "Which one are you?"

"I think you can guess." She hitched the side of her mouth. "I've planned and plotted and figured everything out but then wham! Life comes along and sweeps all the strategically placed pieces off the board."

No response. Watkins tapped his index fingers against the steering wheel. The traffic crawled.

"'Life comes along and sweeps all the strategically placed pieces off the board.'" He spoke the words like he was trying them out in his mouth. "I like that. It's true."

Pia warmed to his appreciation of her insights. More often, she was used to being told she was too dramatic. "Feels like the giant arm of fate has knocked all the pieces off my board lately and I'm always scrabbling around on the floor picking them back up."

She wasn't sure why this was coming out. Maybe it was his sympathetic look. Not pity, but kindness. Maybe it was because he'd shared what happened to him in the war, how he'd gotten injured. That must have been bad. Mostly, because he made a vow to a horse and wanted to keep it.

"Is Regalo one of those pieces?" he asked.

There was no malice in his tone. She nodded in the dark, knowing he probably couldn't see her. "Some pieces I'm recovering and fixing, others I'm going to kick under the sofa and forget." She folded her arms. "I told you my name's Harcourt, Mrs. Harcourt, but that's not going to be so for much longer." The darkness of the cab and the silence of her fellow passenger gave her courage. "A year ago, Ron left me for someone, but not before he cleaned out our savings. Everything's a mess." She sniffed.

Watkins flipped open the console, fished around inside, and handed her a Kleenex.

"I wasn't crying, just so you know." She dabbed her nose and looked around. "This was probably stupid. Trying to find the van."

Watkins's eyes lit up from the oncoming headlights. "Trying's never stupid."

Another exit faded behind them. Pia struggled to move the conversation onto safer ground. "So you grew up with horses?" she asked.

He shifted in his seat. "You could say that."

"Around here?"

"My father was career Army. When we were kids we were stationed in Virginia. That's mostly where I grew up. At least that's where I got my first kick butt introduction to horses. My mother was the horseman in the family. She was whipper-in for the local hunt and was damned determined her two boys would ride, too. I think I was tossed up on the back of a hard-mouthed, ornery pony when I was about five."

Pia laughed. "I think I rode that same pony." The tension between them shrunk a bit.

"I was about fourteen when my father was stationed in Germany. I hated leaving my friends, school, everything familiar. Worst of all, we had to sell my hunting horse. We were based near Stuttgart. Not much foxhunting there. In desperation, I took up dressage."

"Your dad, who called it horse ballet, right?"

Watkins gave a comic shudder. "He was not a fan. If he didn't do a sport, he didn't see any sense in one of his boys doing it either."

The robotic female GPS voice instructed him to take the next exit. Pia eyed the Welcome to West Virginia sign as they glided by.

"We're close," he said. "Morgantown's just over the border."

A swell of energy lit Pia up like she'd just chugged an energy drink.

"I'd better check in with my someone," Watkins said and pushed the auto dial. Pia wondered who he had to check in with. *Parole officer?*

She relaxed when he explained, "My little brother. One of those chess pieces I'd love to knock off the board, but…" he shrugged. "Promised to watch out for him. He's been—"

A lazy voice drawled over the car speakers. "Yeah, where are you? I've been stuck here without a car all day, man."

Watkins dialed down the volume. "I had something come up and I won't be back until very late. I wanted to let you know so you wouldn't worry."

"One of your super-secret missions? Never mind, don't care. Where's the keys to the Ranger. I gotta get out for a while," the voice answered. More belligerent this time.

"Not sure. Look around. I'll be back around—" The call ended.

Watkins shot Pia a sheepish grin. "Every family's got one. Black sheep."

She also would bet a million dollars the car keys to the ranger were not in the house. In fact, a key fob with the Ford emblem hung from the keys in the ignition. *What was that about?*

Watkins pressed the brake, slowing on the slick Interstate off ramp. After another ten minutes along the main road, bright lights blazed from the highway rest stop. Watkins took the turn into the oversized parking lot and headed to the back area where several tractor trailers were parked.

"Are you sure this is it?" Pia looked around, hoping to spot a green horse van.

Watkins leaned forward, peering through the windshield. Pia scanned the lot, crammed with double-axle trailers. A driver slid down from a cab, hiked up his sagging pants, and headed to the convenience mart.

"I don't see a van," she said. "God, I hope we didn't miss it."

Watkins inched the SUV past the trucks lined up in the back lot. No van.

"Drive around by the gas pumps," Pia ordered. "We haven't checked there."

They swung around the back of the convenience store and came out onto another expansive parking area, filled with passenger vehicles, pickups, and panel vans. Watkins stomped the breaks as a minivan door slid open and disgorged a gaggle of kids in front of them.

Pia prayed she'd spot the shipping van they'd been chasing all night.

"Nothing." His voice echoed her thoughts.

"We missed it." She couldn't believe they came all this way.

"Wait." He veered the SUV toward the lot's back corner where the overhead lights didn't reach.

She leaned forward willing herself to see through the dimness. Was there someone parked there? The headlights swept the outline of the vehicle. She squinted and unhooked her seatbelt.

Watkins pulled up facing the vehicle. The headlights illuminated a green horse van. The gold lettering reflected the light. *Equestrian...*

Her hand was on the door handle. She opened it and threw her shoulder so hard against the door, she almost fell out onto the pavement.

"Wait!" Watkins's voice shouted behind her.

Pia lost the rest of his words, drowned out by the thud of blood coursing through her head as she raced toward the vehicle. She was right! They'd found Regalo. The cold air seared her lungs as she reached the front of the van. She grabbed the cold metal of the side mirror and she swung to face the loading door. It was open. The ramp was down. A trail of bedding, like a breadcrumb path, told the tale of a horse having passed.

Pia mounted the ramp in three strides, hoping against hope to be greeted with the familiar, long face. A welcome nicker.

The van was empty.

A pile of fresh manure steamed in one stall. Did we just miss her? Pia grasped the chest bar of the open stall and folded over it, unable to stand, trying to catch her breath and comprehend the disappointment.

"Just my luck," she said to the empty steel walls.

"Hey, you." A male voice hollered from the parking lot into the van. Pia's head shot up. A squat man holding a steaming to-go cup stood at the bottom of the ramp. The headlights from Watkins's SUV went out, plunging everything into darkness as the stomp of boots mounted the ramp.

Chapter 19

Watkins

Watkins sat glued to the driver's seat and watched a squat man in a billed cap approach the horse van. He hesitated only a second and stomped up the ramp. Must be the driver.

Watkins shut off the engine and shoved his door open. *Am I going to have to save this woman twice in one night?*

He made it to the van at a jog. A gruff voice resonated from inside. "What the hell you think you're doing in here?"

Watkins couldn't hear Pia's response, but he had a pretty good idea she wasn't saying anything that would help her cause. The inside was lit up. He headed up the ramp where the man in the cap had his finger in Pia's face. Watkins took in the empty stalls and sized up the situation. "They took her already," stating the obvious as a heaviness invaded his muscles.

The man spun to face him. He was clutching the to-go cup so hard, Watkins was afraid the lid would pop off. "And who the hell are you?" he asked.

"Sorry to ambush you like this. We're looking for the horse you had." Watkins held his hands palm up in a gesture of supplication.

He snuck a sideways glance at Pia's face. In the dim light, her eyes looked glassy.

The man's voice sounded like a rock tumbler, as if the words had to fight through a wall of smoker's phlegm. "Well, like you can see, the horse isn't here, so..." he jerked his head toward the exit.

"Who picked her up?" Pia asked.

The driver pointed to the ramp. "Out."

Watkins tugged Pia's sleeve and pulled her behind him out of the trailer. At the bottom, the man lifted the ramp, slid it back up and locked it in place. Without another word, he headed for the driver's side door.

"Wait." Watkins stood next to him. "Could you tell us where the horse is headed?"

"I'm not saying anything. This one"—he glared at Pia—"threatened me. Said I was hauling stolen property. I've got nothing to do with where the horse comes from or where it's going. I just ship 'em. If you're cops, you can talk to my boss about it."

Jonah shook his head the whole time the man was talking. "We're not cops. We're worried about a horse that might be in a lot of trouble right now."

"Sorry. Can't help you." He rested his to-go cup on the roof and reached for the door handle. "I meet the client here for the pickup. No idea where they're taking the horse. Not any of my business."

Pia stepped in front of Watkins. "Can you at least tell us what the trailer looked like that picked her up?" She leaned against the door to the cab. "Please. I'm sorry about the stolen property crack." Her voice softened. "You see, the mare's special..."

The driver paused with one hand on the door handle. He moved his mouth like the words were bunched up in there but he wasn't letting them out.

Watkins nodded at the man's cap. "I see you served. Special Forces, right?"

The driver fingered the brim. "That's right. The 5th SFG Airborne." He cocked one eyebrow. "You serve?"

Watkins thrust out his hand. "Jonah Watkins. Rangers. Last stationed near Kandahar."

A smile spread over the driver's stubbled face. "SF were the first boots on the ground in Afghanistan back in the day." He grasped Watkins's outstretched hand in a bone-crushing grip. "Tom Gibson. Rangers, huh? You still in?"

"Got out in 2015. Injured. Got a new gig now."

Out of the corner of his eye, he noted Pia lean in, listening. He'd avoided the topic of his job. It put people off. When they heard he worked intelligence, folks would avoid him.

Watkins shifted from one foot to the other. "Sir, we're anxious to track down this horse. If you could give us any help whatsoever, we'd appreciate it."

Tom scratched under his cap. "Don't know much. I was scheduled to do the transfer here twenty minutes from now." He pulled back his shirtsleeve and consulted a large-faced watch. "But when I got here, the trailer was waiting." He retrieved his to-go cup, took a slurp, and winced. "Horrible coffee," he said and dumped it in the grass behind him. "I thought it was weird—transferring a horse at a highway rest stop. But like I said, I'm just paid to haul them. No questions."

"If you tell us what the trailer looked like, maybe we could still track it down on the road?" Pia said. She glanced toward the highway as if hoping the trailer would magically appear.

Tom shook his head. "It was a plain white tagalong. No insignia, no farm name, or anything on the side. After we transferred the horse, I went in for this." He lifted the empty cup. "Didn't even see what direction they took off in."

Pia rubbed her arms and bounced on the balls of her feet.

The temperature had dropped with the sun. They'd driven for hours and now their only lead had gone as cold as the evening.

"Hey, Tom. We appreciate you taking the time to talk to us. I know you've probably got a schedule to keep. I guess we'll figure something else out to find her." He turned to where he had parked the SUV.

Gibson's face softened. "She was a nice mare. Real polite. Never put a foot wrong while I was working with her." He looked at their faces. "Sure wish I could help." He swung open the driver's side door and lifted a foot to get in.

"Before you go—" Pia once again put her hand on the doorframe. "You mentioned we should ask your boss. Is that the wiry guy with a neck tattoo?"

Gibson snorted out a laugh. "Doesn't sound at all like Mr. Schafer. He's a tall, thin man. Gray hair…" Tom waved a hand over his own head.

"No, this guy had black hair. Really dark, like he dyed it. And wasn't that tall," Pia said.

Gibson scrubbed his chin. "That sounds like Sam Becker. Got fired a few days ago for drinking on the job."

Watkins said, "Description fits. Earlier this evening when we went by the office he was there. Drunk, looking for a fight."

"And he's the one who told you I'd be hauling the mare here? How'd he know?"

Pia raked her bottom lip between her teeth. "Yeah. We kind of convinced him to look it up for us—well, the captain here did."

Tom laughed. "I bet he's good at convincing people."

Watkins looked away. A lot of people saw his physique, his military haircut, and assumed certain things about him—that he was brawn and no brain and preferred to solve problems with his fists.

He didn't respond to Tom's remark. He rubbed a hand over his eyes. They felt like he'd been out in a sandstorm instead merely driving all night. "What matters is we find the horse. Maybe we can circle back to this Mr. Schafer, the real boss, and ask him. About the people who picked her up—they must have signed for her, right? Or showed some ID? Maybe mentioned where they were headed?"

Tom shook his head while he spoke. "It was prearranged. I got a text from my boss confirming the owners were in a white van waiting. I was ordered to help load the mare and hand over the shipping invoice to their driver. It was prepaid. They didn't ask to see any papers I had on the horse, they took her and left. I thought it was strange, I have to admit."

"Any name on the shipping documents you had?" Watkins asked.

"No name, just a company. Median Diagnostics."

Pia's face scrunched. "Weird. One or two drivers?" she asked.

"Two. One was used to handling horses. You know, comfortable around them. The other guy, not so much. He kept his distance. Ordered the first guy around, like he was in charge."

"Sounds like a hired horse shipper and someone else, maybe the buyer, who went along to keep an eye on things." Watkins ran a finger along his scar. A habit he couldn't break. "Did either guy say anything to give you a clue where they were headed?"

Tom's brow beetled together. "Not really. Just the boss guy telling the other to hurry up. He seemed pretty put out over having to pick up a horse."

"How's that?" Watkins asked. "Did he say something?"

Gibson slumped against the driver's seat. "Let's see." He tugged at the bill of his cap. "Said something about how rats weren't good enough for a Doctor Zeta anymore. Remembered the name Zeta cuz my wife had a cat with that name. She was Italian. My wife—not the cat. Anyway, thought that was weird, too, but hey." He shrugged and tossed the empty paper cup onto the floor of passenger seat and hauled himself up behind the wheel.

Pia let go of her grip on the door and stepped away. "Thanks, Mr. Gibson, for your help."

Tom Gibson leaned out the window. "Hope you find your dad's horse, miss. Now I think about it, doesn't sound good where she's headed." He started the van and rolled up the window.

They headed back to the SUV. Inside, Pia started shivering. Watkins cranked up the heat and turned to rummage in the back seat. He extracted a silver foil blanket and tossed it in Pia's lap. "Here, use this until the heat gets going."

"A survival tarp? Why do you have…? Never mind." She wrapped herself up in it.

He laughed.

"What's so funny?" she asked.

"You look like a human burrito. You know, the Taco Bell kind wrapped in foil?"

"Yeah, yeah, I get it." She tucked her chin and smiled. "What now?"

He leaned across the seat to get his iPad out of the glove box when a light floral scent struck him. Lilac? It reminded him of his grandmother's backyard when he was a kid. Maybe lavender. He didn't know, but the smell, delicate and feminine, felt at odds with the inside of his vehicle. Her closeness, her warming body exuding the springlike scent caused a strange idea to form in his mind. He imagined placing his face against the soft skin of her neck, burying his nose in her hair.

He tossed around the contents of the glove box, in a hurry to find the iPad and get away from the scent.

"What are you rummaging around for in there?" Pia asked.

"My iPad. Got to notify work I'm probably going to be late." He located it under the vehicle owner's manual and a pile of repair receipts. Before he slid it out he took in a deep breath. Lilac. That's definitely what it was.

"You have to check in with work? You don't just, I don't know, show up late?" Pia pulled the blanket off her head.

"Not if I don't want to get in trouble." He didn't want to offer any further explanation. Leaning against the driver side door, he held his thumb against the ID sensor to unlock it. In a brief message to Abramson, he punched in his geolocation and a note explaining he'd be late.

"Ah, before we go, you want to grab a coffee inside or need to..."

"Use the potty? Nah, but thanks for asking." She stifled a snicker but the blanket's silvery material crinkled and gave her away.

"Well, I do." Watkins pushed open the door and tossed the iPad back on his seat. "I'll be right back."

He jogged to the convenience store and located the men's room. Washing his hands, he looked in the mirror and told himself to stop. He'd been thinking all evening how he enjoyed her feistiness, the fact that she never let him off the hook with a nonanswer. She was a classic beauty, but he'd never seen her with trendy clothes or her hair done in any other way than a simple ponytail. She was so unlike his fiancée. Ex-fiancée. His thoughts drifted back to a spot under the curtain of a Pia's thick hair where her neck flowed into her shoulder. Where the scent of perfume would erupt with moist kisses as her skin warmed. Watkins shook his head. He splashed some water on his face. It was going to be a long ride back.

When he returned to the SUV, the windows were steamed up from the heat being on full blast. He spun the dial down and turned to see her head bent over the iPad.

"What are you doing?" he asked.

She leaned over and held up the screen so they both could see it. "I'm looking up Median Diagnostics. Might be a fake name, but worth a try." The search window served up list of companies with Median and some with Diagnostics in the name ranging from South Korea to Kansas along with references to some medical and scientific papers. "Ugh, we'll have to narrow the search," Pia said.

Her warm breath brushed his ear. "Probably not a good idea to use my iPad, however." He gently slid it out of her hands and looked at the screen. The device was monitored. Every search was recorded, but it was harmless. He'd simply explain if they asked.

Her mouth formed a tight little circle. "Oooh, sorry. I figured it would be easier for both of us to read that screen instead of on a phone."

Watkins closed the iPad and stowed it in the middle console. "It's okay," he reassured her even though he wasn't so sure it was. He pulled out his phone. "Median Diagnostics is a pretty generic sounding name. That may be why they used it." He swiped open the search window. "Hiding in plain sight among a dozen places with the same name. Maybe if we narrowed down the search with geographical limitations. If they're shipping a horse in a small trailer, it's reasonable to assume they weren't going far." Three rows down in the retrievals, a Mid-Atlantic Pathology and Diagnostic Services included one reference to Median Diagnostics. Watkins leaned over to show Pia. "Whaddaya think?"

"Check out the website. See if it looks legit," Pia said.

Watkins clicked the link. A website filled the screen with a professional looking Mid-Atlantic Pathology and Diagnostics Services banner declaring themselves a consultant provider for advanced genetic recombination and diagnostic services.

Pia wrinkled her nose. "What does that mean?"

"Not much. That's the point." He clicked around the site, displaying stock photos of people in a sterile-looking lab environment, leaning toward a computer screen, and holding up a test tube. "There's no info about Median here. Let's see what's on the contact page." A form popped up inviting the website visitor to fill it out in order to contact the lab along with a post office address for mailing. "No physical address. How do they get supplies shipped to them?"

"Or horses." The side of Pia's mouth twitched up. "Looks fake, or at least a shell for a company that's hiding something."

He felt his brows shoot up.

"You know, a company that exists only on paper. Maybe has a bank account or registered owner but no office..."

"How much do you know about shells?" Watkins leaned back and took a look at the woman wrapped like a burrito who continually surprised him. She knew a hell of a lot more about fake companies than the average person.

Pia pulled the blanket down and freed her arms. "More than I want to know. I work insurance fraud. It's helpful for some companies to use a shell for various financial maneuvers if you know what I mean." A smile crept over her face. "Hey, you thought I was just a spoiled brat who played around with her daddy's racehorses, didn't you?" She swatted his arm. "C'mon, admit it. You never asked me what I did for a job."

Watkins looked through the windshield at the looming darkness beyond the streetlights. "Nope. Sure didn't, you're right."

"Why's that?" Pia asked.

He turned to look her square in the face. A "gotcha" kind of smirk slid over her face and made her eyes glitter.

"Maybe because I don't ask personal questions." She expelled a burst of air through her lips, making a noise like a balloon deflating. "I call bullshit on that answer, Captain. I think it's because you assumed some things about me before you knew anything." She picked at the edge of the blanket. "Kind of like what I did with you earlier. The stuff about assuming you knew nothing about horses."

"Then we're even. We can start over." He thrust his hand out. "Pleased to meet you, my name is Jonah. I served in the US Army Rangers and am now an agent of the Department of Homeland Security." He leaned in closer to Pia and lowered his voice. "I knew you were trying to figure that out." He tapped the console containing his badge.

Pia's hand, small and bony like a bird's wing, disappeared in his. "I was that obvious? Darn."

"Let's just say you wouldn't make a very good spy." He pulled his hand away and held it over the temperature dial. "Warm enough?"

Pia shrugged out of the blanket and held it on her lap. She nodded. "Sure. Guess we'd better head home." The spark had disappeared from her voice.

"Don't worry. We'll find her."

Pia turned away and stared out the dark window. "What do you think they're doing with her? A vet, bringing her to a medical lab—that can't be good."

He shook his head. "No. Not at all."

"It just doesn't make sense. Why Regalo? This sounds horrible, but there are a lot of lame or unwanted horses. People donate those horses, so why take a healthy, sound one for medical experiments or whatever she has in mind?" Pia's lips pinched together and she looked down. "You know, when I started looking for Regalo, I thought I wanted her back because she was a gift from my dad. She was a big part of happier times. Sounds dumb like a Hallmark movie or something, but she was a piece of who I was then." She twisted her ring. "That person is gone. But you know what?"

She turned to him and her dark eyes held his. He made an almost imperceptible movement of his head *no*.

"I don't care about all that so much anymore. Not the part about me. It's not about that anymore, I just need to save her." She shifted, angling her knees toward him. "*We* need to save her."

Chapter 20

Pia

It was after midnight when she got home. Deliah had left her car parked near the house with the keys under the mat. Deliah never had trouble finding a ride home, no matter how last minute. Pia took a shower and tossed the clothes she'd been wearing for almost twenty-four hours in the laundry hamper. She made a cup of chamomile tea—like that would help her sleep—and settled down in front of her laptop. She felt so spun up she figured she'd poke around on the Internet for an hour and still get enough sleep before the alarm went off.

The big mistake was punching into the search bar how horses are used in medical testing. What she learned swept sleep totally out of the equation. Horses were used for all kinds of medical experiments, but especially for respiratory research trials, immunology testing, and genetic tracking.

Her imagination ran wild. Regalo, being infected with Lyme's disease or worse, just so they could try out some experimental formula. Pia twisted in her seat, conjuring up a picture of Regalo restrained in a straight stall in some dark lab while a stranger thrust needles into her.

But there was no proof Regalo was sent to a lab. It might have simply been a company name used for the shipping payment. She'd check with the shipping company boss—the real one—in the morning.

Pia pulled her robe tighter around her. The room was chilly. Ryder shuffled in and collapsed at her feet.

"We'll go to bed as soon as I look up a few more things," she said. "I promise."

The dog dropped his head on his paws and let out a sigh.

The only leads were DiMarco's name, his daughter, Caroline, and Aunt-the-vet who may or may not be called Zeta. If she could find the vet's last name, she'd have a chance of hunting her down. She pulled up Facebook, but DiMarco's page held no clues. He had it pretty well clamped down for privacy and besides, he didn't seem overly interested in sharing brags about his family. It featured him and his work at the law firm. Great guy and family man. Pia cupped her chin on her palm and thought. The kid is her best bet.

A quick scan of Caroline's page showed the apple not falling far from the tree. It featured pictures of her mostly—at horse shows, high school sports team photos, and what looked like some very dark party venues. She had a few facts about herself in the Intro, but nothing helpful. There was one picture of family members it looked like—Caroline was in a white graduation robe flanked by a man and two women. The comment boasted: Feeling proud (happy emoji) with mom, dad, and Aunt Zeta at my Honor Society Induction. None of them were tagged. Dead end for getting a last name. How hard could it be to find a vet with the first name Zeta? Turns out, harder than she thought.

"Let's see where else you hang out, girl."

Pia took a sip of lukewarm tea. The stuff was nasty when it was scalding hot, now the herbal mess caused her face to twist in a grimace. "Who drinks this crap? Tastes like weeds." She pushed it away and started several searches through horse-related groups hoping for Caroline to pop up. No luck. She switched to Instagram, which made more sense. She scanned for Caroline, Aunt Zeta, friends...

Pia stretched. Her neck made noises like a bowl of Rice Krispies when she circled her head. Her eyes weren't focusing anymore. But then she saw it. On Alice's post—the kid who worked at the farm where Caroline had the supposed accident. Alice posted about a horse she was leasing—a cute gray that looked a bit underweight. It had garnered a stream of "helpful" advice, not least of which came from Miss Know-It-All Caroline DiMarco. She dispensed her pile of venom on poor Alice, insisting the horse looked sick, helpfully adding, that she ought to know because her aunt, Dr. Zeta Usoro, is an equine vet. Pia smiled. So, the little arrogant shit actually did write something helpful. A search popped up a link to Dr. Usoro's practice right away. No wonder Zeta didn't pull anything up—her full name was Maria Zetta Usoro, spelled with two Ts. It seemed she went by Maria professionally and was Zetta to her friends. If she had any.

She grabbed her phone and texted the information to Watkins. The glowing numbers the corner of her computer screen told her it was one thirty. Oh well, he'd get it in the morning. She stood. Time for bed.

Her phone pinged.

Ryder struggled to his feet. He stood on shaky legs giving her a baleful expression.

"Gotta get this. Might be Captain America," she said.

It was Watkins. She felt a surge of adrenaline.

How did you find her name? I came up empty.

A warmth spread through her chest. He was up, too. She wasn't alone in this obsessive search. She smirked as her fingers poked out the message: **You gotta think like a teenage girl. Epic fail for you.**

He sent back a thumbs up with *Talk tomorrow* underneath.

Entering her office the next day, despite the lack of sleep, Pia floated on a cloud of success. She passed Deliah's glass-enclosed private office on her way to her desk in the middle of the cube farm. It had all the privacy a four-foot partition could provide, crammed up against her neighbors' desks numbering in the dozens. The click of keyboards and ringing phones made it hard to think sometimes. She went to get a cup of coffee and tossed seventy-five cents in the donation jar.

Her boss, Mr. Burke, approached from the opposite direction. She figured she'd give him a silent nod greeting and hurry on to her desk. Damn, she needed the coffee. She slowed to take a sip and looked up. He was standing in front of her.

"Mrs. Harcourt, I'd like a word."

Not good. He sounded too formal. "Sure, Mr. Burke. When did you have in mind?"

He nodded to his office. "Right now. Follow me."

Definitely not good.

Pia stepped into his office and he shut the door behind her. He made a sweeping gesture for her to take a seat as he stepped behind his massive desk and sat.

Was it because she and Deliah took off early yesterday? They both signed out, using their vacation time. Nah, that was minor. He looked serious with his fingers steepled in front of his face.

"I wanted talk to you about the Dankert case."

Uh-oh. That was a mess of a case that landed in her lap earlier that year. It looked like an open and shut fraud case at first—the insurance company was being asked to pay out a huge sum on a personal injury case but something didn't smell right. Supposedly, Mr. Dankert was injured in a forklift accident at his company, but it turned out he was faking his injuries. He found out his wife was having an affair with a prominent physician and blackmailed him into attesting to his injuries. The physician had a very rich wife—someone Pia happened to know from her racing days…

"Something else happen with the case? I thought the insurance company was off the hook for payment?"

Mr. Burke shook himself as if Pia's words shocked him. "No, no. It's fine. In fact, the insurance company was very appreciative of our work. So much so, they've tossed a few additional cases our way. One in particular is—" he spun in his chair to face the computer and wiggled the mouse to bring the screen back to life. "Here it is. When I said I wanted to talk to you about the Dankert case, it was within the context of your, um, connections that helped resolve it. I want you to take this new one because it's right up your alley, so to speak. It's a very sensitive case. It requires someone who can fit in while poking around, not arouse any suspicion."

"Mr. Burke, it sounds like you want me to go undercover or something. The PIs usually do that sort of stuff. I'm more of a cyber spy. You know, dig around in people's online profiles, their credit card bills and financial statements…safe stuff."

He didn't appear to have heard her. He prattled on. "No, you're the perfect candidate for the job. Go, ask some questions. No danger, really. It's billed as a stolen property case for now. Very strange circumstances. The damaged property was donated for a tax write-off, the insurance was prepared to pay out, but when the client circled back to check, no sign of the property. Like I said, odd."

"So, what's the property that went missing? Stolen property cases usually just settle with the insurance and everyone forgets about it."

Mr. Burke harrumphed. "Sadly, not in this case. The owner is stirring up a hornet's nest."

"Okay, where was the property when it went missing? Where are you sending me?"

"The track. A racehorse has gone missing."

Chapter 21

Watkins

Watkins sat in his car in NSA's parking lot and reread the text Pia had sent him in the middle of the night. She was clever going after the teen girls' online profiles to find the information they were after. He had to smile. Maybe Pia should get a job working Intelligence and Analysis at the Agency.

He stowed his phone in the console and made his way inside. Like every morning he greeted his cubicle mate. "Good morning, Marion."

"What's good about it?" she answered. "Oh, before I forget. Abramson is looking for you. I left a note on your desk."

Watkins's desk was uncluttered. Only a US Army mug holding pens and pencils and a small, framed photo of his old unit graced the surface. "Nope, no note. What's it about?"

"Shoot, must have forgot to write it down after all. Abramson was looking for you last night. I was here late and he came by."

Watkins turned to look toward the private office in the corner. The door was shut. "What about?"

"Didn't tell me." Marion hitched a shoulder. "I'm just NSA. Your need-to-know spooky Homeland Security stuff is off-limits for me." Her pronunciation of the O in Homeland was drawn out like a true Baltimore native.

Watkins locked his screen and stood up. "Wonder if he's there now." He approached the office and ran a hand down his tie to flatten it before he rapped on the door with the back of his knuckles. The door swung open. Abramson looked up from his desk.

"Jonah. Just who I wanted to see. Come in."

Watkins closed the office door behind him. "Heard you wanted to talk to me." He preferred getting right to it without a lot of preamble. The boss wouldn't have called him in if it weren't important. Abramson stood and gestured to a small conference table where they both took a seat.

Watkins need not have worried about Abramson setting him at ease with a few questions about the family or inquiries about sports team standings. He placed his hands flat on the tabletop and leaned in. "Do you want to keep working in the cell?"

A flush of heat rose over Watkins's face. "Of course. Is there a problem?"

Abramson compressed his lips. "Might be. That's what we need to talk about."

Watkins sat up straighter. He gave a slight nod.

"You know we're here at NSA's behest? We have to stay in their good graces."

Another nod.

"The agency has afforded us access to their resources—their linguists, special databases...as long as we play by their rules."

Watkins leaned back and crossed his arms. "Look, if I've broken any rules, just come out with it."

Abramson's gaze shifted away for a minute. "Here's the thing. You set off a red flag with a search." He sat in the chair opposite.

"What was the search term? Simple solution, I'll void any further research into something sensitive if that's an issue."

Abramson lifted his head. His expression showed relief. "That's part of the problem. You see, it's a close hold project. Special access."

A noise of disgust mixed with disbelief erupted from Watkins's chest. "What? So they issue a cease and desist on any searches related to a term they won't tell us? How am I supposed to stop doing something I don't even know I'm doing?"

"It was yesterday. Last night actually, on your iPad. An unclassified search on Median Diagnostic Services. A liaison officer contacted me first thing this morning wanting to know what Homeland Security was up to. At the time, I had no idea what he was talking about."

Watkins's mouth fell open but he held back the questions flying through his brain. *If an open source search elicited this sort of attention, what was this Median Diagnostics place up to?*

Abramson continued. "I assured him we weren't stepping into anything they had set up. Apparently they've had Median's Middle East offices in Turkey on their radar for a while. What I want to know is what's Median Diagnostics to you?"

Watkins's shoulders dropped a half inch. "Most likely not the same company. This Median had to be a local organization. I was searching for—" *How to explain to Abramson running around at night chasing down a horse in a trailer so that he didn't sound crazy?* "It was a personal matter. Nothing to do with work."

"Then why were you using a government-issued reader?"

Watkins held up his hand. "I was wrong there. Agreed. I unlocked the iPad to check in at work and the person I was with used it to look up Median."

His boss's face bloomed red starting from the edge of his collar. "Someone else? You mean an uncleared individual? So why were you and this *someone else* interested in Median?"

Watkins paused to consider his choice of words. "We were tracking a missing horse—one that might be in trouble. Just over the border in West Virginia we caught up with the driver of the horse van who told us the horse was handed over to some guys probably from a place called Median Diagnostics, according to the shipping papers. It was a logical next step to look up Median and find out where it's located."

Abramson's face contorted like he detected a bad smell. "And what does this other person know?"

"Nothing. We didn't learn anything and—"

"Good. You make sure your friend doesn't pursue it. Take care of the situation, Watkins."

"I'll be sure to." The words felt slick on his tongue like a betrayal. Pia had opened herself up to him, vowing they would work together to save Regalo. How could he keep her in the dark on purpose?

Watkins assumed a casual pose and moderated his voice. "What's the story with Median? Is there a US -based branch of the same company?"

His boss made one sharp shake of his head. "Not my worry. Besides, it's off-limits. No interfering—"

"But if Median is of concern and has penetrated into the US, it should be Homeland Security's business." Watkins's index finger stabbed the table. "Why are we being shut out? If they insist on keeping us in the dark, we need to initiate our own investigation."

Abramson rubbed a hand over his face. "We are involved. We were brought in when the threat moved from Median's international headquarters to a suspected subsidiary operation here. The one you seemed to have stumbled on."

"Get me the clearance and read me in." Watkins leaned on both elbows. "Are we dealing with a bioweapons threat? Are we working with the Proliferation people on this?"

Watkins words trailed off as Abramson shook his head and sighed like a man who hasn't seen much sleep lately. "No can do. It's a bigot list—someone has to come off the clearance list before we can put anyone else on."

"But you're read in." Watkins's one eyebrow cocked. "The boss, but not the analysts actually doing the job?"

Abramson's face clouded.

Watkins rushed on. "Look, I don't know what this place is up to, but I do know there's a certain veterinarian who is likely involved. If you clear me, I could help—"

"It's not up to me," Abramson stood, signaling the subject was closed. "Median is a restricted file. This is official notification."

Chapter 22

Pia

The smell of the backstretch brought Pia back. Days of schlepping to Pimlico before sunrise, ignoring biting cold or stifling heat, and getting the horses fed, groomed, and worked all before noon. Steaming piles of manure in the dumpster cans outside the shedrows and the sharp tang of horse liniment were scents that held hands with happy memories. A brush gliding over a satin coat, the thrump of galloping hooves, the electricity in the air on race day. The sounds, smells—they all transported her back to the old days. But were they really the good ole days?

Pia fingered the temp badge she was issued in order to slip past the public areas and access the barns and saddling area. It helped to have old friends in the office who remembered her. Mrs. Russell came from behind her desk and gave Pia a hug so hard her bones cracked.

"I heard you got a new job," she said. "Some kind of insurance company according to gossip. What brings you back here?"

Pia had debated telling people she was there to check out a horse for a partnership deal, so they wouldn't be so on guard when she started asking questions, but Mrs. Russell was the track's eyes and ears and would uncover the truth about Pia's mission eventually.

"My company works with the agency that insured the horse that went missing. Did you hear about that?"

"Did I hear? The police were all over this place. Are you working with them?"

"Not directly, but my company keeps in touch with their investigation. The insurance company hired us to determine whether the claim is legitimate. Was the horse stolen, or did someone do something to him in order to file a claim?"

"Doing something, like..." She made a throat slicing gesture. "Wouldn't be a first."

Pia raised her eyebrows but kept silent. Sometimes the best way to get information was to leave a void in the conversation. People rushed to fill the empty air and Mrs. Russell had no problem filling the silence.

"If you ask me," she said, "the whole thing doesn't make any sense. I know the owner. Howie O'Dell is a straight-up kind of guy. He takes care of his horses and he uses an honest trainer. The horse—a big, goofy bay colt named Bourbon Ball—wasn't much of a runner to begin with when he came up lame. Long story short, the vet diagnosed a torn sesamoid. Needed the usual treatment but mostly he was in for a long layup. Maybe the horse would come back, but doubt it." She sucked her teeth. "Anyway, Howie arranged for the big guy to do his layup at a nice place in Baltimore County. The facility supposedly has all the bells and whistles for treating injuries. Thing is, the horse never turned up there."

Pia nodded. She knew all this from the file, but she wanted to hear Mrs. Russell's version. "He left from here directly to the layup farm? Do you have the name?"

"White Oaks Farm."

The name rang a bell. Pia could ask Selma about the rescue. Check up on its rep.

The older woman circled behind the desk and slapped a thick file on top. "Here's all the in and out passes logged for that week. Horse gets loaded on a trailer and taken outta here, but a chit needs to be filled out. They need to check his ID at the gate, make sure they got the right horse." She patted the file like it was a baby's back. "Goes in the computer file, when I get a chance to enter them."

Pia knew the guards at the gate were sometimes lax about verifying the paperwork. She'd shipped her own horses out without filling one out, promising to complete it later. "The police looked through all that?" she asked.

One sharp nod sent Mrs. Russell's glasses sliding down her nose. "You betcha. Went through everything. Security camera footage—what we had working at the time—the gate logs, the whole nine yards."

"So they determined the right horse got on that trailer and left. Who shipped him out? I know when the horse rescues pick up a horse, they come with their own trailer to take possession. Did the"—Pia glanced down at her notes to check the name of the farm—"White Oaks Farm send their own trailer and driver?"

"That's something else strange," Mrs. Russell said. "The farm's van was in the shop so they contacted a local shipper to get BB—that's what everyone called Bourbon Ball."

"A shipper you know?"

"Sure. But wasn't them that got the horse. A different outfit shows up. Drives straight to O'Dell's shedrow. The driver knows which horse he's picking up." Mrs. Russell flipped through the stack of papers and pulled one out. "Had it filled out with BB's tattoo number and everything." She slid the paper across the desk to Pia.

She frowned at the scrawled writing, but it was filled out with information and listed White Oaks as the destination. Time of departure and the date were noted in the right-hand corner. The tattoo number matched. Pia took out her phone and snapped a picture. "Not sure if it will help any, but thanks."

Mrs. Russell returned the slip of paper to her pile. "Thing is, why would anyone take him? It wasn't like he was worth a lot. BB wasn't much of a runner before he got hurt. I imagine Howie didn't have him insured for much..." She raised an eyebrow.

She was fishing for gossip. Pia obliged, wanting to keep the conversation flowing. "Probably for more than he was worth, but certainly not enough to risk going to jail for committing fraud."

"Howie told me he was donating the horse after its rehab. Probably forgot to cancel the insurance. That's the kind of guy he is, though. Paid for BB's rehab himself up front and didn't just dump the horse. Like some other owners might."

"How so?" Pia asked, although she was well aware of how horses get dumped at auctions, riding schools for a write-off donation, or suspicious rescues.

"A lot of other owners don't keep such good tabs on a broken-down horse. They donate them for a write-off and never follow up on whether they got to the rescue or the riding school or whatever. As long as a racer doesn't end up at auction, no one cares. But Howie checked up on BB. Heard from the White Oaks people he wasn't there, but he sure as hell left here."

Thank God there were good, caring owners like O'Dell. But Pia knew there were also plenty of trainers who didn't care about horses not earning their keep and would turn a blind eye to where they ended up—as long as it wasn't an auction that would get them barred from the track. But she had another thought. "Did Howie O'Dell have any enemies? Someone who might want to get back at him through his horses?"

Mrs. Russell's face scrunched with thought. "No one I can imagine. Sure, anyone is bound to make an enemy in the horse racing biz, but Howie is about as nice a guy as you'll meet. Surrounds himself with good people, too. His trainer, grooms..." She continued shaking her head long after her words trickled to a halt.

Pia pulled a business card out of her cell phone case and placed it on the desk. "It's been great seeing you again, Mrs. Russell. I'll swing back around again before I leave today to say goodbye, but if you hear anything more about BB, please let me know. I'm going to wander around, see who's still here from the old days."

"Old days!" Mrs. Russell blew threw her lips. "You don't know from old days. I started working here when Spectacular Bid won the Preakness."

Pia gave the woman a quick squeeze and waved as she headed out the door. It was a short walk to the stabling area. She'd tried contacting a few of her former acquaintances, but many of them had dropped out of the racing business, a few had died, she was sad to learn, and a handful moved their operations out of Maryland to the West Coast.

But old Jenkins was still here—a hard-nosed trainer who ran his stable like the bridge of a battleship. She set out to his stabling area but was disappointed to learn she'd missed him. A hotwalker told her he'd been called back to his farm on an emergency. While she wandered around, she asked a few people what they'd heard about the missing horse, but wasn't sure how much to believe. The track was either a boiling pot of gossip or would close ranks and shut out the nosy outsider. Even if she tapped into someone willing to dish out the dirt, she couldn't be sure how much was true, how much was hearsay, and how much was pure invention in order to make a sexier story. Over the course of the day, she listened to a bunch of screwball theories from a mob boss who lost a bundle on Bourbon Ball and wanted revenge, to a deranged animal rights activist who was stealing racehorses in order to set them free.

Pia dragged her feet through the raked stone as she passed the row of stalls she knew so well. Reaching out her hand, she brushed it along the wood outside of Regalo's old stall, and stopped a moment to peer inside. A big raw-boned gelding occupied it now. He swung his head, ears pinned and teeth bared. She stepped back, slamming into a wheelbarrow.

"I'm sorry," she said, grabbing for the man's arm to steady herself. "Wasn't watching what I was doing."

A short man supported her elbow until she steadied herself. "Be careful of that one." His chin jutted in the direction of the big gelding. "Nasty."

The man was dressed in the track uniform of worn jeans, Timberlands, and a thick plaid shirt worn over a T-shirt frayed around the neck. His hands were scuffed and dirty, and his face was lined from a lifetime of exposure to the sun and wind. His hair, though white, had a yellow tinge. He dropped the wheelbarrow he was pushing, and they both moved a few feet away. Too old to be working so hard still, she thought, and guessed he must be in his late sixties.

Pia straightened her twisted jacket. "Thanks." She looked back at the gray horse. "Maybe he's just hungry. He looks a little"—she struggled to pick the right word—"underweight."

To her surprise, a bark of a laughter exploded out of the man. "I agree! But that's how the trainer likes them to look. Likes them to act, too. Aggressive."

Pia glanced at the cranky horse. "Might have ulcers," she said almost to herself. She turned back to the man who was now looking at her with a puzzled expression. "You're not the new girl Jenkins hired?" He took in her spotless black slacks and stack-heeled boots. Not clothes someone wears working around horses.

"No, I'm here to meet someone." She didn't want to give out too many details. It was harder to keep her story straight if she did. "I was just reminiscing about a horse I used to have in training here. Long time ago. That was her stall." She pointed behind her.

"Clarence Langston." He tapped his chest. "Been here since God created the earth and sky. What was your horse's name? Maybe I remember her."

"I doubt it. She wasn't here long and didn't make much of a splash as a runner. Her name's Regalo de Suerte."

"Gift of Luck, huh?" he shook his head. "Nope, not ringing a bell."

Pia calculated Mr. Langston's command of Spanish was pretty good since he had no trouble translating Regalo's name. "You'd remember her if you saw her. I'd guess you'd say she had unusual coloring. A mix of golden hair over her haunches mixed in with a bay coat."

He shook his head. "No, guess not. And I remember ones going way back. Horses, yes, their people, not so much." He tapped his temple.

Pia knew what he meant. She remembered the names of some of the great horses she'd met and details about their quirks and habits, but the people who tagged along with them had faded into a blur. "It was a long time ago," she said not unlike an apology. "You must see a lot of horses come and go over the years."

His face lost expression like a cloud blotting out the sun. Pia worried she had triggered a bad memory.

"That's right," he said. "I've seen it all. Believe me."

"You've worked here long?"

He flashed a smile. His teeth on the left side were missing. "Too long. Getting old for this kind of thing. Just hanging around for the horses."

Pia shifted, intent on moving off so she didn't keep Mr. Langston from his chores. She was tired of asking about the missing horse and getting nowhere, and besides, her feet hurt in the stupid boots she'd chosen to wear. But she liked this old guy who seemed to have a soft spot for the horses. She scanned the shedrow, taking in each of the horses with their heads hanging over the door.

"Yeah, the things we do for them. They're all great, but every once in a while there's an extra special one," he said.

A *special one*. Without reservation, in the next five minutes she'd blurted out to this stranger the entire story of how she was looking for Regalo, how she had tracked the mare down but now she'd slipped through her fingers. Maybe it was because this old horseman reminded her of her dad and his love of horses. The quiet way he listened as if he had nowhere else to be.

"Don't give up," he told Pia. "Whatever you have to do, it will be worth it." He touched her arm as lightly as the brush of an insect's wing.

The side of her mouth twisted up into an expression that felt cynical at the same fingers of regret clamped her throat closed. She wanted to trust his encouraging words, but it wasn't looking good. "I hope you're right."

"I'm right." He turned to pick up a halter that fell from its hook near a stall door. "You owe it to your dad to keep trying."

She did owe it to her dad to find Regalo and at least make sure she was safe. "I owe it to Regalo, too," she said.

He nodded but said nothing. His gnarled hand ran down the long face of the filly that knocked the halter to the ground.

"You'd have probably liked my dad. You'd have had a lot in common." Pia pushed away from the post she was leaning against, resolved to leave. She had to get back to the office, fill out a report on what she'd learned, but mostly she needed to let this man get back to work. She knew a lot of trainers would fire a worker for hanging around talking when there was so much to get done. "I'm going to head out of here and let you get back to work, Mr. Langston." She nodded at the wheelbarrow. "Don't want you to get in trouble with anyone for hanging around talking to me."

The old man rubbed the back of his neck. "Dunno who would make trouble for me, except my horses when they didn't get fed in time. That red filly there holds a grudge."

His horses? Did he mean that in the sense that he took care of them, or something else? Pia felt her eyebrows inch together.

He laughed, giving a full view of his toothlessness. "Don't worry, miss. You're not the first to mistake me for one of the help." He gestured to five horses at the end of the shedrow. "These are my children. Love every one of them, so I like to do some of the caregiving myself sometimes."

This man dressed like a stall cleaner owned a stable of racehorses. Pia shook her head and felt the heat wash over her face. How stupid of her to assume...

"I apologize. I'm so embarrassed."

He waved her apology away. "The only thing to be sorry about is the fact that you know my name, but I never got yours."

Her mouth dropped open. "I'm sorry. Gosh, I keep saying that. My name's Olympia Murphy." She dropped her married name. "My dad was—"

"Murphy?" His mouth scrunched to one side. "Your dad's not Paddy Murphy?"

"You knew my dad?"

"Not knew him. More like, knew of him. He had quite a reputation."

Pia looked down and shook her head. "A good one, I hope. He took some chances on horses. Had some great runners, but more often he went down in flames." She felt herself smiling.

Mr. Langston had a hardy laugh. "He did that. Got to admire his courage, however. Gutsy guy. I was sorry to hear he passed. He never cut corners where the horses were concerned and never backed down from a fight."

Pia grew up on her dad's dreams of finding the Cinderella racehorse and cut her teeth on his lost-cause campaigns and battles. "He was that," she agreed.

Mr. Langston stepped back to let a groom pass, leading a chestnut dancing on the end of a lead rope. "Your dad helped the girl jockeys get a start here, did you know that?"

Pia did. She knew her dad went to bat for one female in particular who had promise, but was harassed by the old boys network. "He came home with a few bones broken in his hand after a discussion—his words—after some guys jumped her behind the shedrow, trying to scare her off."

"And I heard he ran off that vet for a time. Caught her doping for a fee but could never prove it to the Jockey Club. Almost got her license revoked. That was something." He sucked his teeth with disgust. "She's a real bad apple."

Pia's antenna went up. How is it she'd never heard this story from her dad?

"A vet here at the track?"

"Not the official track vet. No, our track vet, she's a great gal. This one came in special for a few clients. Special, cause she was willing to look the other way for a fee when it came to falsifying papers and mixing up a special cocktail for a slow or hurt horse. Never proved anything, sorry to say."

"So she's still practicing? What's her name?" *There's no way it could be the same vet. What are the chances?*

Mr. Langston scratched the underside of his chin. "Something odd, I remember. We used to call her the Warrior Princess cuz of her name."

"Xena the Warrior Princess?"

"Yeah, that was it. Or something like that." He shook his head. "Can't remember exactly."

"Mr. Langston, could it be Zetta, not Xena? Like Maria Zetta DiMarco or—"

He shook his finger in Pia's face. "That's it. Dr. Zetta Usoro, not DiMarco. Strange name."

Pia's hands shook as she pulled out her cell to text Watkins. "I've been looking for her. She's the one who took Regalo. She's—"

Langston straightened. "She's no one to fool with, Miss Murphy. Especially if she finds out who your dad was. Bad blood between them."

Pia expected him to shake a finger in her face based on the force of his words. She wished she could assure him she had no intention of messing with Dr. Warrior Princess, but she knew that would be a lie. "Does she still come to the track for any clients?"

Langston peered at her from the corner of his eye. He answered with a suspicious tone to his voice. "I might have seen her around. There's always new trainers who don't know her rep."

Pia pulled out her card and gave it Langston. "If you see her, could you call me?" She pressed the card into his hand. "Please?"

Langston's eyes narrowed. "What do you have in mind?"

"I have to meet with her. She's my only hope of finding Regalo."

Chapter 23

Watkins

Watkins pushed open his townhouse door and reeled back as the smell of rancid food slapped him in the face.

"It smells like low tide in here," he said, tossing his keys on the kitchen counter. "I told you to take those crab shells out last night."

Caleb swung his legs around and sat up on the couch. He was still wearing what he had on last night—a Harvard T-shirt and gray sweatpants. The waistband had lost its elastic and caused them to hang precariously around his bony hips.

Watkins pulled out the garbage bag and cinched down the knot to close it. Wrestling it past the recycle bin, he bumped it and set off a clinking rattle as the bottles settled inside. He looked over the lip of the bin and counted six longnecks. Just on the top, where he could see. It had been emptied last night after Caleb's friends went home around eleven.

"I see you've kept the party going by yourself today." His jaw hurt from clenching it.

Caleb lurked in the kitchen entrance, leaning against the wall. He scratched a bare patch of his abdomen like a languid cat.

When Watkins brushed past, he reached out to grab the bag. "I'll take it. Sorry. Just forgot."

Watkins jerked his arm away and turned, protecting the garbage bag like it was full of treasure. "Forgot? How could you with the stink in here?" He stomped through the living room and out to the dumpster across the parking lot.

The evening air cooled the heat in his face. He didn't want to go back inside. The thought of facing Caleb with what he had to say made him stop in place. In the darkened parking lot he watched his breath swirl in clouds around his head. He'd promised to take care of his brother, but he didn't know how. Every effort was met with failure or fights.

On leaden feet he trudged up the front stairs and inside. Caleb was on his knees in the kitchen with a sponge raised in one hand. "Spilled something. Don't worry, I'm cleaning it up."

He bent over a puddle on the linoleum and teetered forward, bumping his head on a cabinet and toppling sideways. The puddle of liquid seeped into his dirty sweatpants.

Watkins hesitated. He should just leave him. Let him deal with it, but his body disobeyed his reason and marched forward to scoop his brother up under his arms. He frog marched him into the spare bedroom.

"Ouch," Caleb squirmed and twisted. "You're hurting me."

Watkins didn't loosen his grip. Instead he shoved Caleb onto the futon bed—still unmade—and pulled off his sopping pants.

Caleb tugged the sheets over his bare legs. "Perv. What's your problem?" His brother's unfocused eyes avoided looking at him.

"Why are you home and not at work?" Watkins had called in a favor with an old army buddy and got Caleb a job working at his café in town. He'd started a few days ago.

"Whaddaya think?" Caleb's words slurred.

"Fired or quit?" Watkins went to cross his arms and thought better of it. His father always crossed his arms while delivering his lectures.

Caleb snorted. "Quit. It was a bullshit job."

"It was a job. You got something better in mind?"

"Yeah. Stop running my life."

His brother's hands scrabbled at the edge of the blanket, tugging at it in an attempt to pull it up over his shoulders and failing. One enormous effort caused the tucked end of the blanket to give way, sending his fist into his face.

Watkins laughed. It was pathetic. Sad even. This was his brother. His drunk, hopeless baby brother but he couldn't stop laughing. The dam of control over every frustratingly ridiculous event of the last few days broke. He couldn't fix anything. He couldn't find a damn horse, he couldn't get his boss to come clean on what was going on in his own office, and he damn well couldn't fix Caleb.

"Asshole." Caleb draped the blanket over his head, slumped down, and turned his shoulder away from Watkins.

He stood watching his brother as his breathing slowed and deepened. He'd probably sleep through the night.

"We'll talk about it tomorrow," Watkins said to the lump in the bed.

Caleb's voice murmured from underneath his cocoon. "Right, Dad. Whatever."

The *Dad* crack was a well-aimed stab. "I'm not Dad."

"Damn straight you're not. Just acting like the same asshole he was. Captain Dad."

Watkins retreated to the doorway. A sound like a sob leaked from under the blanket. He couldn't deal with him right now. When he was sober in the morning, they'd get things straightened out.

He had to get showered and over to Pia's place. She'd invited him over to discuss their strategy for finding Regalo and to share what she'd found out. He cringed, thinking he'd have to hold back on any mention of Median Diagnostics, if she brought it up. It only made sense that she'd want to track it down. He'd have the same plan in her shoes. But now it was up to him to slow roll that idea. To keep her from plowing into something...he didn't even know what. Until he came up with a better plan.

※※※ ※※※

Watkins drove the old Ranger down Pia's long driveway past several fenced acres. He noted the broken board held up with bailing twine and the sagging gate. He headed toward a white farmhouse surrounded by a wrap-around porch, but something caught his eye near the entrance to the barn. Pia stood at the entrance, waving an arm overhead. She motioned for him to come in the barn and disappeared inside.

Under his jacket he wore a pressed white oxford. That and clean loafers were not what he would have chosen to wear if he knew she needed help with the horses. He parked and met her inside. Even in the frigid air, the scent of fresh hay triggered memories of summers as a kid, working in exchange for rides on the better horses. The old bank style barn was constructed when workmanship was a matter of pride. He noted the fine masonry of its stone foundation and huge beams held together with wooden pegs and joints. Built in the days when people made things to last.

Pia appeared around the corner wearing snug black yoga pants and a down vest over a flannel shirt. "Before we go up to the house, I wanted to introduce you to someone." She spun on her heels so fast he had to jog down the barn aisle after her, missing half of what she was saying. A guilty stab shot a flash of heat to his face, realizing he'd missed what she was saying because he was focused on the movement of her hips under the thin spandex. He came up beside her.

"What were you saying? I missed it," he told her.

She stopped in front of a stall and slid open the door. A dark bay mare pulled at her hayrack. Her topline had sunken and she'd gone gray around her eyes. She flicked an ear at the interruption, but didn't turn to greet them. She had to be at least thirty, Watkins figured. Judging by the size of her feet and bone, she wasn't a Thoroughbred, so not an old racer here on retirement.

Pia cocked an eyebrow. "I thought you of all people would appreciate meeting this old gal."

"She looks good for her age," he said. The horse's coat was thickening, getting ready for winter. Watkins stepped close and ran his fingers down her neck.

Pia in her open-toed sneaker things stepped in beside him. He caught a whiff of lilac as she stood beside him. "This is Artio. Winner of the Grand Prix Special in the Dressage Championships, Horse of the Year in 2005, silver medal in Freestyle in the World Equestrian Games—"

He bent over to look at the mare's face again. Yes, the trademark lightning bolt blaze was there, as was the high right rear stocking. "What's she doing here?"

Pia straightened her back in a posture of mock insult. "Like here isn't good enough for her?"

"I didn't mean that. Just how did she end up—" He clamped off the rest of the words that didn't sound any better. "She must be close to thirty years old now."

"My dad saved her. One of his fanciful trades." Pia stepped out of the stall and shook the shavings out of her shoes. "She was used up, crippled up, and dried up from being a broodmare as my dad described it. The owners didn't want to put any more into her, well, you know how it is. Dad brought her home, fixed her up enough for me to ride, and—"

Watkins stopped. "Wait. You're telling me you rode an Olympic dressage horse?" He felt the grin spread across his face.

She gave a casual shrug. "Just walk and a little trot mostly. She was pretty arthritic. Once in a while she'd have a flashback to her glory days and launch into passage." Pia laughed. "I developed a good seat trying to stay on her riding in a jumping saddle."

This woman continued to surprise him. Normally, he didn't like surprises, but somehow this was different.

She hugged herself. "C'mon, I'm freezing, let's go up to the house."

They walked out to the Ranger, trailed by an old lab. Pia introduced Ryder and held the door open for him to jump in the back seat. Watkins cringed at the dirty paw prints on the clean upholstery. Pia hopped in the passenger seat and slammed the door.

"This is a luxury, getting a ride back up to the house." She trailed her hand out an open window, catching the night air. At the house, when they approached the front door, she threw herself against it. The old wood squealed before the door burst open. "Sticks in the cold," she explained.

The dog shoved him aside and strode ahead of Watkins. He retreated to a plaid dog bed in the corner of the living room. Pia shucked off her vest and held her hand out for his jacket. "Go sit in the living room." A head tilt to the right. "I'll get us something to drink and grab my laptop." She hung the outerwear on a coat tree—laden down with coats, scarves, and vests—and headed down a narrow hallway. Watkins walked into a living room that looked like what his grandmom from Virginia always called the front parlor. He was not an expert, but it looked like the furniture spanned a century from an Empire period writing desk, a Victorian couch probably stuffed with horsehair, to a modern leather recliner. He perched on the edge of an ottoman with his elbows resting on his knees. Across the room, a barrister's bookcase held an array of bloodstock volumes on racing Thoroughbreds and the walls were covered with photos in the winner's circle.

Pia appeared with a wine bottle clutched in one hand and two glasses in the other with the laptop clamped under her arm. He jumped to his feet to assist, but stood, unsure what to do. She set the bottle and glasses down on the bare wood of the coffee table. Watkins slid a magazine under the dripping bottle.

"I opened this one earlier, so I figured we'd just finish it," she explained. "Hope you like red." She tilted the bottle to read the label. "Whatever it is."

He filled the bottom third of the glasses and handed one to her. "Thanks again for asking me over."

Pia ditched her shoes and settled on the couch with her legs tucked up under her. "No problem. Like you said, it's better if we work together on this. Texting what we found out is okay, but this way we can make a plan." She pulled the PC onto her lap and opened the lid. After a few keystrokes, she swung it around to show him. "This is what I found."

Watkins got up to join her on the couch. The screen displayed a website for a veterinary clinic. Dr. Maria Zetta Usoro was listed as a staff member. According to her biography, she held advanced degrees and belonged to a number professional organizations. A photo of a woman with very dark hair streaked with silver cut in a style favored by many of the female officers he knew. She wore a severe expression.

"Not going to win many clients with that picture," Pia said. "But look, says here at Cornell she specialized in molecular virology and infectious disease. Bet she was a real party girl."

"Her office is in Towson." Watkins pointed to the contact information.

"Yeah, that's where she's affiliated, but apparently she doesn't really work out of that office. She has a call center that dispatches her to clients. She runs her lab work and stuff through that vet office, but doesn't see patients there. I called. Had to leave a message and said that I'd been referred by someone and wanted a consultation with Dr. Usoro. When her gatekeeper called me back, she asked me a million questions about who referred me before she would book an appointment. I didn't know what to say, so I acted like I had another call waiting and would get back to her. She's not making it easy for us."

Pia also filled him in on her encounter with Mr. Langston and Dr. Usoro's run-in with her father.

"You'd better be careful she doesn't figure out who *you* really are," Watkins warned. "It sounds as if she might have been vindictive enough to take Regalo—whatever she's doing with her—to get back for what your father did years ago. Who knows what else she'd do."

"That's what I was thinking. It finally makes sense, but then it doesn't. I kept wondering why DiMarco's sister would take a healthy horse—sight unseen no less—and ship it to a medical lab. She must have heard the horse's name and knew right away it had belonged to my dad. She obviously had enough run-ins with him back in the day to know that Regalo was a special horse. But why now? My dad's been dead for years."

"Opportunity presented itself." Watkins hoped to keep the focus on Usoro and steer away from the lab's involvement.

Pia's nose was red and cheeks flushed. The wine? Or maybe the fury in her, Watkins guessed. She suddenly looked small sitting on the couch with her legs folded under her. An urge to pull her into his chest and say encouraging words swept over him. Instead, he shifted away on the pretext of reaching for his glass. She leaned forward to refill hers to the brim.

"She sounds like a dangerous nutcase," he said.

He could sense her mind spinning. Then her eyes narrowed on him. "What did you find out?" she asked. It wasn't a question, but more of a demand.

Watkins set his glass down with more care than necessary. If he said nothing and let Pia go after Usoro by herself, she could get hurt. But he also had to tread carefully not reveal intelligence or jeopardize an ongoing sensitive operation. He only knew the laboratory abroad was under surveillance and had to assume they had the affiliate in the US likewise targeted. How could he warn her that the vet was likely involved in something much more dangerous than taking a horse in an act of retribution?

He weighed his words as he chose them. Each one felt like a stone on his tongue, guarding the truth from Pia, not revealing what she had a right to know.

"Dr. Usoro appears to be linked to the Median Diagnostics Laboratory," he said.

Her eyes were glued to his. "Yeah, we figured that much after talking to the driver."

"Median's international reputation is not good."

She tilted her head like a little terrier listening for something. "Not good how?"

Watkins rested his elbows on his knees and stared at the floor. "The Mid-East office is being...*watched*." He turned his head to check her reaction. Her face remained passive, blank. "It stands to reason the US branch may also be involved in some illegal activity."

"Illegal?" A line formed between her brows. "Like illegal drug manufacturing or organized crime involvement or something? Wait. How do you know this? You found out at *work*?"

Watkins let out a sigh and leaned back. "Might be drugs, but I'm afraid it's something much worse. I can't say because I don't know any more than that. I'm shut out." The words felt like lava, spewing from a pent-up volcano. He had shoved the anger and frustration down ever since Abramson told him about the op and warned him, like a second-string player, to keep his nose out of it.

Pia cupped her wine glass and stared at him.

"I'm sorry." Watkins rubbed his palms down his pants legs. "I'm on the outside and being kept in the dark on purpose for some reason and I don't know why."

She blinked, taking in everything he said. "They're keeping stuff from you? That's some kind of bullshit."

Watkins tossed down the dregs of his wine and winced. It wasn't very good. "I was given a reprimand and told in no uncertain terms that Median was off-limits. Before I was warned off, I did manage to find out more about the Mid-Atlantic lab that probably hosts Median as a subsidiary. It does a lot of the usual veterinary support testing, but also had been involved in some antitoxin and vaccine research. Everything checks out as legitimate, unless they're scaling up for sales here. Unlicensed sales."

Pia lips parted a sliver and her eyes grew wide. "Unlicensed. You mean like places that promote fake vaccines and medical supplies?"

"I'm not saying that's the case. I don't know. But a lot of small innocent pieces, combined with the lab's sketchy import and financial records, add up to create a pretty suspicious picture."

Her gaze shifted to her lap. "They test this stuff on horses?"

He heard Pia catch her breath.

He wanted to assure her they didn't, but that would be a lie. "Horses are used in a lot of medical research, especially for metabolic and respiratory diseases. They'd be useful in vaccine research—even counterfeit vaccines."

He sat and let the silence of the room weigh down on him until his shoulders rounded. His words drifted down like toxic ash from a storm. The clock in the hall ticked.

Her words were barely a whisper. "Do you think Regalo's even still alive?"

Chapter 24

Pia

Watkins looked out of place perched on the edge of the Victorian love seat. *He's uncomfortable here,* Pia thought. She had to admit to herself, she was a little uncomfortable with him in her house, too. Not in a bad way—she invited him after all—but because she sensed something was different, something had changed. He was the complete opposite of Ron who would make himself comfortable anywhere and expect others to dance around at his beck and call. He'd only sit in his recliner and refused to drink wine. Only beer and whiskey. Pia glanced at the old, empty recliner that retained the ghostly outline of Ron's body. The sudden resolve to haul it to the dump lifted her spirits.

But what to do about Watkins? She was afraid she'd scared him, like she was going to cry or something. If she did cry, it would be because she was so mad. And frustrated. There had to be a way to find Regalo.

She poured the last of the wine into her glass. "Oops, sorry. I have more." She held up the empty bottle. "Or do you want something to eat?"

He gave her a hopeful look. "Left without grabbing anything for dinner. Maybe we can order a pizza?"

She let out a snort and quickly covered her mouth. Not very ladylike. "No one delivers out this far. C'mon in the kitchen and I'll see what I've got." Pia stood and a fuzzy static zipped through her head. Had too much wine on an empty stomach, she figured. She bent to retrieve the glasses and had to take a step to keep her balance. "Whoa, who moved the floor?"

Watkins took the glasses from her hand. Was he laughing at her? "Lead on. Let's get you something to eat."

The Tiffany lamp shone over the wooden kitchen table. With Watkins standing next to her, she saw the room through different eyes. Wow, how did the cabinets get so worn looking? And the linoleum on the floor had been dug up in the corner by one of the dogs years ago and never repaired. At least there were no dishes in the sink.

Pia opened the refrigerator. Nothing smelled bad, so that was a plus. "Ah, I've got eggs, a chicken breast, some stuff for salad..." She had no idea how to make this into a meal for two.

"Do you have spaghetti?" His was right behind her.

She spun and was within the span of one of his huge arms, holding open the refrigerator door. She paddled back a step. "Sure."

He leaned into the refrigerator and selected butter, bacon, a bagged salad kit. Was he checking the expiration date? His face scrunched.

"Now I need a shallot if you have one, some garlic, and white wine." He lifted a bottle of Chardonnay out of the door and closed the refrigerator.

"Shallot?" Her nose wrinkled.

"Onion's okay." He placed a large skillet on the burner and rolled back the sleeves of his white shirt. "You're supposed to use pancetta for this, but bacon works."

"Hold on," Pia ordered. She pulled a frilly bibbed apron from the back of the pantry door and handed it to him. "Don't want you to stain your shirt."

He looked at the apron like she was handing him her underwear, but slipped it over his head without comment. The ruffles down the sides were a comical touch.

Watkins had a wooden spoon in his hand and shook it at her. "No laughing," he said but his smile made wrinkles appear along his eyes.

"Turn around." From behind, Pia reached her arms around his body to retrieve the apron ties. Body heat radiated from his broad back, just inches from her face as she struggled to get hold of one tie. His hand brushed hers as he slid it along the fabric to help her. She wanted to freeze this moment and rest her head against his back, wrap her arms around his chest and hang on to him, breathing in the male scent of his skin. She definitely had too much to drink, she thought, and took a step back. Her fingers fumbled, but eventually managed to tie a bow. "There. Now you look like Julia Child."

He tipped the wine into the sauté pan and feigned Child's distinctive voice. "I'd never cook with a wine I wouldn't drink," he said as he filled a wine glass.

Pia wanted to find where she left her glass and fill it up again, but she thought that might be a mistake. "What the hell." She filled it halfway. "Can't have my guest drinking alone."

She sat at the counter and watched as he moved around the kitchen from the refrigerator to the stove to the chopping board like a choreographed dance. He gave her little jobs like chopping a clove of garlic or putting water on to boil. Before she could finish her glass of wine, he said everything was ready.

"Angel hair beurre blanc, salad, and"—he looked around the kitchen—"any bread to go with this?"

Pia pulled a boule of Italian out of the old breadbox. That was something she definitely always had on hand. She loved good bread.

"Perfect." He took it from her and his eyes held hers for a second longer than usual. A warmth spread from behind her belly up into her chest. He wasn't calling her perfect, it was the bread, but damn it felt good nonetheless.

She looked away as a slight tapping noise against the window caught her attention. "Sounds like the rain is turning to sleet." She frowned, thinking no doubt he'll feel the need to hurry up, eat, and get home if the weather turned bad.

He turned his face to the window, listening. "I like the sound it makes." Their plates, piled with a buttery pasta creation billowed a fragrant steam over the table, mixing with the scent of warm bread. It surrounded them in an envelope of comfort and security. Pia twirled her fork and held it aloft waiting for the food to cool before taking a mouthful. "Thanks for making dinner." She shoved the loaded fork in her mouth, then realized it was too much. Struggling to swallow, she said out the side of her mouth, "Delicious." Ugh, she was so graceless. But what did she care? It's not like he was interested in her. That's not what they were about after all. She washed it down with a swig of wine.

Time became something no longer measured as Pia sat at her kitchen table and had dinner with someone else. It was such a normal thing to do but it had eluded her for years. If it was late, she usually made something simple and ate it without paying much attention in front of the TV or she grabbed an early dinner with friends after work. Even when she and Ron were married, they hardly ever ate in the kitchen together, which now she realized was so odd. And maybe part of what was wrong. As a kid, she remembered eating almost every meal at this table with her dad sitting where Watkins was and her mom on the end so she could jump up and get something from the stove.

Pia looked down at her empty plate. "My mom was a great cook." She shook herself out of her reverie. "I don't know why I just told you that." She knew her face was flushed. Maybe he'd think it was the overheated kitchen.

"My mom hated cooking," he said. "She was put on the spot to host a lot of dinner parties and other wife-of-an-officer social duties, and always called a caterer. Those parties were awful. As a kid, we were forced to wear a coat and tie and coached by Dad on how to make polite conversation. My brother and I would be excused for the formal dinner and set free to eat pizza in the kitchen. That's where I got interested in cooking. Watching the caterer and bugging the poor guy with a million questions."

Pia wondered what kind of home Watkins grew up in with a mom who hosted dinner parties with a caterer. She thought of her family's huge dinners on holidays that spilled from this kitchen table out to the dining room table with the extra leaves put in. The kids ate with the grown-ups, but at a special kids table. They certainly weren't coached in the art of polite conversation. In fact, the adults didn't observe anything close to polite talk when they started in on the wine. Between her dad's Irish stories and singing and her mom's relatives snaking through the living room for Greek dances, the house was far from gentile conversation. She had no idea what to say to this guy. He was so different.

She watched his eyes track across the kitchen. They landed on the shelf near the sink where her mom's trophy sat. It was a big, silver monstrosity with the figure wearing a bathing cap doing the crawl. The inscription crowed about her record-breaking freestyle event in college.

"You're a swimmer?"

Pia hated that question because her answer was a disappointing *no*. Disappointing most of all to her mom. Pia hated the water. "It's my mother's trophy," she started the well-practiced explanation. "She was a D1 swimmer in college. Slated for Olympics. That's the last big trophy she won."

"Injury?" he asked.

"Pregnancy." Pia pointed to herself. "I'm the reason my mom's swimming career ended."

His expression shifted. Pia could imagine the thoughts whirring through his mind. Clicking into place. Her name, her mother's Olympic bid, the lost chance of a lifetime... It usually only took a few minutes for people to figure it out.

"Olympia. Your name—"

"That's right," Pia snapped. "To remind me what I cost her."

He looked shocked. Pia scrambled to soften her words. "My mom always said it was to assure me I was more precious to her than any Olympic competition, but I knew otherwise. When I didn't turn out to be her swimmer mini-me, she never missed an opportunity to remind me what a disappointment I was. Couldn't help it, I hated the water."

She picked at the fraying edge of the placemat. Watkins was still wearing the ruffled apron. When Pia's eyes rested on the seriousness of his face above the pastel ruffle, she burst out laughing.

Now he looked a little frightened of her.

She wiped her eyes. "Sorry. It's just you in that apron."

He stood, towering over Pia still seated in the wooden kitchen chair. His head almost brushed the low-beamed ceiling. She sat back. Did she insult him?

A second passed. Then he struck a pose and curtsied. "Did Madam enjoy the meal?" He collected the plates, balancing them on his arm like a professional waiter.

"No, let me." Pia stood, knocking the edge of the table. She collected the rest of the glasses and silverware and stood beside him at the sink. She caught their reflection in the dark glass. Even though she was tall, he made her feel petite—her head just above his shoulder height. The ghostly reflections bent together over the open dishwasher. She knew she should not allow a guest to do all this work but somehow it felt natural. After clearing the table and washing up the cooking skillet, he untied the apron and handed it to her.

"Be sure to keep this handy for next time."

Next time. She liked the thought that they'd have a next time. For a few hours, she'd managed to forget about the task in front of them. She closed the dishwasher door and stood facing him only inches apart. She had to tilt her chin up to look him in the face.

"I think you need to have another talk with your boss," she said.

His lips pressed together.

"You need to tell him how you feel shut out. Like he doesn't trust you or something. Do you think that's what it is?"

A quick headshake. "No."

His eyes drifted away from her face.

"Then what?"

He made a move to step around her, but she stopped him by grabbing his upper arm. Her head was clearing from the amount of wine sloshing through her system and it was time she got some answers. "Will you talk to him at least? I know you can't tell me anything, but if you can find out..." Her hands dropped and hung useless at her side. "If we have any chance still of saving her."

Watkins leaned against the counter. "The whole thing doesn't make sense. Abramson recruited me. He came to my hospital room after the—" his hand floated up to touch the scar. "He's the one who asked me to join the cell. He knew I had special skills they needed. I can't figure out why he's shut me out of this particular project."

He looked a little like a kid who wasn't picked for the team. The dejected expression stabbed her heart and took over her brain. Before she realized what she was doing, her index finger lightly traced the scar along his eye and down his face. Her hand cupped his cheek for a heartbeat. The pads of her fingers registered the coarse feel of stubble along his chin. Her face was drawn closer to him with a magnetic force. She opened her mouth and whispered, "Are you ever going to tell me the story behind this?" Her focus went to the scar.

His hand covered hers, but her didn't draw it away from his face. Instead, he brushed his lips across her palm. An eruption of heat started somewhere behind her navel and gushed down her legs, making them wobble.

He dropped her hand and circled her waist with his arm.

"You don't mind looking at it," he said.

She made an almost imperceptible shake of her head. "Why should I?"

He looked away. "Most people find it…"

She turned his chin back to look at her. In the dimming light, his eyes were almost black. His arms snugged around her as his face moved closer.

A noise startled her and they jumped apart. His phone rattled on the tabletop, blaring out "Sharp Dressed Man."

Pia laughed. "Didn't know you were a ZZ Top fan." Her face flamed. *Was he about to kiss her?*

Watkins lunged for the phone like a life preserver. He frowned at the screen. "It's Howard County Hospital." With the phone held to his ear, his face paled as he listened. After hanging up, he held it in his hand and stared at it.

"What did they say?" She took a step toward him. "Is everything okay?"

He shook his head and shoved the phone in a pocket. "I've got to go. Sorry."

"Hey!" Pia stepped in front of him. "Talk to me."

"My brother's in the hospital. They said it's an overdose."

Chapter 25

Watkins

"**I**'M COMING WITH YOU." Pulling on a fleece boot, Pia hopped a few steps to keep from toppling over. She flicked on the outdoor light. It shone on the Ranger covered in an icy film.

"No. Stay here. I'm not sure how long I'll have to stay and I might not be able to get you back home tonight."

"Then I'll drive myself and follow you." She shoved arms into a down coat and hiked it up over her shoulder.

"No way. You've been drinking."

"So have you." She opened the front door and the clatter of freezing rain hitting the walkway made him recoil into the warm house, pulling Pia with him. Inside, he fished the keys out of his pocket. "Let me warm up the truck first, then come out."

She ignored him, stepped outside behind him, and pulled the sticking door shut behind her. "No way. You'll leave without me."

He jogged to the vehicle and let her inside. Once he got the defroster going and scraped over the sheen of ice, he got in and clicked his seatbelt into place. "You're a pain in the ass, you know that?"

Pia looked like a turtle snugged down inside the voluminous down coat with the hood pulled over half her face. "So I've been told," rumbled out from under the lump in the seat next to him.

The roads weren't as bad as he'd feared. Yet.

They pulled in the front parking lot of the hospital and entered an overheated waiting room packed with people. The scream of an ambulance caused everyone's head to turn. The woman at the front desk looked up. "Busy night," was all she said before turning her attention back to the papers in front of her.

Watkins shifted from one foot to the other and cleared his throat. He couldn't afford to politely wait his turn if Caleb was as bad as they made it sound. A nurse came up behind the receptionist and asked if he'd been helped. She shot a cross look at the receptionist.

"I got a call about my brother, Caleb Watkins. He was brought in by ambulance a little while ago."

"Follow me." The nurse strode through the waiting room and held open a door. "He'd be in the other wing with Emergency. I'll find someone who can help you."

Watkins and Pia trailed behind the nurse, whose shoes squeegeed down a long hallway that smelled of disinfectant At the ER desk, another nurse led them to a closed door.

With a hand resting on the knob, she turned to Watkins. "Family only." Her eyes shifted to Pia.

He put his hand on Pia's shoulder. "She is family."

With a curt nod, she opened the door. Even though he was expecting to see his brother in bad shape, the scene of Caleb's pale face with hoses protruding from his nose and wired to a bank of machines shocked him. In a trance, he moved to his side and touched his hand. He felt Pia's presence hovering behind him.

"He was treated with naloxone on sight and is being given fluids for dehydration. We're monitoring his heart and respiration due to the blood loss."

Watkins snapped his head around as the nurse's drone finally registers. "Blood loss? What happened?"

"The patient was brought in unresponsive from the overdose but also sustained injuries to his hand and lower arm."

Watkins peeled back the sheet and saw Caleb's right hand was bandaged up to above his elbow. "Where was he? What happened to him?"

The nurse checked a white board above the bed covered with hourly readings. "You'll have to speak with the officer in charge—the one who found him. I don't know any of those details." She made a hasty retreat from the room.

"She doesn't know dick, leave her alone." Caleb's voice sounded like thin paper rustling. His unsteady gaze landed on Pia. "She your replacement for Stacey?"

Watkins clenched his teeth. He wasn't going to be baited by Caleb. "You want to tell me what happened? When I left, you were in bed."

"Changed my mind." Caleb lifted his bandaged arm. "What's sucks is they can't give me any painkiller for this. Seems they think I have a little problem."

You have a huge problem.

Caleb struggled to prop himself on his elbows. "Look, you can't fix me, bro. You can stop trying." Color surged up his neck. He fell back on his pillow and closed his eyes.

A machine blasted a high-pitched whine. A nurse appeared.

Watkins backpedaled into Pia as the nurse shooed them both out of the room. Outside, his knees seemed to give out as he sunk into a bank of plastic molded chairs. Sitting with his elbows resting on his knees, his head felt like a heavy weight. He sensed

Pia moving to sit down beside him. She shrugged out of her coat, tossed it on the seat, and sat on top of it.

"Who's Stacey?" Her voice pierced the solid shell of his thoughts, blocking out all outside noise.

Watkins sat clutching his head like he was palming a basketball. Her question caused him to tilt his chin to look at her. "What?" He winced. "That's your first question?"

"No. I just thought I'd start with something easy."

He sat up. His hands hung from limp wrists. "Okay. She was my fiancée. That is, until I got blown up and ended up looking like this. Seems Stacey liked everything to be perfect. Perfect jobs, perfect wedding, a perfect couple. I no longer fit the role of perfect husband."

Pia snorts a laugh through her nose.

"It's funny?" he asked. *What's wrong with her? Is she still drunk?*

"Yeah, kind of. I'm picturing this chick who wears matching workout clothes, drives a Barbie mobile, and is never seen in public without full makeup. Oh, and all her friends really think she's a bitch."

He feels his mouth curl up. "You've met her?"

"Bet she thought horses smell, too. Am I right?"

His smile faded. "Dunno. Never brought her to the barn. She broke up with me in the hospital when I landed stateside."

He thought he heard her whisper something under her breath. An orderly pushing a gurney with a wonky wheel passed by them. She touched his knee, but snatched her hand away when he glanced at it. "Now the hard question. Your brother. Is this the first time?"

Watkins blew out a stream of air. "No, but never this bad. He's getting worse."

"And you want to help him?"

His back stiffened. "Of course I do. He's my brother."

"Is what you're doing working?"

Her face was inches from his. Her dark eyes opened wider and looked at him without judgment. Open, caring. His shoulders dropped and he let out a sigh.

"No. Nothing I've done has helped. Caleb is an addict. He's always gone his own way, did things on impulse, never saw the consequences down the road. When I got out of the military and ended up back here, I figured I could help him out, but he lived a couple hours away. I've given him money, bailed him out, but I can't keep him safe. I can't..." Watkins tipped his hands palm up. "He doesn't want my help. In fact, I think he's worse around me."

Pia's hand slid over his and cupped it in her other hand. She didn't say a thing. He didn't want anyone's advice right now. And she was smart enough not to give any. Her hands were warm and delicate surrounding his. He felt his heartbeat slow.

The door to Caleb's room opened. The nurse backed out, dragging a machine. Pia's jerked her hand away leaving his exposed to the cold air. The nurse said, "You might want to check back later. They've sedated him, but we removed the monitors. The attending will check in on his next round and let you know if he'll be cleared for release."

She wheeled the machine to the nurse's station and dropped a file on the desk.

"C'mon, I'll drive you home." He stood.

Pia pulled her coat out from under her and folded it over her arm. "If you have to wait, why don't we go see if the cafeteria is open. We can get some coffee, then check back and see if they're keeping Caleb overnight. You can take me home then."

The hospital cafeteria was closed except for coffee, wrapped sandwiches, and snacks. A lone cashier sat on a stool at the end of a self-serve line, scrolling through her phone. A few people in scrubs clutched coffee cups. Only half the dining area was lit, the other half shrouded in darkness. After paying, they chose a table on the edge of the lighted area and stared out the darkened windows as the freezing rain tapped at the glass.

"This place is kind of creepy at this hour," Pia said.

"Reminds me of the army chow halls."

Pia wrapped her hands around the paper coffee cup but hadn't taken a sip. He could see she was struggling with something.

She tilted her head. "So, the army. Good memories or bad?"

How to explain? "A little of both. Bad food memories to be sure." His laugh sounded forced. She held his eye, not letting him off the hook so easily. "But good memories, too, of the mission, the people..."

"You miss it?" she asked. Did her nose wrinkle just the slightest bit, like she couldn't believe anyone could miss being in the military?

He rubbed his eyes. "Sure. In some ways I miss it. The army defined my life, even before I joined. My dad was an officer; we all grew up on military bases with other military families. It's familiar."

Pia nods like she's taking notes in her head. She looks intent, listening to all the words but her expression says something wasn't adding up. "Caleb grew up in the same family, the same environment, but he's not like you at all."

Watkins pulled the lid off his cup and set it aside. "No." He wanted to say more, but how to describe Caleb to someone who didn't know him? "Even before we left Virginia and lived overseas, Caleb was already getting in trouble. Small things. He had to be with people, be in the center of things almost like he fed off the energy of everyone around him. Caleb attracted people wherever he went. They flocked to him and surrounded him like a cloud. Problem is, he wasn't very discerning about what type of people.

"He took it hard when we moved to Germany and blamed Dad and the army for tearing him away from his friends. It was only later I figured out the move had severed his drug sources, among other things. He didn't adjust to being overseas, never again shone like the brightest star amid a constellation of his peers, and became withdrawn. Sullen. He and Dad started to fight in earnest—not the teenaged rebellion type stuff like earlier."

Watkins dropped his gaze to his hands.

"And I was no help. He'd recruit me to be on his side in an argument, and I'd either walk out or say something he interpreted as being on Dad's side. I was too busy wrapped up in my own ambitions, my own drive to get into my chosen college and—I'll admit it—distance myself from my "troublemaker" brother so Dad's friends would write a recommendation, open doors for me to the academy..." A bitter laugh erupted from his chest. "I was an asshole. Caleb saw it and called me on it, but I was too sure I was right and blew him off."

Pia didn't say anything. Unlike most people who jump in with platitudes and assurances, she just sat there.

"No comment?" he asked.

"I don't have a sibling. What do I know?"

Watkins grunted his approval. His hand went to the scar, stroking the raised surface.

Pia pointed to where the white outline ran along the outside of one eye. "You do that when you're deep in thought."

His hand jumped away as if burned. "Habit."

Like a magnet, her attention was again drawn by the rain and sleet against the windows. A fluorescent light overhead emitted a low buzz and the air was heavy with the scent of burned coffee.

Watkins squeezed his eyes shut. "It happened in a small village in eastern Afghanistan."

Pia turned away from the window. He couldn't meet her gaze as he told the story. The hopes for a successful mission. The sticky bomb slapped so callously on the side of the vehicle. The blast, leaving him in broken pieces. The dawning realization of his betrayal. His promise to the guys that they'd be safe...

"I'd planned it meticulously down to the last detail. But I ended up killing most of them."

"You never could have predicted an attack like that. You can't blame yourself for what a crazed terrorist decides to do," she said.

He held up one finger. "There's where you're wrong. I can and I do. It was my job to ensure the area had been secured. I had a specialist assigned to me who was in charge of the meeting venue to have snipers in place, to sweep the area for explosives, to secure it against any intruders. At the last minute, he moved the meeting location. Without informing me. He said the meeting location had been compromised and he arranged an alternative one. I didn't check up on him, like I should have. My thoughts were too consumed with my own glory if I managed to pull off the most important negotiation toward ending the hostilities in the most violent area of Afghanistan. I was being an asshole. Like Caleb said I was."

Pia's mouth fell open but no words came out. Her face contorted in concentration. "Are you saying this security guy set you up? My God! Why?"

Watkins's mouth hitched up on one side. "I've given it a lot of thought. Had lots of time in rehab afterward. I found evidence later that this guy may have been getting paid from both sides to escalate the violence—to keep the conflict going and keep the demand for weapons flowing."

"Did they catch him?" Pia leaned in. "You told someone what he did, right? What happened to him?"

"I have no idea. I was debriefed. I gave the investigators every detail of the op. They were going after Morrow, but I've never managed to find out what happened to him. Closed files."

"Damn those closed files. Which reminds me—"

Watkins's phone rang a few bars of ZZ Top before he grabbed it. He listened and checked his watch. After he hung up, he stood and tossed a half-full cup into the trash. When he caught Pia's eye, he said, "That's the ER nurse. Since it's almost midnight they're going to keep him overnight." He pulled his coat off the back of the chair. "Let's get you home."

Chapter 26

Pia

Pia woke the next morning with an all-too-familiar dry mouth and pounding head. *A couple bottles of wine will do that.* Even though she didn't get to bed until well after midnight after Watkins dropped her off, she couldn't sleep. Her mind spun like a kaleidoscope, dropping one picture after another in front of her eyes: Regalo trapped with an IV dripping poison into her, Watkins's body tossed into the air by an explosion, her boss's face when she told him she'd learned nothing so far about the missing racehorse... One more picture came to mind and caused her to flinch. Standing by the sink, her face tilted up in expectation of a kiss. *What was she thinking last night?* She flipped over and punched a lump out of her pillow that wasn't there and buried her face in it until she heard Ryder scrabble to his feet. She listened to his toenails click along the hardwood floor and down the stairs. As she sat up and drudged to the bathroom, she vowed for the hundredth time, she'd get a grip on her drinking.

After brushing her teeth to get rid of the film of red wine, garlic, and stale coffee, she let the dog out and leaned against the hall table to check her phone. It was only six thirty, but it felt as if a cold stone dropped into her gut when she saw there were no messages from Watkins. He was supposed to go back to the hospital this morning to get Caleb. Did he get home all right? She hoped he'd update her.

A shower and a twenty-ounce tumbler of coffee did a lot to jump-start her day, feeding the horses and getting to work on time. When she arrived, the office was deserted except for the intern who always seemed to be there. It was early and the bad weather would likely keep even more people away. Booting up her computer, she was surprised to see Deliah's office light snap on. This early? Deliah never showed up before nine or ten. She wandered over to check in with her friend.

Deliah was rummaging in a bottom drawer when Pia knocked on doorframe. Her friend sat up and clutched her chest.

"What the hell!" Deliah said. "I thought I was alone."

"Why you in so early?" Pia entered and took a seat facing the desk. Her eyes narrowed as she took in Deliah's mussed hair and face scrubbed free of makeup.

"If you must know, I came straight here. Got a text from Burke he wants legal to weigh in on the workers' comp case, Norcross versus Bradley Industries." She shoved a stack of folders aside. "And I hadn't finished it. He wants it this morning because the case got moved up."

Pia hung one leg over the arm of her chair. "And you weren't home because...?" Her voice lifted and she made a rotation gesture with her wrist, indicating *C'mon, fill in the juicy details.*

Deliah came around her desk and shoved Pia's leg to the floor. "I don't have time today to feed your need. Get your virtual love life fix somewhere else." Her voice took on the tone of a scolding teacher, but a Cheshire cat smile spread across her face.

Pia stood and walked to the door. She turned to fire back her volley. "Yeah, well keep your story. I've got one of my own. I kissed Watkins last night."

Deliah's head, bowed over her paperwork, shot up. "Hunky soldier guy?"

Pia lifted her chin. "Yeah, hunky ex-soldier guy. I also got the whole story. But you're too busy now to hear it." Pia twiddled her fingers. "Ta-ta. Good luck with your case."

She speed-walked down the hall back to her desk to make her exit more dramatic. It was less than two minutes before Deliah appeared at her desk, now wearing a colorful scarf around her head and a smear of lipstick. She arched her neck, checking that the nearby desks were empty, then sat close to Pia.

"What happened?" Deliah's caramel eyes widened.

Pia took a sip from her coffee tumbler and considered what she'd say and what she should hold back. "I invited him over to compare notes on finding Regalo. He ended up making me dinner." She left out the part where she drank so much she wasn't capable of cooking. *Maybe it was a pity offer after all.* "When we were washing up, I asked him how he got that scar and we might have had a moment." Pia looked at the palm of her hand where he had kissed it. *Did he do that just to be kind? Because she was acting pathetic throwing herself at him?*

"That's when he kissed you? Then what?" Deliah scooted her chair closer.

Pia stared at her palm. "We didn't kiss, not really. It was as if it was going to happen, but maybe I was imagining it. He got a call his brother was in the hospital, and we spent the rest of the night in the Emergency Department." Pia filled her in on the relationship between the two brothers and how Caleb was brought in unresponsive.

"OD? Do you think he tried to kill himself?" Deliah asked.

"No one said suicide, at least not in front of me. But I wondered, especially the way Watkins was acting." Pia lifted her phone and checked her messages again. "He's supposed to go get him this morning. I was hoping to hear..." She shrugged at her own words. Hear what? She wasn't family. He wouldn't call her first.

Deliah fell back against the chair. "Damn. You had a hell of a night."

A few more lights in the offices along the open hallways flashed on.

"Looks like Mr. Burke is in early, too." Pia jutted her chin toward the open office door. "He has me running around the racetrack acting like the private investigators. He's not going to be happy when I tell him I didn't learn anything new."

"On that missing racehorse case?"

"I'm getting nowhere." Pia hugged her arms to her side. "It doesn't even make sense. Why steal a horse that isn't worth anything? The owner was sending it for rehab and was going to donate him."

Deliah pursed her lips and tapped them with one finger. "Hmmm. Seems he's not the first horse in your life to mysteriously disappear."

"Are you talking about the disappearance of this racehorse and what happened with Regalo? My horse hasn't been near a track for years. I don't see any connection."

Deliah tapped Pia's knee and stood. "Look for one. Might be something you hadn't thought of." She glanced over her shoulder. "I'm going to sneak back to my desk before Burke knows I'm here."

"Thanks." Pia sighed and had turned to her keyboard when her phone vibrated. She snatched it up, heart thumping. The text wasn't from Watkins.

Usoro is here at Pimlico. Horse got kicked bad. She may be here a while but no guarantee. C. Langston

Pia grabbed her purse and headed to her car. The track was a haul from her office and the roads were bad. She'd have to drive slow, pray she didn't run into an accident that would gum up the highway, and get to Pimlico before Dr. Usoro finished up and left.

By the time she parked outside the track's gatehouse, her shoulders were stiff from tension and she nearly had to pry her fingers from the steering wheel. She texted Langston, asking for an update on Usoro's status and location. The information pinged back on her screen.

Wrapping up. Shedrow B near the back.

Horses kept up in their stalls due to the icy conditions slammed hooves against the door or rattled feed buckets in agitation. Pia's heart echoed the outside banging with a steady thrum against her chest. *What was she going to say to this woman? How could she confront her and get any information if she didn't want to give it? She wasn't a detective or even a PI.*

Deep in thought, she almost collided with Langston, coming from the opposite direction. He was dressed in a down coat with a strip of duct tape holding a rip closed.

"Good, you made it. She's still here but wrapping things up. What do you have in mind?" he said.

Pia paced while she talked. "To tell the truth, I have no idea."

"You could just come out and ask her where's your horse." He lifted both palms and hunched his shoulders. "The direct approach."

"It's more complicated than that." Pia clamped her bottom lip between her teeth. "I pulled out my dad's old papers and read up on the case against Usoro. There were a couple other complaints against her, but nothing stuck. She's mostly a researcher and only does the clinical vet work to help fund her research, which is pretty sketchy."

Langston's bushy eyebrow crept up a fraction. "Vet work like taking a big payout to administer illegal drugs. So what kind of sketchy research are we talking about?"

"She's studied virology but she's primarily a geneticist. Does stuff called gene targeting. I didn't understand most of what I read, except that you can use it to mutate genes. For good stuff, like knocking out genetic diseases, or other creepy stuff." Pia jammed her hands into her coat pockets. "Maybe if I figure out a way to get her talking about her work, then slip in a question about the lab where she does her research..."

Langston backed up a few steps and leaned back to peer around the corner of the shedrow. "Her truck is still here, but better think of something quick. How about if you say you're a reporter for a horse racing magazine and want to interview her for, I don't know, drug use controversies."

"Not a bad idea, but I'm afraid the topic would make her defensive, given her rep. Maybe I could say I was a vet student and—"

"Heads up." Langston's face signaled *trouble approaching* as a woman matching Usoro's profile barreled past. Her hands were full, carrying an ultrasound monitor, a tote of bandaging supplies, and an extension cord coiled under one arm. She strode to a truck, placed the items in the back, and headed in the other direction.

Pia's mouth felt as if she had been injected with Novocain because her lips were frozen and her tongue was thick and useless. She called out "Dr. Usoro" to her retreating back.

The woman turned. "Yes?" She was average height, shorter than Pia, but stocky. Up close, Pia saw she was much older than the picture on the vet clinic website.

"I heard you were here for a client, and, well, I'm a vet student doing a rotation here at the track...My name's Pia Harcourt."

Dr. Usoro looked away to where the horse or owner was no doubt waiting for her. "I'm in a hurry right now."

Pia closed the distance between them. "It's just that I've read some of your papers on"—she struggle to recall the scientific mumbo jumbo of one she'd seen—"genetic targets for detection of encephalitis viruses and I wanted to ask you some questions."

Usoro paused. She seemed to size Pia up, then made a come along gesture. Pia fell into step beside her. Langston gave a quick salute and faded off in the other direction.

"What's your question?" Usoro asked as they approached a groom holding a big bay with his legs bandaged. The vet didn't pay any attention to Pia and did not seem to notice that she had not answered. She uncapped a syringe and plunged the needle in the horse's neck with practiced efficiency. She then handed the groom several tubes of Banamine. "Keep him in his stall. Administer a five-hundred-pound dose of Banamine twice a day for the pain and swelling. I'll have my partner do a follow-up tomorrow." While Usoro was finishing up with the horse, Pia grasped for a plausible gambit to get Usoro talking. When the woman turned away from the horse, her face registered surprise as if she had forgotten Pia was there.

"I wanted to ask you where you did your research, because I'm looking for my next intern tour and thought I'd like to specialize in R&D, clinical trials," Pia blurted out. The woman's dark eyes bored into her. Pia felt the word babble erupt before she could bite it off. "I like the track okay, but I'm looking for something more challenging than giving inoculations and treating injured tendons. You know?" She hated how she was so bad at this. She punctuated her juvenile ramble with an ingratiating smile.

Usoro put a hand on the horse's neck. "I'm done. You can put him away," she told the groom without taking her eyes off Pia. "I gave that horse an injection of 400 milligrams of quinalbarbitone sodium in case of infection from the tendon tear. It will be followed by cinchocaine hydrochloride for pain. Would you agree?"

Pia played along. "Sounds like the prescribed protocol for that type of injury."

Usoro's lips curled into a smile that instead of being warm and welcoming, caused Pia to take a step back. "Who are you, because you certainly are *not* a veterinary student. If I'd given that combination of drugs, this horse would be dead right now."

Pia's back stiffened. "Okay, I'm not a vet."

Usoro pulled out her phone and checked the screen. She nodded, as if her hunch was confirmed. "Stop wasting my time, Miss Harcourt." She glanced up at Pia and her mouth hardened into a thin line. "Or should I call you Olympia Murphy Harcourt." She swiped the screen blank, shoved the phone into a coat pocket, and walked away.

"You have my horse." Pia flung the words at her retreating back. "The one you got from your brother."

Usoro stopped and turned to her. "It was not my understanding that it was *your* horse."

Pia marched up to Usoro and looked down at the smaller woman. "You knew whose horse it was when you heard her name. My father bought Regalo and that's why you wanted her. I'm here to get her back, whatever it takes."

"Including lying about who you are?"

Pia had to keep her talking. Whatever it took, she couldn't let Usoro walk away because if she blew this chance there wouldn't be another. "Just tell me where I can find her and I'll buy her back. No questions asked." Pia swallowed. "Please."

The vet zipped her coat up to her chin and shook her head. "No."

"Then I'll just go get her at Median Diagnostics. Yeah, we know about that place, too." Frustration welled up inside as this woman with a face like a stubborn pug stared at her without speaking. "In fact," she thrust her face in Usoro's, "there's some other people pretty interested in the lab, too. Government people."

Pia remained rooted to the spot. Her nostrils flared as she struggled to suck in air. She knew she shouldn't have said all that.

Usoro walked away, but before she turned the corner, she tossed over her shoulder chilling words: "The horse is dead."

Chapter 27

Watkins

Watkins hated hospitals. He'd spent too much time in them. He was anxious to get Caleb and go home. The neurologist, Dr. Patel, was a thin man with very dark circles under his eyes. He had fine, long fingers, Watkins noted, as he signed his brother's discharge papers.

Caleb sat in a wheelchair. He hadn't exchanged a word with Watkins.

The doctor handed over a list of instructions he had gone over and laid a hand on Caleb's shoulder. "See you back here in a week. When I do, I'll want to have a report from the clinic as well."

Caleb took the papers handed him and shoved them under his thigh. He tried to roll the wheelchair with one hand, but it only turned in circles.

Watkins thanked the doctor and grasped the handles. His brother sat cradling his bandaged arm. At the hospital front door, Caleb stood and gave the wheelchair a shove so hard it rolled into the wall of the waiting room. He stalked out the front door without looking back.

Sitting side by side in the SUV, Watkins studied Caleb's stone-faced profile. He thought of and discarded a million things to say to his brother and ended up arriving home without exchanging a word. He spoke more to the stray cat, MacArthur, as he unlocked the front door and ushered his brother inside.

Caleb settled on the couch in front of the TV, scrolling through the program menu with the remote. He grunted in response to every question. Watkins figured he'd give Caleb some time alone while he caught up at work. It wasn't like his presence was helping any.

※

The office was humming by the time Watkins arrived a few hours later than usual. He'd asked Caleb to call if he needed anything, so every time his outside line rang, a jolt ran through him as he eyed the caller ID. Not the police, not the hospital...good. But also not Caleb. He hoped his brother would reach out for something. But he was met with silence. What happened that night when he was at Pia's? What had possessed Caleb to get out of bed and walk to wherever he had gone... to find a fix? And how was his arm cut down almost to the bone? Maybe if he had stayed home with him, this wouldn't have happened. Or perhaps just not this time.

Marion stomped in and let out a noise like air escaping a balloon when she collapsed into her chair. She ripped a page off her joke-a-day calendar with a flourish. "Another day closer to retirement," she crowed.

Watkins spun on her. "If you hate it here so much, why don't you quit?"

Marion's coral-painted mouth shaped into a pursed O. "Sor-ry," she said. "I thought you got it was a joke."

His shoulders curved inward as he blew out a stream of air. He was so damned tired. But that was no excuse for being a jerk. He was treating Marion the way Caleb talked to him. Marion's hurt expression made his heart squeeze in his chest. He scooted his chair closer and murmured, "I'm sorry, I'm being an ass."

She made a curt nod. "Your brother?" When she spoke, he noticed she had a bit of the coral lipstick on her teeth as well.

He'd called that morning and told Marion he would be late today because he was picking up his brother. She knew some, probably guessed the rest.

He shoved his chair a few inches away. "Yes, but that's no excuse."

"Now a penitent asshole." Marion rolled her lips trying not to smile. "That's better. What's going on, Captain?"

When she called him Captain instead of Jonah, she was tapping into respect for his service...and that she was ready to put kidding aside.

He glanced around. The analysts sitting at desks nearby were wearing headsets and scowling at their monitors. Others furiously tapped on their keyboards. No one was listening to him. "Caleb was admitted for an overdose. But I'm worried it was more than that. His arm was cut. He's not talking to me and the docs aren't allowed to. Patient privacy."

Marion slid her chair closer and clasped his hand in hers. It was warm. Fleshy and soft. So unlike the memory of his mother's calloused hands, abraded from years working with horses.

He'd never noticed how beautiful her eyes were. They were usually lost in her jowly face overly made up with liner, circles of rouge, and odd-colored lipstick. She heaved her bulk to a more comfortable position in her chair, causing it to squeal.

"You can't fix someone who don't want to fix himself," she said. "You take care of you. Okay?"

Watkins figured she was putting on her tough-love mom act for him. She probably wouldn't follow a word of her own advice if the situation were reversed. He turned the conversation into a peace offering. "Hey, so how many more days until retirement? How short are you?" *Normal. Let's talk about normal things.*

She pointed to her countdown clock. "So short, I'll be able to slip under the door soon." She cackled at her own joke.

A twinge of envy coiled around his ribs. He'd never been jealous of people who were leaving the office. What was with that? The unease he felt over being excluded from the Median lab op rankled him. He'd tried to set it aside, but it was like a crusty wound that kept opening up. "I may be right behind you," he said.

Her penciled eyebrows shot up. "You? Mr. Gung Ho ready to pack it in? No way."

"Yeah, well, seems I might not be as indispensable here as I'd hoped." Watkins hated that he slid his eyes to Abramson's office. He of all people knew better than to undermine a superior by murmuring in the ranks. If he had a beef with him, he needed to march right in there and confront the issue.

"What gives?" Marion asked.

He didn't want to shut her down again with a curt answer, but he also knew he shouldn't air the dirty laundry of how his agency was apparently being excluded from some sensitive information. But he apparently underestimated Marion's powers of observation and was shocked when she asked, "You're not included in the Darren-Abramson boys club? They've been whispering behind closed doors now for a few weeks. All hush-hush."

"Darren's read in?" Watkins's voice pitched upward. Darren was the new guy. Less experienced, and Abramson saw fit to include him? Watkins deserved an explanation. There was something strange going on.

He stood so fast his chair rolled backward, crashing into his desk. "I'm getting to the bottom of this right now."

Marion shot him a thumbs up. "Get 'em, cowboy."

Watkins strode by Darren's desk and knocked on the desktop to get his attention. Darren slid off his earphones.

"What's up?" he asked.

"Come with me. You, me, and Mr. Abramson are having a talk about Median Diagnostics. In his office, now."

Darren's pale face grew paler than normal. "You know about Project Nergal?"

"Not enough, apparently. But we're going to fix that right now."

Watkins gave a one-knuckle knock on Abramson's door before he entered with Darren in tow. He got straight to the point.

"I want an explanation for why I've been excluded from Project Nergal. And not some bullshit about restricted access. There's something else going on."

Abramson stood ramrod straight behind his desk. His gaze went from Watkins to Darren, sizing up the situation. He seemed to study Watkins's face for a moment. "I've been expecting this. After our last conversation, I had frank discussion with the project leader." He lifted his chin, indicating Darren. "We're prepared to read you in, but Mr. Woodhouse doesn't have to be here for this."

"No, he stays." Watkins pushed Darren into the room. "You recruited each of us individually for what we could bring to the table. We're a team. At least I thought we were."

"Alright." Abramson walked to a large safe and spun the combination. When it clanged open, he tugged on the heavy drawer and fished out a folder striped in red and stamped with special classifications. "I put you in for the clearance." He sauntered to the table where Watkins and Darren were seated and dropped the file in front of Watkins.

Watkins cocked an eyebrow. "Old school, huh? Most of this stuff is done online." He opened the folder and started reading.

"Not this project," Abramson answered. "Keeping it especially close hold."

Watkins scanned the description of the project, which typically revealed few details. Project Nergal was a counter-illicit drug operation focused on one individual with ties to both drugs and weapons possibly flooding into the country through Median Diagnostics. Some bad actors had backed the overseas facility and rumor had it the operation had moved to the US to avoid detection, or more likely to test the market for distribution of counterfeit drugs. It was now a domestic problem. Watkins signed acknowledgment of the clearance, closed the folder, and pushed it back across the table to Abramson. "So what's the real bottom line? The reason I've been shut out."

Abramson sucked in a deep breath through his nose. "Here's the deal." He pulled out the chair opposite Watkins and sat. "Nergal is the cover name for Wallace Morrow. The intel community has been tracking him for nearly a decade."

The other two men stared at Watkins.

"Morrow?" A wave of heat flushed through his body. "The only Morrow I know is that SOB who got half my men killed in an ambush. A contract security guy who didn't do his job—"

"He was a triple agent, a plant." Abramson leaned forward and rested his elbows on the table. "Morrow was placed in the unit specifically to scupper the peace negotiations. He was working for an arms supplier who couldn't afford to have demand trickle to a halt. Now he's on to bigger things."

Watkins couldn't believe what he was hearing. He spoke in a carefully controlled tone. "You mean you knew about this guy?"

"The community was watching him."

"Watching?" A dull roar started in his ears. "You mean this guy who killed half my men, almost killed me, you knew about him? And you let him go?"

Darren inched his seat away and sat looking at his hands. Abramson wouldn't meet Watkins's gaze.

"We had to," Abramson was quick to add. "Sources indicated he was the common denominator in a weapons and drug network, and if we took him out too soon..."

"So you let the rat go free hoping he'd lead you to the hawk." Watkins's nostrils flared, sucking in air. "And the hawk is the guy behind Median Diagnostics."

"That's why I didn't bring you in on the project. Because of your history with Morrow."

He gave a curt nod. He understood the logic even if he didn't agree with it. "The mission comes first." But Abramson had lied to him. Kept him in the dark and withheld the fact that Morrow had not been arrested, as he had been led to believe. What else might he be holding back? "So what's changed now?"

"Morrow can be eliminated from the operation, I'm told. The bigger fish is in the net, but that's all I know. The counterterrorism guys are on point for that." Abramson tapped his pencil against the folder. "Darren here has been tasked with penetrating the overseas facility in the hopes that we could make it through their air gapped network and back to their US lab. A few days ago he found the connection and we're on the inside. Inside their computers, that is."

"A court approved penetration? There must be ample evidence that the US facility really is a threat," Watkins said. He shifted in his chair. His worst fears were being confirmed.

"Oh, there is." Abramson turned to Darren. "You can fill Watkins in on the attack tree later. But right now I want to know if you've discovered anything useful yet."

"I'm still wandering around inside, trying to map the network and get to the good stuff. But I'll tell you one thing, there's been an uptick in activity all of a sudden."

Darren explained the cyber breadcrumbs he'd been following that told him the activity level on the system had increased lately.

"Since when?" Abramson scowled. He went back to his desk and had one hand on his secure phone.

Darren looked like a kid in his punk band T-shirts and high-tops, but he had a genius for breaking in and crawling around inside a computer. He knew how to get in and not be detected. If he noticed a change in activity, there had to be a reason. Something was going on at the lab.

"Before Captain Watkins grabbed me to come in here, I saw a bunch of things light up that had been quiet. Files I can't read—yet. But something's up at that place now. Something big."

Chapter 28

Pia

Pia stood outside the shedrow watching as Dr. Usoro turned the corner and disappeared. Did she believe what the vet just said—that Regalo was dead? Maybe it was something aimed to hurt her or, more likely, to get Pia to stop looking. That wasn't going to happen.

A groom, leading a fractious bay mare, was forced to step around her. He shot her a pissed-off look. No sense sticking around now. She headed to the exit, passing the vet's truck where it was parked at the end of the shedrow. She stopped walking and looked around. Usoro was allowed to drive the vehicle inside the stabling area to be able to access equipment and supplies. Pia glanced around. There were no security cameras, no one near this end of the shedrow. She fingered the GPS tracker Wiggins had given her, forgotten in the bottom of her purse. It was illegal what she had in mind. She pulled it out and cupped the device in her palm, pressed against her thigh. Was she really going to do this? Even if she did have the authority to use it, and found out anything important about where the vet was going, the police or Federal agents couldn't use the information.

But she could. Usoro could lead her to Regalo.

An exercise rider brushed past her, dropped his cigarette butt, and crushed it into the raked gravel. He kept walking. No one else around. Just the same, she pretended to drop her car keys beside Usoro's truck, bent down, and scooted the GPS up under the rear wheel well.

She stood and headed to the front office on her way out. If Mrs. Randall was in she planned to find out more about how her dad tried to get Usoro's license revoked. She'd only gone a few steps when her cell phone chimed. It was Ron.

Bank notified me mortgage not paid.

Pia's stomach did that weird thing when she hadn't eaten and had too much coffee. It folded up on itself like it was going into the fetal position. She knew she'd missed a payment. Or two. She was keeping up with the taxes and the interest, hoping for a financial break—maybe a promotion at her job. Or a bonus. Instead, everything was breaking at the farm. A chunk of the mortgage this month went to paying an emergency plumber's bill when the old hot water heater finally crapped out. She figured she'd make it up. Certainly never figured the bank would contact Ron. Shit.

I'm taking care of it, she typed back. Before she could slip her phone back in her pocket, it rang. Ron. This time calling.

Pia sucked in a deep breath, willing herself to stay calm. "I got your message, Ron. I told you—"

"Foreclosure, that's what the bank's talking about. This is no joke, Pia." His voice coiled inside her ear like a worm.

She held the phone away. "If you hadn't cleaned out our bank account, I wouldn't be in this mess."

"It was my money." His voice was taut like a tightrope. He was speaking through clenched teeth.

It was the same conversation that spun around and around and up and down like a carousel but got absolutely nowhere.

"I'm not losing my share of that property because you can't pay the bills."

"It was never your farm." Around and around, Pia thought.

He heaved a big sigh right into the phone. His voice became more even. "We have to meet and work this out. Are you free tomorrow afternoon?"

Ron never considered her schedule before. He usually called with a mandate declaring where and when they should meet. The marriage counselor, the divorce mitigation attorneys, the bankers... She headed across the open area of the track to the main office.

"What do you need to talk to me about? We've said everything already. I'm not selling the farm." Pia's hand holding the phone was sweating. She switched to the other ear and wiped her palm down her pants leg.

"There's been a new development. I want to explain it to you in person," he said. This was the Ron she knew. A condescending jerk.

"What type of new development? You can tell me now." Spikes of adrenaline sent tingling sensations through her body. This was a red flag—when Ron was calm and used his fake politeness, he knew he had the upper hand. And that wasn't good.

"I prefer to discuss the plans—" he said.

"I don't give a rat's ass what you prefer. Tell me and then I'll decide whether I'm meeting you or not."

Pia froze in front of the racetrack exit. The hell with seeing who was in the office. She wanted to get home.

"The zoning's been changed." His words had a ring of triumph.

Pia hung up on him. She barreled through the exit and jogged to where her car was parked.

Pia spent the rest of the afternoon doing whatever backbreaking chore she could find as a way to block out any further thoughts of Ron's conniving plans or the nagging worry that Dr. Usoro did not lie and Regalo was dead. Or, if she were honest with herself, the fact that she hadn't heard anything from Watkins. By five she was covered in a sheen of sweat, smeared with dirt, and had a headache from not eating. She staggered back to the house, showered, and poured a glass of wine while she decided what she could make for dinner. The options weren't great. While she was hanging on the open refrigerator doors, her phone rang. She had texted Deliah about what Ron had told her, asking for advice.

Deliah's image popped up on Facetime. "Hey there. That ex of yours causing trouble again?" she asked. She was dressed in a black sheath dress. A dazzling necklace of red stones and diamonds set off her bright red lipstick and gleaming white smile.

Pia took a gulp of her wine and set the glass down a bit too hard. She avoided giving the obvious answer to Deliah's question—when was he *not* causing trouble? "Going out tonight?" she asked.

Deliah waved a hand, heavy with jeweled rings and looked askance. "You know it. Desmond asked to get together, so how could I say no?"

A million smart replies jumped into Pia's mouth, but she kept them clamped behind her teeth. It was clear to her that Deliah had a lot more feelings for Mr. Desmond Cornell than she let on. "You look nice," she replied while straightening the towel wrapped around her head. "I just got out of the shower and have a date with my laptop tonight. I've got to find out what I can about the zoning change. So far it doesn't look good. Oh, and he lied about the change having gone through. Big surprise. It's still in the proposal stage."

"And you didn't know anything about it?" Deliah stared back at Pia from under her thick, false eyelashes. "What's up with that?"

Pia bit her lip. "Yeah, well, I guess I haven't been paying attention to things like I should." She eyed the stack of unopened mail sitting on the counter. "But listen, maybe you and Desmond could brainstorm tonight on what I could do."

Deliah snorted and her shoulders shook. "Right. Zoning regulations make hot pillow talk."

"Okay, forget it." Pia picked up her glass.

"No, go ahead. Fill me in on what you know. I'll poke around in some legal precedents while Desmond pokes around on me." Deliah pulled a legal pad in front of her and had a pen poised. "Shoot."

Pia filled her in on everything she had found out so far about the proposed rezoning of the area her farm occupied. From what she could tell, it would mean that Ron might be able to press for breaking up and selling the farm. Especially since she was underwater and behind on the mortgage.

Deliah hung up. It left the kitchen feeling eerily quiet. And lonely. Ryder got up and slurped at his bowl.

"You're my hot date tonight, boy. Me and you and the Internet."

She opened her laptop and intended to read the files she'd marked about the zoning commission and the legal fallout from property disputes in divorce cases, but instead her finger tapped the Facebook icon.

She scrolled through pictures of her friends winning ribbons at horse shows, some old college acquaintances bragging about kitchen makeovers, and more than a normal person's share of cat memes passed by in her newsfeed. She swallowed the last of the wine in her glass and got up to pour another. What the heck, she brought the bottle over and set it next to her. A few more minutes, then she'd get to work.

Her finger stopped. Facebook dished up an old photo from years ago of her and Ron, their faces smashed together into the frame of the picture, holding up Solo cups in a toast. When was that? When were they that happy together? She checked the date—five years ago. Where were they? She scanned the background for clues. Then it came to her. It was his summer office party cookout. She could see part of the company banner in the background. Oh, and that really perky intern walking under it in a minidress. Pia remembered now. That intern—what was her name?—spent the evening inserting herself in conversations, drinking a lot, acting like a kid. Well, she was a kid. Pia recalled she was starting her high school senior year that fall.

The wine fog lifted. It came to her. The girl's name was Kennedy Marshall. She heard Ron's voice in her head now, talking about the intern in his office whose parents named her after Jack Kennedy. They were from Cape Cod.

It was time to get to work, but Pia dillydallied, scrolling through some newsfeeds and wondering what happened to Kennedy after that summer. She pulled up the girl's Facebook page and saw a more mature version of the same person. Her profile displayed a woman looking confidently into the camera, her makeup flawless, wearing what looked like a designer dress that hugged every curve. On the sidebar, Pia learned she went to college at University of Maryland and worked at a competitor of Ron's company. That's gratitude. The few thumbnail pictures displayed showed her in various corporate settings, galas, openings...this gal was plugged into the social scene. The page wasn't locked down at all. She probably had a very public setting and was using the platform to drum up more business. What the hell, this was more interesting than zoning regulations. Pia clicked *see all friends*, wondering if she'd recognize anyone, like some familiar faces from Ron's old office parties. She didn't see anyone she knew until...wait. A picture of Ron. It listed only one mutual friend. Was that weird? Pia checked on the mutual friend—no one she recognized. Was Kennedy still in touch with Ron or was it simply an old connection from several years ago.

She should leave it and get back to reading about zoning.

She set up a search of Kennedy's old newsfeed going back to the summer five years ago. How well did she know her husband? He was her husband then after all. And Kennedy was an underage intern. Pia drilled back in time through pictures like a backward running time-lapse photography, seeing the sophisticated Kennedy regress to the teenaged intern before college. Kennedy mugging for the camera with her arm slung around a friend with Ron sitting in a booth in the background. Pia didn't recognize the restaurant. Another featured a dark interior of what looked like a nightclub. She was wearing a dress with spaghetti straps with an arm draped over her bare shoulders. Half of Ron's face was leaning in, whispering something to her. The comments gave no clue as to the occasion. She was seated in a group of people Pia didn't recognize. There were more. Pia spotted Ron in the background in another that looked like a cookout. They could all have been company functions, but strange Pia hadn't been invited to any. She looked closer at each photo for any hint of Ron's presence or any clues to a possible relationship.

Then she saw it. Was that him? She blew up the image and leaned in, almost pressing her nose to the screen.

The image was a typical Kennedy photo, dressed in a short, tight dress with one hand on her hip and her chin tilted up in a defiant look. The comment read, *Not enuf pics of me in this awesome dress!* Apparently friends agreed based on the likes.

But maybe they didn't look at what was reflected in the mirror. Kennedy stood in front of probably a bathroom mirror, but there was another on the back of the open door. That mirror reflected the interior of what appeared to a motel room. The vague image of a man sitting on the bed, shirtless, was visible in the bottom edge of the mirror. Pia copied the photo onto her computer to enhance it. But she knew what she'd find. It would prove it was Ron because she knew the wine stain birthmark just above his left pec. She knew every inch of those shoulders, including the one with the two-inch shiny white scar he got from a waterskiing accident as a kid.

Five years ago, while they were still married, Ron was in a motel room, partially dressed, with a high school girl.

Pia blew up the image of him sitting on the bed in his underwear and copied the original with him reflected in the mirror and stored them away in a special file.

She closed her laptop and waited for the grief. The anger. She closed her eyes and probed around inside waiting for it to wash over her like a cold, rogue wave.

Nothing.

She didn't feel anything at first. After a minute, she cast around again like poking at a bad tooth, waiting for the familiar hurt, anger, disappointment he always spawned, but it wasn't there.

Chapter 29

Watkins

Abramson and Watkins trailed Darren back to his desk. He brought up a display on the triple-monitor and pointed. "Most of the activity has been in this one department."

"I'll take your word for it," Abramson said. He perched on the edge of Darren's desk. "I don't know what I'm looking at."

Darren opened his mouth no doubt to launch into the technical explanation of his tradecraft, but Watkins jumped in. "What set off the activity? Any email or other exchanges on the open side that might be a clue?"

Darren shook his head while Watkins spoke. "No, nothing obvious. Looked like normal stuff to me. I've created a sort of lifestyle profile of the place and as far as I can tell, nothing unusual to account for the increased cryptic activity. The lab's ordering supplies, logging samples for testing, other routine boring stuff." Darren gave a characteristic shrug. "Nothing."

"When you can, send me the messages from the last twenty-four hours," Watkins said. "See if I spot anything unusual. I'm not as close to the project as you are. Maybe something will jump out."

Watkins returned to his desk and noted that Marion had left for a downtown meeting. He became immersed in scanning the new information and did not realize how late it had become. When he looked up from the computer, most of the office had gone home. It was close to five and he hadn't checked in on Caleb. The outside black phone sat in the farthest corner of his desk, accusing him of not being a good enough brother. He snatched the receiver and punched in his home number. His brother had lost his cell phone the night of the OD. Probably left on top of a bar or slid out of his pocket when he collapsed on the street. Watkins expected to hear his own voice on the answering machine and was jolted by Caleb's voice in his ear.

"Yeah?" He sounded tired.

"Sorry if I woke you," Watkins said. "Just checking in. Wanted to know what you might like for dinner. I can bring something home."

"Don't have to check on me."

Watkins pinched the bridge of his nose and held back the sigh that wanted to bleed out. He was tired, too. He made his voice upbeat. "Okay, well then I'll surprise you. I'm out of here in a few minutes."

He expected a *whatever* response. Caleb often reverted to high school vocabulary to accompany his bad attitudes. Instead, Caleb surprised him.

"Dinner would be great. Thanks."

An hour later, Watkins walked into the townhouse with a carryout bag of Mission Barbeque ribs—Caleb's favorite—along with mac and cheese and two pulled pork sandwiches. A six-pack of cold longnecks was tucked under his arm. He set the beers on the counter and noticed the table had been set. Two placemats on each end of the small table were laid with a paper napkin, fork, and knife. Watkins went to slide a beer from the pack, glanced at Caleb, and stowed the pack in the refrigerator.

"Hungry?" he asked. His voice sounded forced.

Caleb struggled to rise from the couch, protecting his bandaged arm, and clicked off the television. He joined Watkins in the kitchen. "Actually, I am now. Haven't felt like eating earlier." He filled a water glass at the refrigerator. "Thanks for getting it."

Watkins placed the carryout containers along the counter. "Help yourself." Their conversation was stilted, overly polite. He studied Caleb's pale face, the slight tremor in his hand as he spooned a glob of mac and cheese on his plate beside a slab of ribs.

"How was work?" Caleb asked. "What you can tell me. I don't want you to have to kill me or anything."

One side of his mouth curved up. It was good to hear him joking around a bit, even if it was the same, tired old joke. Whenever Watkins was around his brother, he felt as if he were on high alert, his skin tingling, waiting for the word or the gesture or God knows what that would set him off. Caleb could fly off the handle in anger or crumple, retreating into his own world.

"Damn, the agency didn't issue me that license to kill yet." He filled his plate with a sandwich and took the last of the ribs. Catching Caleb's eye, he felt a flicker of the old connection they had as kids. Before everything went off the rails. "It's been tough at work lately. Got to admit." He pulled out a chair and sat across from his brother at the small kitchen table.

Caleb held his gaze with his mouth full, chewing. He washed it down with a gulp of water. "Why's that?"

"I'm not sure I'm cut out for this job after all."

His brother ran his tongue along back teeth, making a sucking noise. "Why's that?"

Watkins picked up his sandwich. "It's hard to explain."

"Try." Caleb wiped sauce from his fingers and propped his elbows on the table and leaned in.

He could not remember when his brother had shown any interest in his life. He placed the sandwich back on the plate, picked at the inside with a fork, and wrestled with what to say. "It's hard to tell if I'm making a difference."

Caleb gave a deprecating snort. "Maybe your job is too safe. You're not on the cutting edge of things anymore. Not making life and death decisions."

"Don't want to make those kind of decisions anymore. That's not the problem," Watkins said. He set his fork down.

"You sure? Cuz as far back as I can remember, you were the one in control of everything. Planned everything out. Just like Dad, you made a decision, gave an order, and had absolute confidence that you were right. You never wallowed around in a cesspool of self-doubt like me, second-guessing every decision I ever made. Oh, maybe that's because I made a lot of bad ones. But not you."

"You make a decision, you live with it."

Caleb sat back and crossed his arms. "But you're not living with it. Not at all."

Watkins lifted his chin. "What's that mean?" The tingling was back. He was heading into dangerous territory with Caleb.

"You made a decision in Afghanistan that got men killed. Just wait—" Caleb held up his hand to stop any interruption. "Not saying it was your fault, but I guess you think it was. Ever since then, you've changed. You still think everything is your responsibility, but you don't make the hard decisions anymore. You want everything safe, risk free, with clear choices."

"So what? Maybe I don't want to give orders anymore. Maybe I don't want to be responsible for everything and everyone around me—"

Caleb shot forward, eyes narrowed. "You're not. And that's what you can't get through your head. You're not responsible for anyone else but you." He scoffed. "The night I OD'ed, you felt guilty because you left me alone. It had nothing to do with you. It has never been anything to do with you, big brother. That's the problem, you think it is."

Caleb's face was flushed. He stood to refill his glass.

Watkins cradled his between his palms and wished it were a beer instead. "You are my responsibility," he said. "I promised to watch out for you. I'm sorry if—"

"You're not listening." Caleb sat down and pushed his plate aside. "I've always been compared to you my whole life. No, listen. You had your shit together. Dad always said I should be more like you, but instead I went in the opposite direction and screwed up. Then got bailed out. Lather, rinse, repeat. I never took responsibility for myself because I never had to and because it seemed whenever I did, I made the wrong decision. So I stopped trying." He paused. His chest rose and fell as his breath slowed back to normal. His voice was quiet, modulated when he spoke again. "The other night—the OD. It scared me finally. You know? I've been thinking about it today and when I was lying in the hospital with tubes running out of me, keeping me alive. I've been thinking a lot." His eyes pinned Watkins's and held them. "You want to know what really happened that night?"

"You want to tell me?"

The tight cords of Caleb's throat constricted as he swallowed two gulps. "Jake called me. After you left."

Jake was a friend of Caleb's. One that had gotten him in trouble more than once.

Caleb raked his bottom lip with his teeth. "Jake was down here to see someone in the hospital. At Hopkins in Baltimore. Do you remember Jennine?"

Watkins cast around in his memory for the name. "A girl you dated a few years ago? From the college."

"Yeah. We broke up. She broke up with me. Anyway, hadn't kept in touch so I didn't even know she was sick." His voice dropped. "She died. Jake told me that night and, I don't know, I was thinking all sorts of things like what was my life worth when this smart, nice girl was dead and I was still here? Jake came by and we took off for some bars. I knew it was a bad decision but I didn't care. Life didn't make sense. Jake had some stuff and after a few drinks, well, I hit it pretty hard." Caleb lifted his damaged arm. "Did this in the men's room. Jake found me in there, called 911, and must have taken off. It wasn't an OD, Jonah. I tried to kill myself and now I don't even know why. It scared the shit out of me."

The story sat between them like a dark spirit, hovering over the table.

Watkins stood, pulled a beer from the pack in the refrigerator and twisted off the top. He swigged half before he took his seat again. "What can I do to help?" he asked. It sounded lame. The words rang insincere, but he wasn't equipped to deal with problems of this magnitude.

"Nothing. I want you to do nothing for a change," Caleb said. "You're not responsible. Same as you're not responsible for those men that died because some asshole terrorist decided to blow people up. You're not responsible for finding your girlfriend's horse for her. You're not responsible for the world being in the mess it is and most of all you're not responsible for me trying to kill myself. I am. I'm responsible."

Caleb fell silent. The refrigerator dropped a load of cubes in the icemaker. The kitchen clock ticked. Watkins had the sensation that he'd been encased in cement and suddenly it had cracked open. The light shone in. He could walk out, free of the weight, if he chose to. "Then what are you going to do?" he asked.

Caleb retrieved a pamphlet from the coffee table and pushed it toward Watkins. "The hospital gave me this."

He picked it up. "Drug rehab?"

"I'm on a wait list. I called today and set it up."

He let the pamphlet drop to the table. "You can stay here until they're ready to take you. You know that." He gave Caleb a penetrating stare until his brother dipped his head in a barely discernable nod.

"And there's some other stuff I need to tell you. Some things I've never told anyone before, but it's important. About Dad..."

As the night deepened, Caleb unfolded a tapestry of stories from his past, many of which he didn't know or didn't want to see—stories of abuse, neglect. The brothers sat together at the small table under the one light as the shadows closed in around them. The past they shared and could never deny was lifted up to the surface. Into the light. They had to look at it at last. When Caleb's words ebbed and stopped, they sat in a companionable silence. For the first time in a long time, Watkins felt at peace.

His cell phone on the kitchen counter rang. Watkins reached around to retrieve it, glanced at the screen, and answered. "Hey, Pia. What's going on?"

He turned his back and plugged a finger in the other ear. "What? What's all that noise in the background?" Watkins checked the time on the wall clock. Ten twenty. "Stay there. I'll be right over."

Chapter 30

Pia

Cold water rolled down the sloped barn roof, ran along the eaves. A droplet fell onto Pia's bare head. It streamed down the side of her face and disappeared under the collar of her coat where it continued its course, chilling her body inside and out. Another tapped on the top of her head like a boney finger before she inched away.

The firemen stripped off wet coats and packed away their gear. The chief approached Pia. His shoulders were set in a way that made her brace for bad news.

"Ms. Murphy?" His voice was gentle. Probably the one he used to soothe scared children, rescue cats in trees, and coax crazy people. Pia was certain she fell well into that last category. In the preceding hour she had run into the burning barn twice to open stalls, drag horses out, and try to salvage what she could of her valuables.

"We're leaving, but we'll be in touch with the results of the investigation." Pia stared at his face, wordless, as the sting of tears struck the back of her eyes. The fire chief was a tall man in his late forties with ice-blue eyes made more striking by the dark smear of soot on his face. "I suggest you do not enter the barn again until we can evaluate its structural integrity in the morning."

As soon as he left, she intended to ignore his advice, get her tack out, and inspect how much damage there was to the hay. She was afraid between the smoke and the water, the entire winter's worth of hay might be a loss. Several thousand dollars down the drain. The farm insurance should cover the damage, but there was the deductible to worry about. "Tomorrow?" Her voice sounded like a hopeful little girl.

The chief ran the back of his hand across his forehead, smearing the soot. "Not until tomorrow. An inspector will be out to assess the damage and prepare a report for your insurance company."

The entrance to the barn was a black, gaping mouth. The fire had burned the face of the barn, up one of the sides, and along the front eaves. Pia watched the chief's eyes travel the path the fire took, spreading upward.

"Lucky it didn't spread and take out the roof. If that collapsed, dropping inward, the entire building would go up in a short time. Looks as if it started just inside the entrance."

The firemen had asked her if she stored gasoline or other flammables in the barn. They'd inspected the wiring, lights, all electrical appliances inside like her small refrigerator. Everything had been working right and not a likely cause for the fire. Pia could have told them that. Like all horsemen, she was terrified of barn fires and paid close attention to any and all hazards.

That left only one conclusion. Someone had set the fire. Would Ron do something that drastic to force her to sell? The total loss of the barn would make it impossible to keep the horses and boarding that many of them would require some serious funds. As self-serving as Ron was, she didn't think he was capable of arson.

The chief issued some final instructions she didn't really hear, gave a quick salute, and got in his vehicle. The pumper truck and heavy rescue vehicle made a silent caravan, rolling down her long driveway into the darkness.

Pia tilted her face up to the sky. It was a starless night. A horse in the back field whinnied—probably old Jenny—unhappy to be outside without her pile of hay in front of her in a warm stall. A cloud slipped over the moon, dimming her view. Time to go in. Her feet were freezing in the rubber boots she pulled before running outside. They offered no insulation against the freezing temperatures. She'd need to look for the insurance papers. Call her uncle and let him know what happened. Maybe he could float her another loan until the claim was processed... As she faced the long trudge back to the house she wondered why in the middle of the confusion, when the flames were eating through the barn, she'd only thought to call Watkins. Why was that?

Standing at the entrance to the barn, the thought of returning to the empty house felt like icy hands clenching her heart. She scanned the charred opening to the barn—her refuge, her sanctuary in times of crisis. Now she was ordered not to enter. A scream of frustration she didn't dare allow to release, cemented her feet to the ground.

A mist from the sodden area rose and swirled around her in the frosted air. It mixed with dust from the driveway as a dark vehicle approached. She pulled her coat around her as a hunger of hope rose. But it would be silly for him to come. At this hour? She'd told him not to.

The black SUV's headlights blinded her for a minute before it stopped in front of her. In a flash between the blinding light and the darkness, she was lifted off her feet in an embrace so fierce, she let out a gasp. Watkins set her down and held her at arm's length.

His face was so close she felt his warm breath on her cheek. "You alright?"

The crush of her ribs combined with the sooty air set her on a coughing fit. Her eyes teared, but she nodded. Between hacks, she spun out the story about what happened.

"The horses okay? They got out?" When he craned his neck to look inside the barn, Pia caught his expression in profile. A deep line between his brows and a hollow beneath his cheekbones aged him more than she remembered. He had his own worries—his brother at home now probably—and here she was piling more on.

"I shouldn't have called you. I'm okay. I just didn't know at the time," she said. "The horses got out. They're in the back and the fire was stopped before it did too much damage."

"Any idea what started it?" He walked past her without waiting for her answer and moved closer to inspect the charred face of the barn.

"Not yet. And we can't go in," she warned.

"How bad is it?"

"Bad enough."

His gaze traveled the same track as the chief's had, following the burned marks forming a V-pattern where they were more intense at the bottom spreading up along the sides. Watkins disappeared into the darkness.

Pia followed. Her throat pinched from the acrid smell of wet, burned wood with an underlying chemical blanketing the air. He stood examining the starfish-shaped scorch in the corner. It looked like a black ball with thick legs shooting out of it.

"Looks like it started here, just inside the doorway," Watkins said.

"That's what the chief said, too." Pia tilted her head, gazing up at the rafters. "It was contained before it spread along the roof. Thank God."

Water dripped from overhead.

"The fire inspector is coming tomorrow," Pia said.

Watkins nudged some debris with his foot. He squatted, touched the blackened ash, and brought it to his nose, then stood, brushing the dirt from his hands. "I don't like the looks of it."

The pricking needle of fear and suspicion made a bigger jab at Pia's gut. "Why do you say that?"

Watkins shook his head. "Just let me know what the inspector says." His expression changed as if he were purposefully reshaping for her sake. To look hopeful, encouraging. "You must be freezing. I'll bring you back up to the house, but do you need to get anything else out of here tonight?"

"Nah," she said and held up a framed photo of Regalo. "Before the fire spread, I got the important stuff out of the tack room." Fearing the office would be damaged from fire or water, she'd rescued her dad's bloodstock notes from the files and slipped the picture of Regalo off the nail on the wall. She held it up for him. "Regalo, as a two-year-old."

The photo captured the horse in midair, her tail flagged up across her back and the white of one eye showing.

He took the frame and held for closer inspection. "Never thought to ask you if you had some pictures of her during her earlier life. Looks like she was a handful."

Her heart squeezed in her chest. "That vet, Usoro, told me she's dead."

Watkins handed the picture back. "What do you mean?"

"I'll tell you about it in the house. I need a drink." Before she left the entrance of the barn, she kicked a bucket under the dripping hydrant to catch the water pooling on the frozen ground. "Like that makes a big difference." The lump that felt like cold clay in her stomach threatened to creep up and choke her. She would not cry. Crying does nothing, her mom always said and for once she was right.

Watkins packed the few items she saved from the fire in his SUV and drove to the house. Inside, she dropped everything on the dining room table.

"What'll you have?" Pia asked.

"Just coffee."

Her mouth twitched. "Too bad. I'm having a drink. I earned it." She went into the kitchen and pulled a bottle of wine out of the refrigerator. The racks were pretty much empty. She figured she'd go shopping tomorrow after work, but now she had to stay home for the fire inspector. She retrieved a wine glass out of the dishwasher rack, rinsed it, and filled it to the top. Over the rim of the glass, she watched Watkins turn on the Keurig and select a mug from the rack nearby. Pia set a gallon milk jug on the table next to a sugar bowl and spoon.

He pulled out a chair, which scraped along the floor. Ryder wandered into the kitchen and stood at the back door.

"Don't go far," Pia warned before she opened the back door. The scent of smoke snuck in on the cold air.

"Tell me about what happened. Where did you meet Dr. Usoro?" Watkins asked.

Pia stood by the door, looking out at Ryder. "At the track. I had some friends watching out for her. One of them called me when she came for an injured horse."

She opened the door again and Ryder limped over to a dog bed in the corner.

"Did Usoro know who you were?" Watkins asked.

Pia sat at the table. "Not at first. I wanted to get her talking about what she's researching. I tried pretending I was a vet student, but just my luck she saw through that. I found out later she must have an insider at the track helping her."

"Why do you think that?"

"Because she looked at her phone and suddenly knew who I was. Someone must have texted, telling her I was Patrick Murphy's daughter. So then I just came out with it."

Watkins dropped the empty coffee pod in the trash. He stood at the table as he spooned sugar into the mug. He didn't take a sip, but instead kept stirring. "What did you tell her?"

"When it was obvious she knew who I was, I asked her for Regalo back. I said I'd buy her, whatever, I just wanted my horse back. She was such a bitch. She didn't say anything, just stood there looking smug."

Watkins sat finally. "Then what?"

Pia took another few gulps of wine. She didn't like this feeling that she was being interrogated. The alcohol bit into her empty stomach. "Well, since she knew who my dad was, I accused her of taking Regalo just to get back at him. I wanted to get a reaction out of her. Have her blow up at me or something."

"Do you think that was smart?" He tapped his index finger against his lips. It made her think of her mom when she'd ask Pia a question she already knew the answer to.

She stood and yanked open the fridge to top off her wine glass. "What would you have done?" She didn't join him at the table but instead leaned against the counter.

"I'm not sure. But I don't think making her angry was the right move."

"You weren't there."

He sighed. *I hate that!* He looked like he was trying to get his frustration under control. *Frustration with me?* The heat of rage flooded her muscles.

He took one sip and wrapped his hands around the mug. "I think it was dangerous." He lifted his chin, indicating the direction of the barn. "Did you think it might be possible your conversation triggered what happened out there?"

"You're sure it was arson? Is that it? You think I said something that got her upset enough that she snuck onto my farm this evening knowing I'd recognize her if I spotted her, and set a fire?" Pia looked away until her heart stopped hammering against her chest. "More likely it was my ex." She nodded as if agreeing with herself, warming up to the idea after all. "It's just like him to try to burn me out. He always hated the horses." She pinched her lips shut as her voice wavered. That ring around her throat got tight like a noose under her chin. "Yeah, and he also knows I'm hanging on by my fingernails with the expenses. A good barn fire would be the nail in the coffin."

She needed to blot it out. The thoughts like cockroaches scurrying through her brain. How was she going to pay for this? What if his zoning proposal goes through? Where would she put all the old horses? There were no answers, just more questions. And here was this guy who knows nothing trying to blame her.

"Your ex might have done this?" Watkins slid his hand into hers and pulled her back to the table. It was warm, dry. Big enough to completely cover hers. She didn't resist. Her anger ebbed as fast as a receding wave. Too soon, his hand slipped away.

"You must be tired," he said. "I should go."

"No." The word shot out of her mouth. She didn't want to be alone. "No, I won't sleep anyway. Do you want more coffee?" She picked up his half-full mug.

He held up a hand signaling no way.

She slid the mug aside. "I'm sorry, I never asked you about your brother. In all this stuff going on, I never asked how he's doing, if you got him home from the hospital okay. Is he feeling better?" Her words streamed out like a recording on high speed.

"Well enough to give me advice," Watkins said. His shoulders flinched like he was laughing to himself.

"That's a good thing, right? Means he's better."

Watkins fingered the raised edge of his scar. "He's told me some things. Not good things, but important." He pressed his lips tightly together.

"Yeah? Like...?"

"The OD wasn't an accident. Not entirely. He also told me things I didn't know—or rather didn't want to see—when we were growing up. Caleb took most of the heat in the family. He was different. Dad didn't like different, he wanted conformity." Watkins clutched the saltshaker and slid it back and forth between his palms. "He told me things about my dad. Things he's been carrying all alone."

"What did he say?" Pia asked. She took the saltshaker away and set it out of reach.

She thought he was going to brush her off with a vague answer, but instead he clasped his hands so tightly the bones shone white through his skin. "He beat one of Caleb's friends when they were in high school. The kid was gay and out and hanging around with Caleb. Dad didn't like that and..." He held up his palms. "Army covered it up with the boy's family. I never knew." Watkins blew out a stream of air. "Who knows what he was thinking. For years, I never knew any of this. And there I was, acting as if I had it all together because I was stronger, better than my brother. I tried to help him, but I failed. In the end, he's the stronger one. You know he told me that if he'd wanted to die that night, there was nothing I could do about it. It wasn't my choice, he said."

"You like to protect people like Caleb. Like your men. Like me. But sometimes it isn't your job." She held her breath, waiting for him to tell her it was none of her business, or she was out of line.

His eyes lifted to meet hers. His lips pressed together. "You're right. Caleb's going for help. Real help, not what I can give him." The electricity in the air dissipated like after a storm. Watkins rubbed his chin. "But I'm still worried about you. Confronting Usoro was dangerous."

Pia tossed back the dregs of her glass. "My life is dangerous." She gave a flippant shrug. "Maybe more than yours even. If it was arson, who says it had to be Usoro? In the past few years doing insurance fraud investigations, I've had pissed-off guys slash my tires because we busted their workers' comp scam and a bunch of other weird things."

"But not come to your home. Nothing like burning down a barn."

Pia didn't reply. He was right. This was much more serious, if it was arson. Her horses could have been killed. If it was Usoro, they had to stop her. Get Regalo back home and safe. Her frustration throttled up her anger. At least *she* was doing something to get her back. What was he doing? "You're on me for tracking down Usoro instead of telling me I did a great job finding her. Which you didn't manage to do. Oh, yeah, and I at least did something to get Regalo back. What have you done?"

"Pia, listen. I know you've made some good breakthroughs, but we have to manage our approach to this woman. She's dangerous—"

"I'm dangerous, too." Pia drew her hands back and dropped them under the table. She clenched them together until her fingers cramped. "I'm tired of doing nothing. She said Regalo is dead and maybe she is. Maybe because we've been *managing our approach*"—she mocked his tone—"instead of finding her."

Watkins sat like a lump across the table. The heat bloomed on her face, fueled by the fact he wasn't even fighting back.

"I at least tried," she taunted. "I found Usoro and I wasn't about to let her get away with taking Regalo." Pia stood and jerked open the refrigerator. She poured the last of the wine into her glass, sloshing it over the brim. She ducked to slurp at the edge of the glass until she could pick it up. An expression of disgust flashed over Watkins's face, like he suddenly got a whiff of a dirty cat box. It was as if everything had come loose in her body. The knots were undone, her mind stopped whirring like a pinwheel, and she was ready to take action. Right now. "Hey, and I also forgot to tell you,"—she set the glass down hard and returned to the table for her cell phone—"we can see where she went. I used the tracker."

"What tracker?" His face registered surprise, then concern.

Pia waved away his comment. "I slipped a GPS tracker our PI gave me on Usoro's truck before I left." Her eyes wouldn't focus on the tiny tracking app to get it to open.

Watkins took her phone. "That was reckless. What happens when she finds it? She thinks the police or someone licensed to conduct surveillance is following her." He emphasized the word *licensed*.

"I know, I know." Pia took her phone back. "It's illegal, but I just want to know where she's going. Maybe lead me to whoever's working with her. Besides, she already knows we're after her. And I sort of hinted that we weren't the only ones."

"What do you mean?" The eyebrow over his good eye rose. "What else did you say?"

Pia replayed the conversation in her rattled state. "Nothing really. I hinted that maybe some government officials were interested in her. And Median. That they might be watching the lab—"

Color drained from his face, making the scar stand out. His Adam's apple bobbed up and down with a hard swallow. "You didn't. Tell me exactly what you said about Median and the government investigation."

Her mouth gaped. Too late, she remembered she wasn't supposed to have said anything. He'd warned her, in confidence, hadn't he? She felt airless like she could fly apart in a million pieces.

He looked away. "You may have jeopardized everything."

"I took a chance." Her voice was small.

"A chance?" His words were sharp.

He'd never spoken to her like this.

"You didn't think. Don't for a minute confuse being impulsive with being decisive. You didn't weigh the risk—for the horse, my job, the op, anything."

She took a step and lost her balance. She grabbed the edge of the table. Her fear inflamed her. She was done with not fighting back. "Yeah? Well I didn't sit around for days weighing risk, like you. You won't *do* anything to get her back. I had to make you follow the horse trailer. I have to convince you to talk to your boss. You won't step out and take a chance because you spend all your time planning and plotting until everything's perfect. Well, you know what? A plan is never perfect. Life isn't perfect. You have to just be brave sometimes."

His eyes narrowed. "Brave? Is that what you think you were? You don't have to be too brave when you don't put any thought or work into what you do. It's easy to throw caution to the wind and then blame it all on bad luck when it blows up in your face."

His image swam before her eyes. "You ought to know about things blowing up in your face." The words blurted out and as soon as they did she wanted to call them back. He stood.

"I think I'd better go."

Pia's feet were stuck to the floor. Her brain didn't send anything useful to her mouth. She watched him put on his coat and open the kitchen door. He walked through it, pulling it shut gently. Still, her feet didn't move. The sound of a car door slam, an engine starting. The rumble retreating down the driveway and disappearing under the tap of ice hitting the window. One. Two. Then a dozen. Pia didn't move even when the sound of hail beat on the windows and roof and drowned out every other sound except the now very sober voice in her head. *He will never forgive you.*

Chapter 31

Watkins

Inside the Ranger, the dampness and the closed space released the smell of smoke trapped in his clothes. He didn't bother to go home to change. Instead, he turned down Route 32 and into NSA's almost empty parking lot. At this hour, only the shift workers and a handful of people starting their day early were in.

He craved the orderliness of work. He needed something that was linear, logical, factual to focus his mind on. To shut out Caleb and Pia and everything else that didn't...couldn't be controlled or managed. He'd look through the files Darren had sent, dig into the work and shut out everything else. When he opened the door to his office, he was surprised by the number of people sitting at desks. He didn't recognize a lot of them.

Darren spotted him and slipped off his earphones. "Yo, Captain. Abramson called you in, too?"

Watkins looked around at the unfamiliar faces without answering. Some had their heads down, peering into computer monitors like they were deciphering the Rosetta Stone. Linguists sat with eyes closed and faces contorted in concentration. There was a small group huddled around a desk, speaking in whispers.

"Who are all these new people?" he asked.

"Called in to work Nergal. The overseas HQ has them spun up. But the real action's right here." Darren pointed to lines of code on his screen. "We were able to get in finally. The suspicion is that someone's tipped them. Looks like the operation might be shutting down."

"How do you know?" Watkins perched on the edge of Darren's desk.

"Files started disappearing," Darren explained. "We knew something big was up, so Abramson brought in the cyber geeks to copy off what they could before it all disappears." Darren again pointed at his smudged screen. "They're wiping all evidence from cyberspace, it seems. Research history files, experiments, results, the whole shebang."

"If they are shutting down, that will also include equipment, bio media, specimens...and animal models." Watkins rubbed his eyes. "When did this start?"

"About twelve hours ago," Darren said. "Give or take."

Watkins would have asked if they had any idea why, but he was afraid he knew. Panic sizzled through him. Dr. Usoro tipped the lab that it was under surveillance and they couldn't take a chance that the information wasn't correct. Was Pia right? He had kept quiet about what he knew, waiting, not taking action for so long that it was his fault Regalo was probably dead. Had he tried to protect her, or rather his career?

If Median thought they were found out, they'd shut everything down, let things cool off, and pop up somewhere else where no one would find them for years. If ever.

He stood and headed to Abramson's office. He found the boss huddled with another analyst. The both looked up when he came in.

"Jonah Watkins," Abramson said. "Guess you heard." He gestured to the other man seated at the conference table. "This is Adam Specht. Head of the Special Response Team dealing with Project Nergal."

Specht rose and held out his hand. "Glad to meet you, Jonah. You've all done great work on this, so it will make our job easier going in."

Watkins shot a look at Abramson. He gestured to the empty chair at the table. "Sit down. We can use your experience in formulating our next move."

Watkins sat opposite Specht. He was not a tall man, but fit with thick muscles that corded along his neck, tying in to broad, developed shoulders. A weightlifter, no doubt. Veins along the inside of his arms stood out, tracing the outline of the Marines' mascot, the bulldog. His hair was still cut to regulation.

Specht looked at Watkins under a heavy brow. "The colonel tells me you were Army SF."

Watkins wasn't in the mood to play armed forces one-upmanship or false modesty games with this ex-Marine. "Did he also tell you I led a mission directly into an ambush?" He held Specht in his glare, but out of the corner of his good eye, caught Abramson wince.

"Jonah, you know that wasn't your fault." Abramson dropped a heavy hand on his shoulder.

"No, it wasn't. It was set up by the same man who's running Project Nergal." He shifted so that Abramson's hand dropped away. "What's the SRT's involvement in all this?"

Specht sat back and crossed his arms. His gaze cut to Abramson.

"The SRT is going in," Abramson said. He sat and steepled his fingers in front of his lips. "We've evaluated the situation and think it's worth the risk. If the cyber guys can't break the file codes—providing they manage to pull any of them—we won't have much to go on if they fold up and move elsewhere. No means of tracking them and we'd have to start all over. So we've decided we have to move soon."

"Problem is," Specht leaned in and took up the thread of the conversation, "Median is a smaller operation within a large complex. There's a legitimate lab facility there with civilian employees. We want to go in at night, when there's the least risk of it being occupied, but just the same we have to create a way of ensuring any employees are out of the building."

Abramson spoke up. "Once inside, SRT will download what they can, scan equipment, take air samples, collect intel to ensure Median wasn't also involved in any bioweapons threat. In addition to the counterfeit drug scheme, Morrow had ties across all sorts of criminal and proliferation networks."

"What have you come up with for going in?" Watkins sat forward.

"We'll get our hacker friends," Specht nodded to the area outside the office, "to trip their system. Set off an alarm signaling a fire or toxic leak. Get any people who might be there to evacuate. Then we go in suited up as firefighters. We won't have much time. Forty-five minutes or so, then we declare it a false alarm. Pack up our equipment, which will hold special compartments for what we need to exfil out of there. Later, the law enforcement guys take over."

Watkins nodded. "I'm going with the team."

Abramson opened his mouth to object, but Watkins didn't give him the chance.

"You owe me that much." He waited. This was a line he would not back down from. He'd been shoved to the sidelines for long enough.

Abramson looked at Specht. Something unspoken passed between them. "Okay," he answered. "Have Specht fill you in. The big bosses are meeting tonight to approve the op. After that, we'll know more about dates, timing, and logistics."

"And what's the provision for getting the live subjects out? They've got lab animals in there. Surely their tissue and blood contain evidence of what they've been up to."

Specht frowned and shook his head. "No provision for that. No way. Besides, if the lab got orders to eliminate the project, first stage of shutdown would be elimination of the lab testing subjects. They've probably killed them all."

Chapter 32

Pia

T HE SUN WAS JUST over the horizon when Pia hung the feeder over the fence and called to the old mare. The horse stood at the gate. It was time to come in for breakfast, she'd been out in the cold all night, and she'd had enough of this nonsense. She struck a hoof against the metal gate. The sound rang out in the damp, cold air. Other horses lifted their heads.

"C'mon, Jenny. Come over here and eat your grain. I can't let you in the barn." Pia rattled the bucket, making a swishing noise with the grain in the bottom. Jenny looked cross. Her mud-brown coat was wet along one side. She must have lain down in the damp. Jenny hated to be wet. The old mare cast a sidelong glance and sauntered to the bucket. Her nose disappeared inside and Pia stroked her forelock.

She pulled her phone out of her pocket and checked if Watkins had responded to her text. No, her words sat unanswered in their lonely bubble:

> *I'm so sorry. There's no excuse for what I said, but please, PLEASE forgive me. I was tired and a little*

drunk and maybe angry because what you said was the truth.

She shoved the phone in her coat pocket and went down the fence line, hanging feed buckets for the horses. They were stirred up by the disruption in their quiet routine and the acrid smell of smoke still hanging in the air. After she had filled the water trough and tossed flakes of hay into the pasture, she turned in time to see a car coming down the driveway. Her heart hiccuped when she saw it was a black SUV. Then her insides turned to lead when she realized it wasn't his. The vehicle stopped and a tall man wearing khakis, work boots, and a down vest stepped out. He was very tall with dark hair, graying at the temple. He'd stopped in front of the barn, examining the scorch pattern, when Pia approached.

He held out his hand. "Jim Monroe. I'm the inspector." He pulled out an official looking ID card to show her. "Are you the owner?"

Pia introduced herself. He outlined the procedure for the inspection.

"We've already canvassed the neighborhood," he looked around at the open expanse of fields, "such as it is. Not too many people out here within line of sight, but it turns out your neighbor up the road has a security camera mounted on the front of his property. Tracks everyone coming up and down the road. We'll get permission to view the tape on the night of the fire."

"Sounds like you're already convinced it was arson," Pia said.

He made a tsk noise, sliding his tongue over his teeth. "I'm not saying—officially yet—but the scorch patterns, the high heat stress..." He shook his head. "And you say you didn't store flammable materials in the barn, not even a tractor or machinery that could have leaked?"

"Nothing." Pia sniffed in the cold. "Because I'm terrified of this exact thing happening."

They stood for a moment. Their breath mingled in the frosty air.

"You got any enemies?" The inspector turned to her. "Sorry, I have to ask. It might help the investigation if we can establish a motive."

Pia chewed her bottom lip. Should she say anything about Ron and the zoning changes? She had no proof...

"I work insurance fraud cases. There might be plenty of people pissed off over my part in exposing their scams, but I've never had any real trouble before. Besides, I'm pretty careful about revealing anything about where I live." She looked down and toed the gravel. "But there's some trouble with an ex."

When she raised her gaze, Monroe gave her a *go on* gesture.

"My ex-husband's name's Ron Harcourt. We're in a battle of sorts over the fate of the property here. He wants to sell and develop it to get the money out."

"But you don't."

Pia shook her head. "The final settlement on it is still up in the air. It's my family's farm." She considered explaining how she hoped someday to get the place fixed up, bring in some young horses, maybe find a way to make money from it again. But her throat closed up on words she knew were fanciful ideas now. Her hopes were gone on the cold, smoke polluted breeze.

"Well, I won't keep you from what you need to do today. I'll look around, take pictures, a few samples for the lab, and I'll be out of here."

"When will I hear about the results? The insurance..." She let it drop. Even when the insurance paid out, the deductible was crippling and there were repairs that had to be made that couldn't wait. She'd have to get a loan or something.

"Usually two weeks if we don't run into complications," Monroe said. He looked up and scanned the sky. "Looks like another storm on the horizon. I heard we might get a big one by the end of the week."

"Great." Pia thanked Monroe and waved goodbye. She jammed gloved hands into her pockets and trudged along the ice-encrusted drive back to the house. Inside, she shucked off her coat and sat at the table with a cup of coffee in front of her. What could she do? The bank wouldn't give her another loan to fix the barn when she was behind on the home equity loan. She also knew the taxes were due and the amount in escrow never completely covered it. The old horses couldn't stay out in a storm and she couldn't pay board for that many horses for a few months. And the hydrant was still leaking...the firemen noticed it and warned her it would freeze. She couldn't go to her relatives again. She dropped her forehead in the cradle of her arms propped on the old kitchen table.

Other women would cry right now, but she'd never been allowed to cry or for that matter, express any emotions. It might feel good to sob and scream and get angry, but in her house growing up, such outbursts were never tolerated. Her mother did not condone emotional women—she cast them as weak. She'd prided herself on being tough. And so did Pia.

Yeah, tough, but it didn't get you very far. She spotted the empty bottle of Chardonnay on the counter from the other night and felt a painful memory stab through her gut. And she turned on the one person who was willing to help her. What a jerk she'd been. She fished her phone out of her coat pocket. Nothing from Watkins. But another message from Ron.

Can you meet today? We must discuss the settlement.

Pia's finger hovered over the delete key, but she stopped. She took a gulp of scalding hot coffee, her throat squeezing it down.

Why not? If he was the one who set fire to the barn to force her hand, she was going to meet him head-on over it. Put emotional energy into action, her mom always said. She tapped out her response.

Meet me in 40 at Donegal's. That or nothing.

He responded right away that he would clear his schedule and see her there. Bully for him. What a pretentious jerk.

Donegal's was a casual restaurant nearby that they used to frequent when they didn't feel like making dinner or to grab a few drinks and watch the Capitals hockey game on the big screen. It opened early for the breakfast crowd. Pia considered throwing on her barn coat and heading over right away in order to secure a booth in the back, but no. She decided to change first. She wouldn't show up looking like a beaten down country girl. If she couldn't always act like a ballbusting businesswoman, at least she'd show up dressed like one. Right after she called in to work to tell them she'd be late.

Upstairs, she showered, dried her hair, and selected a pair of black tights topped with an icy-white sweater with a deep neckline. She dug a string of pearls out of the jewelry box and slipped into some high-heeled pumps. Her toes protested over being crammed into the tight fit. Within a few minutes, she had transformed her face from plain farm girl to exotic Mediterranean beauty, accenting her large, dark eyes with liner and selecting a kick-ass shade of red lipstick. She fluffed her loose hair—free of its usual bondage in a ponytail or messy bun—and assessed the effect.

Screw you, Ron, and your lies.

She arrived at Donegal's five minutes late. It couldn't have been planned any better, because Ron had just arrived and was looking around for her when she breezed through the door with her coat over her arm.

His brows shot up. "There you are," he said, looking her up and down. "You look nice."

Pia forced a smile and allowed him to escort her to a booth. She wanted to play it like he was still in control. And maybe let him think she got fixed up for him, because she was desperate to win him back or something. He'd think like that.

Ron lovingly folded his cashmere topcoat and laid it on the seat before he sat in the booth. The waitress appeared to drop off menus and they both ordered coffee.

He opened the conversation, per usual. "I'm glad we could meet finally and have a civilized discussion about these issues."

Pia put down her menu. There was going to be nothing civilized about this conversation, she thought. "You're referring to the zoning change. It hasn't happened, as you led me to believe, and it won't."

His face registered shock, then took on its usual deprecating expression with his half smile and headshake. Like a disappointed teacher or parent, struggling to maintain his patience with a willful but ignorant child. "Yes, you are correct the zoning is a proposal at this stage, but you have to see it's our best option for the property."

"You mean, your best option for taking a share of a farm that was never yours."

The deprecating head shaking continued, infuriating her.

"Your finances indicate this is the only option for saving what's left of the property value. If you're not willing to listen to reason on this—"

"You'll do what?" Pia leaned across the table. She whispered in his face, "Burn my barn down?"

He shot backward. "What? What are you talking about?"

The waitress appeared but he waved her off.

"Someone set fire to my barn last night. You are the only person who has a reason to force me out. It's only a matter of time, Ron, and the fire inspector will prove it was you. He has a video."

He sputtered. "I don't know what you're talking about. That's just nuts. I'd never set fire to your barn."

"Just like you'd never try to swindle a change in the zoning laws. Just like you'd never steal our savings or cheat on me when we were only married a year!" Pia's voice rose. She sensed the waitress hovering a few feet away. Pia turned to address her, "Don't bother with our order. I'll be leaving." She grabbed her coat and stood up. As she passed, Ron snatched her wrist.

"I never cheated on you when we were married. I met Valerie after I moved out. You know that." He spoke, clamping down on her wrist.

Pia shook him off. It was telling he was more concerned about being called a cheat than an arsonist. One he was guilty of, the other, probably not. "You're a cheat but you're a worse liar." She put on her coat and lifted her loose hair to free it around the collar. "And I have proof."

A hint of doubt shimmered across his eyes. Then they narrowed. "Now who's lying?" He seemed to shake off his anger and smiled. "Sit down again. Tell me what you think you've heard or whatever. I'm sure I can explain. C'mon, sit."

Pia had researched the metadata associated with the photo of Kennedy in the motel room with Ron. She had saved that piece of ammunition for the lawyer if things looked desperate. It looked desperate now.

She bent over and spoke in a calm, almost seductive voice. "Three tidbits for you to chew on, Ron: Kennedy, Bradford Motel, underage intern. I wonder what your boss will think of that? It's considered statutory rape—a felony. I also wonder what your parents and your golf buddies and your fiancée, Valerie, will say?"

His mouth gaped. A flush spread over his clean-shaven cheeks. She noted he swallowed hard. It was true. She knew it was most likely true, but here was the proof.

She resumed her seat. It was time she pressed the advantage for a change. "There isn't going to be any rezoning, Ron."

His mouth formed a hard, thin line.

Pia had never been a bully, in fact, she disliked people who abused their power over others but she felt no qualms about striking fear in Ron. She would find out how much fear this caused him. "In fact, you're going to give up all claim to the farm."

He sputtered denials, but they rang hallow. "What's your proof?" The last gasp of a guilty man.

"A picture of you undressed in a motel room with Kennedy." Pia stood. "You can contact my lawyer when you're ready to discuss a reasonable settlement."

Pia walked to the exit, feeling every eye in the restaurant on her retreating back.

* * *

Pia arrived at the office and turned some heads while making her way to her desk. Eric, a summer intern who had stayed on through the fall, remarked, "You look different." He caught himself and flushed, "but in a good way."

Pia said thanks and hurried to her desk where she had a pair of comfortable flats she could change into. While she booted up her computer, she checked the tracking app on Usoro's vehicle. It hadn't been anywhere near Pia's farm, not that she actually believed the vet would be that reckless and unhinged. But...

According to the last twenty-four hours, she had visited two farms, spent approximately twelve hours parked in a residential area—likely her home address—and had headed out this morning at six in the morning.

"What's that?" Deliah stood over her shoulder.

"Jeez," Pia clutched her chest. "You usually sneak up on people?"

"That's not what I think it is, right? Because a GPS tracker placed illegally on a suspect's car is illegal and can't be used in court." Deliah had one hand on her hip.

Pia shut down the app. "Not the missing Thoroughbred case. A personal matter."

"I'm just going to pretend I never saw anything. We agreed? How's that going anyway? Mr. Burke is breathing smoke over how a damn horse could go missing." Deliah cocked her head. "And why're you so dressed up anyway?"

Pia sighed and shoved the spare chair in Deliah's direction. "Have a seat. The last twenty-four hours have been hell. If you want to know, I discovered my husband was cheating on me during my honeymoon practically, someone set fire to my barn the other night, and I got drunk and pissed off Captain America so he'll never speak to me again."

Deliah sank into the chair. "What did you say to him?"

Pia laughed. "Most people would have reacted to the arson news first, but not you."

Deliah's warm hand on her shoulder felt comforting. "I'm sorry. Is everything okay? Do you know yet what happened?"

"Yeah, thanks. The animals got out and it was stopped before too much damage, but..." She shrugged and slumped in her chair. "At first, I thought Ron might have done it, you know, to force me out. Maybe scare me a little. Now, I'm not so sure."

Pia filled her friend in on the details about the fire, what the inspector said, and the fact that she accused Ron that morning. For some reason she wasn't sure why she didn't mention the other business with Ron and the underage affair with an intern. It was still so humiliating.

"Who else would want to do something like that? If it were a revenge sort of thing, why the barn and not your house?"

"The barn was an easier target maybe. Less likely to be spotted in the middle of the night." Pia imagined someone taking the chance that a farm dog wouldn't set off alarms barking or even attack a trespasser. "Maybe afraid the house had surveillance cameras. I dunno. Or it was someone who would know how much a barn fire would scare me. Like another horse person would." She sat. Dejection washed over her. The barn repairs, her humiliating disaster of a marriage, not only losing Watkins, but hurting him so badly. She glanced at her phone for a text. Nothing.

"Watkins came to help you after the fire. So what happened?"

"Ugh." Pia rubbed her forehead. "It was so awful. I was stressed out and, well, drinking. Too much. We were talking about finding Regalo and he said some stuff about me going off half-cocked and blaming it all on bad luck when things blow up—" The words *blow up* caused her to wince. Dreading the sound of them over and over in her head, she confessed the horrible retort she'd flung in Watkins's face.

Deliah's mouth hung open. "You said that?" She twisted in the chair. "You said that to a man who had half his face blown off? That's cold."

Pia couldn't meet her eyes. "Worse thing is, I know he blames himself for that ambush. He told me. He feels responsible for all those guys who were killed."

"You apologized?" Deliah's voice had an edge Pia hadn't heard before.

Her eyes flitted up. "Of course. I've been texting and calling. He won't answer."

Her friend crossed her arms over her chest. "Guess you'd better hike your butt over there in person. Knock on his door until he answers it and apologize in person. A text isn't going to fix that half-assed remark."

The thought of knocking on his door terrified her. What if he didn't answer? What if he did? She didn't think she could face his look of disgust as seeing her again. "You're right," she said. But didn't know when she'd have the nerve to do it.

Deliah's look softened. "Look, he's a decent guy. He knows you were under a lot of stress." She stood and before walking back to her office shook a finger at Pia. "Do it. Don't chicken out."

Pia picked up her phone and under her lines of apology text to Watkins, added one more:

> *I'm coming by your place to apologize in person tonight. Please answer the door. If you never want to speak to me again, that's okay, but allow me to say I'm sorry in person.*

Everything had come apart in her life. It felt like a run of bad luck, but she realized it had more to do with her choices. She had choices and needed to accept that responsibility. She held the phone in her hand, staring at the wallpaper background she'd posted of Regalo in the winner's circle. Regalo. *Are you still alive, girl?*

The phone's vibration startled her. When she answered, the fire inspector's voice blasted in her ear. He was talking above some noise in the background.

"Hello Ms. Murphy? Got some information from that neighbor's camera already. Seems a red Chevy half-ton passed down your road about twenty minutes before the fire broke out. Could only get a partial on the license because of the lack of light and angle." He paused. Pia heard papers flipping. "Here it is—Maryland plate, ends OP79. Ring any bells?"

Pia told him she didn't know anyone with such a vehicle. She knew Ron didn't drive a truck.

"Doesn't prove anything, of course, but it was spotted coming back out a half hour later. There's nothing past your farm and that's an awful long time to take for turning around down the wrong street."

He promised to keep her posted. She thanked him and hung up.

Her life was going to hell, but she still had a job to do if she expected a paycheck. She had to make some progress toward finding Bourbon Ball. If she didn't find a lead at his last known location, the track, then maybe she should check out the rescue facility where he was headed and never turned up. Maybe they'd have some helpful information. She doubted it, but it was worth a try. She called White Oaks and confirmed they were expecting the horse, but it never showed up. Dead end. Pia frowned at the business card she had for White Oaks. It listed the farm name as White Oaks Rescue, but underneath in smaller script, it was described as A *Greener Pastures Equine Care, Rehabilitation, and Rescue Group.*

"While I have you on the phone," Pia said, "can you tell me about Greener Pastures? Is that another farm?"

The woman on the other line seemed distracted, giving orders to someone in the background. "What? Oh, we had some other properties. Greener Pastures was the biggest, but we had to sell and consolidate."

"Just another second of your time," Pia begged. "Could the horse have been shipped there by mistake?"

The woman laughed. "God, I hope not. It's been empty for a year. The guy who bought it wants to develop it. Big bucks." Pia heard a scuffle and shouting. "Gotta go, sorry!"

The phone clicked.

Pia found the contact information and location of former Greener Pastures location and called. A cheery woman on the answering machine informed her that they were very busy taking care of horses and would get back to her as soon as they could. That's odd. Why hadn't they disconnected the phone message? Pia didn't leave a message, but decided to head over there. *I guess in person is the theme for the day.*

Chapter 33

Watkins

It was almost sunset when Watkins left work and drove home. Walking along the sidewalk, he expected to see MacArthur waiting for his dinner. It would be winter soon, and he wanted to trap the cat, get him to the vet, and see if he could convince him to come indoors. He didn't like to think about the cat freezing, or seeking shelter under a car, or being on the losing end of a fight. The bowls he'd set out that morning by the front door were empty, but MacArthur was nowhere in sight.

It left him with a disquiet feeling. It was perfectly reasonable for a cat to disappear for a few days. But MacArthur had always been so predictable, so regular in his habits. Something he relied on every day—seeing MacArthur.

Watkins opened the front door and tossed his keys in the bowl on the bookcase. One of his habits he couldn't break. He sauntered to the refrigerator to get a drink and take out what he'd planned for dinner. The townhouse was quiet. Caleb must be out. He grabbed a beer and sat at the small kitchen table, thinking how tiny it looked compared to the big farm table in Pia's kitchen. He pushed that thought aside, because it came linked with their final conversation while sitting at that table. She had been the one person who never shied away from the scars, who was honest about how she saw him, and yet she was also the one person who was able to hurt him so deeply. Deeper than revulsion over his looks. No, her rejection of him went to the core of who he was. What he believed. Her words were a surgical instrument that cut through any tough exterior and plunged into his softest, most vulnerable innards.

That he'd been afraid to take risks lately.

He wiped the top of the bottle and took a long swallow, waiting for his phone to boot up. It set off a string of chimes as it loaded text after text onto the screen. He glanced at the messages, each one from Pia starting with the words I'm sorry... He turned the phone face down and left it on the table. Upstairs, he decided to change and put in a couple miles before dinner. Passing Caleb's room, he sensed an unusual emptiness. The bed was made, the dresser top was clear, and the chronically overflowing trash can by the desk was empty. Watkins was drawn into the room. He pushed open the closet. The empty hangers jingled against one another. There was an envelope on the desk addressed to him.

He sunk down on Caleb's bed and ran a finger under the seal. There was a single sheet of paper inside covered with cramped, backward-slanting handwriting.

Dear Big Brother—

A spot opened up unexpectedly and they called. Goodbyes are not my thing so I got someone to pick me up. Thanks for your help. Don't worry, I'll show up for the court date.

> PS Hope you find your horse, but my money's on that woman who doesn't put up with your crap finding her first.

Watkins crumpled the letter. His brother was right. Pia had done something. She had been open, honest about her actions, unlike him. He'd tried to control the search, control her...

Was he really like his father—controlling? Demanding everyone comply with his rules? Watkins never felt comfortable leaving anything to chance. It wasn't safe. But was safety an illusion? He'd tried to keep his men safe, but he couldn't. Too many unforeseen variables. He'd tried to keep Caleb safe, but instead pushed him away. He'd tried to save Regalo, but now she was likely dead and he'd alienated Pia by trying to control every step she took. Hell, he couldn't even help a stray cat.

He went downstairs and punched in a number for someone he knew would answer his call no matter the hour.

"Selma Bennett speaking," the familiar voice rang in his ear. "I wonder what it is that could have you calling me this time, Jonah Watkins."

The woman had a direct way of cutting though all the bull. Maybe that's what made her such as good therapist.

"Ah, hi Selma. Jonah here, like you know already. Yeah, I was wondering if you had some time to talk to me." A horse whinnied in the background. It dredged up memories. "I know it's been a while."

He heard what sounded like a stall door being rolled shut and latched. "I got to say, I've been expecting you to call sooner or later. You left before we were finished."

Watkins hung on the line without speaking. Her breathing echoed in his ear.

"You still there?" she asked.

"Yes."

"Are you okay, Jonah?" Her voice edged with concern.

His jaw flinched. "No." He waited and listened to her breathe. "No, Selma, I'm not alright."

"You'd better come now."

He jotted an unfamiliar address on a scrap of paper and grabbed his keys. The address she gave led to a small farm about forty minutes from Baltimore. When he pulled up the drive, he spotted Selma standing outside a small barn. She still wore her hair in a long, white braid but looked as if she had lost some weight. He stopped and got out of the car. Like the first time he met her, she simply motioned him to follow her inside.

The barn was set up with four stalls divided by a central aisle. Just inside the entrance there was a stack of sweet-smelling hay, a feed room area, and some tack hanging on the wall.

"When I had to shut down Pegasus, I brought the old guys here." She gestured to the graying heads with sunken eyes hanging over their stall doors. "My friend owns the place and had room for me."

Watkins ran a hand down the face of a chestnut draft cross. "How are you doing, Selma? I imagine it must have been tough after losing the farm."

"It was." Her hooded eyes were the same piercing blue as ever. "But this is a new phase of my life, that's all." She gestured to his running shoes and sweats. "Not dressed for the barn."

"Left in a hurry."

"Guess we'd better go on up to the house then. I've got a small office space in the front room." She led him to a farmhouse surrounded by mature maple trees and lilac bushes, now bare of leaves in the deep autumn. The front door opened to a hallway of wide-planked yellow pine boards. Selma opened a door to the right. "I'm in here." She gestured for him to enter ahead of her.

The room was contained well-worn leather furniture, a braided rug, and hunt prints on the walls. Behind a modest desk, Selma had hung framed degrees and certificates. The only piece that seemed out of place was a dented, olive drab filing cabinet. "Have a seat. Can I get you anything? Something to drink?"

Watkins waved away the offer. Although he hadn't had dinner, he wasn't hungry. He glanced at the couch and chose instead a straight-backed chair alongside the desk. Selma smiled at his choice and nodded. "Down to business, then," she said and took her place behind the desk.

He glanced over the items littering the surface. Folders, reading glasses, an abandoned half-full cup of coffee... It was strange to talk with Selma over a desk instead of a horse's back.

"Feels odd, like something's missing," he said.

She picked up a pencil and twiddled it between her fingers. "Yup. The icebreakers. Having the horses to draw out the words. You'll have to do your best without them."

He tried to gather his thoughts, but they skittered away like cockroaches under a light. Without looking, he knew her eyes were on him. It was if he were standing on Nordic skis at the top of a black diamond run and couldn't push off. She kept fingering the pencil, but didn't say anything.

He took a breath and pushed off. "I've alienated everyone around me." His clenched hands clung to each other as if for dear life. "The most important people, I've let them down when I thought I was helping. I don't know how to see myself anymore." He sought out her eyes, sought some understanding of his words. He was met with a blank stare.

"How have you seen yourself?"

He ducked his head. "As someone who doesn't make mistakes. Who can't make mistakes."

"Why?"

Watkins looked up under his brow. He felt like a small boy again repeating the words he had to recite for his father. Recite, over and over, with every strike from his belt. "I am responsible."

His gaze shifted to the darkened window. The black panes reflected the figure of a mature man, not a little boy. Funny how the outside did not match the inside sometimes. He looked back at Selma. "I had the words beaten into me." He pinched the bridge of his nose and began the story. "I'm older than my brother Caleb by almost seven years. When he was a baby, I was put in charge of watching him. It was my father who was supposed to, but he didn't care for babysitting. My mother had Thursday evening meetings—I don't remember what for—and left Caleb with my dad. Meaning, she left Caleb with a nine-year-old. Dad would go to his study and drink after telling me I was to watch my two-year-old brother who by this time had become mobile, headstrong, and adventurous. It was one of these Thursday evenings when my dad had polished off a half bottle of Jamison when Caleb discovered he could climb out of his playpen. I was in the kitchen heating up his bottle when I heard him scream. Our house wasn't huge, but it seemed to take me ages to find him. He'd smashed his head on the edge of the coffee table and there was blood all over the living room. Dad burst into the room at the same time and grabbed Caleb. He was cut and bleeding a lot, but we didn't take him to the hospital. Dad got it stopped and told my mother it was an accident. I thought everything would be okay, but it wasn't. That night, after everyone was asleep, he came in my room. One hand covered my mouth while the other grabbed my arm and jerked me out of bed and down the stairs. He kicked open the kitchen door and dragged me behind the shed in the darkest corner of the yard. There, he stripped my pajamas off and beat me. That was the first time."

Selma stopped twirling the pencil. She nodded to go on.

"But it wasn't the last. Thursday nights usually, when mom wasn't home or when everyone was in bed. *I am responsible* was beaten into me every time I made a mistake, received a poor grade, or failed in some measure large or small."

"Did he treat Caleb the same way?"

A laugh tinged with sadness erupted through his chest. "Yes and no. When Caleb was older, he had his turn by the shed but the refrain wasn't the same. Caleb was forced to repeat *I am hopeless*."

A small noise escaped Selma's lips.

"Thing is, my father was revered. Revered. His reputation was spotless. He couldn't be wrong, could he? Caleb and me, we believed him. We believed..."

The clock in the hallway chimed.

"Did your mother know?" Selma's voice was hushed. It wrapped Watkins like a warm fleece blanket.

"If she did, she didn't let on."

"When did it stop? How old were you?"

Watkins's mind cast back over the rocky landscape of memories. When he was beaten, no matter the age, he always felt as if he were a nine-year-old. "I left for boarding school when I was fourteen. A year before that, I suppose. At least it was less often."

Selma's profile was softened, more youthful in the dim light from the desk lamp. He would see that she was struggling to hold a neutral expression, maintain a professional demeanor. She folded her hands on the desktop. "The message was beaten into you. Your heightened responsibility for others."

"Yes, for others. Also for anything bad that happened. It was because I hadn't prepared. Hadn't planned or studied enough. I was blamed."

"And when your father stopped beating you, you took over the job yourself. Beating yourself up for every failure. For not helping

Caleb, for not saving your men... Tell me, is that why you refused plastic surgery for your face?"

His head shot up. "What?"

She patted a file. "Your repeated refusal for reconstructive surgery was noted in Dr. Merkowski's file from the rehab hospital. She recommended the best plastic surgeons in the country, yet you never followed up on it."

He fingered the scar along his face. "I deserved this by making a deadly mistake. I was too wrapped up in my own ambitions and it cost me. My face reminds me to be careful. Not make mistakes."

"Fear of making mistakes has paralyzed you, Jonah. It's kept you from taking risks in life, and living life means plenty of risk."

She held her hand up to stop his protests.

"You risk getting hurt because you can't predict and control everyone and everything in your life. You risk hurting other people as well. We're messy, flawed—or if you believe in the biblical interpretation—sinful human beings. That's how we're wired and there's no one who is capable of threading that needle called life without making a mess of mistakes. The beautiful thing is, when you do, there's grace. There are people to forgive and who will forgive you. As well as forgiving yourself." She shook a finger. "That's one you especially have to work on. Can you forgive others for hurting or disappointing you?"

Watkins pictured the trail of apologies from Pia sitting in his text messages. He thought of the note from Caleb. He swallowed hard. "Yes."

"When you forgive others for hurting you, put their words and deeds in the past. Others will do the same for you. Do you remember when you had so much trouble reaching Regalo when you first started riding her? She hadn't forgiven riders who had hurt her in the past. She held back, fought, anticipated punishment when there was nothing to punish her for...do you remember?"

Watkins nodded. The raw frustration of not getting through to her when he was doing everything right, but he couldn't get her to respond was maddening. It wasn't his fault.

"She had to let go of her past and open up. She didn't know if you were going to hurt her, too, but at some point she had to give up her fear and trust."

The mention of Regalo squeezed his heart. He had failed in his promise to her as well. He knew in no uncertain terms there were no provisions in the op for saving the animals at the lab. But what if he made the arrangements? Some ideas flashed through his mind. He weighed and dismissed them. Without help from the outside, there was no way he could pull it off. Not with Specht in charge, orchestrating every move. Unless... It would be a huge risk.

He smiled at Selma. "This has helped. Thank you." He stood and stretched. "It's getting late and I'm sure you've had a long day." He had a plan. He wanted to test out his idea.

Her tired eyes grew round with surprise. "I hope you'll come back. I think there's more to discuss." She stood and escorted him to the door.

"I will, I promise." He drew her into a brief hug. Her round, soft body was comforting pressed against his. "Right now, there's someone I need to forgive."

Chapter 34

Pia

It was midafternoon when Pia pulled her car up in front of the sign for the Greener Pastures Equine Rescue. It had taken almost an hour to drive from her office outside of Columbia to the countryside of Baltimore County near the Pennsylvania border.

The sign was an impressive carved and painted one planted at the end of the driveway, but the grass around it had grown tall. The driveway was blocked by a length of chain.

She debated turning around, but hated that she had wasted almost an hour driving out here, especially when she still faced going to Watkins's at the end of the day. She got out of the car and approached the barricade. Barns and a storage shed were visible in the distance, but no activity caught her eye. The fields running along the driveway were empty. A bird called from the stand of trees beyond the fields. The place gave off an air of something wrong, something a bit sinister.

Pia didn't spot any No Trespassing signs, so she unhooked the chain, returned to her car, and drove in. If anyone asked, she'd tell them she'd called and was there on a missing horse investigation.

The driveway ended at a large, old-fashioned barn with a stone foundation. The white paint with hunter green trim was probably striking in its day, but was now faded and peeling. Another long, low building that she guessed used to be a cowshed ran at right angles from this one. Its windows were mostly broken or missing. Pia shouldered her purse and stepped out of the car.

"Hello!" she called, feeling a bit foolish. It was clearly abandoned, as the woman at White Oak Rescue had told her. But it made sense to check whether Bourbon Ball could have been taken here in error. God, she hoped not.

Scanning the roof line, she didn't notice any security cameras. Her sneakers crunched on the loose gravel as she crossed the parking area and entered the barn. Inside, the temperature dropped. It was dark, but she sensed movement from deep within the interior. Instead of the usually grassy scent of most horse barns, the air was heavy with the moldy hay, dust, and rodent droppings. Pia clicked on the light on her phone. As her eyes adjusted, she caught an orange cat skulking along the wall. It disappeared in an empty stall.

The stall held aluminum trash bins and a stack of empty grain sacks. It looked as if it were set up as a feed room and used more recently than a year ago. A makeshift shelf contained the usual jars of horse wound ointment, a box of brushes and a hook pick, leg wraps, and a lead rope hung from a nail. She opened the lid of one of the bins. A sour odor of old grain lingered in the bottom. She replaced the lid and brushed her hands together to remove the dust. A corkboard held curled notices of emergency numbers and feeding instructions in faded ink.

The orange cat arched its back, wrapping its body around the doorframe. Pia spotted an empty cat bowl and another with water covered with a film of oily dust. She checked the water hydrant in the aisle and found it was still working. This was all very odd. She filled the cat's water bowl and found a Tupperware container of kibble on the shelf.

The cat dove into its food.

"Been a while since anyone's fed you, I guess."

Pia poked around looking for an office or somewhere used as an operations center. Where was the phone hooked up with the cheery lady handing out that fake message about being busy with the horses? In some empty rental office?

She stepped outside. Tucked alongside the barn, partially hidden behind the cowshed, a two-horse tagalong trailer sat with its tongue resting on a cinder block. Its new, clean exterior was incongruous next to the rusting barns and overgrown parking area. Pia checked inside. There was a pile of dried manure on the left side, but still attracting flies. A horse had been in it recently. She walked around the trailer and took note of the license plate. She'd look up the owner when she got back to the office.

Back at her car, she took a last look around. Someone had been here recently as evidenced by the horse supplies and the trailer. Could there really have been a mix-up and the driver took Bourbon Ball here instead? But where was he now?

It looked as if this place hadn't been run as a legit rescue for years, she thought. The word *legit* echoed in her head. Instead, it smacked of an illegal stopover point, hiding horses for shipment elsewhere—like to slaughter or other illegal operations. The fire inspector's question about whether she had any enemies came back to her. She'd been so focused on Ron being responsible for setting the fire, she never really gave it much thought. Did she make an enemy who would burn down her barn for revenge? Or one who might want to stop her from poking into a fraud case? Like a missing horse?

It was getting late in the afternoon. She was alone on a deserted farm, a long way from the main road. People wouldn't see her car even if something happened. If someone was here, hiding, watching her. She got in her car and hit the locks. Her job had never spooked her before. It would be just her luck to stumble into something very illegal—and very dangerous.

At the entrance, she reattached the chain behind her. There were no tracks on the drive indicating she'd been down it. She wasn't sure what kind of operation was going on, but until she found out, she didn't want to tip anyone off someone had been there.

As soon as she returned to her car, the tracker alerted her that Usoro's car was active. She opened the app and watched the vet's vehicle travel along Route 40 just inside the Beltway circling Baltimore City. Usoro had not been very active that morning. There was one stop at a big racing farm Pia was familiar with that took up several hours. Then she was at a shopping area for about an hour and was now moving west, away from the city. It would only be a matter of minutes for Pia to shoot down the Beltway and follow her. Maybe if she stopped at an open, public area Pia would approach her again. Get Usoro to tell her what she did with Regalo. Or maybe she would lead her to Median Diagnostics…

The traffic was building for rush hour already when Pia turned onto the Beltway and sped along in the fast lane. She kept an eye on her phone, propped on the dashboard, displaying the tracked route. In another ten minutes, Usoro's vehicle came to a stop. Pia slowed down and checked the location. Only about twenty minutes outside the Beltway. If she stayed there long enough, Pia could catch up and park right outside. She noted the address and heaved a sigh of relief as the GPS confirmed the vehicle was no longer in motion.

"Now just stay there until I find you," she said.

In a few miles, she turned into a large strip mall area with a specialty grocery store anchoring one end, a kitchen appliance store, and few fast-food places interspersed. Usoro's car was parked in front of a stand-alone diner. Pia pulled in nearby—close enough to keep an eye on Usoro's vehicle, but not too close to be spotted. She checked the time. Usoro had been stopped for twenty minutes. She could be meeting someone here for an early dinner or simply stopping for carryout. *What to do now?* Having no idea usually didn't bother her—she'd go with her gut. And her gut was telling her to bust in there right now and confront Usoro. She unclicked her seatbelt, but didn't move. *That's a dumb idea.* Watkins had a point. She did tend to rush in, throw caution aside, and leave a lot to fate. And a recipe for bad luck.

That changes today.

Instead, she'd sit tight until she figured out her next move. And speaking of Watkins, a glance at her phone told her he hadn't responded to her threat to come knocking on his door.

Just as she punched the number to call Wiggins and have him run the trailer's license plate, Usoro burst through the front door of the restaurant. A few steps behind her, a tall man grabbed her elbow. Usoro spun on him, shook off his hand, and issued a few terse words Pia couldn't hear. She cracked the window hoping their voices carried. The man wore new looking jeans, a fleece-lined jacket, and had a ball cap pulled down over his forehead. It had an insignia on it, but she couldn't make it out. Usoro had on coveralls as if she had just come from a farm call, but incongruous with her outfit, she was carrying a very expensive looking soft briefcase. They stood to one side of the front door. The man towered over her, but she never stepped back in retreat as they exchanged what Pia guessed were cross words judging by the man's downturned mouth and rigid set of his shoulders, glowering over her. Usoro's back was to Pia so she couldn't see her face.

A few words coasted over the distance to her ears. The man: payment, a deal... Usoro: the wrong one, endangering...

Pia couldn't follow the thread of the conversation, but it was clear the man wanted something Usoro was not willing to give. She turned away, opened her car, and pulled the door shut with the man standing outside it. She started the engine and pulled away. The man gave her the one-finger salute and stiff-walked to his vehicle, anger leaching from his tall frame.

He jerked open the driver's door to a red pickup.

A red half-ton pickup truck. Pia grabbed her phone and clicked some pictures of the license plate. She checked the image, blowing it up to make sure it was readable. It was. Good thing, because the tall man pulled away and headed in the opposite direction from Usoro.

How many red pickups were there in Maryland? Several hundred thousand probably. She rummaged through her notes to find the partial license number of the truck seen the night of the fire. She'd scribbled it down when the inspector called, but now she couldn't find the scrap of paper. Damn. She didn't want to send Wiggins on a wild goose chase for a license search on someone who probably just had a personal beef with Usoro. Besides, the police would be running down that lead. It was their job. She had enough to do, tracking down a lost racehorse. But then again, she really wanted to know who that guy was who was so angry with Usoro. He might be someone worth talking to.

She texted Wiggins and asked him to run a trace on the tall man's license as well as the trailer parked at the rescue. For a justification statement, she linked both searches to the fraud investigation case for Bourbon Ball. A little white lie.

It was getting late. Pia still had to make good on her threat to show up at Watkins's townhouse, and she wanted to eat and freshen up a bit before she tackled that promise. By the time she turned into her driveway, her shoulders ached from driving and her empty stomach was burning a hole through her back. Since she still hadn't been to the grocery store, she'd probably have to rummage through the freezer for that old, frozen lasagna that had been there for months. Her dismal dinner reverie was blown away when she saw a black SUV parked near the barn. An adrenaline dump hit her system, causing a tingling down her arms. Her brain told her it must be the inspector again, but it wasn't. It was him. Watkins was here.

She pulled up beside the SUV just as he emerged from the barn wearing a dark T-shirt that outlined his chest and biceps, tucked into a pair of faded jeans. A wrench dangled loosely in his right hand. As he drew closer, she could see dirt had crept into the creases around his eyes, outlining the scar. She unclicked the seatbelt and stood outside her car. She wanted to ask him what he was doing here, but the words fled her lips and stayed submerged somewhere deep in her chest.

"You were right," he said, holding up the wrench. "The hydrant was leaking, but only needed tightening on the aboveground end. It's fixed."

Pia pointed to new, green fence boards replacing the broken ones. "Why?"

He swiped the back of his hand over his forehead. "It's my way of apologizing. I said some things the other night." His gaze moved from Pia's face over her head, into the distance. "I've been avoiding facing some things." He shoved the wrench in a back pocket.

Pia leaned against the car. "It's me who should be apologizing. Blurting out horrible stuff. I'm so sorry about the—" She clamped her bottom lip between her teeth. "I never should have said anything about the accident. It was horrible."

His eyes sought out hers and held them. "You called it an accident. I've always described what happened as an ambush, an attack, a betrayal...but you're right. It was an accident. It was something I could not have foreseen or avoided and I think I'm done paying for a mistake that was never my fault."

Pia pushed herself off the car and wrapped her arms around his waist, taking in the smell of sawdust and sweat. His hand cupped the back of her head for a moment. When he pulled away, the cold air filled the space were the heat of his body had pressed against her. Had she overstepped the boundary? Too soon?

She flashed a coy schoolgirl smile to lighten the moment. "So we're friends. Good. Because I have a lot to tell you."

Chapter 35

Watkins

WATKINS WALKED INTO THE townhouse, tossed his keys in the bowl as always, but even after a week had not gotten used to the emptiness without Caleb. He'd called the rehab facility and although he was not allowed to speak with his brother yet, they assured him Caleb was doing well. He showered and dressed before leaving for work. He knew the Project Nergal ops planning meetings would take all day again. Like they had been. The operation to evacuate the production and business spaces of the facility was planned down to the last detail and was set to launch as soon as they received notification from the courts that the warrant was approved. The days dragged on, waiting. Time was not his friend. It allowed too much space to worry, go over what he had and had not done. Regret. He hoped that Regalo was still alive, but with each passing day and with what Usoro had told Pia, that possibility drained away.

Homeland Security had categorized the search and arrest necessary to shut down the Median operatives a high-risk op because of the known international criminal elements involved, therefore SRT would take the lead. The planning involved reps from FBI, Homeland, and a cleared point of contact with the police jurisdiction where the lab was located. If all went well, the op would occur after hours when the facility had the least number of employees on site and when the Median Diagnostics crew conducted most of their illegal operations.

At six forty, Watkins made his way down a long corridor to the special conference room set up for the planning operation. A conference table scarred with water rings dominated the room. There was a small gallery for seating around three sides and a platform with a mic'd podium. Behind it, an oversized screen displayed the layout of the lab and vicinity. Exits, vents, and windows were marked, as were assorted outbuildings, parking lot, and the surrounding wooded area. Next to it was a map displaying the location of the lab within the broader context of the area with main highways, police and fire station headquarters, and populated areas highlighted. The lab was isolated down a single-access road, but beyond a stand of trees, it ran alongside the back of a strip mall. The SRT had to take everything into account in order to secure the area.

The mid shift was breaking up. Watkins grabbed a cup of coffee from the side table. Every morning, Abramson made a stop at the local doughnut shop for a jug of joe and a few dozen doughnuts for the planning team. He appeared beside Watkins and plucked a chocolate frosted from the box. His skin sallow and puffy under the artificial lights.

"Looks like they're taking a break," he said to Watkins. "Good, because I wanted to fill you in on some developments."

Watkins followed him to two chairs in the gallery, away from others who were still seated at the conference table. Abramson rested a napkin on his knee and balanced the doughnut on top.

"I wanted you to be the first to know. They got Morrow last night. The international finance guys were tracking his activities, moving money in and out of the country, and got the tip he was headed out of the country via Dulles. They had enough on him for an arrest right there."

Watkins looked at the frosted doughnut with a sheen of condensation in the overheated room. He cast around inside for how he felt about the news. The man who had orchestrated the death of so many of his men was now in custody. At last. He thought maybe he should feel some elated sense of vindication, justice served, revenge even. But he felt tired. Deadened inside.

As if Abramson were reading his thoughts, he rambled on. "He was in the pocket of the rebel faction in Afghanistan, getting paid to keep the fighting going. His paymasters were supplying weapons to them and Morrow was getting a cut. He couldn't afford to have your peace initiatives succeed."

Watkins took a sip of scalding coffee. "What will happen to him?" He didn't really care, but maybe it would be good to let the families know. Especially Brody's family.

"For a start, we have him dead to rights for his part in the counterfeit vaccine scam. The finance guys are pretty sure they can link the proceeds from it back to arms sales and other activities. He'll be spending the rest of his years in prison, I'd guess." Abramson took a bite from the doughnut and swallowed. "We'll keep pressing to get the evidence for a conviction for his part in the assault planning."

※※※

That night, Pia was coming over to his place for drinks before dinner. When he called to invite her, she mentioned she made some progress involving Bourbon Ball, the missing racehorse.

"Oh, and I tracked Usoro to a diner where she met this guy in a red truck," she added. "Same red truck seen passing along my dead-end road the night of the fire. Coincidence?"

"Check six," he said.

"What does that mean?"

"An old fly boys' expression. Means watch your back. Be careful," he said, but hurried to add, "But I know you will."

By seven, they were seated at a small table in his favorite Thai restaurant. The warmth of the spices clinging to everything in the room, mixed with the ambient lighting from the shaded lamp on the table made their table for two feel like an exclusive island. The rest of the noisy restaurant filled with people's conversations, clashing dishes, and a hostess barking orders to the waitstaff receded into the background.

"Wiggins called. He ran the license on the horse trailer I found. It's registered to a guy named Donald Bell. Seems he's now the property owner. He plans to develop the farm, but in the meantime leases it out to make some coin. Turns out he kept the rescue's name since it had a great reputation and he or someone else has been using it as a transshipment holding facility for donated horses before he arranges for them to be sent to slaughter. Nice guy."

"How did you put all that together from just a license plate registration?"

"Not just the plate. Turns out Bell has a long history of scams, mostly out west, so Wiggins decided to set up a camera at the entrance of Greener Pastures. A day later, that horse trailer rolled out and he had someone follow it to Timonium where he picked up a horse. It came back to Greener Pastures, but a day later a big rig pulled in. Turns out it was picking up cargo bound for Canada. The rig was a long-hauler with a manifest to deliver to a feedlot up there. Wiggins said they were stopped at the border. The horses were confiscated pending a fraud investigation."

"You think that's what happened to Bourbon Ball?" he asked and immediately regretted it. Pia's face crumpled.

"Probably. There was evidence a horse had been kept at Greener Pastures probably a few days around the time BB was shipped out of track. Might have picked him up by mistake, thinking he was another horse or...who knows." Pia placed her fork down beside her plate. "They might have counted on no one coming to look for him."

"You stopped other horses from enduring that fate."

"I guess. But the insurance company isn't happy. No body, no payout. The case is still officially open." Pia picked up a spring roll and dragged the end through a dish of hot mustard.

"Fill me in on the story of the guy with the red truck. The one who met Usoro?" He braced for whatever Pia was to tell him about her latest encounter. She had outlined the briefest facts of the meeting, but he wanted to mentally pick the odds and ends of the story that might have been overlooked.

"I'm not sure what to think of him. He obviously had some disagreement with Usoro so that assumes he had some sort of relationship with her. Unless he just spilled a drink on her, but she seemed pretty pissed off. According to the truck's registration, his name is Huey Wright and he doesn't live anywhere near me, so who knows what he was doing that night. He has a clean record, pays his taxes, served a tour in the army... Nothing jumps out."

Watkins took a swallow of water to wash down a fiery mouthful of nua pad prik. He wiped a bead of sweat forming on his eyelid.

Pia munched the spring roll and shrugged. "Dead end. Maybe the fire inspector will come up with something."

"What's he do for a living now, do you know?"

"Done some farrier work, some general construction. Seems he moves around a lot."

"As a farrier, maybe he had a run-in with Usoro. That might explain the fight outside the diner."

Pia picked at her plate. "Maybe."

"You say he was in the army."

She lifted her eyes. "What are you thinking?"

"Not sure yet." Watkins picked up his phone. "Did you look up his discharge record? I have a contact in military records. Maybe she can poke around for me."

"It's eight o'clock. We can look him up—"

"I'll leave a message for her. If there's something there, we'll get more details this way."

Watkins rehearsed the succinct message he would leave with the pertinent details, and was surprised when a throaty female voice answered.

"US Army records service."

Watkins covered the mouthpiece and told Pia, "Go figure, someone's there." He turned his attention back to the person who answered and explained what he wanted. "Is this Dolores? What are you doing working so late?"

Dolores was an old friend. She threatened his request would cost him.

"Name your price." He winked at Pia. "Hey, I'm here with the woman who has a need to know. I'm putting you on speaker. Okay?" He pushed a button and set the phone in the middle of the table.

Dolores's smoky voice came back on. "I can tell you his discharge status. That's public record you can look up yourself, hon. But I figure you'd want to know more when you hear it was dishonorable."

"Dishonorable. What's the cause?"

"Need a freedom of information request before I divulge more, you know that, Jonah."

"You save me the time and give me a hint now. I'll file the papers later if it's going to help."

"You're asking me to bend the law. Not like you."

Watkins hunched over the phone. "It's the new me. Look, this guy is a suspect in a suspicious fire. Might have tried to burn a woman's barn down a few days ago. Just warning you, you'll probably be hearing from a bunch of officials soon when they catch up on the investigation."

He listened as she tapped some keys.

"Well, well. You might be on to something."

"How's that?" His fingers gripped the phone.

"Seems Mr. Wright was a bit of a firebug."

Chapter 36

Pia

The next morning, Pia tapped on Deliah's door and stepped into her office. "I need to vent."

Deliah set her glasses down on the desktop and gestured to the chair. "What's up?"

"Men and horses." Pia slung an arm over the back of the chair. "Failing at both."

"Can't help you with the second one," Deliah said. "As for men, I'd say I'm a bit of an expert. You and the captain still fighting?"

Pia had confided in Deliah about the almost kiss in her kitchen, which had started her thinking about Watkins in a new way. Then the fight. "He came by and we made up. But..."

A smirk curled one corner of Deliah's lips. "But what? No hot make-up sex?"

Pia snorted. "Not even close. A hug and he pulled away. Asked me to dinner, but then nothing. I'm getting mixed signals. Maybe I'm thinking there's something there when there isn't." Pia picked at the sleeve of her sweater. "It all started when we were working together to find Regalo. It was like she was the glue pushing us together. And now, well, the hope is gone that she's still alive. The glue is gone maybe."

"So what do you want me to tell you?" Although Deliah's tone was gentle, the words sounded harsh.

Pia straightened in her seat. "Huh? I guess maybe I thought you'd be—"

"Nope." Her friend shook a finger. "I'm not here for your pity party. You come to me for advice about what you should do, I'll tell you. But not if you're going to sit and feel sorry for yourself and do absolutely nothing about it."

"Ouch." Pia pressed against the arms of the chair to stand. "Sorry. Guess I'll leave."

Deliah waved her to sit. "Not so fast. You want to talk, let's talk. Strategy, action plan, weighing options, but I'm not going to listen to 'I'm a failure' kinda talk. You want something bad enough you've got to go after it and if it doesn't work out, you deal with the consequences later. You want to find that horse of yours, you don't give up when some batshit crazy lady *tells* you she's dead. You want to find out who burned up your place, you confront that red truck-driving guy and find out. Do something, girl."

Pia opened her mouth to object, but Deliah shut her words down with a cross look. She held up a hand, causing her bracelets to jingle down her arm. "I know it's not easy, it might be dangerous, and you'll probably have to break a few laws to find out. But what's the cost of never trying? Of giving up?" One perfectly shaped eyebrow slid up a fraction of an inch.

Pia chewed on her bottom lip. "You're right."

"I know I'm right. And that 'I'm a failure' talk is nonsense. I heard from a reliable source that you got that scamming ex of yours to back down."

Pia snorted. "By reliable source, you mean my lawyer and your lover boy, Desmond, you mean. So much for client confidentiality."

"No, he didn't tell me anything confidential. Just said it looked like old Ron was backing away from his claim to your property and was splitting the assets fifty-fifty." She looked at Pia under her brows and spoke in a conspiratorial tone. "You must know where the bodies are buried on that boy."

"You know it. But live, underage, sexy young intern bodies."

Deliah gave an approving nod. "Use whatever weapons you have to. That's what I say."

Pia knew her friend was right. Doing something was better than sitting around, wondering, worrying.

"Same goes for Captain America. You've got to make a move. If you don't, you might never find out."

Pia pulled up the progress report on her failed attempts to find Bourbon Ball and filled in the new information she learned about Greener Pastures. She added a note, stating that in her opinion the likelihood of the horse's body being found was slim. It was a depressing case without closure. She'd tapped her pal Gary Paulson as a track official to research any horses matching BB's description turning up at auction, but it seemed every direction she turned, she was met with a roadblock. Deliah was right, she needed to do *something*, but what?

Jim Monroe's card with her case number was pinned to her corkboard. Since she'd tipped him off to what they'd found in Wright's military records, maybe the police or investigator found something else to link him to the fire. He had told her to call for updates. Pia pulled down the card and dialed the police investigator's number. A bored-sounding official took her case number and said to hold while he'd check.

An officer came on the line who sounded like an officious high school kid. "In light of what you told us, we went back over the debris found at the site. It didn't yield any new insights or connection in the case."

"What kind of debris?" Pia knew they'd raked the yard for any signs of an accelerant and bagged it all up and took it with them. They tried to discern the tire tracks in the slush, but they were such a mess after the emergency equipment and everyone else had driven or tracked through the gravel, churned up with slush, that it was an impossible task.

"What kinds?" he repeated, like it was a ridiculous request. "Well, nothing helpful." He read from a list: "A plastic dog toy, the arm off of a pair of sunglasses, a horseshoe—"

"Wait. A horseshoe?" Pia asked.

"The scene of the fire was on a horse farm, correct?" He was losing patience with her.

"Yeah, but..." Pia thought it was strange to find a shoe in *front* of the barn, especially when most of her old guys were barefoot. "What kind of horseshoe?"

"What do you mean, ma'am? It's steel, has nail holes, round..."

"Round? Do you have a picture you can text me?"

A sigh brushed her ear. He thinks she's a crackpot. Too bad. In a minute, an image of a heart bar horseshoe pinged onto her phone. It was a specialty shoe, made to support horses that had foundered or needed extra support. Most of them were handmade for a custom fit. None of her horses had ever worn one. It was possible it fell out of her blacksmith's truck, but he hadn't been out to her place for almost two months. She blew up the image, which displayed the shoe front and back. There, in the corner, she spotted something.

"Hey, can you check what it says on the back. There's something engraved." She knew shoes sometimes had the size pressed into the metal, but this was something else.

Another sigh. "Um, looks like letters, ma'am."

"What do they say?" she asked, although she suspected she knew.

"It's stamped H.W."

"They're initials. For Huey Wright maybe?"

It didn't take long for the police to track down Mr. Wright and bring him in for questioning. Pia got a courtesy call from the detective handling the case because she had provided most of the leads. He wanted to know if she knew of any reason motivating the arson—anything that would connect her with Wright, any business dealings with him, any people they knew in common.

"Dr. Usoro, ask him about her," Pia advised. "I witnessed an argument between them a few days ago," Pia faltered. She didn't reveal how she'd come upon them at the diner by following an illegal GPS tracker planted on Usoro's car. "Anyway, Dr. Usoro was in a legal battle with my father years ago and is responsible for possibly killing a horse we used to own." Pia knew she had no proof, other than what Usoro herself said.

The detective grunted. "We'll look into the connection."

Pia thanked him and hung up. If Wright was acting on Usoro's orders to burn down her barn, she wouldn't be surprised.

When she walked out of the office at four, it was almost dark. She crossed the small parking area and clicked open her car door. A man's voice right behind her sent her heart hammering against her chest.

"Should be more careful before you unlock your car. Look around first."

She spun around to find Watkins behind her. He had one hand on the open car door.

"Thanks for the tip, but people don't usually get carjacked in the business park. What are you doing here?"

He shut the door, took her arm, and pulled her away from the car. "Come with me." He led her a few feet to where his black SUV was parked and ushered her inside. The car was still warm. He sat in the driver's seat and turned to her. "I wanted to talk to you."

"Okay, but this feels like some sort of clandestine dead drop. Why didn't you just call?"

Pia searched his face. He didn't give his emotions away, but it seemed he was tense, on high alert for some reason. His eyes were overly quick, taking everything in.

"What is it?" she asked. "What's wrong? Is it Caleb?" She touched his leg.

"No." A grateful smile crossed his face and vanished. "Nothing like that." He drew in a breath and Pia sensed her muscles tightening, waiting. "We found Median lab and we're going in tonight."

Her lips formed the question, *What?* but he hurried on.

"I can't explain, other than to tell you if there's a chance Regalo is there and still alive, I want to get her out. But I need help."

Pia found herself nodding dumbly. A million questions sprang to mind: *Where is the lab? How did he find it? What did he mean, we're going in?* "I thought you were shut out."

His gaze shifted away. "I convinced them otherwise. A few days ago."

The pieces shuffled around in her head like the lottery balls in that spinning wire cage. They came to rest on one troubling thought. "You've known where the lab is for a few days? A few *days*? We could have gone there to get her. Or, you could have told me. Why didn't you?" She hated how her voice broke at the end.

He rubbed both palms along his thighs. "I couldn't. The information was classified, besides, the place is guarded, alarmed, and it's not likely we could just waltz in and take a horse."

"We could have tried. A few days might have been the difference between Regalo being alive or dead."

"The people running Median are dangerous. They called in the SRT—Homeland's SWAT team—along with the local police to secure the area. They hope to make arrests and seize evidence without anyone getting hurt. There's also some innocent folks working there who aren't involved in"—he hesitated, as if choosing his words carefully—"what Median's doing."

"Which is?" Pia asked even though she knew he probably couldn't tell her.

He shook his head. "Illegal medical practices. Very lucrative, so the ones in charge are pretty anxious not to get caught. Problem is, they've been tipped we might be on to them and indications are they've started shutting down, destroying evidence." He looked her in the eye, imploring her to understand. "And that means—"

"Regalo might already be dead. If not, it means you have to hurry."

Watkins gave one curt nod. "Tonight."

It felt like she'd wolfed down a rancid meal. Her gut was heavy, churning. All her muscles drained of strength. She knew where that tip came from. When she mentioned Median to Usoro at the track that day. She might have signed Regalo's death warrant.

"You said it's dangerous, but you're going with them, the SWAT guys?"

His mouth hitched. "There's nothing in the plan to save the animals. I made a promise to Regalo, and I intend to keep it if I can."

"What are the chances she's still alive?"

He looked down. "Not good."

Pia clasped his hand. His fingers closed around it. "But we have to try. What do you need me to do?"

※※※

An hour before she had to leave for the planned rendezvous, she checked the map again for the hundredth time. Watkins had emailed her an address and told her to open it in Google maps. It displayed a strip mall on a rural state route in western Maryland. He had her enlarge it and pointed to the surrounding area.

"I want you to park the horse trailer behind this auto body shop. There's enough trailers and panel trucks sitting back there that you won't look suspicious. Anyone passing will assume you're dropping it off for repair. There's no night guards and only one security camera on the other end of the building. It doesn't face that end," he'd instructed her. Pia replayed their conversation in her head, how he'd planned every detail of the operation for her.

"So I just wait with the trailer?" she'd asked. "What if Regalo's not there? What if something happens inside or the police come by and ask me what I'm doing?" Her voice scaled up a notch.

He slid a hand behind her shoulders and tugged her closer. She leaned, yielding to his insistent pressure. His face moved closer. He whispered into her hair, "You don't have to do this if you're afraid. I'll figure something out, but if she's alive, I wanted us both to be there."

She pulled pack and looked up at him. His face so close, she could smell the hint of his aftershave. His lips moved, shaping the word he never voiced—*together*.

Pia should have wrapped her hand around the back of his head then and pulled him in, pressing her lips to his. She should have fallen into his arms, resting her head against his chest to listen to his beating heart and told him... Told him what?

She shook her head, scattering the memories of earlier that day. Told him what? That she loved him? Did she? Now she had to focus. She had to keep her head looking straight ahead only at the next task in front of her. Hooking up the trailer took twice as long as normal because her hands shook and she fumbled with all the connections. She double- and triple-checked the batteries in her phone, the supplies laid in for the horse in case of emergency, the wrecking bar she stowed under the front seat. She didn't know what she was in for tonight. Watkins hadn't explained a lot. He couldn't answer many of her questions. He only told her she might hear fire engines, possibly police sirens. They set up a signal—he'd text her *go home* if Regalo wasn't there. But when? How long was she supposed to wait?

She'd fed the horses outside and laid in an extra supply of hay in case she was late getting home. Hillary was standing by if she needed someone to fill in. Dark descended over the farm with a quiet that reached into Pia's heart and stilled the anxious thumping. In the pure, dark cold air she looked up at the sky. The stars were bright. The night was still and cloudless.

"Are you still alive Regalo? If you are, we're coming for you. Hang on."

Her eyes stung in the cold. She looked to her house. Ryder was fed and dreaming about chasing rabbits on his bed in the kitchen. The old horses nosed their hay and snorted. A clear moon cast light enough for her to see the outline of the barn, the work that would be done when the insurance came through, the fence line Watkins had repaired. It would be okay.

But it would be better if Regalo came home.

She opened the door of the truck and hopped in. It was a long ride to the rendezvous point behind the strip mall. She wondered what Watkins was doing now. Was he a little scared like she was? Probably not. He'd been in combat. He wouldn't be vibrating with anxiety like an addict trying to hang on without a fix. She started the engine and felt the hum in the quiet night. This was it. She shifted into gear, checking that her phone had the directions programmed. The voice, the calm sterile voice, told her to proceed on the main road. "You'll be keeping me company tonight," she told it. In the dark cocoon of the truck's cabin, alone, she allowed herself to cry.

Chapter 37

Watkins

The team rolled out at nine. They stowed equipment and piled in the van, giving each other silent glances. It was hard to read whether the looks were a plea for encouragement or the face of bravado, saying, *Let's go kick some ass.* In the end, two ways of expressing the same thing. They were scared and needed to know someone had their backs. Watkins knew those looks. He'd seen them in his own men before a combat op.

The men sat along benches in the back of a van alongside firefighting equipment they'd shrug on when they entered the lab. Approximately ten minutes before arrival, the cyber geeks would set off the alarms on Median's computer system, alerting those inside that a fire was detected in a critical lab. Protocol dictated that nonessential personnel evacuate immediately. The local fire station would stage an engine, just before they pulled up and spilled into the facility, ushering any lingering personnel outside and securing the area.

Watkins checked his phone, tracking Pia's progress. She was on her way. Last check, before he shut it off. Specht had ordered a complete communications blackout. No distractions. The op had an internal, secure comms net set up and it was to remain clear in case of an emergency. He had no idea how closely Specht was monitoring the team and would only risk contacting Pia if things went bad. It was up to her now.

Intel confirmed the two Median targets, Erikson and Arslan, were on the premises. They'd been ordered to start shipping out product and destroying any evidence. It was unlikely they'd gotten the word about Morrow's arrest yet.

Watkins sat across from two SRT members, dressed like him in black T-shirts and cargo pants, ready to don firefighting jackets large enough to hide their Kevlar vests and sidearms. His mission was backup—to scour the rest of the facility while the SRT went into the Median lab after the targets. That was fine with him. It worked with his plan to locate Regalo and get her out the back, while most of the security and police were concentrated elsewhere.

Specht sat in the passenger seat, waiting to receive word that the alarms at the lab had been tripped. The timing was essential in order to take advantage of the confusion. The hum of the oversized tires and the grim faces of the other team members triggered Watkins's memories. Men together, driving into an ambush. He shook off the thought.

Specht turned to Watkins and the other agents seated in the back. "Confirmation the alarm's been triggered. We'll arrive in five."

When the van pulled into the parking lot, a fire engine, ambulance, EMT/Hazmat vehicle were staged outside the entrance. A tendril of smoke oozed out of the main entrance. Watkins surveyed the scene while donning the firefighter's overcoat, admiring the efficiency of the SRT's planning. He and Specht passed through the handful of personnel standing outside, while two other team members ushered the stunned workers away from the building.

Specht signaled Watkins to follow. "Median's area is in the back." They passed through a reception area into a large lab with workbenches crowded with air hoods, glassware, and disabled equipment. Specht headed to a door in the back, which led into an airlock. A cipher lock keypad was mounted to the wall to the left of the door. The other two SRT agents joined them. They reported the personnel had dispersed and the local police were keeping the area clear. Specht nodded.

"Video surveillance indicates Erikson and Arslan never came out of the Median lab," the young agent with the blond buzz cut said.

Specht shucked off his firefighter's coat and unholstered his weapon.

"Watkins, you search the remainder of the facility and warehouse. The others with me." Punching in a code, Specht and the two SRT officers entered the airlock leading to Median's most secure area. The door closed behind them with a quiet swish of air.

Watkins crossed back through the general lab into the reception area, but took a right down a long hallway. Open doors revealed various offices, a conference room, and restrooms. He cleared each, determining that no one occupied them. A solid door with a small window stood at the end of the hall. He looked inside. Dim overhead lighting shone on metal shelves filled with boxes, equipment, and what appeared to be medical supplies. According to the floor plan, this was the warehouse. He reached around his side and unsnapped the strap holding his weapon. He shoved the door open with his foot and stepped behind the shelter of the wall. Nothing. He entered the room, searching for a switch that would provide better lighting than the dim reddish glow from the night security lights. He found a plate of switches on the wall inside the door and turned them all on. The cavernous room burst into light. Methodically, he passed down each row, checking that they were empty, then circled to the back of the room. There was a set of double doors. He could feel cooler air leaking from underneath them. He turned the handle and pushed one door open a crack.

The earthy smell of cedar shavings and animal dung hit his nose before his eyes could make out the movement in the cages. He pushed open the door and waited. Rustling, scurrying sounds. He groped for the light switch. When he turned it on, hundreds of tiny eyes blinked and stared back at him. Banks of cages lined one wall. Rabbits, rats, and mice tracked his progress through the room. The room was cool, as special air handlers hummed, filtering the air. His comms gear pinged. Specht reporting. Both suspects were in custody and were being brought out the front door to a waiting police vehicle. His shoulders unclenched a degree. He wouldn't have much time before the team rolled out.

A low nicker from a corner behind some stacked feedbags and bedding. Watkins holstered his weapon and strode toward the sound.

Two shadowy horses lifted their heads and looked back at him.

His pulse throbbed in his neck as he moved quickly to check if it was her, if they were okay. Another low, rumbling nicker caused the mare's sides to vibrate. Sides, that showed her telltale stripes although her coat was dull.

"You're alive, thank God." The whispered prayer caught in his throat.

The mare dropped her head as he ran his hand along her face. There was no sign of hay and her water bucket was empty. Tubing ran along a swivel arm and into a needle taped to her neck.

"What are they doing to you?" he whispered while he traced the tubing to the other end. It ran outside her stall and was secured to the wall. It wasn't attached to anything, but it was clear that the port in her neck was for the convenience of pumping whatever into the mare whenever they needed to, without having to go into the stall. Watkins slipped the needle out of her neck, wound up the tubing, and chucked it onto the floor outside. A fine trickle of blood dripped down her neck.

The other horse stood quietly with his head lowered. He was a tall, lanky bay with a lightning bolt blaze. His lids were half closed over dull, brown eyes.

Watkins grabbed the halter off the hook outside his stall. "We're getting you both out of here," he told the bay horse. He went to the sliding rear doors, which opened to a small, enclosed back lot with a dumpster. Just past the gate was the strip of trees that separated the back lot from the rear of the strip mall where Pia should be waiting with the trailer. He slid open the door and paused to see if any of the agents had been sent around back to survey the area. If they had, it was clear now.

It didn't take much coaxing to get the bay to walk out beside him, but he was weak. Watkins had to move slower than he would have liked. A wash of relief hit him when he spotted the white of Pia's horse trailer visible through the trees. When he stepped through the gap into the parking lot, she jumped from the truck.

"That's not Regalo." Her face contorted with pain. "Does that mean...?"

He handed her the lead rope. "No, she's there. I think you might be looking for this one, too." He searched her face waiting for the transformation.

"Oh, my God. The blaze..."

He pointed to the horse's halter with a rusted nameplate. The letters BB barely legible.

"Bourbon Ball?"

"Let's get him loaded, give him something to drink. I don't know how long they've been in there without food or water."

Pia swung into action. BB loaded like he knew he was going home.

Watkins lifted the trailer ramp and came around to the trailer's side door where Pia stood, stroking the geldings head. "I'll be right back with Regalo. Don't move. The team captured their main objectives, but we don't know for sure who else might be around."

"Okay," Pia answered. Her voice was small. He could tell she was scared.

He headed back to the path through the wood when he heard her call to him.

"Hey, Jonah. Check six."

He smiled and held a thumb up before he ducked back into the trees.

Chapter 38

Pia

She gave BB some water, which he sipped between pulling mouthfuls from the hay net. She snapped a picture of his face and pulled up the file photo she had of BB. It was exactly the same. When he took a breather from eating, she lifted his upper lip and snapped a photo of his tattoo. It was blurred, but confirmed it was him. She sent all the photos to her boss, Mr. Burke, and told him there were new developments in the case. To say the least!

The air was cold enough to see her breath, and the only light came from the security lights mounted on the back corner of the building. She had lost track of time, but it seemed like Watkins should have been back long before now. She sat in the truck but didn't want to turn on the engine to run the heat in case it attracted attention. She was supposed to be parked back here for a repair job. It was pretty sketchy cover, but there was no sense making it obvious it was a lie. BB was quiet in the trailer.

Through the trees, she watched the spinning blue lights on the EMT vehicle as it drove away down the long access road. That was a good sign, she thought. Parked along the back of the facility, she couldn't see what other vehicles might still remain out front or whether there were people still milling around. Watkins said they got the main guys. He said Regalo was in there and he was bringing her right out. What was the problem? He also said to sit tight.

For how long?

Another fifteen minutes passed. Something must have happened. Maybe Regalo was giving him problems. She fingered the syringe with a few cc's of tranquilizer she'd brought with her just in case. Acepromazine—what everyone simply called Ace—had taken the edge off many a fractious racehorse in Pia's experience. She didn't want to ship a tranquilized horse, but if that's what it took to get out of here tonight... She got out of the truck. It wouldn't hurt to look beyond the stand of trees. Maybe she'd spot Watkins coming. She checked that BB was quiet and shut up the trailer. Before she closed the truck door, she pulled the short wrecking bar out from under her seat and slipped it under her coat inside her waistband. Just in case.

Her boots crunched across the loose gravel parking area as she approached the spot where Watkins emerged with BB. It was easy to spot with branches broken back and a deep horse hoof print. She eased a limb out of her way and entered the stand of trees. In a few feet, the glow of security lights in the rear of the building guided her way. There was a fenced enclosure with its gate swung wide open. That must be where he came from. She headed down a slight incline, slipping in the wet grass. At the edge of the parking area she stopped and listened. No panicked calling from BB. Good. But no clop of horse hooves signaling Regalo's approach, either. Not good.

Maybe if she looked inside to see if he needed help? If he did, and she was another set of hands, he'd be happy to see her. If not, well, he'd be furious. She could slip in and take a look without him spotting her, that way, if he was okay, she'd leave and dash back to the trailer.

She took a deep breath, secured the iron bar, which was slipping down her pants, and tiptoed inside the enclosure. Nothing here, just a dumpster. Hugging the wall, she approached the open double door. Voices.

Her heart climbed up her throat. What was going on? Even if the woman was a Homeland Security official or a police officer, it meant Watkins was stopped from bringing Regalo out. She couldn't make out the words. Light shone out the doorway, but she was shrouded in darkness. If she took a look, they probably wouldn't spot her. Pia peeled her back off the wall and turned just enough to peek inside.

Something was wrong. The woman with her back to Pia was holding Regalo. In her other hand, she pressed a syringe to the mare's neck. A syringe with bright pink fluid. Pia knew what that was. It was always colored bright pink to ensure it was never confused with anything else. It would kill a horse in minutes. Watkins had his eyes glued to the syringe with his hands half lifted in the air. A pistol was on the floor between them.

Pia ducked back. Oh, my God. She listened through the whoosh of blood pounding in her ears and recognized the woman's voice. Usoro.

Pieces of her sentences floated out into the still night. *Don't call out or...until after I leave...I will kill her and you.*

Where was everyone? Maybe if she left, skirted around the front, found the guy in charge and told him to come back and save Watkins. But by then, would Regalo be dead? Pia pressed her head against the brick wall, willing a decision to come to her. *What to do?*

Watkins's voice floated through the air, low and devoid of emotion. "Morrow knew the SRT were coming in soon, so he sent you. He didn't want to risk it, so he sent you instead. He set you up."

Pia couldn't hear the rest under Regalo's piercing whinny. She looked around the corner in time to see Usoro lash her with the end of the lead rope.

"Shut up," she ordered. Her hand holding the syringe flinched.

Pia's heart pumped so hard she thought it was going to burst up her throat. She took a breath, but it entered her body in ragged waves. Her hands felt as if her veins were full of amphetamines, making her tremble. She couldn't wait. Usoro's fear and tension pulsated out of the room in electric waves. Something bad was going to happen. Any minute.

Pia crouched and ducked around the corner into the room. She remained hidden by a pile of feedbags. The wrecking bar pressed into the small of her back, scraping the skin raw. She eased it out. If she distracted Usoro, Watkins could grab his gun. If she didn't plunge the syringe into Regalo first.

The mare shuffled, dancing on the end of the lead rope, spun up by the nervous scent in the room. Pia wiped her sweating palms on her pants and hefted the bar. About a third of the length of javelin. Heavier. Could she hit a target from here or would she miss and smash her horse's head instead? She'd have to stand, run a few steps to close the distance. Throw, or take a swing at Usoro? Her legs were cramping. She waited, watching for an opportunity. If only Regalo would move away.

A throaty whinny sounded from outside, beyond the trees. Regalo lifted her head and answered back. She twisted, jerking Usoro off her stance for a second.

Pia leaped from hiding. Her old muscle memory kicked in with a galloping stride as she swung the bar in front of her, smashing it down on Usoro's shoulders. She crumpled to her feet, dropping the syringe and the rope. A surge of fury swept over Pia, crushing her back teeth together as she raised the bar, poised to bring it pounding down again on the woman's back. She braced for a blow but felt resistance. Strong hands wrapped around hers and eased the bar out of her grip.

Watkins kicked the syringe away. He loosened his grip on her wrist and brushed her hair with his lips pressed against her ear. "Stop. It's over."

A clang resounded as the bar dropped to the cement floor, followed by a clattering of hooves.

"Regalo." Pia stomped on the lead rope, stopping the mare in her tracks. She picked it up, reeling in the horse with soft comforting words. Regalo's nostrils were flared, her eye showing white. "It's okay, girl." Her voice broke. Everything inside broke into a million pieces and spilled out. "You're my lucky horse. Everything will be okay."

Watkins picked up his weapon and jammed it into the holster. Usoro laid still at his feet. "Go on," he waved at her. "Get Regalo out of here. Hurry!"

Pia started to the back door with Regalo trotting at her side. She turned in time to see Watkins lift the comms receiver out of his belt and disappear back inside the lab.

Chapter 39

Pia

Watkins drove and Pia let him. At the same time she was both super wired, like she'd downed four energy drinks, and heavy with fatigue to the point of being numb. They rode in silence. Several hours later, the truck and trailer loaded with Regalo and BB turned into her driveway. The horses living out in the fields stood by the fence and watched the unusual activity in the middle of the night.

Earlier, after she had loaded Regalo, a policeman blinded her with his flashlight. She had to walk in front of him *with her hands visible* to where the local police had set up a field headquarters outside the facility. She caught Watkins's eye in the crowd gathered by an unmarked van. She looked for a sign from him, but he gave away nothing. For another hour, the police and Agent Specht grilled her with questions about why she was there, about the horses, and her associations with Median Diagnostics. The police took her statement and ran a search against what she had told them about the stolen racehorse and her association with Usoro. After taking down her contact information, copy of her license, and ordering her to report the next day for a more extensive interview, they let her go.

"So I can take the horses?" she asked.

A uniformed officer called over to a muscular man dressed in black, huddled with a group of SRT agents. "Hey Specht. Lady wants to know if she can take the horses out of here?"

Specht turned with a cross expression. "What? I don't give a damn about the horses. Get them outta here." When he returned his attention to the group, Watkins leaned over and spoke with him. Specht gave him a wave of dismissal, and Watkins jogged to Pia's side.

"I'll drive you," he said and took the keys from her hand.

In front of her burned shell of a barn, he helped unload the horses and turn them out in an isolated back field, far from the others in case they were infected with anything contagious. They worked in silence, tossing in piles of hay and filling water buckets.

When the gate clanged shut, they stood watching the ghostly figures of the two horses in the field, outlined by a waning moon. The night air chilled her back, still damp from panicked sweat. She plucked at her shirt, lifting it away from her clammy skin. Her head throbbed and she wanted to change out of her dirty clothes and fall into bed. But she didn't move. Watkins stood by her side, his shoulder brushing hers. The closeness of his body, his warmth against the frigid air, his quiet presence held her to the spot.

"The police asked me a lot of questions. So did Specht," she said. She expected him to grill her with questions on the way home. Instead, he was quiet as if accepting of whatever the consequences of their actions. She felt rather than heard the rush of air leave Watkins's body.

She turned to face him. "What you did to save Regalo tonight..."

His eyes lifted to meet hers. In the dim light, they looked soft, calm. A small smile tugged at the corner of his lips. "We did save her, didn't we? Just like I promised."

Pia ran a hand up his arm. "Thank you. Especially since I know what it cost." While waiting in the trailer she had calculated the risk of Specht or Abramson finding out Watkins had disobeyed orders and arranged to have her there, threatening the security of the operation and compromising the collection of evidence...all those things the police mentioned this evening. If they knew...and Pia was sure he assumed they did. "If Abramson finds out what you did, will he fire you?"

His face registered surprise. "If. How can he not know? As for being fired, I'll be lucky if that's all they do."

Pia leaned with her back to the fence and tilted her face up to the clear sky. "Someone told me once life's not about luck. It's planning. If you plan right, you make your own luck." She stifled a smirk.

His voice, deep and resonant, was edged with amusement. "Whoever told you that was a self-important, pompous ass." He propped his arms on the top fence board and continued to stare out into the field. "A lot of life is pure luck and we have no power to control it. And we shouldn't try."

"I disagree."

He turned. An eyebrow twitched up. "How so?"

"You said you'd be lucky if all they do is fire you. Well, maybe they won't do anything."

He made a scoffing noise. "Oh, they'll do something all right. But it was worth it."

"Maybe not. Because they don't think you had anything to do with me being there."

Pia watched his expression. His eyes narrowed. A look of realization, then worry swept over his face. "What did you say?"

"I told them I was following Usoro. I admitted to having the illegal tracker on her. As far as they know, I was there on my own. Here's the deal: I was investigating the disappearance of a client's racehorse. I had reason to believe Usoro was involved because of her association with the guy who tried to burn down my barn. They were seen together. So I followed her in an attempt to find BB. It just so happens Regalo was rescued as well."

"You lied to them." Watkins shook his head.

"I didn't lie. I told them about the device. They concluded I tracked Usoro there. I told them about the investigation into BB's disappearance. They figured out I was there to find that horse. They drew their own conclusions." She gave his shoulder a little bump with hers. "C'mon, I didn't want you to get in trouble. To be punished for doing the right thing."

"You took a huge risk tonight. You were lucky."

"Luck had nothing to do with it."

·∗∗∗∗ ∗∗∗∗·

The interview room at the local police headquarters was nicer than what she imagined based on TV shows. There was a large table surrounded by padded chairs, a white board on the far wall, and some attractive prints on the walls. When she arrived, the detective who was looking into her arson case was already seated at the table, huddled over some papers with the younger officer. Maybe the guy she spoke with on the phone about the horseshoe. He looked up when she came in, stood, and pulled out a chair.

"Miss Murphy, this is Officer Escarra. I believe you may have spoken on the phone already," Detective Jesseaume said.

Escarra's ears reddened. Perhaps it was the officious know-it-all.

Pia sat at the table opposite them. She placed her purse on the floor, clutched between her feet. She rested her hands on the table, folded them, then decided it looked too much like she was praying and dropped them into her lap.

Jesseaume was tall, dressed in a dark suit that emphasized his lanky frame. He folded himself into a seat, rolled sideways onto a hip, and pulled something from his suit pocket.

He placed the GPS monitor on the table between them.

Pia sat up and opened her mouth to speak, but thought better of it. She'd consulted with Desmond Cornell, her lawyer and Deliah's lover, for advice before showing up at this interview. Like all good lawyers, he advised her to only answer the questions and not offer anything extra.

"This tracker was recovered last night from Dr. Usoro's vehicle." He pulled the stack of file folders closer and tapped the top one. "I have the full report of your statement from the scene. Tell me, are you a licensed private investigator, member of a law enforcement agency, or legal owner of the doctor's vehicle?"

Pia shook her head. "No, I'm not."

Jesseaume pressed his lips together. "I have a statement from your employer here that you were tasked with recovering missing or stolen goods—a racehorse—and as such were concerned that Dr. Usoro was involved." He raised his dark eyebrows, seeking an answer.

Pia said, "That's correct."

Officer Escarra pointed to a line in the report in front of his boss and whispered something Pia couldn't make out. She had used the tracker illegally, but it wasn't like she was the one stealing horses or setting fires. What was going on? She spoke up. "Could I get a glass of water or something?"

Jesseaume sent the younger officer on the errand and as soon as the door shut behind him, the detective sat back and laughed.

Pia jolted in her seat.

"Miss Murphy, this is the craziest case the Property Crimes Unit has come across." He slapped the folder. "You've got the feds, Homeland, and local police scrambling all across three counties chasing after international criminals, stolen racehorses, and crazed firebugs. Reports have been coming in all morning." He shook his head. "Look, you broke the law with the tracker, but I doubt Dr. Usoro is in any position to press charges. My job today and your reason for being here is to answer any outstanding questions before I put this thing to rest."

Her shoulders, which had been hovering somewhere around her ears, dropped and she relaxed. Escarra returned with a cold bottle of water dripping with condensation and placed it on the table in front of her. She pulled a Kleenex from her purse and placed it underneath. Watkins was rubbing off on her after all.

"All right, let's get started. You tell me everything that happened last night and leading up to your wild horse chase," Jesseaume smiled at his own cleverness, "and Escarra takes notes. Then, we answer your questions and tie up any loose ends."

Pia unscrewed the cap and took a long swallow before launching into a tale that began with selling Regalo years ago and ended with her attacking a woman in a lab involved in international counterfeit drug distribution. But there were still big gaps in the story, which she intended to have answered.

"About Usoro...is she going to be okay? I mean, I hit her pretty hard."

"The hospital reported she is in stable condition. And having a lot to say. Seems she's been charged along with her husband in the counterfeit drug charges."

"Wait. Who's her husband?" Pia asked.

"Turns out the head guy, Morrow. The Homeland guys and intel spooks only let us cops in on so much in this type of operation, but it turns out Morrow was a *nom de guerre* as it were. He's married to Dr. Usoro and has been trying to throw her under the bus for the whole operation."

Pia chewed on this new piece of information. That's why she was associated with Median, but it didn't explain what Usoro was doing with the horses. "If the drugs were counterfeit, why did she need lab animals to test anything? Why the horses? It never made sense to me."

"That's where your firebug Huey Wright provided the answers. He dropped a dime as they say on his old business partner, Dr. Usoro. Seems they had a deal wherein he'd provide donated horses through his fake rescue scam for her to use for a fee. When she complained she needed younger, healthier ones, he pushed back. Wanted to know why. Turns out, she wasn't involved in her husband's drug distribution hub, but was using the lab for her own research. Had some idea she could enhance racehorse performance. Speed them up and evade drug testing with something she was working on called"—he rifled through the notes in a folder—"gene-targeted something or other, I can't make sense of it. Her husband was backing the research, figuring he'd making a killing if she were successful. Even if it didn't work, he likely had a scheme for selling the stuff. Anyway, her pal Huey, who was providing the horse test subjects, had a sweet system going whereby he'd get them donated to his fake rescue, sell them to Usoro, and then take them across the border when she was done with them."

Pia held the cool water bottle against her forehead, which had started to pound. "Those poor horses." The words "gene-targeted" tripped some itch in Pia's mind. She knew Usoro was a geneticist by specialty. Was that it? The fact that Regalo was a chimera—with two sets of DNA—would that make her an especially valuable test subject that Usoro would jump at the chance to get her. It finally made sense. As much as anything that crazy woman did made sense.

"But Wright started taking chances, cutting corners, and that's what got him in trouble," Escarra piped up. His boyish round face didn't match the serious way he conducted himself. "In an effort to lay his hands on younger horses that Usoro would pay more for, he nabbed Bourbon Ball. He knew the horse was going to be donated, but didn't count on the guy checking up on him. That fight you witnessed between Usoro and Wright, that was when she found out what was going on and the fact that he'd brought an investigation down on their heads. Your investigation. You see, Wright was her eyes and ears at the track and elsewhere. And she heard soon enough that things were getting hotter. Wright took matters in his own hands the way he knew best—arson. He figured he'd scare you off or at least have a bit of revenge on you for the trouble you caused."

"He told her who I was that day I confronted her," Pia said. "And he probably also found out where I lived. There are plenty of people who knew me there."

Detective Jesseaume tapped the GPS tracker. "We'll be keeping this," he said but gave her a smile.

She stood to leave.

The two police officers got to their feet. "We'll be in touch if we have any more questions," Escarra said, getting in the last word.

Chapter 40

Murphy's Law Farm and Pegasus Equestrian Therapy Center

One Month Later

Pia had made it a habit to bring a huge thermos of coffee down to the barn each morning for the workmen. They'd made amazing progress tearing out the scorched wood and fire damage, rehabbing the old barn so it was better than ever. The smell of freshly-cut wood wafting on the cool morning air lifted her spirits. The worst of the winter storms so far had passed them by and she'd managed to house the more vulnerable old horses in the few stalls that were spared any damage. Soon she'd have a bank of new ones with fancy sliding doors, wrought iron trim, and new lighting. By this time of the evening, all the workers had left and she retrieved the washed-out thermos that was left each night on a bench.

Regalo and Bourbon Ball had become fast friends, maybe because of their shared ordeal. She was glad O'Dell, BB's owner, gifted her the young horse. He'd recovered and put on weight, but was still a quiet, sweet horse. He never wanted to be a racer, so now he had a chance at a bright, new career—as a therapy horse. Selma Bennett was anxious to get started with him as soon as the vet cleared him for work. Here, at Murphy's Law. Selma had found herself without a home base from which she could run her therapy business and Pia had just the solution. As soon as she gained full, unencumbered ownership of Murphy's Law, they formed a joint venture and this time Pia was careful to read all the fine print. She had learned a lot over the past few months.

Pia dragged the hose to top off the water in the trough, watching as Regalo pushed BB away from the pile of hay. Always a fiery mare, Pia thought. After they unraveled the paper trail, it turned out Selma was still the legal owner. But that was okay. The mare was home, where she belonged, at least for now.

Things were returning to normal. Better than normal. Her farm was safe. She had a new business partner who loved horses as much as she did. And not least of all, she'd evaded prosecution for the tracking incident…probably thanks to Detective Jesseaume. Everything had fallen neatly into place except for one thing.

Watkins.

She didn't know where she stood with Jonah. There was that almost kiss. The hugs. The meaningful glances. But were they expressions of comfort, concern, or a shared triumph and nothing more? Maybe it was Ron. Watkins knew he was out of the picture, but perhaps he thought it was too soon to start something new. *That's the problem, he thinks too much.* She knew Selma intended to gift Regalo to him and that was fine with her. The only concern over that was the fact that Regalo was the glue that held them together. He could change jobs and move the mare somewhere else. The sound of water sloshing over the rim of the trough and onto the hard ground snapped Pia out of her reverie.

She shut off the flow with a twist of her wrist. If only she could shut off feelings that easily.

※※※

Watkins left work early to make it to the vet before they closed. The week after the Median incident as it had been come to be known as, Abramson had strongly encouraged Watkins take a week's "vacation." The time off was actually administrative leave while officials looked into certain irregularities committed during the Median operation. To his relief, there was no further word from the investigation other than it had been closed to everyone's satisfaction. Inwardly he winced, knowing the old Watkins would have spoken up to admit to his wrongdoing, but now he saw that sometimes the end did indeed justify the means. The op was a success and Regalo was safe with Pia.

Pia.

Over the past month he had stepped back, giving her room in case it was only the shared passion over the hunt for Regalo that had thrown them together. He was protecting himself by being the one who opened the gap. She had the horse. Her farm was secure. She didn't need him. But did she want him? Pia has an expressive personality. Should he read her touches as anything more than shared enthusiasm, hope, and encouragement as they worked together during the intense search for Regalo? Stacey's stinging rejection at the rehab hospital haunted his thoughts every time he reached out to Pia, hungering to wrap her in his arms. He couldn't and he wouldn't set himself up for another rejection like that. He'd give her a chance to step back if she wanted. And give himself a graceful exit if necessary.

He pulled in at the vet's and approached the receptionist.

"I'm here to pick up my cat. MacArthur," he told the young tech at the desk. The tiny black cat had shown up on his doorstep again a few days ago, limping on a cut paw and starved. Somehow he'd managed to get him into a carrier to bring to the vet.

The tech laughed and displayed an arm covered with scratches. "Oh, yeah, he's a spicy one."

"I'm so sorry. I warned the receptionist he was a stray."

She waved away his concern. "It's nice you saved him. Most people ignore strays. Or worse."

"Someone once told me you can't save all the strays and lost souls in the world."

Her young face broke into a sad smile and she shook her head, causing her ponytail to swish across her back. "I'll get him." In a few minutes she returned with a carrier whose inhabitant sounded like a possessed demon.

Watkins paid and drove to Murphy's Law. Pia had said she would be happy to take in MacArthur because she needed a barn cat. It was a perfect place for him.

When he arrived, he lifted the growling cat carrier out of the back as Pia rushed up to help him.

"MacArthur returns!" She cried and opened her arms. For the carrier.

Watkins transferred the cat to a huge pen set up to facilitate his acclimation to his new home as chief resident barn cat. He watched Pia move with confidence and grace, all the while speaking to the frightened cat in a silly baby voice that actually made the cat pause and listen. Watkins felt like an angry feral cat himself sometimes and understood how the cat might lap up a kind word. He sat on the small bench inside the entrance and watched MacArthur glaring back at him. "Play your cards right, and you've got a great home here," he told the cat.

Pia sat next to him. "It's been quite a week. Get this, my boss Mr. Burke gave me a promotion. Said I had the necessary connections with local law enforcement, fire investigators, and"—she wiggled her eyebrows—"Homeland Security to do the job of an investigator. The down side is I have to train with Wiggins. But, it will be more responsibility, more money, more—"

"Danger?" Watkins regretted it the second the word slipped out.

Pia stared for a heartbeat without saying another word. Her eyes narrowed, as if struggling to make a decision.

"I've got something else to tell you."

Every nerve sprung to high alert.

"Selma said she's giving you Regalo." She sat back and turned her face to him. A light dusting of sawdust trailed across her cheek. He stopped his hand from rising to brush it away. The pupils of her eyes were large, dark pools. He couldn't read what she was thinking. *Was this it, then? The horse was his. He could leave. Did she want him to leave?* He opened his mouth, but she touched his knee. It sent a wave through his body.

"No, it's okay. She's really your horse. The thing is..."

Her chest rose and fell as she took a breath.

"The thing is, she brought us together."

She hadn't removed her hand. Its warmth soaked through his thigh and radiated up his chest. He watched her lips, trying to concentrate on the words. This was when she would say it was over.

"I'm afraid to lose—" her gaze skittered away. "I hope you'll keep her here. So you'll keep coming to see her."

Pia gave him a sideways glance under a curtain of dark hair. She tucked it behind her ear. The removal of her hand left a cool shadow on his leg.

A far-off whinny from a horse in the field was answered by one of the old ones inside the barn. His brain spun with the words she was saying...that she wanted him to stay.

"Well, say something." Her sharp tone broke the trance like a magician snapping his fingers.

Watkins took her hand in both of his. He kissed the reddened ends of her cold fingers. "You think it's only the horse that brings me here?" He slipped an arm behind her and eased her head down against his shoulder. She snuggled into his embrace and wrapped her arms around his waist. He rubbed the side of his scarred face against her glossy hair and breathed in the familiar scent of lilac. "Besides, you'll need me to help on those cases your boss will be giving you."

"I don't know what I'm doing." Her muffled voice sounded like a young girl. "I'm not sure where this is going." She looked up. "Any of it."

"Neither do I. I don't have a plan. I've no idea where I'm headed. But for once in my life, I'm happy to just find out when we get there."

THE END

The Devil's Luck

Book #2 in the Murphy's Law Farm Mystery Series

Murphy's Law Farm and Pegasus Equestrian Therapy Center

Pia could trace the draft of cold air straight to the broken seal on the kitchen's back door. One more thing to fix.

While she filled the carafe for the coffee pot, she twisted her head to peer out the kitchen window and check the sky. A red slash cut across the eastern horizon, hovering over the paddocks. Red sky at morning, sailors take warning. Her dad's sing-song voice sounded in her ears. Although almost dawn and still shadowy, she could make out the silhouettes of the horses, heads down, cropping at the last bits of green grass for the season.

"Wiggins will be pissed if I keep him waiting," she told Ryder as she poured a waterfall of dry kibble in his bowl. The old dog dove into his breakfast, ignoring Pia's further complaints. "I'll get to his car and have to endure an entire day of him lecturing me on how much his time is worth and how I've wasted the company's money for his expert training when I don't show up on time. Blah, blah, blah."

Pia's stomach lurched at the thought of being trapped in a car with Wiggins while he expounded on the techniques of a good stake-out. Maybe this Private Investigator training wasn't such a good idea after all. But, she had promised her boss she would work with Wiggins for a while so she could make a decision whether to go for licensing. Ugh, was it worth it? His breath reeked of stale coffee and he couldn't utter a sentence without twisting it to have a double—and lecherous—meaning. She ran upstairs to dress in as frumpy an outfit as she could find.

Downstairs, she grabbed her car keys and phone and dropped them into her coat pocket before she bolted out the door. Outside, her hand on the open driver's side door, she hesitated before dropping into the seat. A horse in the distant field was hollering and running the fence line.

Hillary, the farm manager, walked up and stood beside Pia. "What's with him?" Hillary's long, silver hair was tied back in a thick braid. She was dressed in jeans, heavy shoes, and had a pair of work gloves tucked into the waistband of her pants. The two women stood, observing the horse.

"That's Bourbon Ball. I don't get it. He's usually so low key," Pia said with an edge of worry lacing her voice.

The horse approached his water trough with neck outstretched, head low. Snorting, he spun and galloped away. His sides were dark with sweat.

"Just my luck when I'm late." Pia slammed the car door. "I hope he's not colicking." She strode down the long strip of grass between the fenced pastures toward to farthest field that ran along the edge of the woods. Her heels sunk into the wet grass and the hem of her pants was already soaked by the morning dew.

Hillary dogged her heels. "I can take care of him. If you have to get to work—"

"Thanks." Pia waited for Hillary to catch up. "But I can't leave you with a sick horse."

The two women walked side by side and Pia couldn't help but notice Hillary was getting winded from the brisk walk. Despite her rail-thin frame and muscular arms, Pia had to admit her barn help—and good friend—was getting older. Hillary lived alone in the guest trailer, and sometimes Pia worried that she didn't take as good care of herself as she did the horses.

When they reached the pasture gate, Bourbon Ball rushed to them like rescuers. His eyes were wild, the white showing, as he glanced back at the pasture as if the devil himself were after him.

"That's not the normal *I'm anxious to come in for breakfast* behavior. He's acting like he's terrified of something," Hillary said and lifted his halter off the hook beside the gate.

"Coyotes or something you think? I've heard they've been spotted in places around here lately." Pia looked to the woods as if one would magically appear and make sense of all this.

Hillary gave a one-shoulder shrug and slipped the halter on the frightened horse. "Hang on there, Seabiscuit, and we'll get you back to your stall."

By now the horses in the other fields were watching, frozen, heads high and sniffing the air.

"There's definitely something out there." Pia ran her hand over the horse's chest. It came away sticky with damp sweat and hair. "Can you manage him okay?" she asked Hillary. "I want to take a look around his field in case there's, I don't know, a dead animal or something scaring him."

Hillary waved off Pia's concern and led the horse back to the barn. Pia stood and watched the big Thoroughbred dancing and leaping on the end of his lead rope, like a kite. Not like easy-going BB at all. She shook her head and turned back to the pasture. She slipped through the gate, but still managed to smear some rust on her coat sleeve. Sheltering her eyes, she scanned the field. Nothing leapt out at her as strange—no mysterious lumps lying in the grass, no broken fence boards, no fire breathing dragons ready to strike.

"Horses." Pia signed. "Always something." She walked further into the field to get a better look around. A fetid scent rode the current and was gone. Pia lifted her chin and sniffed. Maybe there was a dead animal around. She walked along the fence toward the water trough where Bourbon had been acting strange. The smell came back on a breeze. Stronger. A scent like something rotting at low tide. Some animal climbed in the trough and couldn't get out probably. Ugh, that will be an ugly job dumping out the water and cleaning it, she thought as she strode toward the tank. The edge was about waist-high, so she couldn't see the water until she was closer.

Pia stood next to the trough and looked over the top. A face stared back at her. Eyes open. Black hair, like seaweed, swirled around a gray, bloated mask.

Pia staggered backward. "My God!"

She squeezed her eyes shut, then opened them, hoping to clear the vision. What she saw made no sense. It can't be real. Her heart slammed against her breastbone. A throbbing pulse reverbed in her neck and made a rushing noise in her ears. She straightened her back and walked two steps closer again. Keeping a distance, she leaned in to look.

A woman's body, with knees curled to chest, hovered near the bottom of the trough. A look of horror frozen on her face.

About the Author

Growing up during the Cold War, L. R. Trovillion was inspired to learn Russian, which eventually landed her a career with the U.S. Federal Government. At various times during her life she's earned a living as a translator, language teacher, reporter, editor, and intelligence analyst. Nowadays, she makes her home in Maryland on a small horse farm, which she shares with her husband, dog, and a couple of very needy cats. More often than not she's at the barn spending time with her beloved dressage horse. Please stop by her website at www.lrtrovillion.com and say hello.

Final Thoughts and Thanks

Writing books is a lonely business. I would have quit on many occasions if it weren't for my encouraging, accept-no-excuses critique partners and friends. You know who you are. I also want to thank Jackie Savoye, a consummate horsewoman, who provided such helpful information and insights into life on the race track. Her experiences galloping, training, and caring for horses at Pimlico and other Maryland tracks was invaluable. Additionally, enormous thanks go out to Army Special Forces veteran and author Bill Raskin who helped with military operations and lingo. Any mistakes, of course, are the fault of the author. Lastly, I thank all the horses I've known throughout my life. They have selflessly taught and continue to teach me lessons about what is truly important in life.

If you enjoyed this book, please let me know! Consider writing a short review, share thoughts on your favorite blog, or write to me through my website at www.lrtrovillion.co. While you're there, sign up to receive news about upcoming new books, discounts, freebies, and more.

L.R. Trovillion

Also by L. R. Trovillion

The Maryland Equestrian Series
HORSE GODS: The Show Jumper's Challenge
HORSE GODS: The Dressage Rider's Betrayal
JUST GODS: The Eventer's Revenge
DREAM HORSE: A Short Reads Prequel

***

The Jazz Age Cold Case Mystery Series
A DEATH OF CONVENIENCE
THE DEATH CODE (COMING SOON!)

***

THE MURPHY'S LAW FARM MYSTERY SERIES
NOT YOUR LUCKY DAY
THE DEVIL'S LUCK (COMING SOON!)

Visit L. R. TROVILLION'S WEBSITE (WWW.LRTROVILLION.COM) or Amazon AUHOR PAGE for book descriptions and PURCHASE LINKS.

Made in the USA
Middletown, DE
27 July 2024